PIPING TRADITIONS
OF THE ISLE OF SKYE

Piping Traditions
of the
Isle of Skye

BRIDGET MACKENZIE

For Alex, Tom and Andrew,
pipers and lovers of Skye

First published in Great Britain in 2012 by
John Donald, an imprint of Birlinn Ltd

West Newington House
10 Newington Road
Edinburgh
EH9 1QS

www.birlinn.co.uk

ISBN: 978 1 906566 55 5

British Library Cataloguing-in-Publication Data
A catalogue record for this book is available on request from the British
Library

Typeset by Carnegie Book Production, Lancaster
Printed and bound in Britain by Bell and Bain Ltd, Glasgow

Contents

Introduction

It was planned to include Skye in the volume on the *Piping Traditions of the Inner Isles* (2012), but there was so much material that Skye had to be detached and issued as a separate work. It is hoped to follow this with one on the traditions of the Outer Isles, the fifth in the series.

Although Skye and Raasay are geographically close and would seem to go together, Raasay was included in the Inner Isles book, so that it would not appear as a poor relation to Skye – and the piping traditions of Raasay are surprisingly independent of those of its larger neighbour.

The piping traditions of Skye are dominated by the MacCrimmons and the MacArthurs, two great piping families whose history covers centuries. With the MacCrimmons in particular it is often difficult to distinguish between fact and fiction, and while oral tradition is strong, documentary evidence is sparse. I hope I have steered a safe course through the two, and that I have made it clear when I have used material with no written proof to back it up.

As previously noted, I have tried to make each section complete on its own, and this has led to a little repetition at times. It seems preferable to constant cross-referencing, though I hope the indexes will help readers to find their way about.

I have been greatly helped by many people, and would like to give special thanks to the following, who gave me valuable assistance:

Archie Campbell, Glendale, Skye
Jeannie Campbell, Glasgow
Chrissie Morrison, Uig, Skye
James Jackson, Alness
Dr Angus and Emily MacDonald, Braes, Skye
Jonathan MacDonald, Kilmuir, Skye
Roderick MacDonald ('the Admiral')

Seumas Archie MacDonald, Hunglader, Skye
Donald MacGillivray, Calrossie
Sue MacIntyre, Inverness
John MacKenzie, Uig, Skye
Johndon MacKenzie, Dornie, Kyle
Donnie MacKinnon, Uig, Skye
Dr Alasdair MacLean, Portree, Skye
Cailean MacLean, Bernisdale, Skye
Alistair MacLeod, Highland Council Genealogist
Iain MacLeod, Jersey, Channel Islands
Norma MacLeod, Portree, Skye
Flora MacNeill, Skye
Alasdair and Margaret MacPherson, Kilmore, Oban
Donald MacPherson, Balbeggie
George MacPherson, Glendale, Skye
Finlay MacRae, Dingwall
Dr Barrie J. MacLachlan Orme, Australia
Andrew Wright, Dunblane

It is some years since I met these kind people, and some of them have died in the meantime. I have included their names, as my debt to them still stands, and I apologise to their families if this causes any distress.

Abbreviations

In the lists of tunes, the following abbrevations are used:

J   Jig, preceded by the time signature and followed by the number of parts

GA   Gaelic Air

H   Hornpipe, preceded by the time signature and followed by the number of parts

M   March, preceded by the time signature and followed by the number of parts

P   Piobaireachd (Ceol Mor), followed by the number of variations, including the Ground (Urlar)

R   Reel, followed by the number of parts

RM   Retreat March

S   Strathspey, followed by the number of parts

SA   Slow Air, followed by the number of parts

SM   Slow March

In the sources and bibliography, the following abbreviations are used:

NoP   Notices of Pipers

TGSI   *Transactions of the Gaelic Society of Inverness*

Where names only are given in the lists of Sources in the text, the source was a personal interview.

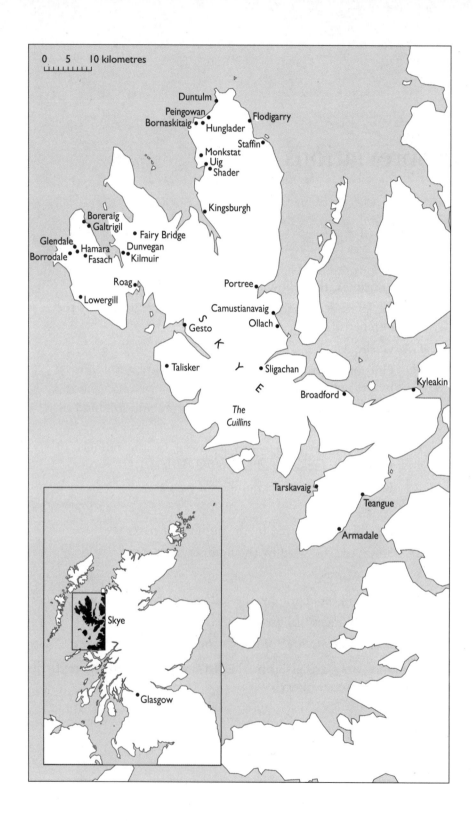

0 5 10 kilometres

Duntulm
Peingowan
Bornaskitaig • • Hunglader
Flodigarry
Staffin
Monkstat
Uig
Shader

Kingsburgh

Boreraig
Galtrigil
Glendale • Fairy Bridge
Hamara
Borrodale • Fasach • Dunvegan
Kilmuir

Roag •

Lowergill

Portree

Camustianavaig
Ollach

Gesto

S
K
Y
E

Talisker • Sligachan

Kyleakin

Broadford

The
Cuillins

Tarskavaig

Teangue

Armadale

Skye

Glasgow

Skye

Today Skye may be reached by road or by sea: the bridge, now toll-free, links the island to the mainland near Kyle of Lochalsh, and there is a car ferry from Mallaig to Armadale, in the south of Skye. The small car ferry which crosses from Glenelg to Skye is still running, but its future is uncertain. This crossing is usually most enjoyable, giving glimpses of wildlife such as seals and otters during the short crossing. All the crossings are notable for the beautiful scenery, weather permitting.

The name Skye is said to be derived from Gaelic *sgiathanach,* meaning 'winged', referring to the many peninsulas or wings of land which jut out from the island. This may be a rationalisation of a pre-Gaelic name.

Piping in Skye

The 79th Regiment traditionally recruited in Skye, many of the men being pipers. Soon after the Battle of Waterloo in 1815, the Adjutant said that more than half the pipers in the battle were from Skye or Tongue (North Sutherland).

Despite religious intolerance later in the 19th century, when the Free Churches denounced music as sinful, and destroyed instruments and written music, the piping traditions of Skye survived. Already by 1800, preachers were opposing pipe music; in 1823, the Rev. Roderick MacLeod of the Church of Scotland, who warned of the 'seductive' effects of piping, recalled his boyhood in Dunvegan, when 'as soon as the services, which were conducted in the open field, were ended, three pipers struck up music, and three dancing parties were formed on the green' (MacRae, *Revivals in the Highlands,* quoted by John Gibson).

The Gaelic Schools Society, who did so much to suppress Gaelic, reported in 1837 that there were still two parishes in Skye where no awakening (to extreme Calvinism) had yet taken place, and 'the bagpipe may still be held at their funerals', but by 1841, the Rev. A. MacGregor, quoted by Alexander Nicolson in his *History of Skye,* was writing that the piper's lament was no longer heard at funerals, although 'a few years ago, as many as two pipers were always present'.

By the middle of the 19th century, a minister recorded with pride that he had just burned the last set of pipes in Skye. Frank Richardson found, as late as 1926, that some of the Skye ministers opposed his presence when he arrived to teach piping to local youngsters.

Piping, however, had not been completely suppressed. In 1877, when the Skye Gathering was inaugurated in Portree, piping competitions were included, and the later formation of the pipe band in Portree consolidated the position of pipers in the community. The gentry encouraged piping, and many of the remaining Skye pipers were army men, or ex-army. They were mostly players of light music, however, and the playing of piobaireachd in the late 19th century had become more of a rarity.

In 1883, Sheriff Nicolson from Skye said that during the American and French wars, Skye alone furnished 100 pipers to the army.

The two great landowners, the MacLeods of Dunvegan and the MacDonalds of Sleat, had, until about 1800, maintained their own hereditary pipers, the MacCrimmons at Boreraig and the MacArthurs at Hunglader, both of whom had piping schools in Skye in the 17th and 18th centuries; and the island has produced pipers, teachers and composers, from the 16th century to the present day.

In Skye Week, held every year in early August, two days of piping competitions include the Silver Chanter in Dunvegan Castle, billed as a recital, but in fact a competition of six invited players in front of a single judge. During the day, pipers compete in the Skye Gathering Hall in Portree for the Dunvegan Medal, and in the evening former medal winners may enter for the Colonel Jock Clasp. Both competitions feature MacCrimmon tunes only, from a list issued by the committee. Meanwhile, in another indoor venue, the seniors play in light music competitions, while the juniors feature in the Skye Games, out of doors. The numbers had fallen badly for a time, but recently have picked up well, and now the problem is to finish before breakfast-time the next day.

The MacCrimmons

MacCrimmon/Macleod Tunes

Piobaireachd Works

These are the MacCrimmon tunes eligible for the Dunvegan Medal (those marked ** are also accepted for the Colonel Jock Clasp competition for holders of the Dunvegan Medal). This list is revised by the Skye Games Committee from time to time. Before submitting a tune, it is advisable to check that it is still on the list.

The Battle of Waternish **
The Earl of Ross's March **
A Flame of Wrath for Patrick Caogach
The Glen Is Mine
The Groat **
I Got a Kiss of the King's Hand **
John Garve MacLeod of Raasay's Lament **
The King's Taxes **
Lament for the Children **
Lament for Donald Ban MacCrimmon **
Lament for Donald Duaghal MacKay **
Lament for Donald of Laggan
Lament for the Duke of Hamilton **
Lament for the Earl of Antrim **
Lament for the Harp Tree **
Lament for MacSwan of Roaig **
Lament for Mary MacLeod
Lament for the Only Son
Lament for Patrick Og MacCrimmon **
MacCrimmon Will Never Return
MacCrimmon's Sweetheart (Maol Donn)
MacLeod of Colbecks' Lament **
MacLeod of MacLeod's Lament **
MacLeod of Raasay's Salute
MacLeod's Controversy
MacLeod's Salute
Mrs MacLeod of Talisker's Salute **

The Pretty Dirk
Rory MacLoude's Lament **
Salute on the Birth of Rory Mor MacLeod
Too Long in This Condition

It is difficult to see the reasoning behind the choice of some of these tunes, which are probably not all MacCrimmon works. Note that the *Lament for Donald Duaghal MacKay* has been on the Skye list only since the Second World War, and was formerly excluded.

Works previously, but no longer, on the list include:

The Fairy Flag
The Half-Finished Tune (Port Leathach)
MacDonald's Salute

Again, the reasoning behind the decision is not clear.

Other piobaireachd works associated with the MacLeods include:

Blar Vuster
The Dispraise of MacLeod – see under MacDonald tunes
Gesto's Lamentation (= *The Young Laird of Dungallon's Salute*)
Lament for Alasdair Dearg MacDonnell of Glengarry
Lament for J. Jersey MacLeod of Skeabost, by D.C. MacLeod
MacLeod of Gesto's Gathering
MacLeod of Gesto's Salute
MacLeod of Talisker's Lament
MacLeod's Short Tune
Patrick Og Macrimmon's Dream of Love
Salute to (or *Lament for?*) *the Rev. Dr. Norman MacLeod*, by
    William Ross, published 1874

The piobaireachd works of Iain Dall MacKay, the Blind Piper of Gairloch, as a pupil of Patrick Og MacCrimmon, may be included here:

The Munros' Salute
The Battle of Glenshiel
Lament for the Laird of Contullich
Lament for the Laird of Anapool
Lament for Lady Anapool
The Unjust Incarceration
Lament for Patrick Og MacCrimmon
Corrienessan's Lament
The Blind Piper's Obstinacy – probably composed in Skye
The Hen's March O'er the Midden – probably composed in Skye

and possibly also

> *The Half-Finished Tune* – probably composed in Skye
> *Lament for Donald Duaghal MacKay.*

The title *Pronnadh nan Miall* (the Squashing of the Lice) is all that has survived of one piece. Two reels, *The Old Grey Wife of Raasay* and *The Miller's Wife*, are said to be the work of Iain Dall, but this has been doubted.

Many of the above MacCrimmon and MacKay piobaireachd works may be heard recorded on CD, played by William M. MacDonald, who won both the Gold Medals in 1956, a pupil of John MacDonald: and by Dr Barrie MacLachlan Orme, in the 19th-century style of Simon Fraser. Both series of recordings have been published by Highlander Music, Beauly (tel. 05603 664899 or 01463 783273).

Notes on the Backgrounds of the Skye Prescribed Tunes

The following notes are not intended to be scholarly analysis, but merely to provide the piper with a suggestion for the mood of a piece. They draw on oral tradition as well as historical documentation. The notes represent a personal interpretation of the titles, and there is no guarantee of accuracy.

The Battle of Waternish

The battle seems to have been a relatively early one in the bitter conflicts between the MacLeods and the MacDonalds in Skye, at the end of the 16th century.

Around 1577, it is said (though the date has been doubted), the MacLeods had committed an atrocity on the island of Eigg, when they set fires outside a cave full of Clanranald's people, all MacDonalds or affiliated to them. All 400 perished, suffocated in the smoke.

In reprisal, the following year, a band of Clanranald MacDonalds made a raid on Skye in the absence of the MacLeod chief. Landing in Waternish, and finding the local people at church in Trumpan, they fired the building and burned the entire congregation. (This was an incident so often reported as a forerunner to a battle that it was probably no more than a story-teller's convention, a formal means of justifying the actions of the eventual victors in the battle – the 16th-century equivalent of the search for weapons of mass destruction in Iraq, in the 21st).

The MacDonalds then started rounding up cattle and other spoil, and setting fire to houses. The MacLeods came in haste to try to stop the attack, but were greatly outnumbered, because of the Chief's absence with many MacLeod clansmen. They brought the Fairy Flag with them, however (talking of weapons of mass destruction), and when they unfurled it, they appeared miraculously numerous and of heroic stature. After some close fighting, the MacDonalds fled for their boats, only to find them stranded by the ebbing tide (surely they could have anticipated this?).

Then, said the Gaelic storytellers, the MacDonalds made a last stand along a wall by the shore, and fought to the death. There are many tales about this battle – one is about the MacLeod blacksmith who was getting the worst of a hand-to-hand fight with a MacDonald. The smith's wife came up behind the MacDonald, and said something 'quite unforgivable' to him. He was distracted, turned his head to look at her, and that was the end of him. All the MacDonalds perished, and to save having to bury them, the victors pushed over the wall on top of the slain.

The battle was then called the Battle of the Spoiled Dyke; its progress can be heard clearly in the music, with the variations depicting the fierce exchange of blows, followed by a helter-skelter chase of headlong flight. It should be played briskly, with plenty of life and vigour.

There is no doubt that the story of the Spoiled Dyke arose from a misinterpretation, by Gaelic speakers, of the Norse name of the wall. Dr Alasdair MacLean's revision of the *History of Skye,* which gives a fuller account of the battle, quotes Donald MacKillop, who thought the name *Millegearraidh* had been misunderstood, as if it were Gaelic *milleadh* 'spoiling' and *gearraidh* 'wall'. It is in fact Norse *milli-garth,* meaning 'the between-wall', i.e. the wall built between the shore and the field above it, to prevent stock on the shore from invading the crops. It is quite a common name in Scandinavia.

This makes it clear that there was only one battle, in spite of a persistent tradition that there were two, the Battle of Waternish and the Battle of the Spoiled Dyke. They were one and the same.

The date, probably 1578, seems too early for this to be the work of Donald Mor MacCrimmon, so perhaps it was by one of the shadowy earlier MacCrimmons, such as Iain Odhar. Or possibly it was one of those works looking back to the glorious past, and we cannot date it. The song on which it was probably based may date from the time of the battle.

Frances Tolmie, in her Journal, quoted in *The Old Songs of Skye*

– *Frances Tolmie and her Circle* by Ethel Bassin, gave the words and music of a song which she collected from a singer, Oighrig Ross, in Bracadale, Skye in 1861, concerning the Battle of Waternish. Interspersed with the refrain *E-ho, ro-ho ro-ho* after the first line of each verse and *O-hi ri-ri, hi-ri ho-ro-ho* after the second, the Gaelic words translate as:

> Do you remember
> (*e-ho, ro-ho ro-ho*)
> the day of the Aird,
> (*o-hi ri-ri, hi-ri ho-ro-ho*)
> or that other
> of Millegaraidh?
> Men were there
> in sad condition,
> lying prone, showing
> the white soles of their feet.
> Many a woman was
> sorely grieving,
> missing her son there,
> having no brother,
> and no man left
> to delight in her.
> May my curse be on
> Clan Ranald.

The air to this song may have given the theme of the later piobaireachd work.

Sources

Alexander Nicolson, *History of Skye*
Alec Haddow, *The History and Structure of Ceol Mor*
Ethel Bassin, *The Old Songs of Skye*

The Earl of Ross's March

The title of the Earl of Ross was associated with that of the Lord of the Isles, when Donald MacDonald of Islay, Lord of the Isles, married a daughter of the Earl, and claimed that this made him overlord of Argyll and Ross, as well as of the entire Western Isles. His claim led to the Battle of Harlaw in 1411, in which he was defeated – but he eventually won the title Earl of Ross for his son, Alexander.

It was Alexander's son, John, second Lord of the Isles, who then lost it. He plotted to bring down the monarchy, and destroyed his own power. The Lordship and the Earldom were forfeit to the Crown in 1475, but the titles were restored two years later, with much of the territory taken away. In the end, John was attacked and beaten by his own son, Angus Og, and both titles were forfeit to the Crown, for good, in 1493.

During the following century, several of the MacDonald chiefs tried unsuccessfully to revive and claim the two titles; one of these was Donald Gorm MacDonald of Sleat, the particular enemy and part-time friend of Sir Rory Mor MacLeod of Dunvegan.

Stuart Letford, in his *Little Book of Piping Quotations*, cites a poem by Iain Lom, probably made in the early 1640s, a song addressed to Donald Gorm Og, MacDonald of Sleat: describing the civilized life of Donald Gorm Og's hall, he refers to:

A harp and a clarsach
And fair-bosomed women
In the tower of the short gaming boards.

The blasting of bagpipes
And Leith organs
With drinking horns filled to the brim;

Wax blazing
All through the night-time,
As they listen to the contention of the bards,

In the hall of the grandson
Of the Earl of Islay,
Of the Hebrides, Kintyre and Ross.

Clearly the family was still associated with the Ross title, as late as the mid-17th century.

Does this piobaireachd work date back to before 1493, or is this title a sarcastic dig at Donald Gorm's aspirations? The latter seems more likely: it must have been galling for the MacLeods to acknowledge that any part of Skye was owned by the MacDonalds.

In the 17th century there were other MacDonald claimants to the Ross title, one being Glengarry in 1653. He said the King (Charles II) had promised him the title and the lands, including Skye, as he wanted to be overlord of the entire Clan Donald. Sir James MacDonald of Sleat put in a counter-claim, with petitions and declarations of rights. Either of these two would-be Earls of Ross might be the Earl named in the title, if it is as late as the mid-17th century – this too seems more likely than pre-1493.

The title went to none of them, but remained with the Scottish Crown.

Does the term March here refer to a particular expedition, i.e. an invasive march, or does it represent the Gaelic word *spaisdearach*, meaning 'walking around'? In former times March was used to mean that particular type of pipe music, which we now, perhaps misleadingly, call piobaireachd. Joseph MacDonald, writing in 1762, certainly used March in this way, but made a distinction between Marches and Gatherings. To him, piobaireachd meant piping in general – as to Gaelic speakers today. The term Ceol Mor was then unknown, being coined probably quite late in the 19th century.

If March is here used to mean an invasive military march, it may refer to the taking of Trotternish in North Skye by a force of MacDonald men who drove the MacLeods back. This established the MacDonalds in Skye, to become the branch later known as the MacDonalds of Sleat. Eventually their seat was at Armadale, in the south of the island, but until the end of the 18th century they lived in Trotternish, North Skye, first at Duntulm and then at Monkstat. The Skye branch of the clan is often called the MacDonalds of the Isles, but this is mistaken: they were related, but those of the Isles were Clan Donald South, based further south, in Islay.

As the title Earl of Ross belonged to the MacDonalds of the Isles, and there is no evidence that the work was made by any of the Mac-Crimmons, it is not clear why it is in the list for Skye. Everyone follows Angus MacKay in this, although his note is confused. He attributes the composition to Donald Mor MacCrimmon, dating it around 1600, although mentioning that the 11th Earl of Ross forfeited his earldom in 1476.

Gesto (1828) gave it the snappy title 'Played at a time when the Scotts were at war in England and obliged to feed on the Ears of Corn for want of Provision, commonly called Kieunidize'. This ties in with the title in the Campbell Canntaireachd manuscript, where the work is called *Chean na Daise*. The meaning is obscure; it probably refers to the end of the haymaking or harvest, in which case the tune was one played in celebration of a harvest being secured.

Seton Gordon tells how in Trotternish in the 1920s, the old custom of drinking the *stapag* was still observed: it was a dish of thick churned cream into which oatmeal had been stirred. This was drunk, or eaten. while two pipers played, in turn, to celebrate the end of the harvest. *Duthaich nan stapag* and *fearann stapagach* were old Gaelic terms for Trotternish ('Country of the stapag', and 'stapag district'). Were the pipers playing *Cean na Daise*? And was this *The Earl of Ross's March*?

Sources

Alec Haddow, *The History and Structure of Ceol Mor*
Simon Fraser, *Piobaireachd*
Seton Gordon, *Hebridean Memories*

A *Flame of Wrath for Patrick Caogach*

Caogach is often translated as 'squinting', but it really means 'blinking, winking' with an involuntary twitch to the eyelid. Around the Games, Patrick tends to be offered as 'Patrick Thingie' by non-Gaelic speakers (along with 'Lachlan MacNeill Wotsit').

Patrick with the twitching eye was a MacCrimmon, younger brother to Donald Mor. In the earliest years of the 1600s, he was sent to be fostered by a family of MacKenzies, over in Kintail, near Glenelg. One of the sons of that family took a dislike to him, and one day when Patrick was bending over a spring of water, his foster-brother stabbed him in the back, killing him. This was a particularly horrific murder, since it broke the ties of friendship, kinship, hospitality and trust, implicit in a fostering.

Donald Mor wanted vengeance for his brother, and asked his chief, Rory Mor MacLeod, to exact it for him. Rory was understandably reluctant to be involved, having just settled his long feud with the Mac-Donalds and having given assurances to the King that he would keep the peace. He kept telling Donald to wait a while and he would do something. But he did nothing, and Donald, after a year, lost patience. He crossed into Kintail himself, found the clachan (small cluster of houses) where the killer lived, and burned it down. According to the story, nine MacKenzies died in the fire. Donald made this exultant piece, his *Flame of Wrath*, to celebrate his vengeance.

He then had no choice but to go on the run, to escape justice, since he could not let his chief appear to condone the deed. He fled to Strathnaver, in northern Sutherland, and the MacKay chief, Uisdean (father of Donald Duaghal), gave him shelter. There are many stories of Donald Mor's narrow escapes from the avenging MacKenzie chief of Kintail, who was, ironically enough, the father-in-law of Donald Duaghal MacKay, but, luckily for Donald Mor, did not like his daughter's husband.

Eventually, after some twenty years of exile, Donald Mor was able to return home to Skye. It is often said that he trained the MacKay pipers in Strathnaver and laid the foundations for the notable MacKay tradition of piping in later years. In the north, they say that he composed

Too Long in This Condition when suffering an attack of homesickness – but some say he made it when attending a MacKay wedding at which he was offered neither food nor drink. Further south, the tradition is that it was not composed by Donald Mor at all, but was made after the Battle of Sheriffmuir in 1715, when MacLeod Highlanders found themselves naked on the battlefield. The same story is told of the Battle of Worcester (1651).

Willie MacLean recorded a tale about a piper he named as Patrick Mor MacCrimmon, who was, Willie said, captured by the English after the Battle of Sheriffmuir, and imprisoned in England. After some months he managed to escape, and made his way north, travelling by night and hiding by day, living off the land and becoming very gaunt and tattered. Eventually he found his way to Achnacarry, the home of Cameron of Lochiel, and ventured into the kitchen. Nobody recognized the unkempt scarecrow of a man with long hair and beard, and their first instinct was to put him out of the house. But Lochiel's piper came in, complaining that he could not get his pipe going, the reeds were giving him trouble, and the new arrival asked if he could have a try. The piper was not keen to let this dirty fellow touch his pipe, but in the end let him look at the reeds. Within minutes the pipe was going, and Patrick told the piper who he was. When he was washed and had his hair and beard trimmed and was given clean clothes, they all said they would have known him anywhere – and eventually he made his way home to Skye, where he composed *Too Long in This Condition*, to commemorate his long ordeal. On the School of Scottish Studies tape, Willie sings the song which goes with the tune, and it has the same Gaelic words as the ditty sung in Sutherland, about the wedding – 'Too long like this, without food, without drink', it goes.

The snag about this story is that at the time of Sheriffmuir (1715), Patrick Mor had been dead some forty-five years. Was it perhaps the Battle of Worcester (1651), not Sheriffmuir at all? Patrick is said to have gone with the MacLeods to that, but there is no tradition of his having been captured. Sir Norman MacLeod of Bernera was, however, captured and imprisoned, escaped and made his way eventually to France, and then home by sea; maybe part of this adventure was transferred to Patrick Mor by the story-tellers, suitably embellished.

In Sutherland, Donald Mor MacCrimmon was piper first to Uisdean and then to his son Donald Duaghal, the 13th and 14th chiefs of MacKay. His presence in Strathnaver in the early decades of the 17th century has always been strongly attested in oral tradition, which said he had come north around 1603; historians scoffed, needing documentary proof. This was found in the Register of the Great Seal, under the year 1614, when 'Donaldo McCrummen lie pyper' (lie = 'the') was named as having fought along with the MacKays against the Sinclairs, at Thurso, two years earlier. He was one of two pipers named – the other was John MacRory – and the *-o* on his name is because the document is in Latin, and the pardon was granted *to* Donald.

Among the pipers he taught in the north was probably Ruairidh MacKay, the father of Iain Dall, the Blind Piper of Gairloch. Ruairidh was already a trained piper when he came south to Gairloch in 1609; it is possible that he was related to the piper John MacRory.

Many years after Donald had returned to Skye, it was remarked that a large number of MacKay pipers came down from the north, all good players of the same high standard, 'as if taught in a school'. It is likely that they owed this excellence to the teaching of Donald Mor MacCrimmon, during his exile.

Around the time of the arrival of Donald Mor in Strathnaver, or possibly a little earlier, the bloodless victory of the MacKays over the Caithness Sinclairs was commemorated by the piobaireachd now known as *Beinn a'Griain* (see below). It is possible that it was the work of Donald Mor for his new patron, but it may be that there was already a tradition of piobaireachd composition in the north of Sutherland.

Sources

Alan Temperley, *Tales of the North Coast*
Register of the Great Seal
Angus A. Mackay, *The Book of MacKay*
School of Scottish Studies tapes

The Glen Is Mine

Peter Reid in 1826 gave this the title *The Glen Is Mine and all that it contains*, and Angus MacKay explained that it was first played when the Earl of Seaforth was riding through Glenshiel with his piper, whom Angus named as John MacCrimmon, one of the sons of Patrick. He did not say which Patrick, and as no John (or Iain) was then known to have been a son of Patrick Og, it was assumed that John was Patrick Og's grandson, Iain Dubh MacCrimmon (c.1710–1822). This is probably mistaken.

Donald MacDonald, who came from Skye, called this work *A MacDonalds' March*, adding 'This Piobaireachd or Pipe March is very simple, the name of which is not known. The MacDonalds claim it as one of their marches'. The word *March* is presumably used here as Joseph MacDonald used it, to mean what we now call a piobaireachd.

Angus MacKay clearly believed that Seaforth had a piper, John Mac-Crimmon, whose father was called Patrick – and often Angus proves to have been right. But when?

A glance at the history of the Seaforth MacKenzies shows that after the 5th Earl, William Dubh (subject of the *Earl of Seaforth's Salute*), had played a leading part in the 1715 Jacobite Rising, his lands and titles were attaindered to the Crown (confiscated). This seems to be what the Campbell Canntaireachd manuscript was referring to in the title *Co gha bhi mi s' leiss Riogh mi*, apparently meaning 'Who will take me now I've been with the King?', which would apply to the Earl or any of his followers.

The Earl was abroad in exile for many years after the Rising, years during which the *Earl of Seaforth's Salute* was composed; he did not return until shortly before his death in 1740. His estates were then sold off by the Crown (1741). Although his heir, the 6th Earl, had his titles restored in 1761, as a reward for not taking part in the '45, he was the last holder of the title, and his only land was the Brahan estate in Easter Ross. The Earldom became extinct when he died, in 1781, although the Seaforth MacKenzies continued at Brahan.

If reliance can be put on Angus MacKay's comment, and if indeed a John MacCrimmon was piper to Seaforth and was riding with him through Glenshiel at a time when it did belong to Seaforth, then clearly this must have been before 1715; so there would be no question of the composer being Iain Dubh, Patrick Og's grandson. It must have been an earlier John MacCrimmon.

Soon after the 1715 Rising, as part of the confiscation procedure, an inventory was made of Seaforth's extensive lands, and his tenants were listed (*Highland Papers* (1916) volume II, 327). Living at Easter Leakichan (now Leacachan), on Loch Duich, in Kintail, was a man called John McCrimmon, paying £21 15s 10d per annum in rent, and £1 17s 6d towards the upkeep of the minister, and as additional rent in kind had to supply the laird annually with a third of a sheep, three stones of butter and six of cheese. This indicates that John McCrimmon was a man of substance, of the tacksman class, with a good holding of land, and some standing in the community. But was this the John MacCrimmon named by Angus MacKay? And was he a son of Patrick Og?

Alick Morrison said that Patrick Og did have a son called John, born in the late 17th century, at Scarista, Harris (this birth-place might be doubted). Was he a piper? It seems very likely. His brothers Malcolm and Donald Ban were pipers, and John may well have been piper to Seaforth, perhaps his piper in the west, just as Sir James Grant kept a piper in Glenurquhart as well as his main piper at Castle Grant, and Breadalbane had a spare at Ardmaddy. There is no other record of Seaforth having a MacCrimmon piper, but he was, at the height of his power, in a position to employ the very best, just as did the Earl of Sutherland at Dunrobin, in 1651.

The *Highland Papers'* inventory of the Seaforth Estates lists two tenants, John MacKay and John Matheson, living at Erbesaig, in the Barony of Ardelf. This is a mile north of Kyle of Lochalsh, and the compiler made a note: 'this being formerly the piper's land, paid neither customs nor rent'. Does 'formerly' mean 'before the Rising', or, possibly, 'before John MacCrimmon came'?

Local historian Roger Miket tells us of a great party that was held at Eilean Donan Castle, Loch Duich, on the eve of the Battle of Sheriffmuir (1715) – 'eve' presumably meaning the night before the local force set out for the south. It was evidently a very good party: MacKenzies, Mathesons and MacRaes ended the evening dancing on the rooftops of the castle. We have to wonder who played for the dancing. There must be a strong possibility that it was John MacCrimmon.

Easter Leakichan is now Leacachan House, on the south-western side of Loch Duich, on the Ratagan shore road, below the pass leading to Glenelg.

On the summit of a hill called Glashven above Bernera, Glenelg, in Kintail, well off the beaten track today, there is a stone which the Ordnance Survey map marks as *Carn Cloinn Mhic Cruimein* 'Stone of the Clan MacCrimmon' (OS Ref. 822 225). It is close to the pass called the Bealach Luachrach (*Highland Papers* 328). It is said that the stone marks the spot where 'nine-nines' of the MacCrimmons were buried, after they fell in battle against the men of Kintail, who were doubtless mainly MacRaes. (The account is in the *Book of Dunvegan*, vol. I (1939) and in *The MacLeods of Dunvegan* (1927), both by R.C. MacLeod.) William Donaldson in *The Highland Pipe and Scottish Society* mentions a report that at the Rout of Glaisbheinn, the MacCrimmons were so numerous that eighty-one called John MacCrimmon fell. Glashven is about four and a half miles due west of Leacachan.

It is known that a 'nest' of MacCrimmons was living in Kintail in the 18th century, presumably based at Leacachan. They were constantly feuding with the MacRaes of Kintail, who were based at Inverinate, on the other side of Loch Duich; in the end, having made the area too hot to hold them, the MacCrimmons from Leacachan emigrated to Ontario en masse. There they were joined in 1820 by Donald MacCrimmon, son of Donald Ruadh and great-grandson of Patrick Og.

In the early 19th century there were many MacCrimmon families living at Glenelg, in Kintail, but these do not seem to have been the same branch as those at Leacachan: the tradition is that they were brought over to Glenelg by their MacLeod landlords, in order to fortify the 'back door' into Skye against possible invasion. Whether this was at the time of the Jacobite Risings, or later, when Bonaparte was the threat, is not clear – but the Bernera Barracks were built at Glenelg in 1720–23, after the Battle of Glenshiel had given the government a fright. The building was occupied by troops until 1797, when MacLeod of Dunvegan bought it for £925 Scots (about £77 sterling). Around 200 people were living there, in or near the barracks, at that time, some of them renting a room at £1 per annum. By the 1830s it had become a refuge, a sort of unofficial poorhouse, for those evicted from their homes in Skye. Today it is a ruin.

It is said that many MacCrimmons were among the homeless Skye tenants who moved to Glenelg looking for somewhere to live; they settled there, having little choice between that and emigration, once they had been evicted. Certainly many MacCrimmons are listed in the Old Parish Register for Glenelg, which is late, starting in 1805.

Angus MacKay's manuscript has two versions of the work *Lament for Iain Ciar* (nos 5 and 97); Iain Ciar was a chief of the MacDougalls, living at Dunollie, Oban, in the early 18th century. Both of Angus MacKay's settings of the lament have a marked resemblance to *The Glen Is Mine;* and Donald MacDonald's setting of *The Glen Is Mine* is similar to that of *Chisholm's Salute*, which seems to have been composed (or made over? borrowed?) in Skye in 1836, to celebrate the election of the Chisholm chief to Parliament. Kilberry commented that *Chisholm's Salute* was 'possibly a crib on *Iain Ciar*', i.e. copying it, to which the Editors of the Piobaireachd Society Book 14 added 'which seems certainly correct'.

But what of the relation between *Iain Ciar* and *The Glen Is Mine?* If, as is often supposed, *The Glen Is Mine* had been made by Iain Dubh, it would have been a comparatively late composition – either late 18th or early 19th century – and so *Iain Ciar* would be the basis for all three works, as it was made by Ranald Ban MacDougall in 1737, when his MacDougall chief died at Dunollie. Yet the *Iain Ciar* version of the tune seems a little more sophisticated, having a Thumb variation with

Doubling, which is lacking in *The Glen*, and it seems odd that *The Glen*, apparently a simpler work, would be based on an older, more evolved composition.

But if, as seems certain, *The Glen Is Mine* was made before 1715, then it would be the prototype, and Ranald Ban MacDougall merely developed it a little further in 1737. Note that both the Earl of Seaforth and Iain Ciar MacDougall were deeply involved in the 1715 Rising, both well to the fore in supporting the Stuart cause, and they fought side by side in the battle of Sheriffmuir. We may assume that their pipers were acquainted.

Angus MacKay provided words to his second version of *Iain Ciar*, and this probably indicates that the tune was current as a song. This is often the case when a theme appears in one place and re-appears in another – not so much a 'crib' as a fashion. Angus' words are:

O Iain Cheir dhiubh slan gu till thu –
O Iain Cheir dhiubh slan gun bith thu –
Slan gun dig thu – slan gun bith thu

Oh swarthy Iain, good health to you until you return.
Oh swarthy Iain, good health while you live,
Good health until you come – good health while you live

This sounds more a salute than a lament, clearly a drinking song to the absent laird. It was presumably sung for Iain Ciar in his years of exile after the 1715 Rising. Maybe it was this, as well as a reference in the MacDougall papers, that led the compiler(s) of the Notices of Pipers to assume two works by Ranald Ban MacDougall, a *Salute* as well as a *Lament for Iain Ciar*, and the second of Angus MacKay's manuscript versions is taken to be the *Salute* – but they are very much alike.

Sources

Notices of Pipers
Roger Miket, *Glen, Kintail and Lochalsh*
R.C. MacLeod, *Dunvegan*
Harris Estate Papers – *TGSI* XLV and LI
Alistair MacLeod, Genealogist, Highland Council

The Groat

The alternative title is *An Grota Misgeach*, the Drunken Groat, whatever that may mean. A groat was a silver coin worth four pence sterling, that is d. (pre-decimal coinage), not p., but the groat went out of use, way back. It was at one time the smallest denomination of silver coin in use in Britain. How a groat could be intoxicated, nobody is sure; it seems certain that at least one word has been corrupted.

Donald MacDonald, himself a Skyeman, thought the work had been composed for the christening of Rory Mor MacLeod of Dunvegan, who was born in 1562. This date would be too early for it to be a composition of Donald Mor MacCrimmon, and brings us into the twilight world of those shadowy figures, Iain Odhar, Patrick Donn and Finlay of the White Plaid, the earliest known MacCrimmons. Even the names are doubtful.

As Rory Mor was not the eldest son of his generation, it could be that this was composed for the christening of his elder brother William, older by two years – if indeed it was a christening piece. And what of the *Salute on the Birth of Rory Mor*? Would a christening piece be needed along with that?

The title of the work as it appears in the Campbell Canntaireachd manuscript is *Marsah na Grantich*, which seems to mean Merchant of the Grants, or possibly Marching of the Grants, but this too may be a corruption. What is the link here, if any, with the Grants?

Suggestions about *The Groat* are:

(a) that a groat, the silver coin, was a levy on each family of clansmen, to mark the christening of the chief's son. It is hard to believe that silver groats would have been available in all the families (even in Dr Johnson's time, two hundred years later, there was a shortage of coins in Skye). This explanation, however, has the merit of possibly fitting the title *An Grota Misgeach*, if we assume that the levy was to pay for the drink consumed at the christening – but this is pure conjecture;

(b) that there may be a link with the Highland custom of slipping a silver coin into a baby's cradle on first seeing the child. As the groat was the smallest denomination of silver coin, it seems likely to have been used for this purpose. The custom is still practised, to bring the infant good luck. This money would not, however, be used to buy drink for the christening;

(c) that the word *grota* is a corruption of a less familiar word, the Gaelic word *cruit*, meaning a stringed instrument, sometimes called a Celtic lyre, often a six-stringed instrument, smaller and more portable than the *clarsach* which gradually replaced it.

We have examples of harp tunes being adapted to the piobaireachd form and played on the pipes, and it is at least possible that *The Groat* was once called *Port Chruit*, a Harp Tune. Among Irish harpers in the

18th century, the term Port did not mean merely 'tune', but had a technical connotation, 'a lesson in music', rather as we use the French term 'etude'. There is some suggestion that it was originally used to describe a tune composed solely for instrumental playing, so that its patterns were not necessarily linked to those of poetry.

When the clarsach took over from the cruit, the latter word probably became obsolete, and so might have been misunderstood and corrupted to a word that was familiar and still then in use, *grota* 'groat', and the stories grew up to explain it. Even among harp-players, *cruit* had already been corrupted to *crot*. A similar process happened with the name which ended up as the *Lament for the Harp Tree* (see below). This theory takes no account of the Grants, however – but *grantich* could be a corrupted form of the word *greanntachd*, 'carving', i.e. an elaborately carved instrument. There is a word *miosganach* which can mean 'made of wood', and this may have been corrupted to *misgeach*, 'drunken'.

Under this third theory, *An Grota Misgeach* would be a late, distorted version of *Port Chruit Mhiosganaich* 'Tune of a Stringed Instrument made of Wood', and *Marsah na Grantich* would be *Marsaill na Greanntaichd*, 'March (= Tune) of the Carved Instrument'. Neat, eh?

In the *Book of the Dean of Lismore*, a collection of Scottish verse from the years between 1310 and 1520, there are many references to the households of great Scottish lords, and the instruments played in their halls were almost always harps. There is no mention of the pipes. One poem, dating from 1427–28, is about wolves, and in it the poet says wolf-skin was used as a cover for the two kinds of harp-like instrument, the clarsach and the cruit, showing that both types were in use at that time.

Whatever its origin, the title *The Groat* seems to be old, and to be associated with feasting among the MacLeods, possibly in the 16th century. This does not necessarily mean that the work for the pipe was composed as early as that, but it may be based on harp music from that time.

See also the *Salute on the Birth of Rory Mor MacLeod,* below.

Sources

Alec Haddow, *The History and Structure of Ceol Mor*
Campbell Canntaireachd, Manuscript
William Matheson, *An Clarsair Dall*
W.J. Watson, *Book of the Dean of Lismore*

I Got a Kiss of the King's Hand

This title, in English, gives English-speaking purists of today a feeling of unease (as does the title *Scarce of Fishing*). They think they are speaking ungrammatically, but perhaps a little learning is misleading them.

This is the unfamiliar idiom of 17th/18th-century Scots English, and what appears to us to be bad grammar was perfectly acceptable then. The word 'got' is here used in the old meaning of 'achieved, managed to achieve', translating Gaelic *fhuair* – which is the verb used in the earliest reference to the work, in the late 17th century (Wardlaw manuscript). Any attempt to replace it by Gaelic *thug* 'gave' is regrettable, and of course 'got to do something' in the sense of 'managed to do it' is still used by Scots throughout the country (as in 'I got to speak wi' the laird', meaning 'I managed to have a word with the laird', or in 'She got a bite of my apple'). This idiom has nothing to do with the American use of 'gotta' meaning 'must'.

In the song accompanying the piobaireachd work, the word *fhuair* rhymes with *chuir* and half-rhymes with *caorach*, and a change to *thug* destroys the internal rhyme pattern, even though *thug* would rhyme with *pog* (see verses below). So, please, let us retain *fhuair* and 'got', and call the work *I Got a Kiss of the King's Hand* (known to pipers as *The King's Hand*, thus neatly avoiding the problem).

Alec Haddow (p. 85) gives a version of the song, as in Angus MacKay:

O thug mi pog, us pog, us pog,
thug mu pog do lamh an righ,
Cha do chuir gaoth an craicionn caorach
Fear a fhuair an fhaoilt ach mi!

Oh I gave a kiss, a kiss, a kiss,
Oh I gave a kiss to the hand of the king,
No one else who has blown into a sheepskin bag
Has had that honour but myself!

If this note was written by Angus MacKay himself, it is surprising that he felt the need to change the wording, but he may have received it in that form – or it may be the work of James Logan.

Margaret Stewart's version (*Piper Press*, March 1999) seems closer to the original:

Fhuair mi pog, is pog, is pog,
O fhuair mi pog a laimh an Righ,
Is ch'd chuir gaoth an craiceann caorach
Neach a fhuair an fhaoilt ach mi.

I got a kiss, a kiss, a kiss, etc.

Note the rhyme scheme, with full and half-rhymes binding all the lines of the verse together – and the alliteration of *fhuair* with *fhaoilt* links the last line with the first.

The vast majority of pipers will have not the faintest idea of what all this is about, nor care, but these internal rhyme schemes in Gaelic and Irish poetry were important, since they were echoed by, and probably the model for, the phrase patterns in the structure of a well-made piobaireachd. With *fhuair* retained, the verse is a nice example of a well-wrought semi-bardic poem; substituting *thug* destroys the structure, impoverishes the verse and is unnecessary.

[Digression: We might compare a modern ditty which goes:

Oh, the big cat piddled in the little cat's eye,
The little cat said 'Cor blimey';
'Oh, I'm sorry, sir, if I piddled in your eye,
I didn't know you were behind me'.

Quite apart from this being sung to an Irish tune (which we call *The Girl I Left Behind Me*, though its Irish name is *The Boyne Water*), the words would suggest its Irish origin, with the neat well-placed rhyming of 'piddled', 'little' (pronounced 'liddle') and 'didn't', and a sub-rhyme of 'cor', 'sorry', 'sir' and 'were'. The lines also have alliterative binding, as 'big', 'blimey' and 'behind' all have different types of alliteration on the letter b. And the 'Oh' at the start of the odd lines is balanced by 'eye' at the ends, supplemented by a kind of end rhyme in the even lines. We also have a repeat rhyme between 'eye' in line 3 and 'I' in line 4, echoed by 'know' in line 4. This quatrain is full of riches. It is most effective when sung with a strong Irish accent. Sometimes you hear it in a debased anglicised form, with slight alterations to the words; this destroys the rhymes and shows that the singer has no appreciation of a literary gem in miniature. The verse is a direct descendant of the old bardic poetry. As Roy Wentworth once remarked, you can get a lot of pleasure from a well-wrought rhyme scheme.]

The origins of *I Got a Kiss of the King's Hand* are found in the Wardlaw Manuscript, where the Rev. James Fraser, minister of Kirkhill, on the Beauly Firth west of Inverness, wrote his account of an incident in 1651. It was written a little later in the 17th century, and is said to be based on an eye-witness account.

He said the Scots army was encamped at Torwood, near Stirling, ready to march south to its disastrous defeat at the Battle of Worcester. The Scots were supporting the attempt of King Charles II to regain his throne.

While they were waiting for all the troops to assemble, the musicians in the army were holding competitions, to find the best trumpeter and so on. When it came to the best piper, however, all the pipers withdrew in favour of John MacGurmen or McGyurmen (= MacCrimmon), piper to the Earl of Sutherland. (MacGurmen was the normal spelling for the name we now know as MacCrimmon, and it was used until the mid-18th century, when MacCrimmon was gradually introduced.)

This John MacGurmen was described as 'the Earle of Sutherland's Domestick', that is, his indoor servant. The Earl himself was not present, but had sent a small force of his men to support the King.

When the King arrived to inspect his troops, he noticed this old fellow standing with his hat on, where everyone else was uncovered as a mark of respect. He asked who it was, and was told 'You are the King, but he is the Prince of Pipers'. The King then sent for John, and when the old man knelt before him, the royal hand was extended, and John got to kiss it. (There, that didn't hurt, did it?). At once he sprang up and played an exultant new tune, called *I Got a Kiss of the King's Hand,* and everyone marvelled.

The Wardlaw manuscript is entitled *Polichronicron seu Policrata Temporum, or, The True Genealogy of the Frasers, 916–1674,* and the account of the incident is on pages 379–80. The wording in the manuscript is as follows:

[At Stirling] there was great competition betuixt the trumpets in the army: one Axell, the Earl of Hoomes trumpeter, carried it by the Kings own decision. The next was anent the pipers; but the Earle of Sutherlands domestick carried it of all the camp, for non contended with him. All the pipers in the army gave John Macgurmen the van, and acknowledged him for their patron in chiefe. It was pretty in a morning [the King] in parad viewing the regiments and bragads. He saw no less than 80 pipers in a crould bareheaded, and John McGyurmen in the middle covered. He asked what society that was? It was told his Majesty: Sir, you are our King, and yonder old man in the middle is the Prince of Pipers. He cald him by name, and, comeing to the King, kneeling, his Majesty reacht him his hand to kiss; and instantly played an extemporanian part Fuoris Pooge i spoge i Rhi, I got a kiss of the King's hand, of which he and they all were vain.

In spite of the confusing pronouns, this is clear enough. The Gaelic verb is *fuair,* the English 'got', and any attempt to change the wording is later. The word *part* must be Gaelic *port* 'tune'. Note the two differing spellings of the name *MacGurmen* within one paragraph. This is entirely typical of the time, when consistency of spelling was not even a consideration.

Note also that the King did not ask 'Why is that old boy keeping his hat on?', but said 'What Society is that?' as if he recognised that a society ritual allowed the old man that privilege. At that time the Freemasons were sometimes referred to as 'the Society', and it seems likely that the King had them in mind.

This eye-witness account, later taken down by Mr Fraser, appears to be authentic – but there is another version, written in 1835 by the Rev. Dr Norman MacLeod, and published later, in *The Messenger*. This says that in 1651, Patrick Mor MacCrimmon (not John) accompanied his chief, Rory Mir MacLeod (known as Rory 'the Witty' and later the subject of *Rory MacLoude's Lament*), and Roderick MacLeod of Talisker, on a visit to London, and they went to see the King, Charles II. Patrick played for him, and the King, delighted, gave Patrick his hand to kiss. Patrick at once broke into *I Got a Kiss,* and the King then knighted Roderick of Talisker.

This account cannot be right. The date is wrong: Rory Mir did visit London but not in 1651, when he was a mere child, too young to go with the army to the Battle of Worcester. His visit was ten years later. Was the visit described by Dr MacLeod supposed to be before Worcester? The King was not in Cromwell's London then. And later in 1651, after Worcester, the King was on the run. From other sources we know that Roderick was knighted on the field of battle, just before Worcester. And the story that the King welcomed the MacLeod party is not borne out by other accounts, which say that when Rory did visit London, after the Restoration, the King, not wanting to give him compensation for the losses of his clan, was less than cordial.

The Rev. Dr Norman was writing for a public whom he wanted to fire with enthusiasm, for Gaelic, for education, for their own history. He wrote lively, interesting articles, showing himself to be a journalist at heart, as he would not let a mere fact spoil a good story. His motive was not the accurate recording of history, it was the stimulation of a downtrodden people, and so we may forgive him.

The privilege of playing with the bonnet on was mentioned again in 1815, when Alexander Campbell visited Donald Ruadh MacCrimmon in his home at Glenelg. He later wrote that Donald Ruadh 'seized the pipe, put on his hat (his usual custom), breathed into the bag, tuned the drones to the chanter, gave a prelude in a stile of brilliancy that flashed like lightning, and commenced *Failte Phrionnsa* in tones that spoke to the ear and affected the heart'. (Diary of Alexander Campbell, Laing manuscript, University of Edinburgh).

Walter Scott had also commented on Donald's habit of donning his hat before playing: 'He plays to MacLeod and his lady, but only in the same room, and maintains his minstrel privilege by putting on his bonnet as soon as he begins to play'.

Willie Gray, himself a Master Mason, said in an interview in 1961 that this custom of donning the hat was 'allied to' the rituals of Freemasonry, but he was careful not to put discussion of masonic practices into writing.

Who was the John MacCrimmon named in what must be seen as the authentic account, that of the Wardlaw manuscript? John living at Leacachan, on Loch Duich, in the early years of the 18th century cannot have been the Earl of Sutherland's piper, who was already an old man in 1651, with his reputation well established. His age means he was not a son of Patrick Mor, but he could have been a brother, cousin or uncle of Patrick, perhaps a brother of Donald Mor. The MacCrimmon family in Harris is said to have been a bottomless well of accomplished pipers (a claim not supported by any provable evidence), but we do not know the names of most of them as early as this.

Sources

Angus MacKay, Manuscript
Alec Haddow, *The History and Structure of Ceol Mor*
Margaret Stewart
Roy Wentworth
Wardlaw MS
Rev. Dr Norman MacLeod
Willie Gray

John Garve Macleod of Raasay's Lament

This is sometimes called *Iain Garbh's Lament,* but in Gaelic MacLeod of Raasay was known as MacGilleChaluim, or 'Gillechaluim, rather than as Iain Garbh. Donald MacDonald called it *Cumhadh MhicGilli Chalum Rasay* in Gaelic, but *MacLeod of Rasay's Lament* in English. This seems to have set the pattern for naming the piece.

John Garve was renowned for his strength and good looks, and for his likable character. When he was drowned in a shipwreck in 1671, Mary MacLeod made a famous poetic lament for him (see below). He had become chief of the Raasay MacLeods in 1648. He was married to

Janet, daughter of Sir Rory Mor MacLeod, and this is the reason for attributing this composition to Patrick Mor MacCrimmon – or possibly to Patrick Og, depending on the date of Patrick Mor's death, which is uncertain, but around 1670. From the maturity and finely developed quality of the work, it is more likely, perhaps, to be late Patrick Mor than early Patrick Og. Simon Fraser attributed it to first one, then the other. Dr Orme, editing Simon Fraser's collection, quoted a diary written by the Rev. John Fraser, Kilmuir, which states that Patrick Mor composed it in April 1661. This date must be mistaken.

Donald MacDonald gave a background story involving a feud between John Garve and Sir Donald MacDonald of the Isles; the latter had got John Garve's sister with child but refused to marry her. John vowed revenge, and to avert this, Sir Donald induced a witch to wreck the boat in which John was returning from Lewis. This version differs in some detail from that of the Wardlaw manuscript.

The Rev. James Fraser of Kirkhill gave us the account of what happened, preserved in the Wardlaw manuscript:

> This April (1671) the Earle of Seaforth duelling (dwelling) in the Lewes (Lewis), a dredful accident happened. His lady being brought to bed there, the Earle sent for John Garve McKleud, Laird of Rarzay, to witness the christening; and, after the treat and solemnity of the feast, Rarsay takes leave to goe home, and, after a rant of drinking uppon the shoare, went aboard off his birling (sailing boat) and sailed away with a strong north gale off wind; and whither by giving too much saile and no ballast, or the unskillfullness of the seamen, or that they could not mannage the strong Dutch canvas saile, the boat whelmd, and all the men dround in view of the coast. The Laird and sixteen of his kinsmen, the prime, perished; non of them ever found; a grewhound or two cast ashore dead; and pieces of the birling. One Alexander Mackleod in Lewes the night before had voice warning him thrice not to goe at all with Rarsey, for all would drown in there return; yet he went with him, being infatuat (foolish), and drownd with the rest. This account I had from Alexander's brother the summer after. It was drunkness did the mischiefe.

As was customary after such a disaster, a witch was blamed. She is said by some to have been John Garbh's wet-nurse, living in Raasay; she stoked up her cauldron until it suddenly boiled over, one version mentioning that she floated a mouse in half an egg-shell on the boiling water, and at the very moment the shell tipped over and the mouse drowned, her chief's ship went down. Her motive is not entirely clear, as the Laird was well-liked and universally mourned, but Somhairle

MacLean said there was a tradition that she was bribed to do it by MacDonald of Duntulm, and this story was embroidered with lurid detail. Clearly the traditions have become entwined, with similar echoes in different versions.

Seumas Archie MacDonald had a Skye story which backs this tradition: John Garve called in at Duntulm on his way to Lewis, and had dinner there. During the meal, his dogs under the table were attacked by MacDonald's dogs, and in the ensuing fight the Raasay dogs were the winners. This annoyed MacDonald (doubtless he had a heavy bet on the outcome) to such an extent that he paid John's wet-nurse to summon her occult powers in revenge. Many well-known witches were drawn in to help her, the same ones who had helped to wreck the Spanish Armada, and some of them flew out to sea and landed on the yards and gunwhale of John Garve's boat. Knowing what their presence meant, he drew his great sword and made a mighty cut at the nearest of them, missed, and split the galley from gunwhale to keel – and down she went. Donald MacDonald said the boat, when found wrecked, had John Garve's sword stuck in the gunwhale to a depth of one-and-a-half planks.

John Garve was about fifty years old, but had no children. He was succeeded by his cousin (Mary MacLeod said it was his brother).

John MacInnes (*TGSI* LVI 1985) said there was a Raasay tradition that some time after the Chief's death, he was seen steering his birlinn between Raasay and Skye and was heard chanting an oar-song as he urged on his spectral crew. The refrain of the song was *Buille oirre ho ro an ceann*, where the command *Buille an ceann* ('Aim the head') is divided by vocables *oirre ho ro,* expressing grief. Of this song, Bella MacLeod (Beileag an Achaidh) could recall only one couplet:

Ged a reidhinn-sa 'na' Chlachan   Though we made it to the Clachan
Chan aithnicheadh iad co bha   They would not realise who it was –
  ann –
Buille oirre, etc   Aim the head, etc

Alexander Nicolson tells of a tradition in Raasay that on every Friday for a full year after his death, one of his sisters, named Janet, composed and sang a new lament to his memory. One of these, the *Raasay Lament,* has survived, a song of poignant sorrow. Sorley MacLean quoted it in his paper 'Some Raasay Traditions', and it appears as Appendix 2 in Norma MacLeod's book on Raasay.

Among the many songs and poems made in memory of John Garbh (Garve), the *Marbh-rann* composed by Mary MacLeod stands out:

Mo bheud is mo chradh	It is harm to me, and anguish,
Mar a dh'eiridh da	what has happened to
An fhear ghleusta ghraidh	the skilful well-loved man
Bha treun 'san spairn	who was strong in conflict
Is nach faicear gu brath an	and will not be seen in Raasay
Ratharsaidh.	again.
Bu tu am fear curanta mor	You were a great hero
Bu mhath cumadh is treoir	strongly built
o t'uilinn gu d'dhorn	from your elbow to your fist,
o d'mhullach gu d'bhroig:	from your crown to your shoe:
Mhic Mhuire mo leon	Son of Mary! it hurts me
Thu bhith an innis nan ron	is that you are in the seals' pasture
nach faighear thu.	and will not be found.
Bu tu sealgair a'gheoidh,	You were a hunter of the wild goose,
Lamh gun dearmad gun leon	your hand unerring and unblemished
Air am bu shuarach an t-or	which was generous in giving gold
Thoirt a bhuannachd a'cheoil,	as a reward for music;
Is gun d'fhuair thu na's leoir	for you have plenty and would spend
is na caitheadh tu.	freely.
Bu tu sealgair an fheidh	You were a hunter of the deer,
Leis an deargta na bein;	by whom hides were reddened;
Bhiodh coin earbsach air eill	trusty hounds were held on the
	leash
Aig an Albannach threun;	by the mighty man of Alba
	[Scotland];
Caite am faca mi fein	where have I seen
Aon Duine fo'n grein	any man beneath the sun
A dheanadh riut euchd	who would challenge you in heroic
flathasach?	deeds?
Spealp nach diobradh	A fine fellow, you did not falter
An cath no an stri thu,	in strife or in battle;
Casan direach	your limbs were straight,
Fada finealt:	long and shapely;
Mo creach dhiobhail	alas, the pity of it,
Chaidh tu a dhith oirnn	you are lost to us
Le neart sine,	by the strength of the storm,
Lamh nach diobradh caitheadh	you whose hand always sailed your
oirre.	vessel hard.
Och m'eudail uam	Alas, my treasure taken from me,
Gun sgeul 'sa 'chuan	without trace in the ocean,
Bu ghle mhath snuadh	was very good to look on
Ri grein 's ri fuachd;	in sunshine and in cold;

Is e chlaoidh do shluagh
Nach d'fheud thu an uair a
        ghabhail orra.

that is what has pained your people,
that you could not reach them in
        that hour.

Is math thig gunna nach diult
Air curaidh mo ruin
Ann am mullach a'chuirn
Is air uilinn nan stuc;
Gum biodh fuil ann air tus an
        spreadhaidh sin.

A gun that does not fail
would suit my beloved warrior
on the summit of the mountain
or the corners of the rocks;
blood would flow at its first shot.

Is e dh'fhag silteach mo shuil
Faicinn t'fhearainn gun surd,
Is do bhaile gun smuid

What brings a tear to my eye
is seeing your land without activity,
now that your dwelling-place has no
        smoke

Fo charraig nan sugh,
Dheagh mhic Chaluim nan tur
        a Ratharsaidh.

under the wave-lashed rock,
excellent son of Calum of the
        towers, from Raasay.

Mo bheud is mo bhron
Mar a dh'eirich dho,
Muir beucach mor
Ag leum mu d'bhord,
Thu fein is do sheoid
An uair reub ur seoil
Nach d'fheud sibh treoir a
        chaitheadh orra.

It is distress and sorrow to me
what has happened to him,
a great roaring sea
leaping around your boat;
yourself and your stout crew
when your sails ripped,
you had not the strength to sail her.

Is tu b'fhaicillich' ceum
Mu'n taice-sa an de
De na chunnaic mi fein
Air faiche nan ceud
Air each 's e 'na leum,
Is cha bu slacan gun fheum
        claidheamh ort.

You were the least reckless,
that time in former days,
of all I saw myself
in a field of hundreds,
mounted on a lively horse;
and no sword was useless when
        you were carrying it.

Is math lubadh tu pic
O chulaibh do chinn
An am rusgadh a'ghill
Le ionnsaigh nach till
Is air mo laimh gum bu
        chinnteach saighead uat.

Well could you bend a bow
behind your head
while making a pledge of valour
not to retreat in battle;
and by my hand! your arrow flew
        straight.

Is e an sgeul craiteach
Do'n mhnaoi a dh'fhag thu
Is do t'aon bhrathair
A shuidh 'nad aite:

This is a sore tale
for the wife you have left behind
and for the only brother
who has taken your place:

Di-luain Caisge	on Easter Monday
Chaidh tonn-bhaidhte ort	a drowning-wave came on you,
Craobh a b'airde de'n abhall	you, the loftiest tree in the
thu.	orchard.

Even in translation the quality of Mary's work shines through. It is thought that John Garve as a child had been one of her charges, along with the Chief's children at Dunvegan. She seems to have been very fond of the children in her care.

Sources

Wardlaw MS
Seumas Archie MacDonald, Trotternish
Alexander Nicolson, *History of Skye*
Norma MacLeod, *Raasay*
Sorley MacLean *TGSI* XLIX
The Poems of Mary MacLeod
John MacInnes *TGSI* LVI

The King's Taxes

The Gaelic name for this work is *Mal an Righ,* which means the King's Rents rather than his Taxes, but in fact they were the same thing.

The year was 1608, and the King (James VI) was trying to subdue his rebellious Highland chiefs. He wanted them to sign an agreement to all sorts of measures – to reduce the number of castles, armed men, war galleys and so on – and among all the clauses was the vexed question of taxes. The King was supposed to get a proportion of the rents collected from the clan tenants, but there were always excuses: the tenants hadn't paid up, or the crops had failed, or the money must have got lost on the way, and his majesty rarely received what he considered his share. So now he proposed a new scheme: he wanted a guaranteed proportion of the rents, calculated in advance and to be paid anyway, whether or not the rents were collected.

A glance at the legal documents of that year shows many references to 'His Majestie's rents' and 'His Majestie's taxes', making it clear that these two were virtually the same.

Not unnaturally, the chiefs would have none of this. They refused to sign the King's agreement. 'Right then,' said King James, 'we'll have a meeting. Come to Mull, and we'll talk it over.'

The chiefs, or their eldest sons, duly arrived at Aros, in Mull, and the King's representative was there to meet them. 'Tomorrow is the

Sabbath', he said, 'in the morning, we'll all go on board my ship for Divine Service, then we'll get down to negotiations.'

They went on board the next day – except for Rory Mor MacLeod, who trusted the King about as much as the King trusted him. He was not going to set foot on the King's ship; so he stayed on shore. He was right, because no sooner were they aboard than the skipper raised the anchor and set sail. The chiefs were taken down to Ayrshire, and clapped into prison until they would agree to sign. They were imprisoned for several months, over the winter. Eventually, they had to sign the Statutes of Iona (and Rory Mor signed, too – in the end). Meantime, Rory Mor went home to Dunvegan, doubtless full of glee. 'Oh, I got the better of him, I saw through his tricks. Pay the King's taxes? Not I.' So the mood of the piece, presumably made by one of his MacCrimmon pipers, is cocky, gloating defiance.

John MacDonald, Inverness, teaching this tune to his 20th-century pupils, told them to play it defiantly, the mood being anger and triumph. Despite this background and this instruction, some judges want the tune to be played as a lament, smooth, plaintive and melodic, and this opinion might be strengthened by the use of what seem to be keening phrases, especially in the first variation. Pipers have to make up their own minds about the mood of the piece, and play it as they feel it.

We assume it is a MacCrimmon work, but which of the MacCrimmons made it? Donald Mor was up in Sutherland by 1608, fleeing retribution after killing his brother's murderer (see above, *A Flame of Wrath*). Presumably Rory Mor in Donald's absence called on other MacCrimmon pipers to take his place. The MacCrimmons are said to have lived in South Harris, and tradition has it (unprovably) that they had a supply of trained pipers available if required. The only one we know by name at this time, apart from Donald Mor and his son Patrick Mor, was the John (Iain) MacCrimmon, who in 1651 was an old man, universally admired for his playing. As piper to the Earl of Sutherland, he composed *I Got a Kiss of the King's Hand*. It is possible, but certainly not proven, that he made *The King's Taxes*, as a younger man in 1608. Different king, of course.

Sources

Records of the Privy Seal
Alexander Mackenzie, *History of the MacLeods*
John MacDonald's pupils

Lament for the Children

There are at least three traditions about the title of this work:

(a) The well-known and widely accepted story, told by Angus MacKay, that Patrick Mor MacCrimmon had eight fine sons, and one Sunday he walked round the head of Loch Dunvegan with all eight of them, to attend church at Kilmuir. Within the year, seven were dead, lying in Kilmuir graveyard, probably victims of smallpox, brought in by a visiting ship. It is said that the grieving father, Patrick Mor, made this lament, basing it on the keening cries of his wife. They were left with the one son, Patrick Og.

(b) General Thomason said there was another story associated with the tune – but lacking the authority of Angus MacKay, it has not been generally accepted. It appeared in Donald MacDonald's collection of piobaireachd, around 1820. Alistair Campsie pointed out that this pre-dates the publication of Angus MacKay's story, but that does not necessarily mean it was older. It seems that three young girls, two of them Campbells and one a Cameron, Lochiel's daughter, went to swim in a deep pool in the river near Lochiel's house at Achnacarry. When they did not return, servants were sent to look for them, but in the end it was Lochiel himself and his wife who found them, all three lying drowned in the pool. It is said that the piobaireachd was made to commemorate them, by Lochiel's piper, who played it at their funeral. It is likely that the General heard this from Keith Cameron or his brother Alexander, who was piper to a later Lochiel. No date is given, and of course it may be that the work was played at the funeral, but was not necessarily composed for it. It may have become associated with that Cameron tragedy, the loss of the young girls, just as in more recent times it has been linked with the nation's sorrow for the tragic shooting of the small children in Dunblane, in 1996.

(c) There is a third possible explanation: the Gaelic title *Cumha na Cloinne* may be translated as either *Lament for the Children* or *Lament for the Clans*. In the 1780s, the two titles were used interchangeably by English speakers, for the same work. It has been suggested that Patrick Mor may have composed the work after the disastrous Battle of Worcester in 1651, when the MacLeods lost 700 of their 800 clansmen in battle against Cromwell, fighting to support King Charles II in his attempt to regain his throne. Not all the 700 were killed: some were captured and transported to the West Indies as slaves, but 700 failed to come home and were lost to the clan. It is supposed that Patrick Mor took part in the battle, and survived to return to Skye, where he composed this beautiful lament for his lost comrades.

Later interpreters have suggested that the *Lament for the Clans* was referring to Culloden, putting the work well into the next century – but it is usually accepted as a mid-17th-century composition.

Is it coincidence that both (a) and (c) involve the loss of seven-eighths of a family or clan, for which the same word is used? Could Angus' story have been symbolic, as were so many Gaelic stories?

It is not possible to be certain. Angus MacKay's tale could have been invented to account for one meaning of the title – and if it was indeed symbolic of the MacLeods' losses at Worcester, the story is no less acceptable. But it would be a shame to destroy anyone's cherished beliefs, especially about a work as beloved and revered as this.

The *Lament for the Duke of Hamilton* and *Blar Vuster* are two piobaireachd works commemorating the Battle of Worcester. Neither is of the quality of the *Lament for the Children*.

Sources
Angus MacKay, Manuscript
General Thomason

Lament for Donald Ban MacCrimmon
It is generally accepted that this lengthy work was composed by MAL-COLM MACCRIMMON, the son of Patrick Og and piper to MacLeod of Dunvegan, in memory of his younger half-brother Donald Ban (Fair-haired Donald), killed at the Rout of Moy in 1746.

The MacLeods had raised two Independent Companies in 1745, to fight against the Jacobites, and one of them formed part of Lord Loudoun's regiment, in the Hanoverian army. Its piper was DONALD BAN MACCRIMMON. Other Skye pipers in the Companies were IAIN MACINTYRE and NEIL MACCODRUM, of whom we know nothing else.

Donald Ban had, from 1730 until the '45, lived in Harris as Mac-Leod's piper there, receiving annually the sum of £26 13s 4d until 1738, when he had a rise to £33 6s 8d. In 1745 he left for Dunvegan and the army. These sums may have been the equivalent of his annual rent, or at least half of it. In the accounts for 1742–43, the sum of £16 is recorded as the price of 'a milk cow allowed Donald McCrimmon'.

This is possibly the earliest occurrence of the spelling McCrimmon (with no *u*), but in the same document there is also MacCrummen for the same man. We find 'the widow McRiman' in 1748 and 1755, but the vast majority of spellings of the name use *u*: McCrumen, MacCrumen, McCumra, McCrume, MacCrummen, MacCruman, MacCruimein or MacCrummon, and other variants.

This was the time when the modern spelling (and pronunciation) of MacCrimmon was just beginning to come in. It was probably introduced when *u* pronunciations were felt to be Scottish vernacular and therefore vulgar, and were being replaced by *i,* much more civilized. It was increasingly common in the 18th century, when those who wrote down names felt themselves to be superior to the common herd, because they were literate. As a result, we find dual spellings of *Drum-* and *Drim-* in placenames, or *Grim-* and *Grum-,* and confusion between *Cul-* (Gaelic *cul* 'back') and *Kil-* (Gaelic *cill* 'graveyard').

Donald was clearly a man of some standing in Harris, as he was one of the witnesses to the Chamberlain's accounts in 1733 and 1735. He is ranked along with the Harris schoolmaster, which gives him professional status rather than that of a servant. He took over as the piper in Harris when his brother Malcolm replaced their father at Dunvegan in 1730, after Patrick Og's death. Malcolm was considerably older than Donald, being his half-brother, the son of the first marriage, born around 1690. It is thought that Donald Ban was born in 1710, to Patrick's second wife, whom he married in 1707.

Malcolm was living at Scarista in 1728, renting a Pennyland (probably the holding known as the Kirkpenny), for £53 6s 8d – a lot of money in those days – and the accounts say 'possessed by Malcolm McCrummen by MacLeods order'.

The next account is dated 1733, witnessed by Donald and others, and it is clear that Donald had taken over not only the position of Harris piper but also the tenancy at Scarista. Donald was never MacLeod's first piper at Dunvegan, and did not replace Malcolm there.

The storytellers said that Donald had a devoted lady-friend at Dunvegan, as well as a wife back in Scarista, Harris. The girlfriend's name has been preserved as Sheila (Sile) MacDonald, living in Dunvegan – but it was later alleged, by her descendants, that she was not Donald's sweetheart, merely an admirer of his playing. As he was leaving for the wars, the story goes, she sang him the song *Cha Till MacCruimein* (MacCrimmon Will Not Return), which must have done wonders for his morale. Donald is supposed to have made the piobaireachd of the same name, from her song, though it is not clear when he had time to do so. He must surely have known the tune already – it was much older than 1745. Was it Sheila who adapted the words to a MacCrimmon context?

The History of Skye tells a somewhat different tale. According to this story, MacLeod's company of some 400–500 men, with their piper, Donald Ban, was gathered in Skye, about to make for Kyleakin in late October, 1745. Donald was uneasy, because although the men were under the impression they were off to join the Prince, he suspected they were being sent to support the Hanoverians. He became fearful of his probable fate, so he went to consult a witch who was handily hard by, on the morning they were to set out. She told him that everything depended on the attitude of his wife: if she willingly helped him prepare and showed proper anxiety for him, all would be well, but if she had no concern for his needs, disaster would follow. It would be no good his asking her for anything, as her co-operation had to be entirely voluntary.

He went home full of foreboding, as it was well known that his wife was lazy and neglectful of his comfort (could Sheila MacDonald have influenced her attitude?). He found her lying on a bench, with the fire not lit and the room untidy, and as he bustled about making his preparations, she ignored him. As the time for departure drew near, he increased his efforts to make her take notice. He took up his pipe, tuned it, put it down, did it all again, but she took no heed. He packed up his belongings, adjusted his hose, took off his brogues and put them on again, fastening them as ostentatiously as possible, after throwing one of them on the floor with a clatter. Still no reaction. He could hear the tumult outside that meant the time had come for him to depart. He lifted his pipe, and as he went out, with a heavy heart, he uttered the Gaelic proverb *Cha ghluais brog, no bruidheann, droch bhean tighe* ('Neither boot nor speech will move a bad housewife'). In his wife's defence, it has to be said that the records point to her being in Harris all through this period, and Donald Ban's home was not in Skye. The story about her may have been based on the wording of that proverb.

Before the battle of Culloden, in February 1746, Lord Loudon, with his Hanoverian regiment, was at Inverness. The Prince was not far away, at Moy Hall, as guest of Lady MacIntosh, an ardent young Jacobite known as 'Colonel Anne'. A certain piquancy is added by the fact that she and Lord Loudon, who were both married, were having a passionate adulterous affair which later caused a great deal of scandalised gossip. They had been carrying on together for some months before this, and resumed their affair after the battle of Culloden.

Apart from their flagrant behaviour, points of outrage included the fact that Loudon, one of the foremost of the Hanoverian leaders, had two pipers in his household who had been sent to him by prominent

Jacobites: 'A piper formerly servant to Lady MacIntosh call'd David Ross now Butler to Lord Lowdoun' was one ground for disquiet, and that 'MacDonald formerly a Piper to young (MacDonald of) Scothouse was a Runner at Lord Lowdoun's' was another, since Scothouse, too, was a Jacobite or Rebel. The affair made even Loudoun a security risk in the eyes of the authorities, in case he had been tainted by Jacobinism.

Eventually he went abroad to escape the gossip, but Lady Anne followed him. He shook her off, in the end, many years after Culloden. She was only twenty-one at the time of the Rout of Moy, renowned for her beauty, her wit and her impulsive behaviour. We have to add that she had been married very young, against her will, to a much older man.

Ruairidh Halford MacLeod has shown that the story of Donald Ban's death, long accepted as the truth, was a whitewash, to cover up what really happened. When word reached Moy that Loudon's regiment was marching from Inverness to capture the Prince, Lady Anne removed her guest, with a bodyguard, to nearby Moy Beag, and to create a diversion, she sent her blacksmith and four others to hold a position in front of Moy Hall. It was a winter's evening, and nearly dark, and the five men hid in some peat-stacks, pretending they were a much larger force, and well-armed – when in fact they had only one gun among the five of them, and only one shot.

This is where the accounts diverge. The five were scurrying around in the dusk, shouting things like 'Keep your men well back', and 'Hold your fire' and 'Bring up the cannon from the rear', to fool the enemy. According to the published account, the blacksmith, Donald Fraser, fired a shot, and as luck would have it, hit the best piper within a hundred miles, killing Donald Ban MacCrimmon as the Hanoverians bravely advanced.

What really happened – and proof has now been uncovered – was that Loudon's men were young and untrained, and consequently nervous and trigger-happy; so he split his force, sending thirty men with an officer by a different route to Moy, in a futile attempt to prevent word of their approach from reaching the Hall. These thirty saw men among the peat-stacks, and opened fire, but hit nobody. The main body of Loudon's men, some 1,200 of them, about a mile away, heard the firing, and panic set in. Five companies turned and ran; the rest stood their ground, but lost their heads. They began 'dropping shots' says Loudon's report to Cumberland, 'one of which killed a piper at my very feet'.

This version was supported by two other contemporary accounts, and by oral tradition.

So poor Donald Ban was killed by random so-called 'Friendly Fire', shot in the back by someone on his own side. He may have been the only casualty of the Rout, and victim of incompetent leadership and indiscipline, though some sources say four others in the regiment were injured. Loudon himself seems to have had a narrow escape. His men picked up Donald's body and fled, taking it on a cart for burial in Inverness. There is a tradition of the grave of Donald Ban being at Moy, but it has not been found, there or in Inverness. It was an ignominious end for a fine piper – but, as Seumas MacNeill remarked, it did give rise to one of our best piobaireachd works.

The false account was made public rather than the true one, to preserve morale in the Hanoverian army. It was current for the next 250 years.

Donald Ban's wife in Harris, whose name was Rachel, referred to in estate documents as his 'relict, the Widow McRiman', was paid £100 compensation by the chief, MacLeod of Dunvegan, when Donald was killed; and MacLeod personally saw to it that she received £50 per year for the next five years, and after that, £25 every year, until 1789, when the Harris estate was sold. She was also supplied with meal for the feeding of her children.

It is generally accepted that the Lament was composed by Donald's elder brother, Malcolm, because he was the Dunvegan piper at that time, but Simon Fraser, apparently drawing on the (lost) work of Niel MacLeod of Gesto, stated that the composer was Donald Ruadh, Malcolm's son; Donald Ruadh, however, was a child of six in 1746 when his uncle died. It is an odd claim for Gesto to make, since he was a friend of Malcolm's other son, Iain Dubh, who must have known who made the Lament.

Simon Fraser's comments are even more strange in that someone – was it himself, his father, Gesto or Iain Dubh? – was at pains to diminish Malcolm in the history of the MacCrimmons: Fraser said, for example, that it was Donald Ban who succeeded Patrick Og as piper at Dunvegan, and that Malcolm (the elder half-brother) came later. It can be shown that Donald Ban was never the Dunvegan piper, and that Malcolm held the post for some thirty-seven years. The motives of Gesto (or whoever) are not clear, but may have been bound up with Freemasonry. Perhaps Malcolm had rejected membership, or had mocked the masons, and Gesto, a fiery man, resented this – but Iain Dubh was Malcolm's own son. Plenty of sons, of course, fall out with their fathers, but in the Gaelic world of 18th-century Skye, to repudiate a father's claim to fame could bring only disgrace to the son. It seems much more likely that the rejection of Malcolm was the work of Gesto, for whatever reason.

A Gaelic poem, *In Praise of MacCrimmon's Great Pipe*, was made by Alasdair Mac Mhaighstir Alasdair (Alexander MacDonald), probably in 1746. It refers to Donald Ban as 'the fair-haired man from Skye', and depicts him solely as a military piper.

Sources

Ruairidh Halford-MacLeod
Culloden Papers vol. v
Cumberland Papers Book 12
More Culloden Papers vols iv–v
John Gibson, *Traditional Gaelic Bagpiping*
Simon Fraser, *Piobaireachd*
Alasdair mac Mhaighstir Alasdair

Lament for Donald Duaghal Mackay

It should be noted that Donald's by-name was not Dougal or Dugald, as pipers so often call him, but Duaghal, and the middle -*gh*- is not pronounced. 'DOO-al' is close to the Sutherland pronunciation. The meaning is not entirely certain, but seems to be associated with the Black Arts (witchcraft). It might be translated 'Black-avised'. Some say it means 'fierce'. Donald was very dark in complexion and hair, with black brows meeting above his nose, a sure sign of alliance with the Devil. As a result, he was reputed to have had many affairs with beautiful witches in Sutherland, especially in Dornoch, but this is no surprise, as he had affairs with innumerable women in the north. 'Lock up your daughters – and your wife' was the cry when His Lordship was seen approaching.

It is an oddity that only in the piping world is he known as 'Donald Duaghal': historians do not recognise him by this name and always call him '1st Lord Reay', and in the tales told in the north, he is simply 'His Lordship'. Donald Duaghal must be the oldest of his names, as the other two date from after 1628, when he was ennobled.

He was 1st Lord Reay, and 14th Chief of the Clan MacKay, in Strathnaver, which was at that time the name for a large area covering most of North-west Sutherland. Born in 1591, he succeeded his father Uisdean as chief in 1614, was knighted in 1616, and became Lord Reay in 1628 (he received the title in exchange for services rendered to King

Charles I, i.e. the king owed him money). He was a nephew of the Earl of Sutherland, his mother being a Gordon, the Earl's sister.

In 1626, Donald raised a regiment of mercenary soldiers, and took them to Germany to fight for King Gustavus Adolphus of Sweden against the Holy Roman Emperor. His motive was solely to make money, and he was not, as has sometimes been suggested, a fanatical Protestant; he said once that if the Swedish king did not pay up, he would fight for the Catholics against him. The regiment, known as 'MacKay's Invincibles', was a great success, as Donald was a born leader, but it was not the money-spinner that he had expected. When he died in 1649, he was nearly bankrupt, but three monarchs, the Kings of Sweden, Denmark and Britain, owed him thousands of pounds (one estimate made the total more than £30,000, a huge amount in those days).

He was a colourful character, intelligent, lively, innovative, warm-hearted, well educated, an affectionate father and an excellent leader of men. He had his weaknesses, however – extravagance was one, guilelessness another, but his greatest weakness was for women. He was forever getting himself needlessly embroiled with scheming females, some supplied by his enemies in the English court, others of his own choosing. These women nearly managed to ruin him, more than once. He was married respectably three times, and dubiously twice more, but was a poor husband who had many affairs, resulting in a large number of illegitimate children. One of these was a daughter who, according to oral tradition in both Scotland and Canada, married the piper Ruairidh MacKay: their son was Iain Dall, the Blind Piper of Gairloch.

On his return from Germany, Donald Duaghal became involved with the Stuart cause, and in particular with Montrose. In 1649 both Donald and Montrose were in Bergen, trying to raise a force of Norwegian mercenaries, when they received news of the execution of Charles I. Donald was already unwell, suffering from heart problems, and it is said that the shock killed him. The King of Denmark, who was also King of Norway, sent a frigate to bring his body back to Scotland, landing it at Tongue, on the north coast. The King probably felt it was the least he could do, since he owed Donald a small fortune, which he would now not have to repay. Donald was buried in the vault beneath St Andrews Kirk in Tongue: the church itself has since been rebuilt, but the vault is still there.

The style of the Lament seems not unlike that of some of Iain Dall MacKay's work. A pupil of John MacDonald, Inverness, said John had told him that when competing in Skye, he had offered *Donald Dua-ghal* as one of his tunes, and had it turned down by the Skye judges. They said it was not composed by a MacCrimmon. It is, it seems, only since World War II that *Donald Duaghal* has been on the Skye list of MacCrimmon tunes.

The Skye judges were probably right. Those who say it must be a MacCrimmon work argue that it is by Donald Mor, since Donald Mor was piper to Donald Duaghal's father, in Strathnaver, and fought alongside Donald Duaghal at Thurso in 1612. And so he did. What they forget, or ignore, is that Donald Mor died about ten years before Donald Duaghal, so he cannot have been the one. So, they say, it must have been Donald Mor's son, Patrick Mor. But Patrick never met Donald Duaghal, and, more to the point, Patrick's chief, MacLeod of Dunvegan, wanted nothing to do with Donald Duaghal.

In 1649, when Donald died, he was deeply embroiled in the cause of Montrose, fighting against the government forces. MacLeod of Dunvegan was anxious to avoid being drawn into any involvement with Montrose and Donald Duaghal, and with good reason. The bitterest enemy of Donald – and of Montrose, too – was the Earl of Argyll, and it so happened that Glenelg belonged to Argyll at this time. Glenelg was held by the MacLeods, and it was vital to the defence of their lands, as it commands the back-door into Skye – but they held it only by the grace and favour of Argyll. This made it important for MacLeod not to offend Argyll in any way, and the very last thing MacLeod wanted was his piper, Patrick Mor MacCrimmon, coming up with a magnificent lament for Argyll's enemy.

So it seems unlikely that Patrick made the lament, and Donald Dua-ghal probably had no lament at all until more than fifty years later, when his grandson, Iain Dall MacKay, the Blind Piper of Gairloch, was looking for a suitable title to please his Munro patron at Foulis Castle, near Dingwall. Iain wanted to stress the links between the Strathnaver MacKays (his own family) and the Munros of Foulis, and Donald Dua-ghal was the obvious choice: Donald's sister had married the heir to the Munro chief, who had been Donald Duaghal's close and loyal friend. The work was superb, the link between the families was emphasised, the Munro chief was flattered, Iain was rewarded, and everybody was happy – except those who regard this as heresy.

It has been said that this work was not played in competitions until Calum Piobaire MacPherson introduced it by playing it in the big three-day competition at the Glasgow Exhibition of 1888 – which he won. It is not clear where Calum Piobaire had heard it – did his father play it?

Sources

Ian Grimble, *Chief of MacKay*
Oral tradition in Sutherland, Caithness and Canada
Alan Temperley, *Tales of the North Coast*

Lament for Donald of Laggan

Described by Seumas MacNeill as 'a masterpiece in miniature, one of the most beautiful piobaireachds we have', this work is a general favourite.

It commemorates Donald MacDonald of Laggan (1543–1645), who spelled his name MacDonald, although his son took the later Glengarry spelling of MacDonnell. Donald lived at Laggan Achadrone (or Achadrum), in Glengarry, close to Invergarry Castle, in the Great Glen, and although he left there when he succeeded to the title of Glengarry, he had been known as Donald of Laggan for so long that the designation went with him, and it was his lifelong name.

His son and heir was Alasdair Dearg MacDonnell of Glengarry, who died before his father and so did not succeed to the title. Another miniature masterpiece was composed to commemorate him, too.

Stories were put about by Donald's enemies, the MacKenzies, who told everyone that Donald was worshipping heathen idols, and cited 'evidence' of his having had wooden images re-painted for his orgies. This was a calumny invented to discredit him, because he was a Catholic. At that time, 'papism', heathenism and witchcraft were intensely topical, as we know from the records of the Presbyteries of Inverness and Dingwall, in the second half of the 17th century: long passages are devoted to discussions about sorcery, the sacrifice of bulls and worship of graven idols. Some of these practices were said to date back to pre-Christian times, but some were relics of more recent Catholic ritual.

Even today, some local customs retain echoes of them: a well on one of the islands on Loch Maree is still believed by some to have healing powers, especially for those afflicted with mental illness, and the Clootie Tree near Munlochy, on the Black Isle in Easter Ross, always has fresh pieces of cloth tied to it, to bring about cure for illness, despite the uneasiness of the local ministers.

Donald's daughter (Alasdair Dearg's sister), Iseabail Mhor, married Sir Rory Mor MacLeod of Dunvegan, and it seems safe to assume that the *Lament for Donald of Laggan* was composed by the MacLeod family's piper, Patrick Mor MacCrimmon. Iseabail Mhor was already a widow when her father died. The tradition is that she loved this lament so much that she had it played by Patrick Mor outside her bedroom door every night, until she fell asleep. Like her father she lived to be 103, so that was a lot of performances of *Donald of Laggan*.

Alick Morrison (1974) said that the widowed Iseabail Mhor retired to a MacLeod dower house in Harris, where Patrick Og was then the Harris estate piper. According to this story, it was Patrick Og who played *Donald of Laggan* to her every night, at Scarista. This version has not received general acceptance, and there seems to be little evidence to support it.

Sources

Piobaireachd Society Book 8
Alec Haddow, *The History and Structure of Ceol Mor*
Records of the Presbyteries of Inverness and Dingwall
Alick Morrison, *The MacLeods, the Genealogy of a Clan*

Lament for The Duke of Hamilton

Angus MacKay was confused when he wrote that this work was made by Patrick Mor MacCrimmon in memory of a Duke of Hamilton killed in a duel in Hyde Park in 1712. Patrick Mor had been long dead by then.

If it is by Patrick Mor, as seems likely, it was probably made for William, 2nd Duke of Hamilton, who fought bravely at the Battle of Worcester in 1651, supporting King Charles II against Cromwell. He was one of the staunchest allies of Patrick Mor's clansmen, the MacLeods of Dunvegan, and this lament would have been doubly welcome in view of the terrible losses suffered by the MacLeods at Worcester. It might be regarded as a lament for all the clansmen killed that day. Patrick Mor himself is said to have been present at the battle, but this is not certain.

The piobaireachd *Blar Vuster* commemorates the same battle (and see also *Lament for the Children*).

The background of the lament is sad. The 1st Duke of Hamilton had been beheaded by Cromwell in 1649, and some accounts say that his younger brother William had been forced to watch the execution. The brothers had been close, and, whether or not he had witnessed it, the death affected William deeply. His brother had left only daughters, so William inherited his brother's titles and lands (and his debts), and he felt guilty that he had deprived his nieces of their father's possessions. He became profoundly depressed, and before the battle in 1651, he made a will leaving everything to his eldest niece, Anne; clearly he did not expect, or even want, to survive the coming conflict. He had five girls of his own, but no male heir, and he does not seem to have worried about depriving his own daughters. In his youth he had been a light-hearted young fellow, but his brother's end had destroyed his pleasure in life.

As soon as the battle began, William, on horseback at the head of his cavalry, flung himself into the fray with wild, reckless and probably suicidal intensity, and the King was unable to restrain him. He fought with great courage, always aiming for the centre of the action. He deliberately sought danger until eventually he was badly wounded and could not stay on his horse. A foot-soldier saw him fall, and dragged him to the shelter of a cart nearby; he lay beneath it until the battle was over. Still alive, he was taken later to the town of Worcester, where the surgeon found a musket-ball had shattered his leg. The wound was infected, and little could be done for him.

He lingered for two weeks, but probably lacked the will to live, and on 12 September 1651, he passed peacefully away. He left huge debts, inherited from his brother, but he returned the title and lands to his nineteen-year-old niece, who became Duchess of Hamilton in her own right, known to posterity as 'Duchess Anne'.

Presumably word was sent to Dunvegan, or more probably to Sir Roderick MacLeod at Talisker. The Chief at that time was a child, too young to go to war, but Sir Roderick, his guardian, had led the MacLeod clansmen, as their commanding officer.

Clearly this work should be played as a battle piece, with plenty of vigour, action and galloping horses.

Sources

Rosalind Marshall, *The Days of Duchess Anne*
Angus MacKay, Manuscript
I.F. Grant, *The MacLeods*

Lament for the Earl of Antrim

It is not certain which of the first three Earls of Antrim is the one named here. We might eliminate the second and third on political grounds, plus the fact that they had no known connection with the MacLeods or the MacCrimmons. The doubt remains, however, and it may be wrong to concentrate on the first Earl.

He was Ranald (or Randal) MacSorley MacDonnell, descended from the MacDonald Lords of the Isles. The MacDonald Clan history says he was known as Ranald Arranach because he had been fostered by a family in Arran, and 'perhaps had a residence there'. We assume this was the island of Arran on the west coast of Scotland, not the Irish isles of Aran. Arran is conveniently close to the north coast of Ulster.

He was created Earl of Antrim in 1620, and died of the dropsy in 1636. His wife was Alice, a sister of the great Irish patriot Hugh O'Neill, Earl of Tyrone (possibly the subject of the *Lament for Hugh)*. This was when O'Neill was trying to resist the English invasion of Ireland in the 1590s – in the reign of Queen Elizabeth I of England.

Elizabeth's aim was to subdue Ulster, and Hugh O'Neill, with his ally Hugh O'Donnell, began a titanic struggle to repel the English. Ranald MacSorley of Antrim, his brother-in-law, was a friend and supporter. They needed all the help they could get, and Irish sources say that Rory Mor MacLeod, and Donald Gorm MacDonald, in 1594, joined forces to send troops to Ireland. After a short campaign, Donald Gorm withdrew, and the MacLeods, needing more men, came home, too, but the following year, Rory Mor collected 600 armed men and returned to Ulster. They raided in Connaught, helped to defend Sligo Castle, and were at the successful siege of Armagh, where their archers were said to have turned the tide of battle. The Hebridean force was well appreciated by the Irish leaders. The Irish accounts give an interesting description of their distinctive appearance, one of the earliest references to Scots wearing the belted plaid.

On their return to Skye, it seems – though this is recorded only in MacLeod tradition – Hugh O'Neill sent a token of his thanks, a magnificent chalice, now known as the Dunvegan Cup. It is said that one of the O'Neills brought it over in person, but it could hardly have been Hugh, who had his hands full in Ulster. So who came with the gift? Ranald of Antrim? He was Hugh's kin, and his friend, and chief of his own branch of the MacDonnells, and Hebridean by descent. Admittedly he was a MacDonald, but at the time there was an uneasy truce between the two clans, just before the bitter feud between them broke out again.

Later, in 1603, Ranald MacSorley changed sides. Things were going badly for the cause, and Hugh O'Neill was about to surrender. James VI was now King, and Ranald, with Hugh's approval, threw in his lot with him, as a Scot.

Both James VI and Charles I proved loyal friends to Ranald, defending him in various plots to discredit him. In 1615, the king gave him a seven-year lease of Islay, but he tried to force 'Irish ways' on the people, who hated him. 'Irish ways' may be a euphemism for Roman

Catholicism. The king persuaded him to try Scottish ways instead, and eventually created him 1st Earl of Antrim as a reward 'for reducing these barbarous people to civility' i.e. for civilising the Hebrideans. This was the man who prided himself on his Hebridean blood, and admired the hardiness of the islanders. He told his children that he wanted them to grow up like that, and so did not allow them to cover their heads or wear shoes or socks at all, in any weather, until they were past eight years old.

The Lament is said to be the work of Donald Mor MacCrimmon, and may have been for a personal friendship, as Donald had been in Antrim in 1593, studying music, presumably with the famed harp-players there. It is likely that they played a form of harp-music with a structure similar to that of piobaireachd, and Donald may later have applied the theory of this to the pipes. It certainly seems a possibility that he met Ranald MacSorley on this visit, and Donald may have been among the MacLeod soldiers sent to Ulster a year or two later. It is said that Ranald always went out of his way to help any Scotsmen in Ireland, and Hebrideans were especially welcome.

If the composer was Donald Mor, he would have been back from his exile in Sutherland at the time of Ranald's death. It is not certain when Donald himself died – probably around 1640 – but he would presumably have been in Skye when the Earl died in 1636.

The elder son of Ranald was the second Earl, who became the Marquis of Antrim but was often still referred to as the Earl. He is unlikely to be the subject of this title, for the same reason that the *Lament for Donald Duaghal MacKay* is unlikely to be a MacCrimmon work (see above): in the late 1640s and early 1650s, the Dunvegan MacLeods did not want to risk offending Argyll, who allowed them control of Glenelg. Both Antrim and Donald Duaghal supported Montrose, and were bitter enemies of Argyll. The third Earl, younger brother of the second, also supported the Royalist cause, so it does seem more likely that the Lament was for the first Earl.

Sources

Rev. A. and Rev. A. MacDonald, *The Clan Donald*
Michael Hill, *Fire and Sword*
David Stevenson, *Alasdair MacColla and the Highland Problem*
S.J. Connolly, *The Oxford Companion to Irish History*
R.F. Foster, *The Oxford Illustrated History of Ireland*
Alec Haddow, *The History and Structure of Ceol Mor*

Lament for The Harp Tree

Although this is almost certainly not a MacCrimmon work, it has its place in the Skye competitions because the composer of the tune was Rory Morison, known as the Blind Harper, and he was harper to the MacLeods of Dunvegan from about 1682 to about 1694. He offended his chief and was expelled from Skye, to spend his later years at Glenelg, but may have been allowed back not long before he died. He was at Dunvegan when he made this tune, as harp-music, to which he set the words of his song, *Feill nan Crann*, 'Harp-Key Fair'.

The curious title *Lament for the Harp Tree* has been explained by Professor William Matheson, in his book on the Blind Harper: the Gaelic word for a harp-key, used for tuning a harp by tightening or slackening the strings, was *crann*, and there is also an old Gaelic word *crann* which meant a tree. These two old words became mixed up, and what had been intended to be Harp Key became Harp Tree. Simple as that.

In fact, it is not quite as simple as that, as Donald MacDonald muddied the waters with his title *Cumhadh Chraobh na 'n Cheud*, apparently meaning Lament for the Tree of Hundreds. This is not unlike Angus MacKay's *Cumha Chraobh na'n Teud*, Lament for the Tree of Strings, believed to be a kenning for a harp. Professor Matheson's emendation to *Cumha Crann nan Teud*, Lament for the Harp Key, seems to make the best sense.

Rory Morison had lost his harp key, or pretended he had, and in 1685 he composed an amusing song, a mock lament for this lost key, about his panic on losing it and his quest for a new one. He was forced, he sang, to equip a boat and sail off into the Minch, visiting the island of Barra to enquire about a new key and buy one. The crew of the boat, he said, was made up of nubile young lassies from the district, whom he named, with sly comments and plenty of *doubles entendres*. This is entertaining even when we do not know the girls; it must have been hilarious to those who did, especially as the harp-key seems to have been a symbol of his manhood. Whether he had really become impotent, or was feigning it for the humorous effect, we cannot tell, but at times the imagery is pretty clear, as, for example, in the second verse of the song, where he says:

> *Chan fhasa leam na'm bas*
> *a bhith fo thair nam ban;*
> *chan fhaod mi dhol 'nan dail*
> *on dh'fhailnich air mo ghean;*

's e their iad, 'Ciod am feum
a dh'fheudas a bhith ann?
Chaidh ionnstramaid o ghleus
on chaill e fhein a chrann.'

'I find it as difficult as death to suffer the scorn of women; I may not go near them since my ability to please them has failed me. "Of what use can he be?" is what they say, "His instrument is gone out of tune since he lost his harp-key".'

The final verse of the song, is more explicit, when the girls had stolen the harp-key from the fair, and examined it:

Thuirt nighean Mhic Leoid
gum bu leor siod mur bu ghann;
thuirt Meig nigh'n Domhnaill Ruaidh
gum bu truagh e bhith gun cheann;
bha Nic Mhaol-mhoire 'g raitinn
gum bu stailinn bha 'sa' chrann,
's nam faigheadh e 'na ruagairean
gum biodh e shuas air ball.

'MacLeod's daughter said that it would do if it was not too small; Red Donald's daughter Meg said it was a pity it had no head. The MacInnes wench kept saying that the harp-key was made of steel, and that if it got in her shift it would be up at once.'

Clearly Rory Morrison's affliction had been cured. We might wonder if Rory's later banishment was because his songs finally overstepped the boundaries of decency.

It is not certain whether Rory composed the tune of this song himself, or if he was using an older air. The title may suggest it was his work – or maybe the title inspired him to make the song. But it was not a MacCrimmon tune, it was a song, the reason why the piobaireachd sings along, and as a lament it is light-hearted and mocking.

There is an obvious link between *Lament for the Harp Tree* and *Corrienessan's Salute*, both being based on the same theme tune. They are not quite two settings of the same work, but more like two creations based on the same theme – rather as *Too Long in This Condition* is not a setting of *MacFarlane's Gathering*, but clearly related.

Both *Lament for the Harp Tree* and *Corrienessan's Salute* reveal their pedigree, being descended from a song, through harp music. When *The Harp Tree* was set as a Clasp tune, the ladies' cloakroom at the Eden Court theatre in Inverness was full of women singing away like larks, unable to get it out of their minds. And a piper playing

Corrienessan at the Games may find himself accompanied by an impromptu choir around the platform.

Some pipers feel that the *Lament for the Harp Tree* is too long for its content, and they suggest that it was not intended that all the available variations should be played; some, they argue, were probably meant as alternatives, to be played at the discretion of each individual piper. The same has been said of *His Father's Lament for Donald MacKenzie*. This judgement is not based entirely on length (no-one thinks it of the *Lament for Donald Ban MacCrimmon,* for instance), but on the players' feeling that these works do not hang together as an artistic entity when all the known variations are crammed in.

In 1693, Rory Morison was, apparently, invited to entertain at a great deer-hunt held by the fifteen-year-old Lord Reay, in the mountains of Sutherland. This was Donald Duaghal's grandson, 3rd Lord Reay. He had guests, a party of Irish lords, who brought their Irish harpers with them. For their enjoyment, the deer-hunt was arranged, and after the kill, the harpers played their music in the great mountain corrie known as Corrienessan. Rory sang his song, *Lament for the Lost Harp Key,* for the entertainment of the company.

This hunt was such an event that even local place-names were changed (e.g. the big strath nearby took the name Strath Corrienessan, and the river became the Corrienessan River). The name of the song became *Corrienessan's Salute.* We know all this from local tradition and because Rory's friend, Iain Dall MacKay, mentions it in his poem *Corrienessan's Lament,* made in 1696 in the form of a piobaireachd poem.

It must have been after this, but we do not know when, that the two piobaireachd works were made. They could be harp compositions made over, or could be based directly on the song. We do not know, either, who did this. It could conceivably have been Patrick Og Mac-Crimmon or one of his pupils, but there is no evidence, other than that Patrick certainly knew the Blind Harper at Dunvegan. It seems likely that the two piobaireachd works were made by two different people. It could be that one was based on the original song and the other on the subsequent harp tune.

Simon Fraser maintained that Patrick Mor MacCrimmon composed *The Harp Tree,* and his son Patrick Og then made *Corrienessan* as a 'parody' of his father's work, calling it *Lament for the Great Music (Cumha na Ceol Mor).* He told his father it was a lament for the proper way the music should be played, and he had composed it 'as near as I can to yours'. It is not clear quite what this means, nor what the purpose was, nor the reason why Patrick Og would feel the need to parody his father's work – nor, indeed, just what is meant by 'parody' in this context. A similar claim was made about the *MacGregors' Salute*, which Simon Fraser said was made by Patrick Mor, then parodied by his son with *The Red Hand in the MacDonald's Arms*. Fraser may have had this from Gesto, or from his father, his mother or his teacher, Peter Bruce.

Another related work may be *Corrienessan's Lament*, possibly the work of Rory Morison's friend, Iain Dall MacKay. It seems to have come down, until the late 19th century, as a Ground and 1st variation, but was then made over, with other variations (of suspicious regularity) added, probably by Dr Charles Bannatyne, in the 20th century. George MacKay from Sutherland had a much more irregular version, which appears to be older.

Sources

William Matheson, *An Clarsair Dall*
Ian Grimble, *Chief of MacKay*
Simon Fraser, *Piobaireachd*
Piobaireachd Society Book 14

Lament for MacSwan of Roaig

This seems to be a vintage MacCrimmon work, from the Golden Age of piobaireachd composition, in the mid-17th century. It was composed on the death of the 21st Laird of Roaig (or Roag), a place a few miles south of Dunvegan, in the parish of Duirinish, Skye. The MacSwan family had lived there for generations before this, and their descendants are still living in the same place. It is not now the original house, as that burned down in the 1920s, but its replacement was built on the same site.

Donald MacSwan was married to Florence, tenth daughter of Sir Rory Mor MacLeod of Dunvegan, and that is why the work is often attributed to Patrick Mor MacCrimmon. By the time Donald MacSwan died, around 1650, Sir Rory Mor was dead, and the chief who had just succeeded was his grandson, Rory Mir, still only a child.

A better reason for attributing this lament to Patrick Mor is the quality of it. Clearly the work of a master, its elegance and deep feeling make it impressive.

Donald MacDonald, of a Skye family, wrote that the tune was 'composed by MacSwan's own piper and very old' – does this mean it was based on a much older tune, possibly a song? Or was it the piper who was very old? Donald MacDonald did not name MacSwan's own piper, and we assume, for no real reason, that he was one of the MacCrimmons. Is it possible that Patrick Mor, being piper to a mere child at Dunvegan, had time to take on a position as MacSwan's piper as well, because of the marriage link with the MacLeods? There is no record of this, and probably, if it were so, Donald MacDonald would have mentioned it.

This was around the time when Patrick Mor made the *Lament for the Children*, and his (presumed) cousin or uncle, John MacCrimmon, composed *I Got A Kiss of the King's Hand* – and we know John was old in 1651. Perhaps MacSwan's piper was John, and he went as piper at Dunrobin after his laird died – or possibly it was yet another MacCrimmon, whose devotion to his laird enabled him to produce this beautiful lament, one of the saddest and loveliest of the MacCrimmon works.

Source
I.F. Grant, *The MacLeods*
Mr MacQueen, Roag
Donald MacDonald

Lament for Mary Macleod
Mary MacLeod, known in Gaelic as Mairi nighean Alasdair Ruaidh (Mary daughter of Red-haired Alasdair) was born around 1610, some say on the island of Bernera, Harris, others say at Rodel, Harris. In one of her poems (*Tuireadh*), she says she was brought up at Ullinish, near Bracadale, in Skye, apparently fostered by a milkmaid in the service of Rory Mor of Dunvegan.

She lived much of her life at Dunvegan, where she was 'nurse' in charge of MacLeod's children and those of other Highland chiefs, children under the fosterage of MacLeod. The term 'nurse' (Gaelic *bean altruim*) does not mean a nanny as we understand it today, nor a wet-nurse, but more a sort of foster-mother-cum-governess, responsible for the children's education and well-being. It was a position of responsibility and trust, and often the nurse was related to the family. From the deep feeling of her poems to her various charges, we can tell that she was a warm-hearted and affectionate woman – when she was allowed to be.

She belonged to the line of the Bernera MacLeods, and had a life-long devotion to her first laird and kinsman, Sir Norman MacLeod of Bernera. He gave her a house there, known as Tobhta nan Craobh, at Risgary, in the east of Bernera, looking out over the sea to Harris. It is now a grass-covered mound. When she lived there, we do not know; possibly before she went to Dunvegan.

She was clearly an intelligent woman, but was not given a good education, being a mere woman and from a poor (though well connected) family. From listening to the chief's bards at Dunvegan, and other poets in Skye, she learned how to compose excellent bardic poetry. She was probably not literate, but at that time very little poetry was written down, and bards stored their verse in their heads.

She had no formal training as a bard; we know this, because she was a woman. Women were not permitted to be bards or to compose in the formal metres of the bards. They were allowed to make, and sing, a type of verse known as *cronan,* often translated as 'lullaby', but meaning more like 'rhyme', or 'informal song', with simple metres. Mary was not content with this, however, and began to experiment with the full bardic genre. This was the beginning of a long wrangle between her and the official bards at Dunvegan, which seems to have eventually led to her being expelled from Skye.

Her case was not helped by the fact that her bardic verse was better than theirs, and they did their best to prevent her from trespassing on their male preserves. She ignored them, and went her own way, building herself a considerable reputation as a poet, which meant that in later years her work was remembered and written down, when theirs was not.

Another bone of contention between her and the bards was that she seems to have bent the traditional rules of poetic composition, creating new and exciting metres. They would have resented this, as it broke down the rigid system under which certain metres earned set rewards. It has been suggested that when Patrick Og made the well-known piobaireachd lament in her memory, with its unique method of variation, he introduced this touch of the unusual in tribute to her own innovations in her poetry.

Today Mary is regarded as an important Gaelic poet because she represents the bridge or link between two types of Gaelic verse which had previously been separate, the 'classical' formal court poetry and the more ordinary vernacular songs. Her work has been described as 'vernacular high-style panegyric, distinguished by its rhetorical assurance, the clarity of its imagery and its declamatory eloquence' (John MacInnes). For an example, see *The Lament for John Garve MacLeod of Raasay*, above.

In the end she was sent out of Skye, possibly because she had riled the bards so much that they persuaded the chief to have her removed from Dunvegan. It is not certain that this was the reason for her banishment, and some say it was because she made a derogatory poem about the Dunvegan chief, comparing him to his disadvantage with her own beloved Sir Norman of Bernera. This is conjecture, however, as the poem has not survived, if indeed it ever existed, and we have no reference to it.

In the edition of Mary's works, *Gaelic Songs of Mary MacLeod*, edited by J. Carmichael Watson in 1965 for the Scottish Gaelic Texts Society, the poems published are:

Posadh Mhic Leoid ('*The Wedding of MacLeod*'), an imaginary poetic bicker between Mary and Lady MacDonald from Trotternish. [60 × 2-line stanzas]

Mairearad nan Cuireid ('*A Satiric Song to Tricky Margaret*'), a woman who had spread a slanderous report that Mary was pregnant. [16 × 2-line stanzas, each ending with the refrain: *Hi riri o hiri o hi o.*]

Marbhrann do Fhear na Comraidh ('*An Elegy for the Laird of Applecross*'). This was Roderick (Ruairidh) MacKenzie, who had been one of the children in her care. In this song she refers to herself as laying aside her harp when she heard of Roderick's death. [14 × 6-line stanzas]

An Talla am bu ghnath le Mac Leoid ('*MacLeod's Wonted Hall*'), in praise of Sir Norman MacLeod of Bernera. [16 × 3-line stanzas]

Marbhrann do Iain Garbh Mac Ghille Chaluim Ratharsaidh ('*Elegy for John Garve MacLeod of Raasay*' who was drowned in a violent storm). [12 stanzas, of 5–8 lines] (see above, *Lament for John Garve MacLeod of Raasay*)

Tuireadh, a rinn Mairi nighean Alasdair Ruaidh goirid an deis a fagail an Sgarbaidh ('*A Plaint*, made by Mary daughter of Alasdair the Red soon after she was left in Scarba'). This song refers to Mary having been wakened every morning by pipe music, when she was at Dunvegan. [15 × 2-line stanzas, each line alternating with a one-line refrain, and each stanza ending with a four-line refrain]

Luinneag Mhic Leoid ('*MacLeod's Lilt*'). A song in praise of Sir Norman of Bernera, composed in Scarba. [14 × 8-line stanzas, with a four-line refrain. The last two lines of each stanza is repeated as the first two of the next]

Cronan an Taibh ('*The Ocean-Croon*') in which Mary compares the sound of the sea to that of 'the great resounding pipe, all music surpassing when Patrick's fingers stirred it'. The rest of the poem laments her misery and praises Sir Norman and his wife. [28 × 3-line stanzas]

An t-Eudach ('Jealousy'), a ditty made by Mary in jealousy of an Islay woman who, according to Mary, enticed her sweetheart from her. This seems to have been made in Mull. [13 × 2-line stanzas, with a two-line refrain]

Cumha do Mhac Leoid ('Lament for MacLeod'). This is Mary's lament probably for Rory Mir, her chief at Dunvegan (subject of Patrick Mor's *Lament for Rory MacLoude*). (see below). In it Mary refers to the deaths, close together, of Rory and his little son Norman. Some, however, say this was for a later Rory MacLeod, who died in 1699, and for his brother Norman (who was not in fact dead). [14 × 8-line stanzas]

An Cronan ('The Croon'). Said to have been sung by Mary to little Norman MacLeod, her chief's son, when he was ill and had begun to recover. She refers to the continuous sound (*gairich*) of the pipes at Dunvegan. [24 stanzas of 5–7 lines]

Fuigheall ('A Fragment') in praise of Sir Norman. [16 × 3-line stanzas]

Do Mhac Dhomhnaill ('To MacDonald'), addressed to Donald Gorm Og MacDonald, who became MacDonald of Sleat in 1695. [15 × 5–7 line stanzas]

Luinneag do Iain mac Shir Tormoid Mhic leoid air dhi thombaca fhaotainn uaidh (*'Song to Iain, son of Sir Norman MacLeod, on his presenting her with a snuff-mull'*.) A song in praise of that family. This son was John of Contullich, subject of the piobaireachd *Lament for the Laird of Contullich*. [8 × 8-line stanzas, with an 8-line refrain]

Marbhrann do Shir Tormod MacLeoid ('Elegy for Sir Norman MacLeod', who died in 1705). [19 stanzas of 5–8 lines]

Cumha do Shir Tormod Mac Leoid (Lament for Sir Norman MacLeod). [17 × 3-line stanzas]

A paper given by William Matheson to the Gaelic Society of Inverness in 1951 (*TGSI* XLI) cleared up a number of misconceptions about Mary MacLeod, and is regarded as authoritative.

Alick Morrison (1974) said that Mary was living in Bernera until the death of Sir Rory Mor at Dunvegan, and that she was nurse to the children of Sir Norman of Bernera, not those of Sir Rory; on the death of Sir Rory, the widow, Isabella, daughter of Donald of Laggan, moved to the MacLeod dower house in Harris, presumably at Scarista. Mary MacLeod was summoned from Bernera to come and look after her. Living in Harris at that time, said Alick Morrison, was Patrick Og MacCrimmon, who was the Harris piper until his father's death around 1670. It was in Harris, not Dunvegan, that Mary heard Patrick Og play (not Patrick Mor), and in Harris that she composed her praise of his piping ability. When the Dowager Isabella died, Mary returned to Bernera, where she lived out the rest of her life. This theory is not generally accepted, and takes no account of Mary's exile, to which she herself referred in one of her poems.

Mary was sent to live in Mull, but apparently this was not far enough away, and she continued to compose poems which reached Skye. William Matheson published three more poems believed to be Mary's work when living in Mull. She was then banished to a small remote island, Scarba, in the Firth of Lorne, well out of harm's way. There she lived in primitive conditions, an embittered and humiliated woman, cut off from the civilised society she had enjoyed at Dunvegan.

There is a tradition in Harris that her exile was not in Scarba but in Pabay, on the west side of Harris, from which she could see another small island, Scarp. Some think she was never in Scarba, and that the name was confused with that of Scarp. Her brother lived in Pabay: she may have been put under his supervision. In one of her poems (*Luinneag Mhic Leoid*), however, she says that she had never expected to find herself in Scarba, looking across at Jura. In the same poem she mentions that she could see Islay from her place of exile ('sitting here on a hill, miserable and anxious, I gaze upon Islay'). Neither Jura nor Islay is visible from Scarp. There is little doubt that she was for a time in Scarba, but possibly she was moved to Pabay later, to join her brother.

Eventually, in her old age, a new chief allowed her to return to Dunvegan, and she spent her last years there. She became a kenspeckle figure around the place, a small waspish old lady, dressed always in MacLeod tartan (or so we are told by later generations). She had a black cane with a silver handle, and used to walk round Dunvegan, nosing into things, and if anyone annoyed her, she would whack them with her cane. But it was her tongue, and her satiric verses, which were feared more than her cane – she was a sort of female Seumas MacNeill, witty and biting – and she seems to have dominated the Dunvegan household in her last years. One of the people she liked, however, was Patrick Og MacCrimmon, and her reference to his excellent playing is well known:

Ach piob nuallanach mhor
Bheireadh buaidh air gach ceol,
An uair a ghluaiste i le meoir Phadruig

But the great resounding pipe
That would get victory over all other music,
When it was stirred by Patrick's fingers

[The word *nuallanach* is sometimes translated as 'roaring', but that is hardly a compliment when applied to the pipe: 'resounding' or 'singing' is better.]

Mary MacLeod died probably in 1705, not long after Sir Norman's death. She was apparently in her late nineties, though we cannot be sure as the date of her birth is uncertain. Even in death she was having a dig at her enemies, as she is said to have left a will which asked for her to be buried lying face down, beneath a pile of stones. This was the traditional burial for a witch, and perhaps she was saying: 'You treated me all my life as if I were a witch; now you can bury me as one, and I'll come back and haunt you – you're not rid of me yet.'

Tradition has it that she was buried in the little church of St Clement, at Rodel, in the south of Harris; the tower of the church can be seen from her former home in Risgary, Bernera. Her grave is believed to be in a small side-chapel on the south side of the church, where she lies beneath the floor. The grave is not marked. It is close to the tomb of the MacLeod chief, Alasdair Crotach.

Alick Morrison, however, said she was buried in the graveyard outside the church, which perhaps is more likely. On the hillside just above the church there is a mausoleum containing the graves of the MacLeods of Bernera, including that of Mary's beloved laird, Sir Norman. Close by, to the west of the mausoleum, is a stone by itself, with no inscription. It is tempting to suppose that this was where Mary lies, but we have no evidence.

Mary's understandable bitterness is neutralised by the exceptional sweetness and lyrical quality of the lament made for her by Patrick Og in 1705. That, and her own skilled and polished verse, form her memorial.

Sources

William Matheson, 'Notes on Mary MacLeod'
J. Carmichael Watson, *Gaelic Songs of Mary MacLoed*
Duncan MacLean, Ardrishaig
Alick Morrison, *The MacLeods, the Genealogy of a Clan*

Lament for The Only Son

One tradition associates this work with John MacIntyre of Rannoch, who made *The Prince's Salute* and other compositions, but there seems to be no evidence to support the claim. Donald MacDonald said 'Nothing is known of this, except the air and the name'. As a Skye man, he might have been expected to have heard local traditions about the tune.

Colin Cameron was the eldest son of Donald Cameron, and therefore likely to know of traditions his father may have received from his teachers, the MacKays of Raasay, who in turn could have had them from the MacCrimmons. Colin attributed the *Lament for the Only Son* to Patrick Mor, and this has led people to suppose that the title refers to Patrick Og, the only (surviving) son of Patrick Mor. As Patrick Og outlived his father by some fifty years, this cannot be right.

If Patrick Mor was indeed the composer, and Colin Cameron's note is all the evidence we have, perhaps we should look not among the MacCrimmons themselves, but among their patrons, the MacLeod chiefs at Dunvegan. One of them, to whom Patrick Mor was piper, was Rory Mir, Rory 'the Witty' or 'Frivolous', grandson of Sir Rory Mor.

Rory Mir was the subject of *Rory MacLoude's Lament*, made by Patrick Mor in 1664 (see below), and he had just the one son, his heir, little Norman, who died young after being in poor health for all of his short life. He was one of the children in the care of Mary MacLeod at Dunvegan, and she nursed him through at least one serious illness, from which he recovered. While he was convalescing, Mary made a long poem called *An Cronan* for him, and sang it to him.

In it she says:

An naigheachd so an de	Yesterday's news
Aighearach e:	is joyous:
Moladh do'n leigh	praise to the doctor
Thug malairt do m'cheill . . .	who brought relief to my spirit . . .
Cha ghearain mi fein	I myself will not lament
Na chailleadh 's na dh'eug	those lost and those dead,
Is mo leanabh 'nan deidh	for my child is left alive and well.
comhshlan.	

After praising the MacLeod family, she goes on:

A Chriosd, cinnich thu fein	In Christ's name, may you yourself
An spionnadh 's an ceill . . .	grow in vigour and in wisdom . . .

He recovered from this illness, but died later, when still a child, probably in 1664, not long before his father. Rory's only other child was a daughter, and he was succeeded as chief by his brother, Iain Breac. It seems likely that the *Lament for the Only Son* was made in memory of young Norman, son of Rory Mir, in 1664.

Mary MacLeod composed a poetic elegy for Rory Mir, in which she said:

Ach a Ruairidh mhic Iain,	Oh Rory, son of Iain,
Is goirt leam fhaighinn an	it is sore to hear the news of you,
sgeul-s' ort,	
Is e mo chreach-sa mac t'athar	my grief is that your father's son
Bhith 'na laighe gun eirigh;	is lying still, never to rise;
Agus Tormod a mhac-san,	and Norman, your son,
A thasgaidh mo cheille –	treasure of my heart –
Gur e aobhar mo ghearain	the cause of my grief
Gun chailleadh le cheile iad.	is that they are both lost, together.

See also *Rory MacLoude's Lament*, below.

Although the evidence in favour of this explanation of the title seems compelling, it has to be pointed out that if the work was indeed made by Patrick Mor MacCrimmon, it is the only one of his known works which uses a semi-tone in the scale; indeed it is the only known Mac-Crimmon work to do so. Iain Dall MacKay, who was a pupil of Patrick Og, regularly used a scale with semi-tones, but it may have been an innovation introduced into piobaireachd by him. This may make it unlikely that the *Lament for the Only Son* was composed by Patrick Mor.

It will be noted that the assertion of Simon Fraser that the *Lament for the Only Son* was a title with religious significance (see below) has not been taken into consideration. It is likely that this association was made later, based on the title, and it must be doubtful if the Only Son was a reference to Jesus Christ at the time when the composition was made. Simon Fraser tied it in with 'Primitive Christianity', a heresy which he maintained was practised by the MacCrimmon family, and especially by Patrick Mor. He probably based this theory on information he found in works (now lost) written by Niel MacLeod of Gesto.

Sources

Alexander Mackenzie, *History of the MacLeods*
Mary MacLeod's poems
Colin Cameron
Alexander Nicolson, *History of Skye*
Simon Fraser, *Piobaireachd*

Lament for Patrick Og MacCrimmon

Patrick Og is believed to have died in 1730, probably at Boreraig, the farm which the family held for a time by virtue of their position as piper to MacLeod of Dunvegan. Patrick was the teacher and friend of Iain Dall MacKay, the Blind Piper of Gairloch, who composed this magnificent Lament. It is not a MacCrimmon composition but Patrick Og being the subject, and the composer his pupil, justifies its inclusion in the Skye list.

If the story told by Angus MacKay is true, we do not know exactly when the work was made. The tale is well-known: Iain Dall, at home in Gairloch, heard that his beloved teacher in Skye, Patrick Og, was dead; in his grief he composed the Lament, only to find out later that the rumour was untrue, and Patrick was still living. This could have been at any time before 1730, but the maturity and assurance of the work suggest that it was not long before that, when Iain was at the height of his powers. Patrick was in the 1720s not a young man, probably just coming into his seventies, as far as we know.

Angus MacKay goes on to tell how Iain Dall went over to Skye to see Patrick, and played him the new work. Patrick liked it, and asked what it was called. When told, he was amused, and said he would have to learn it himself. It is hard to accept this story. Surely in those deeply superstitious times, when death was greatly feared and portents were seen in the most trivial of happenings, it would have been considered the worst of omens to play a man his own lament when he was still alive. Would Patrick really have found it amusing – if Iain had had the bad taste to do it? It would have been worse than opening your newspaper and reading your own death notice.

In any case, the whole story might be suspect, possibly an invention of later times – but why? Perhaps because, in later times, there was a feeling that to play an A Mach variation on a lament was unacceptable, akin to dancing at a funeral, but if the subject of the lament turned out not to be dead after all, an A Mach could be played with impunity. Some play one on *Patrick Og*, some do not, but at least the story frees them to make up their own minds. Even now, however, there are those who would never play an A Mach on any lament, and consider that to do so ruins a perfectly good funeral.

George Stewart has pointed out the musical similarity between the well-known Doubling of the second variation of *Patrick Og* and the equivalent Doubling in the *Lament for Mary MacLeod*. As Patrick Og (the man) composed *Mary MacLeod* (the lament), and as these two variations are unique in piobaireachd, it seems unlikely that this resemblance is accidental. It may well be that the lovely Doubling in *Patrick Og* was Iain's tribute to his teacher as a composer.

Some say that G.S. MacLennan based his reel *Mrs MacPherson of Inveran* on this Doubling, simply altering the timing and the rhythm.

If the story of the false rumour is untrue from beginning to end, then the Lament can be dated to 1730. Roy Wentworth showed that Iain Dall was probably then living in Gairloch, at Engadal Glas (now called Flowerdale Mains), a farm up the glen past the Gairloch laird's house, now known as Flowerdale. We do not know whether Iain was able to go to Skye for Patrick's funeral, nor whether his lament was played on that occasion. It may be that Iain could not attend, as 1730 was the year of his own laird's marriage, and he was required to be in Gairloch to help entertain the guests. He did, however, in his poem to celebrate his laird's marriage, say that he was not present at the wedding (in Easter Ross), though he attended the subsequent parties at Flowerdale when the bride was brought to her new home. Had he perhaps been in Skye for Patrick's funeral? We will probably never know.

An eminent historian commented that Scotland has produced no composers of any high calibre other than the pipers; when pressed he gave his opinion that the *Lament for Patrick Og MacCrimmon* was possibly the finest piece of music ever composed in Scotland – and he was not a piper.

Sources

Angus MacKay, Manuscript
George Stewart
Roy Wentworth

MacCrimmon Will Never Return (Cha Till MacCruimein)

This work, once well-known and popular, has gone out of fashion and is now rarely heard. The Gaelic song on which it was probably based has come to the fore, presumably because it has been recorded by several fine Gaelic singers, notably Margaret MacDonald, of the group known as Albany.

The story behind the song concerns Donald Ban MacCrimmon, half-brother of Malcolm, both of them sons of Patrick Og, and both noted pipers. Malcolm was piper to MacLeod of Dunvegan, and in 1745 was sent to the Hanoverian army, as piper to Captain Donald MacDonald of Castletown's Independent Company, where the Sergeants included Malcolm's brother, Farquhar MacCrimmon (spelled McCrumen in the Muster Roll of June 1746). The 2nd Column of the Privates, called Centinels, included Archie and Duncan McCrumen, and the piper, Malcolm, was described as being 'Sick at Moy' – he had caught a fever. Interesting that he, a Hanoverian piper, was sick at the Jacobite stronghold of Moy.

Malcolm was later captured by the Jacobites at Inverurie, and thrown into prison, whereupon the Jacobites' own pipers said they would not play unless Malcolm was released. In the event, they did play while he was still a prisoner at Stirling, but they had obtained the promise of his release. He later returned to Skye.

Meanwhile, his brother Donald Ban had been summoned from his home in Scarista, South Harris, where he left his wife. For the rest of the story, see the *Lament for Donald Ban MacCrimmon*, above.

One version of the story of Donald Ban's departure to the war tells how he was reluctant to leave, and was playing this piobaireachd as he went, and this inspired his sweetheart in Dunvegan, Sheila Mac-Donald, to compose the song *Cha Till MacCruimein* – or, rather, to put new words to the old song (see above). These words, as still sung today, were published by Angus MacKay, and later in *Cuairtear nan Gleann*, the paper known as 'The Traveller', published by the Rev. Dr Norman MacLeod. His well-known and influential article on the MacCrimmons appeared in 1840. He quoted the song in full. The refrain goes:

Cha till, cha till, cha till MacCruimein,
An cogadh no sith cha till e tuilleadh,
Le airgiod no ni cha till MacCruimein;
Cha till gu brath gu la na cruinne.

MacCrimmon will not return, not return, not return,
In neither war nor peace will he ever return,
With neither money nor goods will MacCrimmon return;
Will never return until the day of the judgement.

There are four verses, each followed by this refrain.

Sir Walter Scott made his own version in English, and it cannot be regarded as an improvement on the Gaelic. It starts:

MacLeod's wizard flag from the grey castle sallies,
The rowers are seated, unmoored are the galleys;
Gleam war-axe and broadsword, clang target and quiver,
As MacCrimmon plays 'Farewell to Dunvegan for ever!'

and it finishes:

Too oft shall the note of MacCrimmon's bewailing
Be heard when the Gaels on their exile are sailing;
Dear land ! to the shores whence unwilling we sever;
Return, return, return, we shall never!

The three intervening verses are of much the same standard – somewhat embarrassing to the modern ear.

In 1998, Malcolm White gave a paper at the Piobaireachd Society Conference, in which he said that the Clan Gregor has a strong tradition that Rob Roy MacGregor's piper played *Cha Till* at his funeral on 28 December 1734, and this was reported in the *Scots Magazine* and in the Edinburgh newspaper, the *Caledonian Mercury*, at the time. What we cannot know for certain is whether this was the same tune as the MacCrimmon *Cha Till*; it may have been not a piobaireachd work but simply the air of the underlying song.

Cha Till was originally called *Cha Till Mi Tuilleadh* (I Shall Never Return), a standard phrase, which was changed to *Cha Till Mac-Cruimein* later, when the words to it became *Ged a thilleadh MacLeoid, Cha till MacCruimein* ('Even though MacLeod return, MacCrimmon will not return'). If Sheila MacDonald put the MacCrimmon words to the tune, she was re-writing a very old song.

Allan MacDonald says that the MacIvers of Kintyre had a song called *Cha Till Mi Tuilleadh* as far back as the 17th century, long before the Skye song, but it became known as a Skye song because the MacCrimmon tradition was so strong.

The *Inverness Courier* had a report in January 1841, about an emigrant ship at Helmsdale, Sutherland, taking people 'from the upland parts of the strath' (of Kildonan), bound for America. The emigrants had been forced out of their homes, and were distraught with grief, 'the sorrow of the women being loud and open'. As the vessel moved slowly away from the quay, the pipes played 'We Return No More', after a long prayer had been said in Gaelic. The *Courier* correspondent had gone on board for the first leg of the journey, as the ship was due to call in at Cromarty, where he meant to disembark, but the night proved stormy and they had to take shelter behind Tarbat Ness, to avoid the full force of an easterly gale. The passengers were terrified – and 'suddenly, as if by common consent, they raised a Gaelic psalm tune which mingled, with wild and pathetic effect, with the roar of surf and wind'. At first light, the correspondent went ashore at nearby Portmahomack – one night at sea was enough for him.

This account shows that the MacCrimmon version of *Cha Till* was not universal, even as late as the mid-19th century.

Sources

Ruairidh Halford-MacLeod, *TGSI* LV
Malcolm White
Allan MacDonald
Inverness Courier

MacCrimmon's Sweetheart (Maol Donn)

This is one of the few instances of the Gaelic name of a piobaireachd work still in use by those who do not speak Gaelic, as there has always been uncertainty about the English form of the title. Until about 1850, English speakers called this *A Favourite Piece*, and this was its name when they submitted it for competitions. Around 1850, or a little before, the new name *MacCrimmon's Sweetheart* began to find favour, though many continued to call it *Maol Donn*. It is pronounced something close to 'Mull Down'. The stress is on the second word.

Nobody seems to know where the name *MacCrimmon's Sweetheart* came from, but presumably it was coined in Skye by some MacLeod devotee, possibly the Rev. Dr Norman MacLeod. It is doubtful whether the MacCrimmon link is genuine, but it cannot be disproved.

Yet another name was *The Widow's Grief*, and the work is sometimes played at funerals, notably in 1868, when Donald Cameron's coffin was borne through the streets of Inverness. Some, however, say that *The Widow's Grief* was another name for *The Old Woman's Lullaby*.

Another problem is the precise meaning of *Maol Donn*, which seems to mean literally 'Bald' (or 'Bare') Brown One'. There are plenty of theories to explain this:

(a) it is the name of a 6th-century prince of Dalriada, son of Connel of Kintyre, and the composition has been claimed as a Kintyre work; it might seem a curious designation for a prince – bald and brown-skinned? – but that is probably not the meaning of his name. Early Celtic nobility often had names preceded by Mal- or Mael-, meaning 'Lord', and Maol could be a corruption of this. In that case, Donn is probably a form of 'Donald', the whole name meaning 'Lord Donald' – two of the early kings of Dalriada were called Donald;

(b) it is a reference to a smooth brown shell picked up on the shore by Ronald MacDonald of Morar, and he would be the composer of the work – Peter Reid said this;

(c) it was the name of a hornless brown cow belonging to a poor widow with many young children. When the cow died, she had no means of feeding her family, and the song, sung in Lewis, expresses her grief – hence the alternative name, *The Widow's Grief*, taken from the Gaelic song. The work is very effective played as a lament, as Rona Lightfoot demonstrated at a recital to the Inverness Piping Society;

(d) it is a place-name, that of a bare brown hill; but where?

(e) it is a corruption of a Gaelic phrase, by English speakers: Alec Haddow suggested that *Maol Donn* might have once been *Mo Ghaoil Dhonn*, 'My Brown Sweetheart' (the Gaelic pronunciation is much closer to Maol Donn than the spelling would suggest). This has the merit of relating to the English *MacCrimmon's Sweetheart*, and also it echoes phrases commonly used in Gaelic poetry, referring to the pipe as the player's sweetheart or lover – words like *leannan* and *gaol*, the language of love. Why brown? In the old days when pipers made their own instruments, they often used laburnum (before cocos and blackwood came in from overseas) – and laburnum wood is brown. By this theory, MacCrimmon's Sweetheart was his pipe, and its Gaelic name meant My Brown Sweetheart.

This last possibly makes the best sense, though it might be thought a little far-fetched. We will probably never know if any of the above is right.

As if the problem were not confused enough, further complication is added by this work appearing in Angus MacKay's MS twice, once (volume I.60) as *Cumha Mhuil Duin* 'Maol Donn's Lament', and once (volume I.4) as *Blar na Maol a' ruidhe* 'The Battle of Red Hill'. His Index listed it as *The Battle of Milduin*, but then *Milduin* was crossed out, and *the Red Hill* inserted. It is clear that confusion was caused by the similarity of the Gaelic words *donn* 'brown' and *dun* which can mean 'hill'. See also below, *The Battle of Red Hill*.

Sources

Peter Reid
Rona Lightfoot
Margaret Stewart
Alec Haddow, *The History and Structure of Ceol Mor*
Angus MacKay, Manuscript

MacLeod of Colbecks' Lament

This was always the old form of the title, rather than the modern *Lament for MacLeod of Colbeck*, because it solved the problem of whether to add the final *s* to Colbeck – he was known as Colbecks in the 18th and 19th centuries. Gradually, as people forgot that he had this final *s*, they changed the title, but the original solution was to write *MacLeod of Colbecks Lament*, omitting the apostrophe altogether. Sometimes it was written *Colbex*.

The reason for the final *s* was that it was a plural – there was more than one Colbeck. The family had two estates, both called Colbeck. One was on the island of Raasay, the other was a sugar plantation in Jamaica, which they named after their home in Scotland. This was not uncommon in the 18th century, and where there were two holdings of the same name, the owner simply added *s* to his designation, and everybody knew what it meant.

MacLeod of Colbecks was a Raasay man. In 1793, 'Mr MacLeod of Colbeck' (with no *s*) was listed among the Highland gentry who became Members of the Northern Meeting, but it is not clear whether this was the father or the son. Both were called John, and it was the father who started the sugar plantation.

When the son left Jamaica to return, a wealthy man, to Scotland, he made his home in Edinburgh, where he lived at Inveresk before moving to a large mansion, Ballencrieff House, in East Lothian. He married a daughter of the laird of Raasay, and himself claimed links with the MacLeods of Lewis. This claim has cast doubt on his connection with Raasay, but the line given in his application to the College of Heraldry for a coat of arms is spurious in parts, and was probably concocted for his own aggrandisement after he became affluent.

Colonel John of Colbecks raised the MacLeod Loyal Fencible Highlanders (or the Princess Charlotte of Wales Highlanders) in 1799, and became their colonel; but he was already a colonel at least three years earlier, and probably had attained that rank when in the Dutch Brigade as a younger man. As soon as the Fencible Highlanders were raised, they were sent to Ireland to quell rebellion there. It was a short-lived regiment, being disbanded on its return to England in 1802. John Mac-Kay, the composer of this lament, had been the regimental piper, and served abroad, presumably in Ireland, for a short time.

It seems that the family's original holding was Colbeck, the estate or farm now known as Caol, in the north end of Raasay, on the east coast of the island. The narrow channel of water separating the north of Raasay from the south of the neighbouring island of Rona was called Caol Beag (Little Strait), now known as Caolrona (Rona Strait). The narrows to the south of Raasay are called Caol Mor (Big Strait), in contrast. Sometimes the farm is called Caolrona, often abbreviated to Caol, but the older form, Caol Beag, would be anglicised to Colbeck.

Note that the comments on the family given in the Piobaireachd Society Book 10 are confused and misleading. Norma MacLeod, in her book on Raasay, offers a more coherent and accurate account.

The Lament is the work of John MacKay, Raasay, piper to the MacLeod chief of Raasay. John made it in 1823 on the death of Colbecks, whose wife was a daughter of the Chief. They had a family of several daughters and a son, but the son died before his father, so that in lamenting the death of Colbecks, John was also lamenting the end of that line of the family.

John MacKay left Raasay shortly after composing this work, moving with his family to Drummond Castle – so this was probably the last composition he made in his native home.

Sources

Seumas MacNeill
Dr Alasdair MacLean
Norma MacLeod, *Raasay*
Alick Morrison, *The MacLeods, the Genealogy of a Clan*

MacLeod of MacLeod's Lament

Henry Whyte, using his pseudonym 'Fionn', said this lament was made by Patrick Mor MacCrimmon when his chief, Sir Rory Mor MacLeod, died in 1626. On Rory's death, said Fionn, Dunvegan lost its charms for Patrick, and 'he could no longer remain within its walls. He got up, seized his pipes, and marched off to his own home at Boreraig, consoling his grief by playing as he went a Lament for his Chief, which is one of the most melodious and plaintive tunes on record.'

Most of this is taken from the writings of the Rev. Dr Norman MacLeod, who in 1840 published an article on the MacCrimmons, drawing on Angus MacKay's book and its historical notes. The Rev. Norman gives the full Gaelic words of the song associated with the tune, which begins: *Tog orm mo phiob is theid mi dhachaidh,* 'Hand me my pipe, and I will go home'. They are the start of a fine Gaelic song.

Alastair Campsie's book gives the English translation, made by Dr John MacInnes, of the whole article.

It is unkind to cast doubt on this touching account, but Patrick Mor was probably not yet MacLeod's piper in 1626; it was more likely Patrick's father, Donald Mor, back from his exile in Sutherland, and there is no evidence that the MacCrimmons were living in Boreraig as early as this. But there is no proof, so we might as well accept the flight of fancy (no proof of that, either), and we may enjoy wiping a pleasurable tear from our eye, without all this unnecessary fuss about historical accuracy.

Sources

Henry Whyte
Alistair Campsie, *The MacCrimmon Legend*
I.F. Grant, *The MacLeods*
Ruairidh Halford-MacLeod, *TGSI* LV

MacLeod of Raasay's Salute

Angus MacKay, himself a Raasay man, said this was a Salute on the birth of James MacLeod of Raasay, in 1761, but Angus seemed uncertain whether the composer was Angus MacKay, Gairloch or his son, John Roy. If it was indeed made in 1761, the composer was Angus MacKay, Gairloch, the son of Iain Dall, the Blind Piper, as John Roy was not then born, or was still an infant. Angus is also said to have composed the *Desperate Battle of the Birds* and *MacKenzie of Applecross' Salute* – and some say he made *Mary's Praise*, but this is doubtful, as the story supporting the claim cannot be true.

James MacLeod of Raasay was the 12th Chief, and brother-in-law of John MacLeod of Colbecks. He was the eldest of three brothers who had ten beautiful sisters, most of whom made advantageous marriages.

James grew up to become an enthusiastic and somewhat guileless young man, apt to throw himself into grandiose schemes which he could not afford. He became Commanding Officer of the local regiment of Volunteers, formed as a defence against possible invasion by Napoleon, and seems to have relished this experience of military command, to the amusement of his more sophisticated fellow-officers.

Later, he plunged the estate deep into debt by ambitious schemes for expansion and development in Raasay, and died a comparatively poor man, in or around 1824. He had had John MacKay as his piper until shortly before that, but John had left Raasay when the estate became too impoverished to support him.

James MacLeod seems to have been a likeable if unreliable fellow, but his character in later life is irrelevant if the Salute was made to celebrate his birth.

There seems little reason to include this work among the MacCrimmon compositions.

Sources

Angus MacKay, Manuscript
Alexander Nicolson, *History of Skye*
Norma MacLeod, *Raasay*

MacLeod's Controversy and *MacLeod's Salute*

These two works, together with *MacDonald's Salute*, form a trilogy of works said to be linked to the end of the long feud between the MacLeods of Dunvegan and the MacDonalds of Sleat. Other works, such as the *Battle of Waternish, The Desperate Battle (Cuillin)*, and *The Dispraise of MacLeod* are possibly part of the same conflict, all belonging to the period in the late 16th century, and on into the first years of the 17th.

There had been trouble between the two clans for many years. In an attempt to reconcile their differences, a sister of Rory Mor MacLeod, called Margaret, was married to Donald Gorm MacDonald. Poor Margaret lost an eye in an accident, whether before or after her marriage is not clear. Donald Gorm decided to reject her, after the year's trial ('handfast') marriage that was the custom then. He returned her to Dunvegan in the most insulting manner he could devise, mounted, so they say, on a one-eyed horse, escorted by a one-eyed groom and a one-eyed dog.

Donald Gorm then married a sister of MacKenzie of Kintail, another bitter enemy of Rory Mor. Rory remarked that they had forgotten to light a bonfire to celebrate the wedding, but he would light a fire to mark the divorce, and he fell on Donald Gorm's lands with fire and sword.

The War of the One-Eyed Woman raged in Skye for the next two years, until, it was reported, 'scarcely a hoof remained on mountain or machair', and the people were reduced to eating vermin to keep alive.

In the end, King James VI intervened, and in 1602, after negotiations by the other Highland chiefs, a reconciliation was achieved. A great feast was held at Dunvegan, to which the MacDonalds were invited. It lasted for six days, and according to a contemporary poet, everyone got drunk twenty times a day.

According to tradition, Donald Mor MacCrimmon went out to meet the approaching MacDonalds and piped them into the castle, playing

MacLeod's Salute. It must have been a tense moment. Later, at the feast, he played the *MacDonalds' Salute*. What is not clear is where *MacLeod's Controversy* came in; it seems a tactless choice of title, in the circumstances – it was probably given with hindsight.

An occasion such as this was a great opportunity for poets and storytellers to embroider the detail, and much of the story is probably just that, fictional embroidery. But the two clans were reconciled, and the war did not break out again, so there is some truth in it.

Traditionally, Donald Mor was the composer of all three works, and they do seem to be all in the same style. *MacLeod's Salute* and the *Controversy* both have what came to be known as the 'Donald Mor run-down', the run of four notes (D-B-A-G) which may be a characteristic of his work. Not all players include it, however, and this might suggest it was a later insertion. And it must be pointed out that this run-down appears in other works.

Lachlan Ban MacCormick in Benbecula, who used to play many old settings, had one for *MacLeod's Salute* which was completely different in its timing from the modern version ('which is rubbish', said Lachlan). His setting did have the run-down, timed a little differently to that of the Piobaireachd Society. He said the work was called *Lament for Donald MacLeod of Grisirnis* (Greshornish, in Skye), based on an old Irish tune and named after a well-known pirate. Lachlan said this was also the origin of the term *The Rowing Tune*. This tradition of a link with MacLeod of Greshornish was also given by Simon Fraser in Australia, probably from the lost manuscript of MacLeod of Gesto – who was related to the MacLeods of Greshornish.

Because the *Salute* is sometimes known as *The Rowing Tune*, some judges insist it be played with a regular rowing rhythm; it has even been suggested that the run-down represents the dripping of water off the oar-blades as they are lifted out of the water.

Another suggestion is that the word 'rowing' does not rhyme with 'owing' but with 'vowing', and refers to the almighty row or feud which had just ended. This seems unlikely, not least because the verb 'to row' in the sense of 'to quarrel' did not come in until centuries later.

Sources

Piobaireachd Society Books 10 and 12
Alec Haddow, *The History and Structure of Ceol Mor*
Seumas MacNeill
Duncan Watson

Mrs MacLeod of Talisker's Salute

Colonel John MacLeod of Talisker, the husband of the lady named in this title, may have been the subject of a lament, *MacLeod of Tallisker's Lament,* of which Simon Fraser gave us the Ground, possibly based on Gesto's (lost) manuscript. It is not certain which MacLeod of Talisker this was, and Sir Roderick, knighted on the field before the Battle of Worcester, could be the one. John and Roderick were from different branches of the MacLeods.

John MacLeod had been a keen Hanoverian who served in Loudoun's Regiment during the '45 Rising – the one which was at the Rout of Moy in 1746, the occasion when Donald Ban MacCrimmon was shot by someone on his own side, and everyone else ran away. After Culloden, John of Talisker joined the Dutch Brigade in Holland, before retiring to his home at Talisker, in the west of Skye.

There he was visited by Dr Johnson and Boswell, in 1773. Thomas Pennant had been there the previous year. Johnson was full of praise for Talisker's culture and learning, and described him as agreeable and polite, a very pleasant man. His tenants might have disagreed, as he treated them harshly. Boswell said he was 'bred to physick and had a tincture of scholarship in his conversation' – his brother was a professor at Aberdeen University, who later became Principal of King's College.

John's own studies had been interrupted by the '45 Rising, when he became a Captain in one of the MacLeod Independent Companies. After Culloden, he was assiduous in the rounding up of Jacobite fugitives, and played a large part in the capture of both Flora MacDonald and Captain Malcolm MacLeod.

When the Independent Companies were disbanded, Talisker became a Captain in Drumlanrig's Regiment of Foot, for service in Holland (known as the Dutch Brigade), and was promoted to Major in 1751. Later he was in Keith & Campbell's Highlanders, and possibly served under Prince Frederick of Brunswick in Germany. It is not clear when, indeed, if, he became a Colonel.

His first wife was a daughter of MacLean of Coll, and Dr Johnson said she was 'skilful in several languages'. She was much captivated by the eloquence of the learned Doctor at her dinner-table, and Boswell said that as a result of her having lived so long abroad, she had 'introduced the ease and politeness of the continent into this rude region'. She had had a library of good books put in Dr Johnson's room at Talisker, which pleased him greatly. He was impressed by the efficient way she coped when some sailors were found half-drowned, washed up on the

Talisker shore; without fuss she had them revived, warmed and fed, so that all of them survived.

After her death in 1780 (or thereabouts), the Colonel married a woman called Christina MacKay, daughter of a merchant in Inverness. Some said that she was his housekeeper, and that she trapped him into marriage. She seems to have been less cultured than her predecessor.

In 1786, John MacLeod of Talisker was described as 'extremely corpulent', and his house as 'the seat of plenty, hospitality and good nature' by an official from the Fisheries Society, who were planning to build a village at Dunvegan, in an attempt to stem the flow of emigration from Skye. The following year, the committee of directors of the society arrived, and Talisker joined them on Loch Bracadale, meeting them in his boat 'rowed by boatmen in uniform, with a bagpiper in the bow'. Who was the piper? The village was never built, and emigration rates increased.

When Dr John Clarke visited Talisker in 1797, he found the Colonel and his lady waiting to receive the party in the old hall, where there were kilted servants, peat fires and all kinds of local produce to eat – and a wood pigeon was perched on the deer's horns in the passage. Dr Clarke wrote of the 'parental kindness' of his hosts.

Colonel MacLeod died in 1798, at the age of eighty, and Ronald MacDonald, a grieve in Minginish, composed an elegy in Gaelic, in his memory.

After Christina was widowed, she moved into her 'jointure house' (similar to a dower house, arranged as a dwelling for a surviving spouse, by their marriage settlement) when she had to give up Talisker House to her husband's heir, his nephew. She was then known as 'The Dowager of Talisker'; she became stout and heavy in her old age, and very autocratic with her servants, though still most hospitable to visitors at Talisker. A formidable woman, by all accounts, and a great character. She died on 2 March 1820.

It is not certain which Mrs MacLeod of Talisker is the subject of the Salute, but it is generally assumed that it was Christina, the second wife. Among her visitors was probably Donald Ruadh MacCrimmon, and he is taken to be the composer. He had returned from America in the early 1790s, to live for some years in Skye, until in 1811 he moved to Glenelg. It is not known exactly when he made this work, if he did, but it was probably in the early 1800s, in Skye.

Another possibility is that it was Donald's brother, Iain Dubh MacCrimmon, who composed this Salute – but tradition attributes it to Donald Ruadh.

Talisker had been the scene of many meetings of the 'Talisker Circle', a group of poets and musicians of Skye who included Iain Dall Mac-Kay and probably also John of Contullich, between 1672 and 1733. It excluded Mary MacLeod, being a mere woman. It is thought that it was here that Iain Dall learned the art of composing bardic poetry, and that at Talisker he made his *Song for Hector MacLean.*

The MacLeods who were the hosts of these meetings were not the same branch of the family as Colonel MacLeod in the 1770s. The tenancy of Talisker had gone to another branch, after the death of Donald MacLeod in the 1740s.

Below Talisker House, nearer to the shore, there is a well, previously known as Cuchulain's Well but later as the Piper's Well. The tradition is that the trickle of fresh water which filled the household pails was sometimes slow in a dry season, so the piper would accompany the water-carrier and play to entertain her (him?) while they waited.

Sources
Hugh Barron
Alexander Nicolson, *History of Skye*
Dr Johnson, *Journey to the Western Isles*
James Boswell, *Journal*

The Pretty Dirk
One of the stories behind this title is that MacLeod of Dunvegan was about to visit the Clanranald chief in South Uist, and his piper, Patrick Og MacCrimmon, was to accompany him there. His job was to produce a new tune suitable for the occasion, and he made this little composition and named it for the gift that his chief was taking to Clanranald.

Another version is that he and his chief were visiting Clanranald when Patrick admired an ornate dirk belonging to their host. Clanranald told him that if he could instantly produce a new piobaireachd work and play it to him, the dirk was his – and Patrick at once played this piece. This story assumes that Clanranald was knowledgeable enough to know a new piece from an old, and that Patrick had a tune ready in his mind for emergencies such as this. Possibly the shortness of the piece might support this account.

The Piobaireachd Society Book 11 has a modified version, in which the chief who awarded the dirk is MacLeod himself, and Patrick Og was given a day in which to produce the new tune.

All these stories are probably apocryphal, invented to account for the title, for which the real explanation has been lost. Little is known about the rewards paid by patrons for piobaireachd compositions or performances, but some itinerant pipers made a living by travelling from big house to big house, entertaining the owners, for due reward.

One of the stories about *Mary's Praise* describes how the wife of Lord MacDonald of Sleat rewarded a performance of the work by giving the piper a hairy sporran, but how much reliance can be put on that is doubtful.

In one of his poems, the *Ode of Consolation* (1734), Iain Dall MacKay said that the MacDonald chiefs, through the years, had given him silver and gold, but did not specify whether this was for pipe music or poetry, or both. In his *Song for Hector MacLean*, Iain said modestly that his reward for the poem would be cloth to make a coat, and homespun cloth would do, but he may have been hoping for something finer. Elsewhere, in his poem *Corrienessan's Lament*, he referred to his profession as a piper and bard, and said he was normally obliged to claim reward for his services because of his blindness. Presumably the rewards for a pipe tune were much the same as for a poem or song, given for both the composing and the performing of the work.

Other than these sparse references to the rewards of piping and composing, the prizes given at the big competitions are what we know in any detail, whether cash prizes or the Prize Pipe, or various items of Highland dress awarded for placings in the prize list – and sometimes the prize for third place was an ornate (or pretty) dirk. The word 'pretty' did not have the feminine connotations it has today: probably 'handsome' or 'fine' would be used nowadays.

We might wonder why the Highland Societies offered a Prize Pipe for first place. The winning piper must have had a good pipe of his own already (unless, as is known in some instances, the pipe belonged to the laird whose piper was competing, and had to be returned when the piper left his employ. In such a case would the Prize Pipe also belong to the sponsoring laird?). Surely it would usually be a mistake to abandon a successful instrument in favour of a new one. The Prize Pipes, however, were made by good craftsmen, such as John Ban MacKenzie, and the Highland Societies paid high prices for them. There are examples of thirsty pipers selling or pawning their prizes, preferring to take the money rather than change their instrument.

Sources

Iain Dall's poems
John MacKenzie, *The Beauties of Gaelic Poetry*

Rory MacLoude's Lament

This Rory was the second of three MacLeod chiefs of that name. The reason for the unusual spelling MacLoude is that it appears in the manuscript source for this work, the Campbell Canntaireachd, and it is used nowadays to help to distinguish the work from *MacLeod of MacLeod's Lament,* and other MacLeod pieces.

Rory MacLoude was known as Rory Mir, in contrast to his grandfather Rory Mor. Mir is often translated as 'witty', but it really means 'fun-loving, pleasure-seeking'. The modern term 'playboy' is close to it.

Born in 1636, Rory was only a child when he succeeded as the 17th chief. When, in 1651, his clan sent a force of MacLeod clansmen to join the army in support of King Charles II, Rory was too young to go with it. He was brought up to be a Stuart adherent, and grew up at Dunvegan to become a jolly, cheerful man, wildly extravagant and self-indulgent, but well-liked by his people. In 1810 he was described in a letter by a Donald MacLeod as having been remembered as 'a man of uncommon liveliness and wit, and many anecdotes are still in memory of his humoursome pranks' (quoted by I.F. Grant).

Ten years after the battle of Worcester, Rory went to London to see the King, hoping for compensation for the huge losses suffered by his clan in the campaign to restore Charles II to his throne. To his disappointment the King, who was much trachled by hopeful claimants, gave him the cold shoulder, and Rory vowed that the MacLeods would never again support the Stuart cause.

He then consoled himself by plunging into a life of debauchery. The writer of the Wardlaw manuscript, a Presbyterian minister, was not amused, calling him a 'prodigal vitious spendthrift'. Rory remained in the south of England for two and a half years, spending a great deal of money that was not his, on wine, women and racehorses. He had been in debt all his life, and this never prevented him from being a cheerful spender.

In the end his debts drove him home to Dunvegan, and his wife and family. He was married to Margaret, daughter of Sir John MacKenzie of Kintail, and their son Norman was born not long before he left for London. It may have been partly the feeling aroused in him by the child's ill-health which drove him to his excesses. Norman was his only son, and there was also an older daughter (see above, *Lament for the Only Son*).

Rory died in 1664, only two years after his return. The cause is not known, but it may have been something nasty he had picked up in

London, exacerbated by his grief for the death of his young son, earlier that same year. Rory was only twenty-eight when he died.

Although his character may seem pretty weak and despicable, he was well-liked in Skye, and cheerfulness and generosity, even with other people's money, are always popular in a chief. On his death, Mary MacLeod made a poetic elegy for him, and the Blind Harper, Rory Morrison, referred to him in a poem as 'no empty-handed miser', putting it tactfully. Patrick Mor MacCrimmon, having composed the *Lament for the Only Son* for poor little Norman, found himself soon afterwards making *Rory MacLoude's Lament* for Norman's father.

Joseph MacDonald, in his Treatise of 1762, gives a few bars of this work, with the comment 'This is a very soft lament', a curious description.

Sources

I.F. Grant, *The MacLeods*
Alexander Nicolson, *History of Skye*
Alexander Mackenzie, *History of the MacLeods*
Mary MacLeod
J. Carmichael Watson, *The Gaelic Songs of Mary MacLeod*
William Matheson *TGSI* XLI
Joseph MacDonald, *Compleat Theory*

Salute on the Birth of Rory Mor MacLeod

Donald MacDonald published this work in 1820, with a note saying that it was composed 'by MacCrimmon' to mark the birth of Roderick Mor MacLeod, in Dunvegan Castle, in 1715. Donald was a Skye man, but he must have known that this could not possibly be right. There were three MacLeod chiefs called Roderick or Rory (Gaelic Ruairidh), and the last of the three died in 1699.

Rory Mor was born in 1562, two years after his brother William. The title of this piobaireachd work cannot be taken at face value, as he was certainly not Rory Mor before he grew up, whether the by-name refers to his physical size or to his greatness as a chief; so whenever the salute was made, the title must have been added later, or changed at a later date.

Since Rory was not born as the all-important heir to the chieftain-ship, his birth would not have been regarded as particularly significant. No-one could have foreseen that the death of William in 1590, followed by that of William's son John in 1595, would make Rory the next chief, and the title must have been given to this work with hindsight: the thinking seems to have been that since Rory became the greatest of all the MacLeod chiefs, he must have a piobaireachd work in honour of his birth (see also *The Groat*, above).

Margaret Stewart, in her article on Gaelic piobaireachd songs (*Piper Press*, November 1998), lists some piobaireachd titles, or alternative titles, which seem to her to be the first lines of songs. Among them she includes *An ann air mhire tha sibh* ('are you merry-making?'), the Gaelic name given by Angus MacKay for *Salute on the Birth of Rory Mor MacLeod*. The Rev. Neil Ross was of the opinion that the Gaelic phrase meant not 'merry-making' but 'beside oneself with rage'.

The Campbell Canntaireachd manuscript has the odd title (in English) *MacLeod's Dog Short Tail*, the origin of which is obscure. It must be a corruption – but of what? The Gaelic word for a dog is *cu*, sometimes confused with *cumha* 'lament' – but the Short Tail is a puzzle.

Sources

Alec Haddow, *The History and Structure of Ceol Mor*
Margaret Stewart
Rev. Neil Ross

Too Long in This Condition

For background to the composition of this work, see *A Flame of Wrath for Patrick Caogach*, above.

The relation of *Too Long in This Condition* to *MacFarlane's Gathering* is close, yet they are not two settings of the same tune. John MacDougall Gillies was asked by the Provost of Dumbarton to write down the work he knew as *MacFarlane's Gathering* or *Togail nam Bo*, from the playing of two brothers, Donald and John Leitch. John MacDougall Gillies said it was a work known and played for generations in his native Glendaruel, and he refuted any suggestion that it was a re-make of *Too Long in This Condition*. The Gaelic title, *Togail nam Bo,* means the Lifting of the Cattle, which indicates that it is not a clan gathering tune but one associated with cattle-rustling, endemic in MacFarlane territory, around the area of Loch Lomond and Loch Long, especially in the 17th century.

It seems that *Too Long in This Condition* and *MacFarlane's Gathering* were two separate works, but both possibly based on the same song, versions of which were probably current over most of Scotland. A parallel development may have been when the three works, *Chisholm's Salute, Iain Ciar's Lament* and *The Glen Is Mine,* were all composed probably based on one song (see above, *The Glen Is Mine*).

Piobaireachd Works not on the Skye List

The above are the tunes prescribed for the Skye competitions. Of those no longer on the list, we have:

The Fairy Flag

This work appears to be very old. It is undoubtedly closely linked to the MacLeods and Dunvegan, and we have to assume that the reason it is now omitted from the Skye list is that nobody ever played it. If it were to be submitted by a competitor, it would be most unlikely to be selected, as judges would not want to be embroiled in the complications of judging it against the more conventional tunes, even if they were themselves familiar with it.

By the criteria of other more conventional works, this seems to be wild and without structure, but Barnaby Brown has related it to the construction of early Welsh harp tunes which use modes and mode-patterns rather than the more obvious echoed and half-echoed phrases to bind their work together. *The Fairy Flag* is what is known as a 'bottom-hand' tune, weak on melody but strong in the old patterns, and full of interest. These compositions are not easy to listen to unless the listener has some background knowledge, but with that, they are fascinating.

The tattered remains of the Fairy Flag are kept under glass at Dunvegan. Examined scientifically, the flag has been shown to be made of white or cream silk, of Middle Eastern origin, probably from Syria. This means that it might have been brought back from the Crusades, and would have then been regarded as a holy relic, at least until the Reformation. We might have expected it to be lost or destroyed during the Reformation, but perhaps its association with the powerful MacLeod family, and its importance in clan history, saved it. Or maybe it was hidden away during the dangerous years.

Associated with the flag is a story that it once belonged to a Viking leader, Harald Hardratha, who brought it home from Constantinople in the 11th century (Thomas Pennant, writing about Skye in 1772, made much of this). As Harald was an ancestor of the Norseman called Ljoth who (supposedly) gave his name to the clan MacLeod, and as Harald is known from Norse sources to have been in Constantinople, there may be a grain of truth in this tradition, and it ties in with the Middle Eastern origin. Harald, however, is linked to a story of the Vikings' raven banner, which when unfurled showed a raven apparently flapping its wings as the flag moved, and serving as a call for help in battle from Odin, the most powerful of the Norse gods. It may be that the link between Harald and the Fairy Flag is merely a blending of the two tales.

Recent work on the DNA of descendants of major Highland clans has shown that the MacLeods were of Gaelic descent rather than Norse, a result which came as a surprise. The MacDonalds, MacDougalls and others were shown to have Norse genes from their common ancestor, Somerled, but not the MacLeods. This discovery, if reliable, gives the lie to the Harald Hardratha connection – and indeed to the link with Ljoth.

There are, of course, other versions of the origin of the Fairy Flag, possibly merely shieling tales, but possibly invented to divert attention away from the holy relic aspect which could have endangered the flag, and towards the less risky clan history.

One story says that an early chief of the MacLeods fell in love with a fairy maiden (as early chiefs tended to do). He married her, and they had a beautiful son. One day, the nursemaid in charge of the baby was tempted by the sounds of music and merriment in the hall below, and she left the baby in his upper room, and crept down to watch the entertainment. She stayed much longer than she intended, and when she rushed back upstairs, she found the child wrapped against the cold in the fairy flag. The chief's wife said it had magic properties, and if waved in battle (like the Vikings' raven flag) it would bring victory to the MacLeods.

Of course, as a fairy woman, the chief's wife was unable to live out her life in the mortal world, but had to return to her own people. She and her husband parted at the Fairy Bridge, between Dunvegan and Waternish.

Stuart McHardy tells a tale which appears to be related, although it does not mention the flag. He relates how, back in the 13th century, the third MacLeod chief, Malcolm, married the daughter of the Earl of Mar, and they had a son, Iain, a sturdy, bonny child with a happy temperament. One day, however, he was left sleeping in an alcove, behind a curtain, and when his mother went to lift him, he had vanished. All the household was alerted and searched high and low, to no avail. Many said the fairies had taken him, but nobody knew, and he was missing for a year.

Then, the following summer, a girl called Morag, who was the daughter of MacLeod's MacCrimmon piper, was up at a shieling with other young folk, when she caught her skirt on a jagged rock, and ripped it. At once she sat down to mend it, and as she was sitting on a rock near an old ruined fortress, peacefully sewing, she became aware of a musical humming noise, somewhere in the ground beneath her.

It seems that her musical knowledge enabled her to amplify the sound by sticking her needle in the ground and pressing the taut thread to her ear (a 13th-century iPod?); by this means she made out that the music was a song, about a kidnapped baby. At once she ran to the castle to tell the laird's wife, and MacLeod determined to try to rescue his heir.

On taking advice from old women with supernatural powers, he decided it must be done at Hallowe'en, and duly on the night, he took a posse of men, and led by the piper MacCrimmon (which MacCrimmon, in the 13th century?) and by Morag herself, he marched to the ruined fort. Gradually as it grew darker they were aware of a chink of light from within the old walls, and looking in, saw an old hooded woman sitting beside a cradle. The father, MacLeod himself, moved some stones and climbed in, to find that the woman was human, not fairy, and that he knew her as an elderly woman from Colbost who had been lost from the shore in a storm while out gathering shellfish. Clearly she had not been drowned but had been taken by the fairies to nurse the little child. She was relieved to be rescued, and MacCrimmon played the party back to the castle, playing the tune of the song that Morag had heard through her needle (he must have been a quick learner).

The flag plays no role in this story, but the piper is further to the fore, and the two stories have common elements.

As far as we know, the flag was waved three times, but the first time it was ineffective. This was at the Battle of Bloody Bay, off the north coast of Mull, in 1480, when the MacLeods supported the wrong side, and the chief was killed. Perhaps the fairies were confused: both sides in this fight were mostly MacDonalds, and the battle was on the sea. Maybe the flag doesn't work on water.

The second waving worked, at the Battle of Glendale in 1537, when the MacLeods intercepted a large army of marauding MacDonalds, and were having a hard time against them. The chief's mother, one of those parents who have to interfere in their children's business (you meet a lot of them at the Games), came hot-footing it over the hill from Dunvegan, bringing the flag with her, and as soon as she waved it, the MacDonald chief, Donald Gruamach, was killed and the MacDonalds were beaten back. The fact that contemporary sources insist that Donald died of natural causes before the battle is not allowed to spoil the story. (See also *The Desperate Battle (Cuillin)* and *Donald Gruamach's March* below.)

In 1578, at the Battle of Waternish, when the MacLeods had too few men on hand to repel an invasion by vengeful MacDonalds, the unfurling of the flag had the effect of making the very blades of grass change into armed men as soon as the folds of the banner met the breeze. As the flag seems to have worked well even though the MacLeod chief was not present, we might wonder why the MacLeods did not take it with them to the Battle of Worcester in 1651 – but perhaps the battle had to be a MacLeod fight, and anyway, the flag probably works only on Hebridean soil.

Thomas Pennant, writing in 1772, visited Dunvegan, and was shown the Fairy Flag. Of its origins, he said it had been bestowed on the MacLeod family by Titania the Ben-shi, or wife to Oberon the King of the Fairies. 'She blessed it at the same time with powers of the first importance, which were to be exerted on only three occasions: but on the last, after the end was obtained, an invisible being is to arrive and carry off standard and standard-bearer, never more to be seen. A family of clan y Faitter had this dangerous office, and held by it, free lands in Bracadale.' Clan y Faitter was probably a family called MacPhedran or MacPhadruig.

Pennant goes on to describe three occasions when the flag was used: one was clearly the Battle of Waternish, the second preserved the heir to the family, and the third to save Pennant's own longings, whatever that might mean – but, he adds, the flag was then so tattered that Titania did not seem to think it worth sending for. A bad moment for the MacPhedrans in Bracadale?

It is not known who composed *The Fairy Flag*, but it does seem to be old, and does not appear to have undergone re-modelling, as so many piobaireachd works seem to have. It is probably safe to say that it will never be as popular as *Mary MacLeod*.

Sources

Alec Haddow, *The History and Structure of Ceol Mòr*
Alexander Nicolson, *History of Skye*
Stuart McHardy, *The Well of Heads*
Barnaby Brown

The Half-Finished Tune (Port Leathach)

Angus MacKay tells the story of how Patrick Og was composing this work, and managed the Ground and one or two variations, but then he stuck. His talented pupil, Iain Dall MacKay, was hiding behind the door, listening to Patrick struggling with the tune. He went away and finished it for him, whereupon the delighted Patrick said it should be called the *Half-finished* (or possibly the *Half-Each*) *Tune*.

John MacKenzie, in *Sar-Obair,* tells a different tale. In his version, Patrick's unfinished work was known and played in Skye for two years, before Iain Dall took it upon himself to finish it for him – and Patrick was deeply annoyed and resentful. John MacKenzie has several rather wild tales about the relation between Patrick and his blind pupil, and indicates that Patrick was so jealous of Iain that he tried to kill him.

There were stories about the bullying of Iain Dall by his fellow-students, and he must have suffered from their cruelty. It is possible that the title *Port Leathach* is a corruption of a Gaelic word *leathachas*, meaning 'unfair treatment, injustice', referring to the victimisation of Iain. If so, the tale of the half-finished tune arose from a need to explain the corrupted name, and there would be no truth in it.

The work might have been composed as an exercise in composition, set by Patrick Og as part of his pupils' training in the creation of piobaireachd music. There is evidence that in 18th-century Ireland, the Irish harpers used the word *port* to mean 'a musical lesson or exercise', rather than simply 'a tune'.

Another work apparently belonging to Iain Dall's time as a student in Skye is *The Blind Piper's Obstinacy;* its use of so few theme-notes has led some commentators to suppose that it, too, was an exercise in composition.

Sources

John MacKenzie, *The Beauties of Gaelic Poetry*
Angus MacKay, Manuscript

MacDonalds' Salute – see above, *MacLeod's Salute*

MacLeod/MacCrimmon Works not on the Skye List

Blar Vuster

This title ('The Battle of Worcester') is remarkable for the rendering of the English name Worcester into phonetic anglicised Gaelic. There is no *v or* w in Gaelic, and *Bhuastair* might be expected. *Blar* means 'battle' or 'battlefield'.

Although the work appears in several sources and under different names, the Piobaireachd Society editors preferred the Campbell Canntaireachd setting, where it is called *Blar Vuster*. In the book *Ceol Mor* it is called the *Camerons' Gathering*, and in *The Music of the Clan MacLean* it appears as the *MacLeans' Gathering*, or *The End of the Great Bridge*. Since all three of these titles are already familiar attached to other tunes, it was thought preferable to use *Blar Vuster*, despite its bizarre spelling, and avoid further confusion.

The Campbell Canntaireachd text has no Siubhal variation, and no Taorluath, but that was typical of this type of composition, in the 18th century. They were known as Gatherings, and usually had the fosgailte form of Crunluath variation, if they had a Crunluath at all. Joseph MacDonald made a distinction between these Gatherings and what he called Marches, which seems to have referred to all other kinds of what we now call piobaireachd.

It is not known who made this work, nor whether it was made specifically for the battle of 1651, or was adapted from an older work. Note that the *Lament for the Duke of Hamilton*, and possibly the *Lament for the Children*, arose from the same battle.

Sources

Alasdair mac Mhaighstir Alasdair (Alexander MacDonald)
Rob Donn MacKay
Piobaireachd Society Book 3
Joseph MacDonald, *Compleat Theory*

Lament for Alasdair Dearg MacDonnell of Glengarry

This is presumably omitted from the Skye list because it is too small to be used in competition with more substantial works, although it is universally regarded, as is the *Lament for Donald of Laggan*, as a 'masterpiece in miniature' (Seumas MacNeill).

Alasdair Dearg was the eldest son of Donald of Laggan (see above), but died around 1619, predeceasing his father, so he did not succeed to the Glengarry title. He was married to Jean, daughter of the 11th Cameron of Lochiel (see *The Young Laird of Dungallon's Salute*). Their son Angus became the heir to Glengarry.

Not much is known about Alasdair, other than that he was at odds with his father. In 1615 he was captured by Sir James MacDonald of the Isles who was leading a rebellion against the Crown, a rising which Donald of Laggan had refused to support. Alasdair was released only when he promised to join the rebellion, which he duly did. Like many of his line, he seems to have had an aggressive and volatile nature, reflected in his by-name Dearg, which probably means 'fiery, hot-headed' rather than referring to a colour (*ruadh* would normally be used if the meaning was 'red, red-headed').

Sources
Piobaireachd Society Book 11
Brian Osborne, *The Last of the Chiefs*

MacLeod of Gesto's Salute
This is a piobaireachd work with seven variations, and appears in the manuscript of Angus MacKay as well as in the Campbell Canntaireachd manuscript of 1790, where the setting is 'somewhat confused' (Piobaireachd Society Book 15). Oddly enough it is not in the Gesto Canntaireachd book of 1828, but there is another work there, called *MacLeod of Gesto's Gathering*, which appears to be the tune we know as the *Gordons' Salute*.

(See also Gesto, below.)

Gesto's Lamentation
This title appears in Gesto's manuscript as the name of the tune known elsewhere as *The Young Laird of Dungallon's Salute* (see Gesto, below).

MacLeod's Short Tune
Very little is known of the origins of this title. Angus MacKay called it *Port Gearr Mhic Leoid, a taunt on MacLeod,* but it is not the tune known as the *Dispraise of MacLeod*, to which he gave the name *The MacLeods Are Disgraced*. As the Piobaireachd Society editors put it (Book 6), 'nothing is known of the occasion of the taunt or of its nature'.

In the Campbell Canntaireachd manuscript, this is one of several works with the heading 'One of the Cragich', and the exact meaning of this is not known. It may mean that the work is rough and unfinished.

Patrick Og's Dream of Love
This title is found in Gesto's book of 1828 – see Simon Fraser, below.

Salute to (or *Lament for*) *The Rev. Dr Norman Macleod*
The Rev. Dr Norman MacLeod was a well-known writer of articles and books in Gaelic, in the first half of the 19th century. He was a leading light in the Church of Scotland in his day, being both Moderator of the General Assembly and Chaplain to Queen Victoria, among many other honours. This tribute to him, whether a salute or a lament, was composed by William Ross, the Queen's piper, probably when Dr Norman died in 1862. It was published in 1874, in William Ross's collection. See also the MacCrimmons, below.

Checklist of the Known MacCrimmon Pipers

There is an annoying tendency for comments throughout the centuries concerning MacCrimmon pipers in Skye to refer to 'MacCrimmon', with a variety of spellings but no indication of the first name. Sometimes it is 'the MacCrimmon', which adds status but not clarity. The following MacCrimmons are known to posterity:

The earliest MacCrimmon on record was **Sir Jhone McChrummen**, who in 1533 was in Inverness as witness to the signature of the MacLeod chief, on a legal document. The title 'Sir' indicates that he was a university graduate, who would have been literate in both English and Latin. He was almost certainly a clergyman, but could possibly have been a lawyer. It is not known if he had come to Inverness with MacLeod from Skye, or whether he was living in Inverness at that time. There is no evidence to link Sir Jhone with piping, unless he was 'Evanus piper', named in a Skye document of 1541 (see below).

From 1557 on, there is ample evidence of MacCrimmons, with various urban spellings of the name, such as **McGuirman**, living and working in Inverness. They had strong links with the Frasers. None of them is recorded as having been a piper, but that could mean only that they did not make their living as pipers.

The first MacCrimmon named as a piper was **Malcolm Makchrwmen**, in Balquhidder in 1574 (see below).

Finlay of the White Plaid was named (a) in Gaelic poetry as being alive at the time of the Battle of Waternish (1578-ish), and (b) in the Bannatyne manuscript, written in the mid-18th century, as having lived in Harris in the late 15th century, one of three brothers, Patrick, Angus and Finlay – who was not a piper but a warrior. The name Finlay does not appear again in the main line of the MacCrimmon pipers, as might be expected.

The name Finlay may have been used by MacLeod of Gesto, to support his theory that the MacCrimmons were descended from the Italian family called Bruno: the birth-name of Giordano Bruno, who died in 1600, was Filipo, and Finlay (Fionnlaidh) was probably the nearest Gaelic equivalent.

Iain Odhar ('sallow'), Finlay's son according to Bannatyne, was said to be piper to Alasdair Crotach MacLeod of Dunvegan (died 1547). The *History of Skye* says Iain was the first of the MacCrimmon pipers, living 'about the beginning of the 16th century'. Alasdair Crotach was said to have assigned Boreraig to the MacCrimmon family, and to have started a piping college there, but there is no record of MacCrimmons at Boreraig before 1710. Simon Fraser, probably following Gesto, said Iain was the son of Petrus Bruno, from Cremona, who had settled in Ireland – Petrus was a nephew of Giordano Bruno (see below). Iain might possibly have been 'Evanus piper', named in Skye in 1541.

Patrick Donn ('brown') may have been a cousin, or nephew, of Iain Odhar. He is also said to have been a piper in Harris. Note that the Italian name Petrus Bruno translates into Gaelic as Padruig Donn.

Donald Mor ('big') may have been a son of Patrick Donn, but he is generally held to be a son of Iain Odhar; he was probably born around 1575, possibly in Harris. He became piper to Rory Mor MacLeod of Dunvegan, and tradition has it that he was in Antrim around 1593, learning from famous harpers there. Later, he was possibly in Antrim fighting with a force of MacLeod clansmen for the Irish cause. He was piper to Rory Mor in 1602 when the MacLeod/MacDonald feud was settled. Forced into exile in the north of Sutherland to escape retribution after avenging the murder of his brother in 1603, he remained in the north for some twenty years, becoming piper to the chief of MacKay and teacher of many MacKay pipers. He was the first of the Skye MacCrimmon pipers to be recorded historically in his own lifetime, when his name appeared in a list of Sutherland men pardoned in 1614, as piper to the MacKay chief. He returned to Skye early in the 1620s, and resumed his position as piper to Rory Mor. It is thought that he died around 1640. For his compositions, see above.

Patrick Caogach ('with a twitchy eye') was the younger brother of Donald Mor, murdered by his foster-brother in Kintail around 1602. His brother avenged his death a year later (see above).

John MacCrimmon, known in 1651 as 'the Earl of Sutherland's domestick' (indoor servant), was at that time an old man, piper at Dunrobin Castle, in East Sutherland. His exact relation to Donald Mor and Patrick Mor is not certain, but he may have been a brother of Donald Mor, or his cousin. He may have taken over as piper at Dunvegan in Donald's absence, but there is no evidence of this. He may have been piper to MacSwan of Roaig. He was of Donald's generation, and in 1651 was described as an old man, much venerated as 'the Prince of Pipers' by other players ('old' could mean anything over forty). He served with the Sutherland contingent in Charles II's army at the Battle of Worcester. His fate is not known. He was a good composer (see above, *I Got a Kiss of the King's Hand*).

Patrick Mor ('big', 'elder' or 'senior'), born around 1595, died around 1670, was a son of Donald Mor. He was piper to four MacLeod chiefs in succession. Angus MacKay said he had eight sons, of whom seven died young. He is thought to have gone with the MacLeod men to the Battle of Worcester in 1651, and survived, but there is no proof of this. A fine composer, whose work is considered to be the Golden Age of piobaireachd (see below). According to Simon Fraser, drawing on the works of Gesto (now lost), Patrick practised a form of religion known as 'Primitive Christianity', and was not only bi-lingual in English and Gaelic, but was also literate, writing poetry as well as a manuscript about his beliefs. There is no evidence to support this, other than Sir Jhone McChrummen being a graduate in 1533.

Patrick Og ('young', or 'junior'), born around 1640–45, died 1730, was the son of Patrick Mor and said to be the sole survivor of Patrick's eight sons. He is also said to be the first MacCrimmon piper *in Skye* whose existence was recorded in his own time. He seems to have succeeded his father around 1670 as piper to MacLeod of Dunvegan. He was renowned as a piper, composer and teacher of piping, his most famous pupil being Iain Dall MacKay, the Blind Piper of Gairloch, who was with him in Skye from about 1678 to 1685. In 1688, the Skye accounts referred to a bonnet which the MacLeod chief, Iain Breac, sold for 14 shillings to 'Patrick MacCrumme the piper' – the earliest reference to this piping family in Skye. Note the spelling MacCrumme, with no final *n*. Patrick was probably the tenant at Boreraig in the late 17th century but his name does not appear in the Rentals, which do not list Boreraig at all; this might mean he was living there rent-free.

He was in Galtrigil from 1706. In 1710, £13 was paid to an unnamed piper in Boreraig, but Patrick Og was then in Galtrigill. He seems to have been a friend of Mary MacLeod at Dunvegan, who named him as an excellent piper, in one of her poems. He was not a prolific composer, but on Mary's death in 1705, Patrick made a lament in her memory. He may have composed *The Pretty Dirk*. On his death at Galtrigil, his pupil Iain Dall composed a fine lament (see above).

Patrick Og, who was illiterate, married twice and had a large family, some children of his first wife possibly born in Scarista, Harris, before he took over as piper at Boreraig. Some of his sons were:

Angus, said to be a piper, who died in 1730.

Patrick, died young.

John, who lived at Easter Leacachan, Kintail and probably composed *The Glen Is Mine*, before 1715. His family emigrated to Ontario, mid-18th century (see above).

Malcolm, born around 1690, died around 1767, was tenant at Scarista, Harris, in 1728. He took over in Skye as piper to MacLeod in 1730, on the death of his father. Serving with one of the MacLeod Companies in the Hanoverian army in the '45, he was captured by the Jacobites, whose pipers then refused to play unless he was released. He survived the campaign, and is believed to have composed a lament for his brother Donald Ban in 1746. From 1751 he held the lease of Borrodale and half of Boreraig.

Donald Ban ('fair-haired'), born around 1710, son of Patrick Og's second marriage, was MacLeod's piper in Harris, after his brother Malcolm went to Skye. He was never MacLeod's principal piper in Skye. He served as piper to John MacLeod's Company in Lord Loudoun's regiment in the '45, and died February 1746 at Moy, shot accidentally by his own side. He was commemorated by a fine lament probably composed by his brother Malcolm (see above).

Donald Donn ('brown') of Lourgill (or Lowergill): some say he was the youngest son of Patrick Og, others that he was the son of Patrick's son Farquhar. He has also been described as a nephew of Patrick Og.

Farquhar, possibly the youngest son of Patrick Og, served as a sergeant in the same Company as his brother Malcolm in the '45. He was probably not a piper. He may have been the father of Donald Donn of Lowergill.

Annag, in the mid-18th century married Hugh MacPherson, a piper in Glendale (see below). She may have been a daughter of Farquhar, and grandaughter of Patrick Og, but this is not certain. Her descendants were the piping MacPhersons of Glendale.

Bess, daughter of Donald Donn of Lourgill, married Duncan Rankin, piper to MacLean of Muck; she was said to be a better player than her husband. They later went to Coll, where they spent the rest of their lives. She died in the 1790s.

Iain Dubh ('black, dark-haired'), born at Boreraig in 1732, was the elder son of Malcolm and grandson of Patrick Og. He took over the Boreraig lease in 1766–67, when his father died, and moved there after his brother Donald left in 1772. After Donald had gone to America, Iain Dubh decided to follow him, but on reaching Greenock, changed his mind and returned to Skye, where he lived at different houses (e.g. Trien, Hamara, Boreraig) until he died in 1822. He is believed to have given MacLeod of Gesto many tunes, possibly as many as 200, for his collection, and may also have taught John MacKay, Raasay. He taught piobaireachd to Niel MacLeod of Gesto and Alexander Bruce, and is thought to have been a friend of Hugh Archibald Fraser, father of Simon.

Donald Ruadh ('red' or 'red-haired'), born at Boreraig in 1733 or '34, was a son of Malcolm, grandson of Patrick Og, and younger brother of Iain Dubh. He succeeded his father as piper to MacLeod in 1766/7, but it is not known why the post went to Donald rather than his elder brother Iain. It is said he was sent to Charles MacArthur to learn his 'particular graces'. In 1770 Donald threw up his lease on Boreraig, closed the piping college and in 1772 emigrated to North Carolina, with 'followers' from Skye. He fought bravely for the British in the War of Independence, in which he lost an eye, and reached the rank of Acting Captain, but this was never ratified, and he remained a lieutenant. He lost his property in America in the war, and in 1783 moved to Nova Scotia, where he had been offered a grant of land. He became a ferryman, but was unable to make a living.

He returned to Britain before 1790. After a spell in a debtors' prison, he was rescued by the Highland Society of London who were planning a new piping college, which never materialised; he returned to Skye and lived there, apparently with his brother Iain Dubh, until in 1811 he moved to Glenelg, as piper to a land-owner named Bruce. There he was visited by Walter Scott and by Alexander Carmichael, who both left accounts showing how greatly he was venerated as a piper, composer and teacher. He taught both Alexander Bruce and Archibald Mac-Arthur of Ulva, and probably composed *Mrs MacLeod of Talisker's Salute* (see above). He died in 1825, in Glenelg. (Simon Fraser gave an account which attributes the *Lament for Donald Ban MacCrimmon* to Donald Ruadh rather than to his father, Malcolm, but the account is suspect in several details and must be regarded as unreliable – see below).

Patrick Mor of Duirinish, son of Iain Dubh, was said to have been piper at Dunvegan and was later a piper in the Black Watch. As a young man he served in the American War of Independence, and later in the Peninsular Wars under Sir John Moore at Corunna. He was a big strong man, and a good boxer. He went to West Africa where he died, leaving no family.

Mrs Ealasaid MacKinnon was the daughter of Iain Dubh by his first wife, and said to be a good piper. Angus MacKay described her in 1838 as 'a worthy gentlewoman who now keeps a school for females at Dunvegan', and said she was 'at the present day able to go through the intricacies of a piobaireachd'. Angus also said that MacCrimmon's daughters were able, in his absence, to superintend the instruction of the students at the Boreraig college. He added that although the pipe 'appears rather an unfeminine instrument, yet in the Highlands women certainly did play, especially after the harp went out of use, and they were, sometimes, proficient, too'. (The above comments were probably written by James Logan, though by implication attributed to Angus MacKay).

Donald, eldest son of Donald Ruadh, around 1820 emigrated to Ontario where he joined his cousins who had gone out from Kintail (see above, *The Glen Is Mine*). This family is said to be 'heavily into Freemasonry'.

Patrick (1780–1837), cousin to Patrick Mor of Duirinish, was a son of Donald Ruadh, but probably not a piper. He died in Sierra Leone while with the army.

Ey (Hugh) Malcolm MacCrimmon lived at Dalintober, Campbeltown, in the late 18th century, and was known there as an authority on pipe music. He seems to have been a lawyer rather than an active piper, serving as Sheriff Depute in Kintyre. He was born in Skye around 1737, and died in Campbeltown in 1822. Not much is known about him, but the dates suggest he might have been a brother or cousin of Iain Dubh and Donald Ruadh. In the 1770s he judged a competition between John MacAllister and the 1st Piper of the Western Fencible Regiment, held in Campbeltown to decide which of them was the better player and therefore to be given the higher rank. He gave the decision to MacAllister, who went on to win the national competition in Falkirk in 1783.

Malcolm MacCrummen was a piper in South Carolina in the late 18th century. His exact relationship to the sons of Patrick Og is not known. It is thought that religious intolerance of music forced him to leave South Carolina, but the details have been lost.

John Gibson quotes, in translation from Gaelic, a report by Calum MacLeod, *Sgialachdan a Albainn Nuaidh*, in which he says that a MacCrumen piper emigrated from Lowergill, near Glendale in Skye, in 1830, going out to Cape Breton, after being evicted by a removal order from the government. He was, said Calum MacLeod, the composer of the tune they call *The Lowergill Crofters' Farewell to the Isle of Skye*. It is not known who this MacCrimmon piper was, nor what became of him, and the tune (at least under that name) has been lost. Presumably he was a descendant of Donald Donn.

Iain MacCrimmon in Canada has published over a hundred pipe tunes, in three volumes of *Music for the Great Highland Bagpipe*. His best known is probably his jig *Murdo MacDonald of Stornoway*.

Euan MacCrimmon, present-day piper, and his father **Roddy**, are descended from Iain Dubh, and have a house and holding of land at Boreraig, although their home is now in Inverness. Euan won the Gold Medal at Oban in 2005.

Possible MacCrimmons in Ireland

If the MacCrimmons were in Skye by the late 16th century, how long had they been there? Were they in Harris as well, before that, and was one of each generation the Dunvegan piper, as tradition tells us? Was William Bannatyne correct in saying they were one of the three families already in Harris at the time of the Norse settlement, probably in the 11th century, or earlier? Did he in fact say this? Would it account for the Lewis legend? They were not *provably* in Scarista, Harris, until 1728, but there may be evidence of them not far way, in Rodel, before that, in the 17th century. Earlier, for all we know, they could have been living peacefully – and unprovably – in Harris, unrecorded by officialdom.

Hugh Cheape has said that, in his view, the MacCrimmons were 'almost certainly of Irish rather than Scottish Gaelic origin', an opinion which appears to be supported by historical evidence (see below).

What we do know about the history of the Western Isles is that, in the 13th century, there was a migration of artistically gifted families from Ireland to the Scottish islands. This migration was politically motivated: throughout the 12th and 13th centuries, the big estates of

Ireland were increasingly taken over by Anglo-Norman lords from England, and during the thirteenth, the country was in a state of conflict as the Irish leaders strove to maintain their own power and status. To add to the confusion, the Irish church had lost its monopoly on literary composition, and the big Irish landowners had begun to encourage laymen to take up the creation of poetry, stories, history, genealogy, art and music, and to have these subjects taught to young men.

The Irish overlords set up a system of tuition, a kind of apprenticeship scheme, under which all the subjects considered to make up native Irish culture were taught under the auspices of the overlord, who paid the tutors. Naturally this was regarded by the incoming English as subversive, and it is clear that they considered all this Irish learning, including the music, to be a means of political resistance – as it undoubtedly was.

Irish bards soon learned that it was not a good idea to name specifically any lord to whom a praise poem was addressed, as the ruler might have changed within weeks, and if the poet had declared his allegiance, he would then be marked out as being a rebel. Times were difficult for men of artistic talent, and made more so when the Anglo-Norman churchmen brought in by the newcomers began to object to the secular tuition of students.

The position of these men of talent was made even more uneasy by the constant in-fighting among the Irish leaders, each small kingdom within Ireland having its own ruler and its own feud over the succession. This weakened the Irish resistance and let English influence flood the country. Some of the bards, historians and musicians, seeing the writing on the wall, felt obliged to maintain their own positions by working for the new overlords; many of their lords and masters knuckled under, too, and kept their positions by paying homage to the incomers, retaining their poets and musicians in their courts. Some did not, however, and they were replaced by Anglo-Norman rulers; it was their poets and musicians who moved out, unable to accept foreign overlords. Many left Ireland during the course of the 13th century.

The natural place for them to go was the Scottish islands, where the people spoke the same language and pursued a similar way of life. We know that the MacMhuirich bards settled in the islands at this time (see *TSGI* XLIII, 1966). As the O Muirgheasain family, they became the bards to the MacLeods of Harris and Dunvegan: 'their Irish ties were so strong that they did not shed the O in their names as long as they continued to compose bardic verse' (Derick Thomson).

Derick Thomson (*Introduction to Gaelic Poetry*, 21) makes it clear that, long before the invasion, Irish and Scots Gaelic poets had had this interchanging circuit, with poets of both countries travelling among the great houses in both lands. 'The two countries formed part of the same culture region. When the Irish poets and musicians were forced to flee the country, they naturally moved to the area which was virtually an extension of their own, a region they knew well, where their own poetic and musical traditions were practised.' It is certainly possible that MacCrimmon musicians were part of this movement out of Ireland. The precedent of the O Muirgheasain bards moving to Skye may have influenced the MacCrimmons in their choice of destination.

One difference between the poets and the musicians of this period was that the top ranks of the bards were literate and wrote down their own work, whereas music was still passed on by ear, the only written proof of its existence being references to it in contemporary verse. Where it is mentioned at all, it is harp music, which was used to accompany the reciting of poetry and the singing of songs. It was an art which earned high rewards.

Irish musicians, possibly MacCrimmons, were probably not pipers at this time,* but they may have been harpers, playing a type of 'classical' music with a structure similar to that of piobaireachd. The music of the harp is bound up with the making of song and poetry, and the patterns of internal rhyme in the verse are echoed in the phrase-patterns of piobaireachd. Unfortunately this type of harp music has been lost, and with it a probable step in the development of pipe music. We know it existed from a few clues that have survived, such as the names of metres and variations used at the end of the 17th century, closely resembling the variation names of piobaireachd. Some of these terms go back to the 6th century when they were the names of different poetic metres.

When, around 1593, Donald Mor MacCrimmon went to Antrim to study music, as tradition tells us, it is pretty certain that he was

---

* The Irish had pipers as well as harpers, but their pipers were classed as a form of rough and bawdy entertainment, along with jugglers and acrobats. Clearly they were not taken seriously as musicians, and their rates of pay were considerably lower than those of the harpers. It is not certain exactly what form harp music took, but it was serious music, and ranked with poetry as a highly paid medium. This seems to date back to the 6th century, and to have lasted until the 15th, or even later.

with the famous Antrim harpers, who would have had a profound knowledge of the form of music which Donald later composed as piobaireachd. We do not know what this kind of music was called – possibly cruitaireachd.

We cannot be sure when purely instrumental music was introduced. Much of the early harp music was accompaniment to song or poetry, and followed the patterns created by the rhyme schemes in the verse. When freed of these restrictions, did the music retain the same patterns? It seems likely, at any rate in its beginnings.

It was in the time of Donald Mor that the first piobaireachd works seem to have emerged. Some are said to be older, but cannot be proven to be so. The flowering of the piobaireachd form appears to have begun in his lifetime, and that was just when we know the new Italian variation form, and perhaps also a fashion for instrumental music, was sweeping Ireland – and Donald was in Ireland among the Irish harpers.

It was at this time, too, around the end of the 16th century, that the Highland chiefs began to build large halls and to hold court in them, as if they were royalty. This was when the pipe began to take over from the harp as an indoor instrument: the larger space of a hall required a louder instrument than the small stringed instrument known as the cruit. A bigger harp, the clarsach, had been introduced, in the previous century, but it had the disadvantage of being more difficult to transport than either the cruit or the pipe, and it was the pipe which now became the fashion for the households of powerful chiefs.

In the old poetry of Ireland, back in the 9th century, the poets gave names to the different metres they used, and usually each separate poem was composed in one metre throughout. Certain metres were used for certain purposes, e.g. one called *crunluth* was an elaborately decorated metre considered suitable for a poem in praise of a great king; other metres – one was *coronach* – were for elegiaic verse or laments, and so on. Each metre had its own patterns of internal rhyme and alliteration which closely resemble the patterns of phrase and grace-note in piobaireachd today.

The music was probably similar in those early times: certain types of 'metre' were used for certain purposes. Possibly it was not until Italian influence came in during the late 16th century that instrumental music took the form of a theme with variations, each variation using a different metre.

The existing music affected by the innovation of the theme-and-variation structure would have been the music earlier brought over, in the 13th century, based on the patterns of Irish poetry. As long as it was harp music, it would be closely bound to the sung forms of Gaelic poetry, but when it was transferred to the pipe it had to become instrumental music, and it took on the new form of Italian instrumental music. The patterns taken from the poetry continued within it but were no longer structural in the way they had been previously, and the new instrument required a new structure.

This is, of course, merely a theory, and it will not please those who prefer to regard piobaireachd as a pure, unsullied product of Highland genius, arising like a shivering Venus from the waters of the Minch. Maybe the genius lay in combining these incoming influences into a Scottish entity, unlike anything found elsewhere in the world.

* * * * * * * * * * *

There is little direct evidence that MacCrimmons were among the Irish cultural refugees of the 13th century. The name Crimthann has been cited as a possible forerunner (the *th* being silent), and Crimthann is well attested as the name of a talented Irish family of rulers and men of learning, but, unfortunately, the name Crimthann, with that *i* as the stressed vowel, is not compatible with spellings such as MacCruimein, where, until the late 18th century, the stressed vowel was consistently *u*. (The same argument would apply to derivation of MacCrimmon from Cremona.)

Edward MacLysaght, a recognised authority on Irish surnames, said there was a name which emerged in modern Ireland (among English speakers) as Cremin, Cremeen or O Cremin, but in Irish is O Cruimin, with that vital *u*. The name was traditionally associated with a branch of the powerful MacCarthy family who ruled West Munster, to the west of Cork, in the south-west of Ireland, the district now known as East Kerry. The name O Cruimin, said MacLysaght, is severely limited to that one small geographical area, and is seldom found outside West Munster.

This branch of the MacCarthy family, in West Munster, lost its fight with the incoming English towards the end of the 13th century. Other branches of the MacCarthys compromised, and by accepting English overlordship, built up their own power to become, eventually, the Earls of Desmond; but the branch to whom the O Cruimin family was attached did not. The West Munster MacCarthys were deprived of their lands and their influence, and dropped out of the picture.

We do not know if these O Cruimins in West Munster were part of that 13th-century MacCarthy court, nor even if they were musicians, but if they were, it is very likely that some of them had to leave Ireland at the end of the century, when their MacCarthy masters were put out of their lands. They would have found themselves branded as rebels, with no status, no employment and nowhere to go: their choice was to bow down to the new overlords, or leave Ireland.

Edward MacLysacht derives the name Cruimin from Irish *crom*, 'bent, curved', but in Scotland, the consistent *u* spellings led folk-etymologists to believe that the name was based on Gaelic *gorm* 'blue', quoting the Highland surname Blue as evidence. It seems, however, that the name Blue, particularly common in the Knapdale district of Argyll, is derived from MacGhilleghuirm, an early form of MacMillan, with links to the MacLennans, and it has nothing to do with the MacCrimmons.

Another Irish name, MacGorman or O Gorman, may be derived from Irish *gorm*, 'blue', or may be from the name of an early Irish saint. Irish MacGorman could give a later Hebridean name MacCruimein. Originally the Gormans came from Slievemargy in County Leix; they were driven out by the Anglo-Normans and settled at Ibrickan, in West Clare, and in County Monaghan. This was a family who had been powerful rulers, and by collaborating with the new overlords they re-built their wealth and influence, until in the 15th century they were hereditary marshalls to O Brien of Thomond, one of the foremost rulers in the country. The MacGormans were noted for their hospitality and their patronage of Gaelic poets.

These MacGormans are less likely to have been the ancestors of the piping MacCrimmons: they had no need to flee to the Hebrides, as they had compromised with the invaders, and they managed to retain their social position as rulers – and they were of the classes which were patrons of poets and musicians, rather than being themselves gifted artists.

Evidence of Early MacCrimmons in Scotland

Early MacCrimmons, variously spelled, are on record in many parts of Scotland, including Inverness (1533, 1557, 1562), Balquhidder (1574), Strathnaver (1614), Taymouth (1697), Aberfoyle (18th century), but there is little evidence to link them directly with the Harris and Skye piping family – apart from Sir Jhone McChrummen's link with the MacLeod chief in 1533. One of the Balquhidder MacCrimmons was in 1574 described as 'Malcolme pyper Makchrwmen in Craigroy', along with 'John tailzoure Makchrwmen in the Kirktoun of Balquhidder'. Malcolm seems to be the earliest MacCrimmon piper on record, though it is not known for certain if he was one of, or related to, the MacCrimmon pipers of Skye.

The wide distribution of a very small clan may suggest that in early times, the MacCrimmons were valued for their specialist knowledge and skill, presumably as musicians, and that this led to their employment by important families all round the country. A similar pattern is found among the Beatons, who were doctors, and the MacMhuirich poets. Probably those with skills in music, medicine or poetry were sought after by the big land-owners, and their presence in a household became an indication of prestige.

The MacCrimmon Name

The MacCrimmons traditionally associated with South Harris were a small clan, and it has been said that all of them today (including such variants as MacCrum, Crum, MacGorman, MacGurman and many others) are probably related and of common origin. This is true of several other small clans in the west, such as the MacQueens, the MacRailds, the MacMhuirichs, and the Boyds.

How the name MacCrimmon arose depends on which theory of their origin is favoured. A reported legend, printed in *An Gaidheal* in 1876, linked them to a family in Galson, in the west of Lewis, in Norse times, and led Dr George Henderson to suggest a Norse name Hromund underlying the later MacGurmen/MacCrimmon names. Hugh Cheape has pointed out that this tale features the MacCrimmon hero as a Lewisman of Norse descent, known not for music but for exceptional cunning and ingenuity.

By the 12th century there were so many people in the islands of mixed Norse/Celtic blood that they were known as Gall-Gaels, 'foreign Gaels' or 'Norwegian-Gaels', their numbers becoming so great that they were a powerful force. The Western Isles are still known in Gaelic as the Innse-Ghall 'Islands of the Foreigners', a reference to the Norsemen. An estimate of some 20,000 Gall-Gaels in the 13th century may be exaggerated, but they were numerous enough to be of political importance. It is possible that the MacCrimmons were Gall-Gaels, but there is no other evidence.

Dr Henderson's derivation from Hromund assumes that the C/G in the name was taken from the ending of the preceding Mac-, but the C/G spellings are found so consistently that this seems unlikely. There are occasional R forms, e.g. McRiman in the Harris Accounts in 1755, but the same person (Donald Ban's widow) is elsewhere in the same accounts spelled McCrummen or McCrumen.

This *u* of MacGurmen is found consistently in the older spellings – even in the extraordinary *Makchrwmen* of 1574, the *w* represents the *u* spelling. The spelling *McCrooman* appears in the Earl of Breadalbane's accounts, dated 1697, where *oo* is clearly the pronunciation of that *u*. The oldest spelling we have of the name is that Sir Jhone McChrummen, who witnessed a document for McCloid of Downveggan, in Inverness, in 1533; the stressed vowel is *u*.

A family called McGuirman was living in Inverness as early as 1547. There is no evidence that they were related to the piping family in Skye, but the clan was so small that a blood link seems likely. MacGuirmans, with varying spellings of the name, are recorded frequently in Inverness throughout the 16th and 17th centuries. They had close ties with the Frasers in and around Inverness. MacGuirman seems to be the urban form of the name. In the Harris Estate papers of the 17th century, the name is rendered as McCumra, which some took to be McCumraid, a Gaelic form of Montgomery.

This spelling may have been influenced by that Montgomery name. Mc Crumme appeared as the surname of Patrick Og in the Skye records in 1688. The MacLeod estate papers later spelled the name McCrummen.

Spellings with *i* are rare before the second half of the 18th century (see below).

MacCrimmons in Harris

In the rentals and accounts of the Harris Estates in the late 17th and early 18th centuries, there appears a family called Mc Cumra, who had small holdings of land at Rodel, in the south of Harris. This name was later spelled McCumrad, leading some to identify it as McCumraid, the Gaelic for Montgomery but there were no Montgomery families in Harris at that time. Alistair MacLeod, the genealogist with Highland Council, who has a vast knowledge of Highland names, thinks that Mc Cumra was a form of MacCrimmon, and that it was later corrupted into an apparent form of Montgomery.

The rental lists for Harris are mainly in patronymic form, that is, they list the generations as single names, with no set surname. The exceptions, of which Mc Cumra appears to be one, are the surnames of families apparently employed directly by the Harris estate, under the chieftainship of MacLeod of Dunvegan, Skye. Most of these estate workers appear to have been brought into Harris from elsewhere. The fact that no patronymic line is given for this Mc Cumra family in Rodel suggests that they, too, had been brought in from outside Harris, to work for the estate – whether as pipers, we do not know.

The Mc Cumra family, living in South Harris (but at Rodel, in the south-east of Harris, not at Scarista, in the south-west), has some of the given-names we know among the piping MacCrimmons: Iain/John, Angus, Malcolm, Rachel. When the last of the Mc Cumras died in the early years of the 1700s, a piper was brought in from Uist to be the official Harris estate piper, which might imply that they had held this office; they feature in the Harris accounts for at least thirty years – but it cannot be shown for certain that the three generations of Mc Cumras who appear in the Harris Estate Papers were related to the pipers at Boreraig and Galtrigill. Unfortunately, only the rent-payers' names are listed, so we do not have the names of family members other than the tenants themselves.

In the Harris records, the first provable MacCrimmon piper (spelled MacCrummen) is Malcolm, son of Patrick Og; he is listed in 1728 as having been granted the tenancy of a pennyland of ground at Scarista, probably the holding known as the Kirkpenny – and the factor was careful to record that this tenancy had been awarded at the personal order of the chief, MacLeod of Dunvegan. The implication is that Malcolm had been brought over to Harris as the chief's Harris piper, and that he was not himself a Harris man. He had probably been living in Skye before 1728.

In 1708, the chief had 'encouraged' a piper named Hugh MacLeod to come from Uist to Harris as the chief's Harris piper, by offering him the excellent salary of £40 per year (other MacLeod estate's pipers in Skye received £10). Hugh MacLeod remained the Harris piper for several years, being named in the estate accounts until 1711. After that, annoyingly, the factor began to list all the estate servants, foresters, ferrymen, musicians, etc, as one entity, with their joint salaries as a lump sum. Their names are no longer given, so we do not know exactly how long Hugh remained in his position. He may have been there until 1727 or '28, for all we know. The very fact of the importing of Hugh MacLeod tells us that there were no accomplished MacCrimmon pipers in Harris in the early 18th century.

If Malcolm was brought over from Skye in 1728, only two years before the death of his father, Patrick Og, it looks as if the tradition of an endless supply of trained MacCrimmon pipers at Scarista at that time may be a myth, though it may have been true earlier – we have no early records to tell us.

When Malcolm replaced his father at Dunvegan, his younger half-brother Donald Ban took over as the Harris piper – and it seems he too was sent across from Skye, as he does not appear in the Harris accounts before that. He figures there from 1730 until 1745, when he was summoned to be piper to one of MacLeod's Independent Companies, fighting for the Government. Killed at Moy in 1746, he left a widow in Harris who was supported by the MacLeod estate until 1779. Donald Ban was never the Dunvegan piper, and he and his brother are the only MacCrimmon pipers named as being in Harris. The questions needing answers are: were they related to the MacCumra family at Rodel, and/or to 'the Widow' Rachel who was at Scarista in the 1680s? And were Angus Mc Cumra and his son Murdo, living at Rodel, the Harris pipers before Hugh MacLeod was brought in?

Distribution of MacCrimmon Families

As we have seen, the MacCrimmons may have come to the Western Isles in the 13th century, from Ireland, when political upheaval drove talented families to seek a living overseas. The Gaelic language spoken in Scotland at that time gradually diverged from the Irish, the differences becoming more and more marked, as we might expect. The written language, however, continued to be based on Irish literary practice, and as late as the 17th century the written form was more Irish than Scottish, concealing changes taking place in the spoken language. Even into the 18th century, poets such as Iain Dall MacKay were using a form of poetic Gaelic closer to Irish than to Scottish. It was archaic even then, but still understood in Scotland, and would have been regarded as venerable and dignified, suitable for formal verse – rather as biblical language, the English of the 17th century, was used for ceremonial occasions right into the 20th century.

A small and geographically limited family in Ireland, with the name Cruimin (O Cruimin or Mac Cruimin), associated with a big clan, is what we would expect if they were musicians to a chief. If this family was uprooted in the 13th century, a few family members probably remained in Ireland, but there is no lingering trace of a tradition associating Irish Cruimin families with music.

Once in Scotland, established in the islands as musicians, the expected pattern would be to find 'pockets' of them attached to different powerful families, as the lairds sought trained professionals to join their households and enhance their prestige. This is indeed what we find: never numerous, the MacCrummens appear in the records all round Scotland, but only in little groups of one or two families.

We have mentioned a university graduate called McChrummen at Inverness in 1533 (associated with the Dunvegan chief); and other MacCrummens at Balquhidder in 1574, one of them a piper; this was land belonging to Campbell of Glenorchy. One was in Strathnaver, Sutherland, in 1612 – Donald Mor himself, stated specifically to be a piper. There was a family of McGrimans in Strathdon and Huntly, and another in Buchanan, near Drymen. Most seem to have been associated with big estates and important lairds, and to have moved there possibly as estate workers – but were they musicians?

From the 16th century on, there were McGuirmans in Inverness, recorded first in 1547 – one of them was a brewer who was fined for over-pricing his ale. Their line was later spelled McGuirman or (occasionally) McCruiman, and can be traced in a continuous line right through into the 19th century. They seem to have been involved in Freemasonry in Inverness, and may have been connected by marriage to the Frasers, the branch which produced Hugh Archibald Fraser and his son, Simon – or indeed by non-marriage, as a 'natural' child was born to a Fraser father and a MacGuirman mother in 1733.

Other than the Balquhidder piper in 1574, the only piping Mac-Crimmon named in the records before the time of Patrick Og was the well-known reference to 'Donaldo McCruimmen lie Pyper', in 1614, listed among the followers of the Chief of MacKay who were pardoned for the MacKay attack on Thurso in 1612.

The Register of the Great Seal in Edinburgh shows that the government issued this pardon, since they had unofficially encouraged the MacKays to attack, in order to put a stop to the activities of a coin forger, Arthur Smith, working in Thurso and undermining the Scottish currency. The strong oral tradition about Donald Mor's exile among the MacKays makes it clear that this Donald was none other than Donald Mor, grandfather of Patrick Og.

The pardon gives us a list of the forty-four men who had attacked Thurso in 1612, under the leadership of the MacKay chief's eldest son, Donald Duaghal MacKay (named in the document as *Donaldo McKy feodatorio de Far*: the final -*o* denotes the dative case in Latin, the pardon being issued *to* him, and feodatorio means feu-holder, feuar or laird. Far is the district of Farr, near what is now Bettyhill, on the north coast, east of Tongue.)

Donald Mor is listed as *Donaldo MacCrummen lie pyper* (this is one reading: another is *MacCruinnien*. There are six successive minims and no dots, which probably indicates that the scribe wrote *MacCrummen). Lie* = 'the'. His name appears above that of *Joanni McRorie lie pyper,* John son of Rory, who may have been related to Rory MacKay, former piper to the MacKay chief. As a very young man in 1609, probably in his mid-teens, Rory MacKay had gone to Gairloch, where his son Iain, later known as the Blind Piper, was born in 1656. Rory's father was called Duncan, but it is likely that Duncan's father was called Rory, and possibly this John was his son, a great-uncle of Iain Dall.

In 1692 we have mention of a Robert McGriman in Banchory, and his line can be followed down through generations of McGrimans in Strathdon, Strathdee and Deveronside, moving on to the Huntly area in the late 18th century. Most of the McGrimans and McGrimmons in that district stemmed from Robert in Banchory in 1692. We have no way of knowing if Robert was the first there, or merely the first to find his way into the records. The *i* of *McGriman,* however, as early as 1692, and the persistent G spelling, may suggest that this is a form of the name Grimond, which appears to have originated in Perthshire, or possibly in Orkney, and may or may not be the same name as *MacCrimmon.*

There were a few McCrimans in Glassary, near Lochgilphead, Argyll, in the 1780s and 1850s, and a John McGuriman was married in North Knapdale in 1780. The spelling of his name reflects an intermediate stage between McGruiman and McGuirman.

Travelling in Skye, Thomas Pennant in 1772 spelled the name Mac-Krumen, while a year later, another Skye visitor, Dr Johnson, used the more modern Macrimmon.

The 19th century saw a vast movement of Highlanders to Glasgow, and there are MacCrimmons, MacRimans and MacGormans there from 1820 on – and a Duncan McGorman married in Glasgow in 1708. Whether the MacGormans were indeed the MacCrimmons is doubtful, and the fact that there were very few Protestant McGorman baptisms may indicate that the McGormans were Roman Catholics, more recent immigrants from Ireland.

Considering the population of Glasgow in the 1800s there are surprisingly few McGrimans, McCrimmons and McRimmons. Greenock had a few in the very early 1800s, all of whom belonged to one family – some of them later moved from Greenock to Irvine, Ayrshire.

There were McGrimans in Paisley, one family in the 1790s, the rest (three marriages) in the mid-19th century. At Aberfoyle we find a family called McCrumen, two brothers, Donald and Patrick, with children

Alexander, Duncan, Marie and Merjerie, all born between 1702 and 1718. Were they brought in because of specialist skills such as music? It is not known what became of them. They disappear from the records, and may have emigrated.

In the parish of Buchanan, in West Stirlingshire, was the seat of the Dukes of Montrose. Here, not far from Drymen, we find Duncane McGrimmen; apparently he married twice, having a son Donald in 1666, and a daughter Jenat by a different mother in 1669. And in 1674, Agnes McRumen married James Buchanan. Was Agnes the sister of Duncane? It seems likely that he was employed by the Graham (Montrose) family at Buchanan Castle, but in what capacity we do not know. Nor is it clear how much reliance we might put on the different spellings of the name.

Edinburgh gives us only three marriages, all in the early 19th century, and no baptisms, while Perth yields just the one marriage, dated 1823. Edinburgh spelled the name McCriman, and Perth MacCrummen. These spellings were often at the whim of the person writing the names, who would have his own ideas about the form of the name, probably based on his own hearing of the pronunciation. The owner of the name would have little say.

At Campsie, which included Lennoxtown, many Highlanders made their homes, and in the 1830s we have Angus, Duncan, Donald and Christian, all married with young families. They may have been siblings. Similarly, at Cardross, Alexander, Roderick, Dorothy and Norman, all spelled McCrimon, were married in the years 1832–51, and may have been siblings.

The distribution of MacCrimmons, with their differing spellings, is sporadic and never prolific, following a pattern we might expect if individual members of the family had taken up posts on large estates, and remained there for a generation or two. The biggest accumulations are in Skye and in Glenelg, which was virtually an extension of Skye. Unfortunately the Registers for both the Skye parishes and Glenelg are late: Glenelg starts around 1805, Duirinish in the 1820s, so that we cannot trace any of the piping families of MacCrimmons. Even though we know that Donald Ruadh was living in Glenelg from 1811 until his death in 1820, he does not appear in the Old Parish Register: he was already married and had had his family, some of them in America, long before he took up residence in Glenelg, so none of the entries refers to him. Similarly, we do not find reference to Iain Dubh in Duirinish.

None of the MacCrimmons whose marriages and baptisms are on record were in the islands, other than Skye. This may be because the island records are not always complete, or because the MacCrimmons were not in the islands, except for Skye.

The only MacCrimmons recorded in Harris are Malcolm, there for two years, 1728–30, and Donald Ban, 1730–45, both apparently having come over from Skye, yet this is the piping family so strongly associated with Harris in tradition. Having records only from 1678 onwards, we cannot say for certain that there were no MacCrimmons there earlier; but if there were, their traces are indistinct and uncertain. The Harris accounts, dating from 1678 on, use the patronymic system, and very few surnames are found in them. Most of the surnames there were those of estate employees, and they included the McCumra family, who may have been MacCrimmons. It is not known in what capacity they served the MacLeod estate. They may have been the Harris pipers.

The (19th-century) registers for Glenelg and the Skye parishes generally spell the name MacCrimmon, with the odd MacCrimon or MacCrummin. The numbers are substantially higher than elsewhere, and in Glenelg must have represented a large percentage of the total population. Almost certainly they moved there from Skye, either transplanted by the MacLeod laird of Dunvegan at a time when he needed to maintain his defences – probably in the mid-16th century, and again in the 18th – or migrating there when the Bernera Barracks were abandoned in the 1790s, so that some accommodation became available for evicted families.

Of all the recorded MacCrimmons who spread so thinly across the country, only two outside Skye are known to have been pipers: Malcolm at Balquhidder in 1574, and Donald Mor in exile in Sutherland, fighting for the Chief of MacKay in 1612. The rest might have been pipers or might not, we just do not know. We have to bear in mind that even important pipers such as Calum Piobaire MacPherson at Cluny were officially recorded as 'Labourer' or 'Ag.Lab.' in the 19th century, obscuring our recognition of the distribution patterns.

Some of the known MacCrimmons may have been harpers, others estate workers with different responsibilities – but the pattern of their spread is consistent with the theory that they were employed by various big lairds for their specialist skills, and they never settled anywhere in large numbers, other than in Glenelg.

We must, of course, also remember that many of the MacCrimmons emigrated, especially to Canada, and this mass movement in the late 18th and early 19th centuries has distorted the patterns. Many of the MacCrimmons now living in Ontario are descended from John

MacCrimmon from Kintail, who was probably a son of Patrick Og, and may have composed *The Glen Is Mine* (see above).

If in the 13th century the Cruimin family made their way from Ireland to the Scottish islands, the name O Cruimin might well lie behind all the early spellings of MacCrimmon. There is evidence that the Irish patronymic O, from Ua, meaning 'grandson' continued in use by some of these immigrant families in the islands, before they became established and adopted the more Scottish prefix Mac 'son' (which was also used, though less frequently, in Ireland).

There is no problem with the many spellings of the name, all with *u* or *oo* (or *w*) as the stressed vowel. Even the form *Mc Cumra* is acceptable, as names with *r* + another consonant, especially *m*, *n* or *l,* often had the *r* displaced; this happens in many languages and is called metathesis. It rouses little comment among linguistic experts. In the case of Mc Cumra, the name has also probably been influenced by Mac Cumraid, the Gaelic for Montgomery. MacGurmen and similar spellings with a *G* are equally accepted as normal: *g* and *c* in anglicised spellings of Gaelic names are interchangeable, as the pronunciation of Gaelic *g* is close to English *c* or *k*. We find this in the name MacInnes ('son of Angus'), which is sometimes pronounced (and spelled) McGinnis or even Guinness. Similarly, *d* and *t* are often exchanged, or *b* and *p*.

Postscript: oddly enough, Edward MacLysaght listed another name, Mac Crum or Mac Cruim, which, he said, 'came to County Down from Islay, Scotland'. This opens doors to much speculation. When? Whereabouts in Islay? Links with Proaig? Links with Conisby? When was this family in County Down?

See also below, Simon Fraser, Gesto and the Bruces.

History of the MacCrimmons

The word 'shadowy' often crops up when the earliest MacCrimmons are discussed. Some of us believe in Finlay of the White Plaid, Iain Odhar and Patrick Donn, some do not. The terms Odhar 'swarthy' and Donn 'brown' seem to imply a darkness of complexion in the family, but that does not necessarily mean that they were of Mediterranean origin, as has been suggested; there can be other reasons for a swarthy skin, such as liver disease, or an outdoor life.

If we accept that Finlay, Iain and Patrick existed, we have problems dating the three of them. Their lives have been moved forwards or backwards to suit various theories, and it is too easy to use these as evidence: for example, Finlay's white plaid has been said to mean that he was a druid, practising a heathen religion, when all it really tells us is that he may have been known for wearing a distinctive plaid of a pale colour, and any reason given for this is speculation.

There does seem to linger about the family a whiff of unorthodox religious belief, heavily fostered by Simon Fraser and A.K. Cameron, but it is difficult to accept Finlay as a late follower of Celtic heathenism. An explanation may be that the beliefs described by Fraser, which seem so weird to some modern readers, were rooted in the rituals of Freemasonry, but it is difficult to ascertain just what these were, especially as early as 1800. Simon Fraser's comments do not always inspire confidence, and those of A.K. Cameron in Montana were even more extreme (see below, Simon Fraser).

Much of the speculation about the early MacCrimmons is rooted in the story that they came from Cremona, in Italy. This seems to be a clear case of folk-etymology, however. Tommy Pearston's visit to Cremona in an impartial attempt to find evidence, for or against, was unsuccessful. The origins of this story appear to lie with either MacLeod of Gesto, in the early 1800s, or the Rev. Dr Norman MacLeod, in the 1820s. For details of Gesto, see below.

Dr Norman MacLeod (1783–1862) was an eminent and popular clergyman who was not only Moderator of the Church of Scotland but also Chaplain to Queen Victoria, among many other important church offices; as an authority his position was unassailable, and he had a huge following, especially in Skye. He wrote (in Gaelic) in the 19th century, about his clan and their pipers, among other topics associated with Highland history. Known as Caraid nan Gaidheal (Friend of the Gael), which seems to have been a self-awarded title, he published a Gaelic newspaper, which he called *Cuartair nan Gleann,* 'The Traveller of the Glens'.

His life-work was to try to relieve distress among the Highland people, especially in the famine years of the 1830s and 1840s. He promoted the Church of Scotland's educational work, and made the Gaelic Bible available to all who could read it. He tried to inspire the downtrodden people by writing many articles in Gaelic, on history, geography, current affairs, literature, any topic to show that Gaelic was a language of dignity and worth, and capable of being used as a medium for education. He also wanted to develop a formal standard Gaelic prose, and was one of the first to do so. He had a huge influence on Gaelic writing for the next hundred years, and was widely respected and loved. The trouble, for us, was that his main aim was to hold his readers' attention, much as a journalist does today, and he tended to insert snippets of interesting though inaccurate information.

As a clergyman, his word was accepted without question. To Dr Norman we may trace several of the MacCrimmon myths, most of them put forward in an article he wrote in the *Traveller* in 1840. This drew heavily on Angus MacKay's historical notes, but it seems that at least four misconceptions about the MacCrimmons came from Dr Norman's pen, in the 1840 article and elsewhere:

(a) (probably) the Cremona connection – unless he took that from Gesto. Dr Norman was quite restrained about this, saying merely that the first MacCrimmon came with MacLeod from a town in Italy called Cremona, and was a harper, 'a renowned musician in his own day and generation'. He added: 'He took the name of his birthplace and those who descended from him they called the MacCrimmons.' No mention of the Bruno family, heresy, Ireland or unorthodox religious beliefs at Boreraig, nor of Miss MacKinnon. Had he ignored these, or were they added later? Note that Gesto died in 1836, and Iain Dubh MacCrimmon in 1822, both before the publication of Dr Norman's article;

(b) the distortion of Pennant's 1772 description of a tacksman's house in Skye, turning it into a depiction of a 'college' or piping school with rooms dedicated to the teaching of students and their practising – a complete fiction which has been applied (inaccurately) to descriptions of later piping schools across Scotland, thanks to Dr Norman;

(c) the story of Patrick Mor going to London to visit the King and being well received there (see *I Got A Kiss of the King's Hand*, above), which is refuted by that told by another minister, the Rev. James Fraser. Not only is the Fraser version earlier, but it is supported by the historical context;

(e) the assertion that Patrick Og had twenty strong and powerful sons of whom only two survived, Malcolm and Donald Ban. This would mean that after the '45 Malcolm was the sole survivor, which is not true; we might wonder how credulous his readers were.

To what extent Dr Norman was inventing these stories, or drawing on contemporary sources, we cannot tell. Some seem to have originated with Angus MacKay's manuscript. Gesto, whose work has been lost, was apparently a similar mine of misinformation, and there were probably others. But Dr Norman did not appear to apply any discrimination in reproducing them, being intent more on holding his readers than giving them historical truth. Did he have direct access to Angus MacKay's manuscript? The stories were perpetuated by many later writers, and became part of the myth attacked by Alistair Campsie in 1980.

Another of his mistakes was to refer to Donald Ruadh MacCrimmon as 'Captain Donald', when we know that his army rank was Lieutenant. This may have been based on contemporary usage: a MacQueen ancestor of mine in Skye went to America with Donald Ruadh, as one of his 'followers', recruited by him into the army in the late 18th century, and the family, who later accompanied him to Nova Scotia, still refer to him as 'Captain Donald'. During the American War of Independence he had for a short time been an Acting Captain, but the promotion was not confirmed. He spent much of his latter years in Skye petitioning for his army pension to be raised to that of a Captain, but in vain. Presumably he encouraged people to call him 'Captain Donald'.

In 1808, it was reported in the British newspapers that the Highland Society of London wanted to establish Donald Ruadh at either Fort Augustus or Fort William as the Professor of a National Academy of Pipe Music. They suggested that 'His Royal Highness' (the Prince of Wales), as Commander-in-Chief of the Highland Regiments, could promote Donald from half-pay Lieutenant to permanent full-pay Captain, 'which to him would be equivalent to a salary'. The report added that he 'is now in the vale of years'. This scheme came to nothing, but must have encouraged Donald to renew his requests for status as a Captain.

Dr Norman MacLeod said that when General Norman MacLeod of MacLeod came home from India, he (the Reverend) heard 'Captain Donald' play *Failte Ruairi Mhoir* (*Rory Mor's Salute*) on the battlements of Dunvegan Castle, and he adds 'I can never forget the impression the whole scene made on my youthful mind' (quoted by Alexander Nicolson, *History of Skye*). To this, Mr Nicolson commented 'Another member of the family was Captain Peter MacCrimmon who also had distinguished himself in the American War and is reputed to have been a man of gigantic stature and enormous strength.' This was Donald's nephew Patrick, and it is possible that the rank of Captain was transferred in people's minds to the more famous uncle.

It has been suggested that one reason for this persistent use of the term 'Captain' was that Gaelic speakers had problems with the spelling and pronunciation of the rank of 'Lieutenant', and it seems that many used 'Captain' for anyone of officer rank. This would account for some of the confusion surrounding Captain Donald.

Mr Nicolson went on: 'Owing to the magic art that this family possessed, we need not marvel at the gorgeous webs of fancy that tradition has woven around them.' Hugh Cheape has shown how the development of the fairy legends may have been a means of explaining the rise of the MacCrimmons from the lower ranks of society to their later prestige, and he links the White Plaid to their humble beginnings – the lower the station in life, the less colour in the clothing, it seems. (But would it then have been worthy of note, in a by-name? Presumably everyone of similar lowly status would be wearing one – and as he rose in status, surely Finlay would have discarded his pale plaid, which would not have distiguished him from the common herd.)

Another source which may be approached with caution is the so-called MacLeod Bannatyne manuscript, which was written in the 18th century. There is a useful note in the *History of Skye*, where Dr Alasdair MacLean, revising Alexander Nicolson's text, added:

> the Bannatyne manuscript (MS History of the MacLeods in the Dunvegan Muniments) is believed to be the work of Sir William MacLeod Bannatyne, well known as an archaeologist, and son of Roderick, a great-grandson of Sir Norman MacLeod of Bernera. However, it was possibly re-written by Bannatyne William MacLeod of the Glendale family. Although the latter lived most of his life in India, he may have inherited a draft from his cousin, Sir William MacLeod Bannatyne. This manuscript should not be confused with another of the same name – the Bannatyne Manuscript by George Bannatyne was published in four volumes (1928–34), edited by W.T. Ritchie for the Scottish Texts Society. [The latter was much older and has no relevance to Skye.]

Sir William may have had access to traditions handed down from the MacLeods of Harris within his own branch of the family, in Bernera, but we cannot be sure of this. As an eminent and titled scholar, his word carried weight, much as did that of Dr Norman as a minister, and few would have questioned his conclusions. He (if it was he) said the MacCrimmons were one of three families living in Harris before the Norsemen came, i.e. probably before the 10th century – but this has been doubted.

Perhaps it should be noted that the MacLeod genealogy given in the manuscript, deriving the clan from the Norse kings of Man, is a fabrication, presumably made in order to link the name MacLeod with Leod (Norse Ljoth), son of Olaf the Black, giving the MacLeods a dash of royal blood.

The Italian Link with the MacCrimmons

Italian influence rears its head so consistently that we should look more closely at the Cremona tradition.

The story is that a man from Cremona, Giordano Bruno, who was burned at the stake in Rome in 1600 for his heretical religious and scientific views, was the uncle of another Bruno, called Petrus – who, to escape the religious persecution of the family (whose heretical opinions he presumably shared), left Cremona and for a time wandered through Europe before he settled in Ireland, where he had a son, Iain (Odhar?).

There, we are told, he founded a piping (or harping) school in Ulster, before he was discovered by a MacLeod chief from Dunvegan, and he and Iain were brought over to Skye, complete with heresies; Petrus passed on his religious unorthodoxy to his descendants, notably Patrick Mor – and to the Laird of Anapool, who was not related to the MacCrimmons.*

How much of this story of Petrus is history, how much a mere farrago, twisted to fit theories invented late? We have to ask ourselves many questions. Was Petrus confused with Giordano, or was it believed that both had to flee for their lives and each, separately, wandered through Europe? Did Petrus leave before Giordano was burned at the stake? And (crucially) did either of them, or indeed any of the Bruno family, belong to Cremona? In those days, there was no unified country of Italy, and the states of Venice, Naples, Cremona and others were separate entities. Giordano was born in Nola, near Naples, nowhere near Cremona, not even in the same state, and he was known sometimes as Giordano Nolano. At no time, it seems, did he live in Cremona, and there seems to be nothing to link the Bruno family to Cremona in any way.

---

* The first Laird of Anapool, or Arnaboll, was Donald Munro, third son of Hector Munro II of Eriboll, who was given the tack or lease of Arnaboll, around 1650. Arnaboll is on the west side of Loch Hope, in North Sutherland. Donald had no male heir, but his daughter Marion inherited the farm in her own right, and it was her husband, her cousin Donald MacKay of Skerray, who became the second Laird of Arnaboll. He was the subject of the Lament composed by Iain Dall, his second-cousin. Marion and Donald had two sons, John and Hugh, neither of whom appear to have lived at Arnaboll, but let the farm to tenants. We assume that the Laird mentioned by Simon Fraser was the second of Arnaboll, and his contact with the heresies may have been in Edinburgh when he was training to be a lawyer: he graduated in 1678.

Giordano was born in 1548, given the birth-name Filipo; he lived at Nola, outside Naples, until as an adolescent boy he joined the Dominican order. He was an independent and outspoken thinker, and at the age of twenty-eight, after being ordained as a priest, he was charged with heresy, a capital offence in those days. He fled the country and spent the next fifteen years wandering through Europe, living at different times in Switzerland, France, England, Germany and what is now Slovakia.

All this time he was writing philosophical, scientific and religious treatises, poems and dialogues. There are reports that when in Switzerland he became a Calvinist for a time, but soon began to question the Protestant doctrines; later, in Germany he became a Lutheran, but the same thing happened. Both of the Protestant faiths excommunicated him. When, in 1591, a year after he had gone to live in Venice, he was denounced to the Inquisition for heresy, he had nowhere to turn; after years of imprisonment he was sentenced to death by a court of the Inquisition, and was burned alive at the stake, in Rome, in 1600.

He is remembered as one of the martyrs of the scientific world, hated by the Church for his questioning of their mediaeval beliefs about the nature of the cosmos and of God. One of many branches of learning for which he became famous was the science of mnemonology, methods of training the memory, and he could perform such astonishing feats of memory that many assumed he was using witchcraft. There is no suggestion that he had any interest in music.

He seems to have had a brother Giuseppi, said by some to have also been a priest. Giuseppi's son was Petrus Bruno (presumably what was known in Scotland as a 'priest's get'). According to some accounts Petrus too spent some years wandering from city to city throughout Europe, until eventually he fetched up in Ireland. Some say he settled in Dublin and set up a school of harpers there, others say he was in Ulster, with a piping school. It is possible that the careers of the two Bruno men, Giordano and Petrus, have to some extent been fused so that the biographical facts have been transferred to the nephew from the more famous uncle (or vice versa).

When Giordano Bruno was in England, in the years between 1570 and 1574, he was living in the house of the French Ambassador in London (having quarrelled with his fellow-scholars in Oxford). At that time the advisers of Queen Elizabeth I ran a particularly efficient system of espionage which supplied her with intelligence about her enemies all over Europe, including the Catholic church on the continent. Elizabeth herself was skilled in decoding cryptic messages, and it is said that she knew more about the Spanish navy than did the King of Spain himself. The whole system, with its elaborate codes, cyphers and symbolism, was known as the Rainbow Scheme. Even the stylised portraits of the queen painted during her reign were to some extent symbolic, and contain mysterious messages decipherable only by those trained to read the symbols.

It has been shown that during his stay in England, the heretic Giordano Bruno was recruited into the Rainbow Scheme by Elizabeth's spymaster Walsingham, and worked for the Protestant cause, under the name of Henry Fagot, by supplying the court with information about the French Catholics.

The system of strange symbols and codes used by the Rainbow Scheme is reminiscent of the weird explanations given by Simon Fraser in Australia for his interpretations of what he calls seantaireachd (= canntaireachd), which he declared to be a 'secret' name. These explanations are often dismissed in modern times as too eccentric to be taken seriously. The Rainbow Scheme, which undoubtedly existed in England in the late 16th century, is even stranger, and the implication is that we should look more seriously at Simon Fraser's theories.

One of the claims he made, almost certainly drawn from his Gesto material, now lost, was that the MacCrimmon family embraced a form of Primitive Christianity which may have followed the religious doctrines of Giordano Bruno – and it was probably Gesto who claimed that Petrus Bruno was a direct ancestor of the MacCrimmons. If we set aside the alleged link with Cremona, could there be something in this?

Simon Fraser said that Patrick Mor MacCrimmon wrote a manuscript about the failure of Christianity, and that it was lost when Patrick died, as it was buried with him. He also claimed that the Laird of Anapool was a believer, though he did not specify which Laird of Anapool – and he used the corrupt spelling *Anapool,* where the name should be *Arnaboll* (Angus MacKay knew it as *Arnbol*). This spelling suggests that it was drawn from a late source.

There is an alternative name for the *Lament for the Laird of Anapool,* and that is *In Praise of the Rainbow,* cited in the Piobaireachd Society Book 9, although the source is not known. This recurrence of the Rainbow theme seems a remarkable coincidence in view of Giordano's involvement with Elizabethan espionage. To Simon Fraser, the work was called the *Lament for Giordano Bruno,* or *for Uncle Giordano,* and not *for the Laird of Anapool.* The use of 'Uncle' links the title to Petrus Bruno.

There is, however, another possible explanation: the Gaelic for a rainbow has several forms, and one is *braon-bogha*, where *braon* means 'rain'. Could this *braon* have been a corrupted echo of the name Bruno? The Sutherland Gaelic dialect pronunciation is similar. If this were so, then the apparent link with the Rainbow Scheme is without significance.

It looks as if someone much later than the 16th century built up this picture of the MacCrimmon link with the Bruno family, and the involvement with heretical religion. This could have been Gesto himself, who spent so much time in the libraries of Edinburgh. He may have taken up hints of MacCrimmon unorthodoxy and created a theory which embraced Cremona and both of the Brunos, Giordano and Petrus. If he had access to the written evidence of Giordano's involvement with espionage, he could have linked the MacCrimmons and Anapool to the Bruno family – it was, it seems, not Simon Fraser who gave the title *In Praise of the Rainbow* to that Lament.

The Rainbow Scheme in late 16th-century England, with its elaborate symbolism and mysterious secrets, was closely bound up with early forms of Freemasonry in England, and later sects, such as the Rosicrucians, based their beliefs partly on theories first put forward by Giordano Bruno. Both Gesto and Hugh Archibald Fraser (father of Simon) may have been active masons in Inverness in the late 18th/early 19th century. Proof is hard to come by, but there is evidence that some of Gesto's many legal hearings, in his prolonged litigation against MacLeod of MacLeod, were held in the Masonic Lodge in Inverness.

The name of Petrus Bruno was presumably not simply plucked out of the air. We cannot be sure that he was an historical person, that he really existed, around the end of the 16th century. And, if he lived at all, was he in Ireland?

The names of the Bruno family appear to be picked up in the names of the (putative) early MacCrimmons: Filipo and Finlay, Petrus Bruno whose name translates into Gaelic as Padruig Donn, and John/Iain (Odhar). If these are fictional characters, it would seem that someone, possibly Gesto, carefully created the link, in order to graft the story of the Italian family of Bruno onto that of the MacCrimmon pipers in Skye.

We cannot be certain if the Cremona story came to us from Gesto or from the Rev. Dr Norman, but it was Gesto who said he had received a lot of information from Iain Dubh MacCrimmon, grandson of Patrick Og. On the other hand, Dr Norman is known to have published several unsubstantiated claims about the MacCrimmons, and Joseph Mitchell, later in the 19th century, said the Cremona theory stemmed from

Dr Norman. Joseph, a well-known civil engineer in the north of Scotland, was a leading light in the Freemasonry movement, in Inverness.

If Dr Norman started the Cremona story, he could have passed it to
Gesto when they were both in Edinburgh, in the 1830s. It may have
been Gesto who then developed it by linking the MacCrimmons to
the family of Giordano Bruno, adding details of unorthodox religious
belief, possibly in line with the beliefs of Freemasons at that time. Or
do the beliefs and scientific theories of Giordano Bruno lie behind the
apparently weird theories propounded by Simon Fraser, presumably
following Gesto?

Simon Fraser gave the story which he almost certainly took from
Gesto's writings, rather than from the Rev. Dr Norman: in Simon's
version, Petrus Bruno left Italy because of religious persecution, and
after various wanderings settled in Ireland. He was a harper, a professional musician, and in Ireland he developed the music we now call
piobaireachd, and he devised a system for singing it in vocables which
he called *seanntaireachd*, a system based on the English language (why
English, when he was using a pseudo-Gaelic name for the system?).
Petrus' son was John, perhaps later known in Gaelic as Iain Odhar.
The MacLeod chief, on a visit to Dublin, met this family and took them
all back with him to Skye. It is not clear if they were supposed to be
playing harps or pipes at this time – indeed, it is not clear what time
this was.

To us nowadays this story is nonsense, and the direct descent of the
MacCrimmons from the Brunos strains our credulity. When living in
Ireland, we are told, Petrus used the name Cremmon (i.e. 'from Cremona' – note the convenient doubling of the *m*), rather than Bruno, it
is not apparent just why; if he wanted to conceal his family origin, why
point to it by naming the supposed town of his birth?

To add to our discomfort, we are told that when they came to Skye,
one of them, presumably John, married a Skye girl called MacKinnon,
and rather than take her name, her husband emended his own from
Cremmon to MacCrimmon. This strains our credulity to breaking
point, especially as surnames as such had not yet replaced the patronymic system in the islands. And the name MacCrimmon was not in
use in that form until the late 18th century (see above).

As Hugh Cheape told the Gaelic Society of Inverness, there are
traditions in both North Uist and Skye which maintain that the first
MacCrimmon in Skye was a harper, before the pipe was adopted as a
serious instrument. Dates are vague, but a person called Evanus Piper
was witness to a grant of lands to MacLeod of Dunvegan in 1541 – was

he a MacCrimmon? He must have been piper to Alasdair Crotach, who died in 1547. Was Evanus possibly the Sir Jhone McChrummen who had witnessed the chief's signature in 1533? The Latin spelling Evanus is assumed to represent Gaelic Eoin (= Ewen), rather than Iain (= John), but in the Gaelic version of the Bible, the name John is always translated as Eoin, so Evanus could be the Latin equivalent of Iain, which was sometimes spelled Eain.

In 1533, Sir Jhone McChrummen, possibly a clergyman, acted as witness to a deal done by MacLeod of Dunvegan in Inverness. We cannot be sure if Sir Jhone belonged to Inverness or had accompanied his laird there from Skye. If a priest, he is perhaps not likely to have been a piper, but the possibility cannot be ruled out: he might have been Evanus Piper. The title 'Sir' tells us he was a university graduate; other witnesses to the same deal in 1533 are described as 'parsoune', but he is not, and he may have been a lawyer. Alasdair Crotach was the MacLeod chief associated with the introduction of Petrus Bruno to Skye: could Evanus Piper have been Petrus' son John? Is it possible that all three Johns were the same person, a piper in Skye? It was Alasdair who was reputed to have started the Boreraig school and to have granted an early lease of Boreraig to the MacCrimmon family – but evidence for this has not been found.

The Balquhidder piper, Malcolm Makchrwmen, in 1574, is the earliest example of a MacCrimmon known to have been a piper, but he was not in Skye. Was he of the Skye family? We do not know. Certainly at that time we have no contemporary references to MacCrimmon pipers in Skye, and it was to be more than a century before Patrick Og was named as piper to the MacLeod chief and living in Skye. We do have evidence of Donald (Mor) MacCrimmon in Sutherland in 1612, and he is the earliest of the proven Skye MacCrimmon pipers on record – but he was not in Skye at the time.

We must pause, however, to consider these claims further. Did Petrus Bruno in fact settle in Ireland? Did he create a system of canntaireachd for singing pipe or harp music? Was there any form of sung vocables of that kind before this? The answer to the last is yes, there was – and it was Italian, and still in use in Petrus' time.

In the 11th century, a monk called Guido (he lived from approximately 1000 to 1050) was in Arezzo, which is in Tuscany, south of Florence, and not geographically linked to either Cremona or Naples. Guido was a music teacher, and invented a system now referred to as Solmization, whereby singing could be taught quickly and sightreading made easy, by using syllables which applied to any musical key. The modern tonic sol-fa system is based on it, but was not in use until the early 19th century.

Guido's scale was used for hundreds of years, particularly for teaching Gregorian chant. His scale was modal, with six notes, called ut, re, mi, fa, sol, la, and the intervals between them were full tones, except for that between mi and fa, which was a semitone. The resemblance to the modern sol-fa is obvious, but did Petrus Bruno, or indeed anyone, create a separate system for the harp, later adapted to the pipe scale? May we assume that canntaireachd was basically an Italian system, just as the theme-and-variations structure was originally Italian?

Italian Influence

Putting aside the fanciful connection with the Bruno family, allegedly from Cremona, we have to consider the possible influence of Italian music and musicians on the development of piobaireachd, probably in the late 16th century.

There is a strong tradition that piobaireachd form evolved in Skye, and we know that Italian musicians had come to both Scotland and Ireland in the 16th century, giving rise to a fashion for Italian music which swept through both countries. Among other kinds, it included not only the introduction of instrumental (as well as sung) music, but also a form with theme and variations, developed first in Italy and then in France and Ireland, before it reached Scotland. Could this have been the link with Italy, to which the convenient resemblance of the name Cremona to MacCrimmon was hitched?

There is evidence that this fashion for Italian music reached western Scotland via Dublin, and this would have given added impetus to the Petrus Bruno story. Add the Italian system of sung vocables to the mix, for extra spice.

Even if the by-name Donn is not to be equated with Italian Bruno, both Donn ('Brown') and Odhar ('Swarthy') have been cited as 'proof' of Italian blood in the MacCrimmons in the 16th century, suggesting olive-skinned or 'Mediterranean' complexions in the family. This has been explained by hypothesising a marriage between a MacCrimmon daughter and an Italian musician in Skye, but the evidence seems thin.

Even less convincing 'proof' is that the features of Simon Fraser's mother, Mary Anderson, said to have MacCrimmon blood, 'suggested Italian origin'. To judge from her photograph, taken in her later years, she was a typical Highland woman, whose looks suggest the Western Isles as much as Italy.

Persistent rumours of Italian blood/music/culture/influence among the MacCrimmons are probably too strong to be dismissed entirely. It seems likely that the Italian influence, if any, came into the family after it was established in the islands, whether in Harris or in Skye. We know that a daughter of MacLeod of Dunvegan spent some time in Edinburgh as a Lady-in-Waiting to Mary Queen of Scots, and that Italian musicians were a feature of the court there at that time. Did she return to Skye bringing an Italian with her? Did he marry a MacCrimmon? It is possible.

Equally possible, and perhaps more likely, is that reports of a MacCrimmon marriage to an Italian musician were symbolic, as was often the case with Gaelic tradition, not to be taken literally: it was a way of putting into concrete terms the fact that the MacCrimmons absorbed Italian music into their own, that some form of Italian music entered the family's musical tradition. Could this have been the casting of piobaireachd in the form of theme-and-a-succession-of-developing-variations? This was undoubtedly an Italian fashion, affecting European music of many kinds.

Similarly, the alleged arrival of Petrus in Ireland from Italy, and then his moving to Skye, might be symbolic, putting into concrete terms the abstract idea of a cultural invasion. This was clothed in the convenient resemblance of Cremona to MacCrimmon, and the rest was developed by a busy imagination.

The MacCrimmons and Freemasonry

Simon Fraser gave details of religious beliefs which he ascribed to Patrick Mor, and many modern readers find them unacceptably weird. If, as has been suggested, they are founded in the Freemasons' rituals, they would be difficult to trace, but it is a possibility, and Fraser's father and grandfather in Inverness may have been involved in the Freemasonry movement. Simon said that his sons were all masons, but implied that he himself was not.

Pipe Major Willie Gray, himself a master mason, linked the late MacCrimmons to Freemasonry; far from finding the weird theories unacceptable, he embraced them with enthusiasm, and believed that they were important in the creation of piobaireachd. He implied that the privilege of a piper putting on his hat before playing was based on masonic ritual – and this is attested as a piper's privilege at least as early as 1651. In more recent times, according to a Scottish MacCrimmon, some MacCrimmon descendants in Canada are 'heavily into Freemasonry'.

One of the earliest recorded members of St Andrew's Lodge in Inverness in 1739 was 'the Laird of Mackleod'; this was MacLeod of Dunvegan, probably Norman, XVIII Chief, son of Iain Breac.

A link between Gesto and Inverness seems to have been his friend-ship with Hugh Archibald Fraser, father of Simon and (according to a descendant) a lawyer in Inverness, about to be promoted to 'magistrate' when he decided to emigrate – and both Gesto and Hugh Archibald were possibly involved with the Freemasons of Inverness. Gesto also had frequent correspondence with his Inverness lawyers (not Hugh Fraser) about business affairs and his law-suits, which were heard in Inverness. It may have been through membership of a masonic lodge in Inverness that Gesto met Hugh Archibald, but Simon Fraser said his father was then only sixteen, a little young to be a mason. The link could have been through Hugh Fraser, possibly the father of Hugh Archibald and also said to have been a lawyer.

It is hard to believe that Petrus Bruno passed his religious beliefs on into the Highlands, and we can understand why Dr Norman left them out of his account, if indeed he ever came on them: as a minister, and a prominent leader of the Church of Scotland, he would have had to disassociate himself from such heresy – or were the Protestant clergy allowed to be masons? If Dr Norman was himself a mason, he was discreet about revealing their mysteries, and his version of the Cre-mona story certainly differs from that of Simon Fraser. It is the sheer variety of Simon Fraser's theories which makes us gasp, the mingling of Christian, pagan, Norse, Greek and so on, but some people, especially practising masons, have no difficulty in swallowing the mixture.

Canntaireachd/Sean(n)taireachd

Two things in particular stick in the throat. One is the changing of the Gaelic name *canntaireachd*, which means 'singing, chanting', or 'the art of the singer', for the system of singing piobaireachd in vocables, used before staff notation was introduced; this was converted by Petrus Bruno to *sean(n)taireachd*, said Simon Fraser, on the grounds that *sean(n)taireachd* contains the letters of the name Christ, where *canntair-eachd* does not. Is there any justification for accepting this? Apart from the unlikelihood, the standard Gaelic spelling of Christ is *Criosd*, using an *o* which is not in *sean(n)taireachd*, a term which is Gaelic in form, but is not a Gaelic word with any real meaning. It has the appearance of having been coined by a non-Gaelic speaker. A.K. Cameron said that the system of sean(n)taireachd – which he spelled *sheantaireachd* but pronounced 'shen' – was in English, but did not explain why. The implication is certainly that the term *canntaireachd* was older, and was adapted to *sean(n)taireachd* to suit someone's theories.

It was claimed that the whole canntaireachd system was based on vocables found in the Bible – that is, the Bible in English. A Gaelic translation of the whole of the Bible was not available until 1801, but the New Testament appeared in a form of Gaelic in 1767. It was not widely accepted, as its Gaelic seemed unusual, not a form spoken in the Western Isles, probably based on an earlier translation into Irish Gaelic (1603). Ministers used to make ex tempore translations during services, most of their congregations being unable to read either language. These oral translations were preferred, being in the local dialects, to the published versions.

It seems clear that Gaelic-speaking congregations were not expected to understand the English Bible, and that Gaelic translations of one kind or another were usually available. There was no necessity for any of the MacCrimmons to base their alleged 'sea(n)ntaireachd' system on the English Bible. The link with Genesis chapter 3, verse 24, quoted by Simon Fraser as containing all the vocables of sean(n)taireachd, is detailed and clearly based on the (English) written word, and as such seems unlikely to date back to 17th-century Skye.

This claim that the MacCrimmons in Patrick Mor's time based their system of vocables on the English Bible necessarily implies that they were not only English-speaking but also literate in English, and there is no real evidence that this was so. References to their literacy are few, and mostly later, but Sir Jhone, in 1533, as a university graduate must have been literate, probably in both English and Latin. Certainly Donald Ban seems to have been able to read and write in the 1730s, when he witnessed the MacLeod accounts for Harris. At the very least, he could sign his own name, using an anglicised spelling, possibly copying a written model. His father, Patrick Og, however, was illiterate, saying in 1724 that he could not write. In 1791, one of the two MacCrimmon brothers, probably Donald Ruadh, had to make his mark rather than sign his name on receiving his salary as piper – and there is evidence that he learned to write some time after this, in adulthood, around 1800. Less convincing is Seton Gordon's story of MacCrimmon (unspecified) writing a tune in the wet sand of the beach as the tide began to ebb, and telling his pupils he expected them to be able to play it before the incoming tide washed it away (*A Highland Year*, 1947).

The other sticking point is that link of the name MacCrimmon with

Cremona: it is too slick, too obviously false and too unlikely, as well as etymologically unsound, as early spellings of MacCrimmon had a *u* rather than *i* or *e*. This fancied Cremona link seems to have been the basis of the whole theory, passed by Gesto, via Hugh Archibald, to Simon Fraser and A.K. Cameron, who then developed it further – so far as we can tell.

Summary of Theories

We might then reconstruct the (theoretical) forming of the tradition: the introduction of Italian form into the MacCrimmon music led to stories of a marriage between an imported Italian musician and a MacCrimmon girl; the fortuitous resemblance between the Italian place-name Cremona and the surname MacCrimmon (a resemblance that would not have been valid before the late 18th century, as MacCrimmon was spelled with a *u* before that) led to the creation of a theory whereby the Bruno family, allegedly of Cremona, was identified as the Italian family to which the bridegroom belonged. As the Brunos were not known to be musicians (although different stories have made them either harpers or pipers), but were well-known as religious heretics and scientific theorists, it was then said that the MacCrimmons embraced a type of religion known as Primitive Christianity, and all sorts of religious symbolism was read into their music; the name Seantaireachd was substituted for Canntaireachd, and verses of a religious nature were attributed to Patrick Mor.

The development of these theories is fascinating, and it is notable that not a word of it can be proved, or, for that matter, disproved. Even the descent of Simon Fraser's mother, Mary Anderson, allegedly a MacArthur, cannot be proved: it was claimed that she was a grandaughter of Charles MacArthur, the piper to MacDonald of Sleat and pupil of Patrick Og MacCrimmon, and that she was a niece of one of the piping MacCrimmons, though it is not specified which one. We have no way of verifying this, and it could be that Mary was the grandaughter of a Charles MacArthur (of whom there were many) and related to a MacCrimmon, not necessarily of the Skye piping family.

In all this miasma of unproven theory and unconvincing allegations, we have to keep our eye on one important provable fact: that *many of the piobaireachd settings which Simon Fraser gave us are first-class*, and do seem to support his contention that Gesto had them from a MacCrimmon source. If not, what was the source of these settings? Simon Fraser cannot have invented them himself.

Add to this the remarkable playing of piobaireachd in the Fraser style by Hugh Fraser, pupil of his father Simon, and by Hugh's pupil, Dr Barrie Orme: both left us recordings which show clearly a very fine tradition of playing the music in Victoria, Australia, which owes nothing to 20th-century Scotland.

See also below, Simon Fraser, Gesto and the Bruces.

Sources

Rev. Dr Norman MacLeod, *Cuartair nan Gleann*
Fred MacLeod, *The MacCrimmons of Skye*
Thomas Pennant, *A Tour in Scotland*
Lesley Alexander
Robert Bruce Campbell, *The MacCrimmon Pipers of Skye*
Ruairidh Halford MacLeod
Hugh Cheape, *TGSI* LXII
I.F. Grant, *The MacLeods*
Bannatyne MS *TGSI* L and LI
Alexander Nicolson, *History of Skye*
Alistair Campsie, *The MacCrimmon Legend*
Canon R. MacLeod, *Book of Dunvegan*
Alick Morrison *TGSI* XIV
Highland Society of London's Records, NLS. Deposit 268, p. 141, and
    Public Records Office, Record Group 8, vol C 1883
Derick Thomson, *Introduction to Gaelic Poetry*
Jeannie Campbell, *Highland Bagpipe Makers*
G.C.B. Poulter, *The MacCrimmon Family*
Alistair MacLeod, Inverness
G.F. Black, *Surnames of Scotland*
Simon Fraser, *Piobaireachd*
Robin Flower, *The Irish Tradition*
Edward MacLysaght, *Surnames in Ireland*
John O'Donovan, *The Annals by the Four Masters*

Iain Dall MacKay

Possibly the most renowned pupil of the MacCrimmons was IAIN DALL MACKAY, the Blind Piper of Gairloch. He was several years in Skye under the tutelage of Patrick Og, probably from 1678 to 1689, or thereabouts. In his poem *Dan Comhfurtachd* (*An Ode of Consolation*), composed many years later, in 1734, he recalled that he personally had known six of the MacDonald chiefs, and named them, so that we know he was in Skye by 1678. He was a member of the Talisker Circle of poets and musicians who used to meet at Talisker House and enjoy the hospitality of James MacLeod, and after James' death, that of his son Donald, until Donald died around 1740.

As well as giving rise to several piobaireachd works, Iain's visits to Skye inspired two of his best poems, the *Song to Hector MacLean* and *Dan Comhfurtachd*. In his old age, when he was in his nineties, he visited Duntulm Castle when the young Sir James MacDonald was entertaining his friends. The old man had been accustomed, in the time of Sir James' father, to dine with the family in the upper hall, but on this occasion he was told to eat with the servants in the lower room. As if this were not sufficient insult, the young chief then sent down a message that he wished the old piper to play for him as he had played for his father – but not to come upstairs, just play from the floor below. This was too much, and Iain uttered a verse in reply (for details, see notes to the *Lament for Sir James MacDonald,* below).

PILGRIMAGE

My grandson played me a piobaireachd
– quite clever for only eleven –
so I said I would take him to Boreraig,
to see where the MacCrimmons had flourished,
living and playing and teaching,
composing incomparable music,
filling the place with their grace-notes,
and leaving it resonant with melody.
I'd inspire him, young Roddy, to practise
when he saw where his ancestors dwelt.

We set out from Glasgow one evening,
sat up all night long on the train.
For me it was a Near-Death Experience,
but Roddy slept sound just the same.
Inverness on a wet summer's morning
did nothing to make me feel better
as we dashed to the train running westward,
a wonderful trip through the mountains
– if it hadn't been raining so heavy,
couldn't see a damn thing of the Highlands
with the cloud reaching down to the sea.

At Kyle the hire car was waiting,
it cost me an arm and a leg,
but a driver was there at our service.
Disappointing to find he was English,

and (of course) new to the district,
never heard of the bleeding MacCrimmons
('What's them, then? One of they boy bands?')
and hadn't a clue about Boreraig.

I wasn't too sure where to find it
and we took a long route around Skye,
the rain beating wet on the windscreen,
the wind blowing cloud from on high.
The driver said this route was scenic,
but how would he know, in the downpour?
And three times we stopped for poor Roddy,
the roads were too much for the lad.

As the downpour eased off to a drizzle,
the midges came out for a feed.
I bought a map from a kiosk in Roaig,
just the corner of Skye I might need,
it showed the way over to Boreraig
so we set off around by Kilmuir.

Patrick's eight sons on that Sunday
walking to church with their father,
then seven of them lay in the graveyard –
I told Roddy, who, pale-green, just nodded.
On, winding down by the lochside,
looking across at Dunvegan,
remembering all that had happened,
old Donald Mor and Dame Flora,
MacDonald's Salute, Silver Chanter.
Roddy grew paler and paler
and said he had heard it before.

Then 'Boreraig' appeared on a signpost.
Heart thumping – the end is in sight.

We got out and looked round in the drizzle,
Midges attacking our ears –
Boreraig? *Boreraig?* Was THIS it?
A great empty space, and dreich with it.
A lone cairn, which we knew had nothing
to do with MacCrimmon, erected
by the Piobaireachd Society or some such,
long after the days of the pipers.

But where did they *live,* those MacCrimmons?
It must be that building there, yonder,

and we walked through wet heather and found it,
a bothy, alone in the landscape,
deserted and desolate, abandoned,
battered, secured with a padlock –
and nobody sane would imagine
that the great Patrick Mor had his dwelling
in this sordid structure. Oh, *Boreraig*.

Not a soul to be seen, houses empty,
not a smoke from a chimney, no cheer,
holiday homes for the exiles?
No-one to ask about pipers,
rain falling coldly, no comfort,
no chance of a cuppie to warm us.
Not an echo of music remaining,
not a gracenote to say they were here . . .

The driver said 'This what you came for?'
and I had to admit that it was.

So we turned and went back where we'd come from,
and it cost us an arm and a leg –
when I thought back on Boreraig, I reckoned
I just might get legless again.

But I do think it's awfully important
for youngsters to see where their forebears . . .

Well, maybe not.

MacLeod of Gesto and Simon Fraser

The importance of Simon Fraser lies in the settings of piobaireachd works which he preserved and handed on, his links with Niel MacLeod of Gesto, the MacCrimmons and the piping Bruce family – and in the transmission of the old style of playing, with its rich ornamentation. Some of his settings probably reflect the music as played in the early 19th century, before it was 'standardised' in the Piobaireachd Society's publications; this early style of playing was passed to Simon's son, Hugh Fraser, and Hugh's pupils. The so-called 'Fraser style' is thought to be based on the teaching and singing of Iain Dubh MacCrimmon, and that of the Bruces, who were MacCrimmon pupils. It gives us an idea of the richness of ornamentation in the music of that time, and opens our minds to different ways of timing and phrasing.

Simon, however, wrote that he learned 'most of the tunes in MacKay's and MacDonalds books' when he was a pupil of Peter Bruce, so possibly up to eighty of his settings could be of a period later in the 19th century – but played in the earlier Fraser (or Bruce) style. He had about 125 settings in all, some of them quite early (see below).

Simon Fraser's Sources

First, let us clear up a source of confusion: there was a manuscript (or manuscripts), apparently belonging to Niel MacLeod 11th Laird of Gesto, containing both music and historical theories, and we know it was in existence in Edinburgh in the 1830s. When this Gesto died in 1836, the manuscript passed to his son Norman, who took it to Australia. On his death, some ten years later, the manuscript seems to have disappeared. Some say it 'passed to' the Fraser family, and Simon Fraser said he had later sold it to someone in Canada, before it vanished – but his account of this, in a letter of 1929, is confused. He appears to have had access to the MS at some point. It is usually referred to as the *Gesto Manuscript*, and is believed to have contained about 200 piobaireachd works written out in canntaireachd vocables, with also a great deal of theory about the music and the alleged religious history of the MacCrimmons.

Simon Fraser tended to refer to it as the 'Gesto MSS', implying that there was more than one manuscript, although he often used 'MSS' as a singular noun. The Rev. Alexander MacGregor, who saw the manuscript in Edinburgh in 1835, said later that it appeared to be written in several different hands, and on different kinds of paper, and parts of it were very faint. Perhaps it is correct to call it MSS, in the plural. Note that the Rev. Alexander said there was 'one old-looking leaf' of MacCrimmon notation, i.e. written canntaireachd, at which he did not look closely.

In 1849, Sir John Dalyell wrote in his *Musical Memoirs of Scotland* that Niel MacLeod had 'furnished me with some notes and observations in manuscript on the pieces'. He did not say which pieces these were. Roderick Cannon, in his *Bibliography of Bagpipe Music* quotes the *Celtic Magazine* for 1883, which printed a copy of a manuscript found at Skeabost House – this was reprinted in the *Piping Times* in January 1970. References to the 'manuscript', including the copy used by J.F. Campbell in 1880, appear to be to the published edition of 1828 rather than to Gesto's earlier work.

The *Gesto Collection*, however, is completely different: Niel

MacLeod's grandson, Dr Keith Norman MacDonald (who lived for a time at Skeabost House), edited and published in 1895 a big collection of pipe music, all of it Ceol Beag, with no piobaireachd included. It contains 340 pipe tunes adapted for the piano, marches, quicksteps, strathspeys, reels, song airs and laments, described in the Notices of Pipers as 'probably the best publication of pipe music for the piano' (which seems to damn it with faint praise).

In addition to the above, there were two other Gesto works: in 1826, Niel MacLeod is believed to have prepared for publication an edition of piobaireachd and theories, a selection from his manuscript(s). As far as is known, this was in canntaireachd syllables rather than staff notation. It reached the proof stage, with two known copies, before it was 'suppressed' because it contained too many 'secrets' about the MacCrimmons. These may have been Masonic secrets, which he was not supposed to make public. These two proof copies, known as *Gesto 1826*, were both taken (separately) to Australia, and both disappeared. One was given to Hugh Archibald Fraser, the father of Simon Fraser: Hugh Archibald was a friend of Gesto. He emigrated in 1828, taking his proof copy of the book with him. He left it to his son Simon, who lost it. The other copy went to Gesto's son Norman, and it vanished after his death.

After publication of the 1826 edition was suppressed, Gesto prepared and published a book of twenty of the piobaireachd works in canntaireachd vocables, with no theory or historical notes, and no secrets. This is *Gesto 1828*, the only Gesto work known to have survived. It appeared with a paragraph of introduction, the wording of which varies, because it was changed for a reprint in 1880. The first edition has: 'Pibereach or pipe tunes, as taught verbally by the McCrimmen pipers in Skye to their apprentices. The following as taken from John McCrimmon, piper to the old Laird of MacLeod, and his grandson the late General McLeod of McLeod, at Dunvegan. By Captain Niel MacLeod, Gesto, Skye.' Note the inconsistent spellings of both MacCrimmon and MacLeod within one paragraph. Some transcripts adjust the spellings and cannot be used as proof of the spelling of MacCrimmon at that time.

Simon Fraser's position in the piping world

Simon Fraser, who was born and spent his life in Australia, has not been taken seriously by the piping establishment in Scotland. There are reasons for this: his apparently weird religious theories have been regarded as unacceptable, and many of the worthies of the Piobaireachd

Society, following the example of Archibald Campbell of Kilberry, have been hostile to Fraser and his family. Kilberry's successor as the Society's music editor, Archie Kenneth, was one of the few who took a real interest in Simon Fraser's settings. When two representatives of the Piobaireachd Society, said to have been possibly James A. Center and Malcolm MacPherson (grandson of Calum Piobaire), visited Simon Fraser in Australia, they reported back that they had had discussions on piobaireachd with him, and that, in their opinion, he knew very little about it. This seems to have sealed the matter for the Society, and Simon Fraser was ignored for many years.

Simon was taken seriously by a few aficionados such as Dr G.F. Ross in India, A.K. Cameron in the USA, and Dr J.D. Ross Watt in South Africa, all well out of the mainstream of piping, and all dismissed as cranks by the establishment. In Scotland, Dr Charles Bannatyne, also despised by Kilberry, claimed (mistakenly) to be the only man in Britain who understood the canntaireachd used by Simon Fraser, but he may have been unaware of the exchange of music and theory between the Frasers and Pipe Major William Gray, whose knowledge and experience of piping was widely respected. Willie Gray had many MSS of Fraser settings of piobaireachd, some of which he bought after the death of Simon Fraser: many of these are now in the National Library of Scotland, along with examples of Fraser's correspondence. Willie Gray gave tapes of himself playing the Fraser settings to the archives of the School of Scottish Studies, in Edinburgh University.

Dr Barrie J. MacLachlan Orme, a friend of the Fraser family and a pupil of Hugh Fraser, set himself the unenviable task of breaking through the wall of apathy, to ensure that Simon received his due as an authority on the MacCrimmon tradition of piobaireachd. His task was made easier by the quality of the settings left by Simon Fraser – and more onerous by the nature of the religious theories in which Simon had shrouded them.

In 1979 Dr Orme published *The Piobaireachd of Simon Fraser with Canntaireachd*, with a second edition in 1985 which was on sale in Britain, and known as 'The Red Book'. It fell into a resounding silence, many of the piping establishment simply ignoring it, though lack of publicity meant that many of them knew nothing of the book's existence. The few who were enlightened enough to study it included Archie Kenneth and Thomas Pearston, two respected members of the Piobaireachd Society; they were impressed by the excellence of the settings and the clear, fair-minded introduction by Dr Orme. Judging by the quality of the music written down by Simon Fraser, and by the way he wrote it, in both staff notation and canntaireachd, it is difficult to understand how James A. Center and Malcolm MacPherson (if his visitors were they) thought he knew little or nothing about piobaireachd: presumably they must have antagonised him so greatly that he 'clammed up' and refused to reveal his knowledge – which he regarded as his family secrets, to be guarded jealously.

Dr Orme, himself no mean player and a good judge of piobaireachd, made several audio and video tapes of the playing techniques he had been taught by Hugh Fraser. He had also been a pupil of Dan MacPherson, a former Seaforth Highlander who came from a well-known piping family in Glendale, Skye (see below). These tapes reflect the teaching of the Bruce family from Glenelg; Peter Bruce, most talented son of Alexander Bruce, emigrated to Australia, possibly in 1846, though some say it was in 1853; he later became the teacher of Simon Fraser. The tapes are of great interest, as they illustrate the 'old' movements and 'obsolete' techniques used in former times, techniques which under the influence of the Piobaireachd Society, and of Kilberry in particular, have now been dropped. Hearing the richness of these lost movements, we might think that so-called standardisation has impoverished the music.

In 1951, Hugh Fraser visited Scotland, bringing with him about twenty volumes of his father's manuscript settings. He gave one to James Jackson, who was a pupil of Willie Gray; James' father was another James Jackson who went to Australia and became a close piping friend of Hugh Fraser. James junior, who lives in Easter Ross, still has this one volume, and the other nineteen were deposited in the NLS.

All of this material was, however, under strict copyright, until in 2006 it was released by Dr Orme, who had satisfied himself that serious interest was at last being shown in Simon Fraser's work. He was previously unwilling to allow its publication, knowing that it would be held up to ridicule or worse, but the interest of serious scholars such as Dr Alex Mackenzie, Dr Angus MacDonald, Niall Matheson, James Hamilton and John D. Burgess, convinced Dr Orme that the time was ripe for Simon Fraser to take his place as a piobaireachd authority. Whether the Piobaireachd Society will bring itself to re-consider Simon Fraser remains to be seen.

Early in 2007, Dr Orme died, shortly before the publication of his book *Ceol Mor in the Style of Simon and Hugh Fraser of Australia*, which he called his Third Edition, or Tutor, dated 2006, the year he completed the background work. It contains a full Tutor of the movements of the Fraser style of playing, illustrated in both staff notation and canntaireachd vocables. Forty-seven piobaireachd works are given, with brief notes.

Background of Simon Fraser (1846–1934)

Dr Orme gave us an excellent account of the life of Simon Fraser, and I am grateful to him and his wife Mary for permission to use this material. The relation between the Fraser family and MacLeod of Gesto is vital to our understanding of Simon's sources, and the teaching of the Bruces of Glenelg played a part in this. It is not easy to confirm or deny the authenticity of the material passed down in the Fraser family, and some of it has probably become distorted through time and distance – as would be expected.

Simon Fraser was the eldest son of Hugh Archibald Fraser. Family tradition claimed that Hugh Archibald had been a lawyer in the district of Inverness until at the age of thirty-two he left for Australia. Hugh Archibald's father, possibly also called Hugh, was said to have been a lawyer, too, and descendants in Australia maintained that Hugh Archibald was a leading figure in Inverness, being about to become a 'magistrate' when he decided to emigrate in 1828.

The family's claims would indicate that Hugh Archibald had been prominent in legal circles in Inverness, but his name has not been found in any of the contemporary sources: he is not named in the Old Parish Register, nor the records of the law courts, nor in the local newspaper (the *Inverness Courier*), nor in the Militia lists of the time. There is reason to believe that both Hugh Archibald Fraser and his father may have been freemasons in Inverness, but their names are not found in the masons' records (which list mainly office-bearers, and do not give full lists of members). If indeed he was as wealthy as the family believed, surely he would have left some mark on the life of Inverness, if only a comment when he departed.

The claims of his grand-daughter, Blanche Jebb, linked him to the Frasers of Dalcrombie and Dalcrag, and a newspaper obituary in Australia in 1893, when Hugh Archibald died, stated that his father was Alexander Fraser of Dalcrag, a sheep-farmer, with no mention of Hugh Fraser, lawyer. This Alexander married a Fraser of Dell, and their recorded family did not include Hugh Archibald – but Alexander had at least one known illegitimate child born to a servant in his household, and it is possible that Hugh Archibald was another. The newspaper obituary must have been based on information from family members in Australia.

The connection with Dalcrombie is more obscure: there were no Frasers of Dalcrombie until 1808, when Sir William Fraser of Leadclune bought the Dalcrombie estate. Sir William, a wealthy and influential merchant in London, had a half-brother, Hugh, who was a prominent lawyer in Aberdeen, and the family tradition of an important lawyer may stem from this connection. Certainly, when Hugh Archibald emigrated in 1828, taking with him a substantial amount of money, Sir William's son, the second Sir William, had just died, leaving his substantial wealth to his brother, John James: possibly Hugh Archibald was well paid by the family to take himself off to a distant land, in order to remove any possible claim to the inheritance. It was a pattern found in other Highland families.

There were Frasers in Dalcrombie who were sub-tenants: they may have styled themselves 'of Dalcrombie' while living there, although they were not, strictly speaking, Frasers of Dalcrombie. They had links with the Frasers in Dalcraig.

The uncertainty about the origins of Simon Fraser's father suggests illegitimacy in the line, and it would explain the conflicting family traditions.

Dalcraig and Dalcrombie are estates which lie some twenty miles to the south-east of Inverness, on the east side of Loch Ness. The legal records of the time show that there was a Hugh Fraser living in the 1820s at Abersky, a farm near Dalcrombie which belonged to a branch of the Frasers of Erchite. He is referred to in the Minutes of the Burgh Court of Inverness as 'Mr Hugh Fraser of Abersky', who was called in as an expert witness to value some farm steadings, in a dispute over their ownership. He is named also in several legal cases when he sued, or was sued by, his landlord over minor matters to do with the estate. Nowhere is his status defined, but the designation 'Mr' indicates that he belonged to the minor gentry of the local Frasers. He seems to have been a factor or agent for the Abersky estate – and some sort of legal training would be required as a qualification for an estate factor. An interesting detail of this Hugh Fraser is that he 'declined to take the oath', which indicates religious unorthodoxy of some kind.

Although Hugh Fraser at Abersky was of the Fraser gentry, it is difficult to trace his birth and antecedents. Possibly his birth, or that of his father, was illegitimate: the Frasers usually recognised their baseborn offspring, and saw to it that they were well maintained.

Hugh Fraser at Abersky may not have been Hugh Archibald, father of Simon Fraser. A factor of that name was living at Abersky after 1828, when Hugh Archibald is known to have left for Australia – but he may not have been the same Hugh Fraser (the name was frequently found in that district).

Simon claimed that his family was related to David Fraser, who fought in the Rising of 1745, and was piper to Lord Lovat. David was the piper who was to have been apprenticed to the MacCrimmons, had the '45 Rising not intervened. He died in 1812, and both Hugh Archibald and his father may well have known him. His home was near Beauly, ten miles west of Inverness, and he was said to have been active both physically and mentally until shortly before his death in old age.

Simon's grandfather, allegedly Hugh Fraser, is said by his descendants to have been married to a cousin of Captain Niel MacLeod of Gesto, but she has not been identified. She may have been a daughter of Gesto's aunt Flora, his father's sister who married another MacLeod, Captain William, V of Hamar, in Skye. They had family but details are not known.

Hugh Archibald, born in 1796, was introduced to Gesto in 1812. The Notices of Pipers say that he and Gesto went together to Donald Ruadh MacCrimmon for piping lessons at this time, but Dr Orme wrote that Hugh Archibald, though able to sing piobaireachd in canntaireachd, was not himself a piper. Simon Fraser wrote that his father never had time to learn to play the pipes because he had to travel so much, a remark which has not been explained. Hugh Archibald used to play piobaireachd on the Jew's Harp, an instrument well suited to the music as it can be played using the pipe scale. Through his friendship with Gesto, he met Iain Dubh MacCrimmon in 1812; Alexander Bruce, pupil of Gesto, who became Gesto's piper, completed this group of piobaireachd enthusiasts.

It was from Gesto and Iain Dubh that Hugh Archibald learned to sing canntaireachd. Simon had a triple link with the MacCrimmons: his father's acquaintance with Iain Dubh and possibly also with Donald Ruadh; his mother's claimed descent from the MacArthurs and Mac-Crimmons; and the third was that his teacher, Peter Bruce, was the son of Alexander, a pupil of both Gesto and Donald Ruadh MacCrimmon. All three sources seem to have passed MacCrimmon material to Simon, who amalgamated this wealth of material to form his collection of settings of some 125 piobaireachd works.

Simon was told by his father that he, Gesto and Iain Dubh had sessions when Iain sang MacCrimmon piobaireachd, and Hugh Archibald wrote it down in canntaireachd syllables, apparently for Gesto.

Why was it Hugh Archibald who wrote the tunes down? Why did Gesto not do it himself? He was fully literate as well as being familiar with the music. The Gesto manuscripts seen by the Rev. Alexander MacGregor in Edinburgh in the 1830s were written by several different hands, and on different kinds of paper. We might ask if this tradition as reported by Hugh Archibald's son is accurate: it is possible that someone, unfamiliar with Scottish legal terms, saw (or heard) the phrase 'Hugh Archibald Fraser, writer' and took that to mean he was the writer of the canntaireachd, i.e. a physical writer, the man who wrote it down, rather than a lawyer. The term 'writer' was used, in Inverness in the early 19th century, to mean a person with legal training but not yet a fully fledged solicitor. It could be used of someone articled to a firm of solicitors, before he qualified. It certainly did not denote a prominent lawyer on the verge of becoming a magistrate, as claimed by Hugh Archibald's great-granddaughter.*

Possibly writing out the canntaireachd vocables was regarded as a menial task, so that Gesto gave it to the young Hugh Archibald rather than undertake it himself. As a trainee lawyer, Hugh Archibald would have been accustomed to copying out legal documents by hand – and at that time Gesto was suffering from breathing problems, which interfered with his piping. He may not have been up to the sustained work of transcribing the music from the singing of Iain Dubh, which would have required prolonged concentration as well as physical stamina.

When Hugh Archibald Fraser emigrated to Australia, he took with him, according to his grand-daughter, a large sum of money, some £30,000, even possibly £40,000, a very great fortune in 1828. In the next fifteen years he lost it all, according to family tradition, much of it through betting on horses. If Hugh Archibald had as much money as that, or was about to become a baillie, he would have been a leading citizen in Inverness, yet his name appears nowhere in the Inverness records. The reason for his emigration was said to have been his health:

---

* In Inverness there were many writers, a substratum below solicitors but above agents; they acted as factors or business representatives, even bankers, but did not represent clients in court. There was a definite distinction between the different ranks, but sometimes 'writer' and 'solicitor' are used loosely as if equals, and this has led to confusion. 'Magistrate' is not a term used much in Scottish legal circles, although the whole panoply of the law, the top ranks of sheriffs, solicitors, procurators, as a body, are occasionally referred to as 'the magistrates of Inverness'. In early-19th-century Inverness, 'magistrate' was used of a baillie, the equivalent of an alderman in England, a civic rather than a legal dignitary.

he needed to live in a warmer climate, according to family tradition. This is often a euphemism for tuberculosis, or the threat of it.

Hugh Archibald left for Australia in 1828, shortly after a memorable night of piping with Gesto, John Ban MacKenzie (who had won the Prize Pipe at Edinburgh in 1823, and was one of the leading pipers in the country), and Captain Simon Fraser of Knockie (who had in 1816 published a book of traditional fiddle music which had great influence). Knockie is not far from Dalcrombie, and John Ban was living at Tulloch, Dingwall, at that time.

Not long before he left, Hugh Archibald attended the funeral of MacDonnell of Glengarry, and heard the first performance of *Glengarry's Lament* when the composer, Archibald Munro, played it, with five other pipers, at the graveside.

A letter from 'Lochgorm' (believed to have been a great-grandson of Gesto) to the *Oban Times* in 1916 refers to a competition held at Kyleakin, in Skye, at which Gesto, Alexander Bruce and Iain Dubh MacCrimmon contended, the winner being Alexander Bruce. It is not clear when this took place, but it must have been before 1815, when Iain Dubh was described as being too old to play. It would be interesting to know who judged this competition.

Hugh Archibald Fraser in Australia

Dr Orme has told us what happened to Hugh Archibald in Australia. He went first to the Hunter River Valley, in New South Wales, where he managed to lose his entire fortune within fifteen years. He lived there in some style, with a household of servants. Conditions in that area were harsh in the 1830s, when agriculture was severely affected by both drought and flooding. The family tradition also says that Hugh Archibald squandered much of his fortune by betting on horses.

In 1844, when he was nearly fifty, after his bankruptcy, he met Mary Anderson, aged seventeen, and they sailed for Hobart, Tasmania, where they were married. The eldest of their twelve children, Simon, was born in February 1845; family tradition says the birth was on board a ship just off Port Arthur, Tasmania.

The family settled at Port Arthur, south of Hobart, Hugh Archibald taking a position as overseer of the penal settlement there. His predecessor had been much hated by the inmates, but the new governor treated them more kindly, and he was well-liked. This is another family tradition, borne out by the testimony of descendants of some of the convicts.

After two years at Port Arthur, Hugh Archibald was caught outside one day by a severe snowstorm. He was close to death when he was rescued and revived by some of the local aboriginal people. Although he recovered, his health was affected, and his doctor advised him to move to somewhere warmer. In 1847, he and Mary and their first two sons, Simon and Peter, left Tasmania, to settle near Mansfield, Victoria, about 140 miles north-east of Melbourne.

Simon's mother, Mary Anderson, came from Lochailort, on the west coast of Inverness-shire. She was only fifteen when she emigrated, and had been employed at the Lochailort Hotel. Her mother, or possibly her aunt, seems to have been another Mary Anderson, in her thirties, a servant at Irine House (now Roshven), a few miles from Lochailort. Simon Fraser said his mother was a daughter of Norman Anderson, who passed on to her his intimate knowledge of piobaireachd and its alleged secrets. The only Norman Anderson on record in Scotland at that time lived at Tarskavaig, in Sleat, Isle of Skye, and it may not be coincidence that the official home of the piper to MacDonald of Sleat was also in Tarskavaig – which is a tiny settlement. Mary, however, was not a daughter of Norman's marriage, and she too may have been an illegitimate child.

Mary junior claimed descent from Charles MacArthur, piper to MacDonald of Sleat, a leading player, teacher and composer in the 18th century. There is no record of her birth or existence in that family, and it is possible that she was merely the grandchild of a different Charles MacArthur.

Simon Fraser later wrote: 'My great-grandfather on my mother's side was Charles MacArthur who was taught by Patrick Og MacCrimmon at Dunvegan for eleven years. He was a favourite pupil and Patrick Og took great pains to teach him all he knew. When Charles had finished his tuition, he returned to his farm at Peingowan, where he was the last of the hereditary pipers to the MacDonalds of the Isles.'

The wording of this inaccurate statement is reminiscent of a passage in Logan's Preface to Angus MacKay's *Ancient Piobaireachd*. Simon Fraser may have used this in support of his mother's claims.

Similarly unproven is a further claim that Mary Anderson's MacArthur mother was 'a niece of MacCrimmon' (unspecified). There were many MacCrimmons who were not directly of the piping family, and there are also many instances of expatriate Scots making unprovable claims about their ancestry.

Another claim made by Fraser descendants was that Hugh Archibald's alleged father, Hugh Fraser, knew Colin Campbell of Nether

Lorne, who around 1790 wrote the Campbell Canntaireachd piobaireachd manuscript. This too is unprovable. Many of the Fraser claims
are impossible to prove (or disprove), for lack of hard evidence. While
they cannot be condemned as false, perhaps judgement should be
reserved until further information is uncovered.

Hugh Archibald and his young family settled on Mount Battery Station, near Mansfield, Victoria.* Hugh was the manager of the station,
employed by Dr John Pearson Rowe. It was wild mountainous country,
covered with dense bush, and Dr Orme says it was infested with bush-
rangers, criminal outlaws on the run. Another hazard was the hostility
of the aborigines, who attacked white settlers. Hugh Archibald's job
cannot have been easy.

Hugh Archibald Fraser died at the end of 1893, aged ninety years.
He moved from Mount Battery to Delatite, not far away, during the
childhood of his son Simon. The fact that none of his twelve children
was named Norman, as might be expected in the Highland naming
system, appears to support the theory that Mary Anderson's birth was
possibly illegitimate.

Life of Simon Fraser

Born in Tasmania in 1845, Simon grew up in Victoria, at Mount Battery and Delatite Stations, where his father was manager. He learned
from an old aborigine the art of plaiting strips of leather to make whips

---

* Hugh Archibald's death certificate in 1893 listed his children as:
  Simon Alexander, aged 50
  Peter 48
  Isabella 46
  John 44
  Mary 42
  Hugh 40
  Alexander 38
  William 36
  Donald 34
  Elizabeth 32
  Thomas 30
  David 28
  This does not tally with the account of the dance band with Simon's sisters,
  there called Hilda and Queenie, presumably family nicknames.

and bridles, and he became an expert forty-strand plaiter, his whips much prized. He was also a skilled maker of pipe-bags. An all-round musician, he played the violin, accordion and concertina. At a Ball in 1874, he played the concertina and Peter Bruce the pipes. Simon had his own dance band, his sisters Hilda on the piccolo and Queenie clarinet; his son Ralph played the piano, Hugh junior violin, Simon himself violin, Simon junior harp. Simon senior was a 'skilled violin maker, and fearless and capable' as a steeplechase rider.

Simon married Flora (Florence) MacMillan in December 1872, daughter of a piper, John MacMillan. They had met at Wappin Station near Bonnie Doon, Victoria (now under the Eildon Weir reservoir). Flora was born in 1851, and lived with a family of MacRaes at Fernhill, where Simon later worked. The MacRaes wanted to adopt her, but instead she married Simon. Flora figures very little in accounts of the family, but she had three sons, John (known as Jack), Hugh Archibald junior and Ralph, as well as two daughters. She died in July 1928.

When Simon was eight he had a dangerous illness, known as the Black Croup, which killed many children, probably a form of diphtheria. His mother, in despair for his life, sang the *Lament for the Children,* in Gaelic, or possibly in canntaireachd vocables, at his bedside, and prayed for his recovery. This made a deep impression on the sick child, and on his recovery he asked her about the strange words he had heard. She then gave him all the secrets. 'She got the whole thing from her father (Norman Anderson) by listening to him explaining it to his friends' – but elsewhere Simon said her father 'taught her all the notation and secrets' before she was fifteen, because she was so keen to learn them. Neither Mary nor her husband Hugh Archibald was a piper, but both could sing piobaireachd in canntaireachd.

When Simon was forty he 'decided to learn the bagpipes seriously' – presumably he had played previously but was not very good at it. He started lessons from Peter Bruce, who taught him 'in exactly the same way as the MacCrimmons taught their pupils, and he knew their secrets and history as well. He taught me', wrote Simon, 'how to correct the beats [bars] in MacKays and MacDonalds books. He played most of the tunes in these books'. Simon rode forty miles from Mansfield to Benalla for his lessons, and forty miles back. Bruce made him sing the Notation (canntaireachd) and memorise it before playing it on the pipe.

It is not entirely clear how many tunes Simon learned from Peter Bruce: 'most of the tunes' in Angus MacKay's and Donald MacDonald's books would amount to about eighty works. Presumably Peter played these in the style he had learned from his father, Alexander Bruce, with a MacCrimmon background.

Then Simon Fraser, never short of confidence, issued his triple challenge:

1. Who could plait a whip better than he?
2. Who could ride steeplechase better than he?
3. Who could play pibroch better than he?

There were no takers, though there were plenty of good pipers in Australia at that time.

Around 1900, he retired from farming, and moved first to Benalla, and then to Warnambool, a Scottish community in West Victoria. There he set up as a bagpipe and fiddle maker and repairer, and a teacher of pipe and fiddle music. He made reeds from Indian cane, and pipes from briar, cocos, African blackwood or ebony. He liked ebony and said it gave the sweetest tone. Sometimes he gave the big drone only two joints instead of three, not as elegant, he admitted, 'but they work as well'.

When in Warnambool, 'he realised he had left his copy of the unpublished proof book (1826) of Gesto's in his workshop on the shelf in Benalla'. There were only two proof copies, and Gesto's son had had the other, lost when Norman died in 1847. It seems extraordinary that Simon would forget a book he used so extensively and must have valued. When he returned to Benalla to recover it, he was told that children had destroyed it. He said the proof copies had 100 pages each, of MacCrimmon history, traditions, scales and vocables, and fifty tunes in 'the old and new canntaireachd, selected by Gesto from his manuscript of about 200 tunes, some written down by Hugh Archibald from Ian (sic) Dubh MacCrimmon'. Note that he uses the term canntaireachd, not seantaireachd. If all this material was contained in 100 pages, there cannot have been much space for the theories and history. This was the book which Gesto's friends had persuaded him not to publish.

In 1914 Simon's eldest son, Jack, died. He had been a champion piper, dancer and pipe band player in Victoria, married with four children. His death was a grievous blow to his father.

From 1920 to 1930, Simon lived in 'Mr Sprague's house' in George Street, East Melbourne, where he was very active in writing manuscripts of pipe music, which he sent all round the world to correspondents in Montana, India, and South Africa – and to William Gray in Scotland (who collected ninety tunes from him). Was he writing these from memory, or was he now in possession of the Gesto MS? If so, when, and from whom did he obtain it? Norman MacLeod, who inherited it from his father, Niel of Gesto, died in 1847, when Simon was only two years old. Did the MS remain in the MacLeod family until Simon was an adult? If so, how did it come into his hands, if indeed it did? He did later say, in a somewhat confused letter, that he had owned the MSS (sic) but had sold it to a man in Canada – who has not been identified, but is assumed to have been a MacCrimmon.

Simon taught his sons Hugh and Ralph the art of whip plaiting, and also to play the pipes and fiddle, and passed on all the MacCrimmon material; they had lessons, too, from Peter Bruce, whose 'masterpieces were *John Garve MacLeod of Raasay's Lament* and *The Prince's Salute*'.

In 1907, James A. Center arrived in Victoria, son of a pipemaker and player. He became a great friend of the Frasers but died of the flu in 1919. This does not accord with some nasty comments made about and by Center – Simon had a low opinion of his playing, saying he was not nearly as good as his own son Hugh – and it may have been Center who said Simon knew very little about piobaireachd. Possibly there was some confusion with Jack Senter, a cousin of James A., who was a close friend of the Frasers in Australia (Jack changed the initial letter of his name from C to S when he emigrated).

Also in 1907, James Center sent to Dr Charles Bannatyne a copy of *Sir James MacDonald's Lament* in 'Seantaireachd' – did Bannatyne get this name from Simon or from Center? Bannatyne wrote to Simon: 'I am the only man in Britain who understands the pipers language and till I heard of you I thought I was the only man in the world.' This was typical of Bannatyne. Of course he was not the only man in Britain who understood canntaireachd. The two Ross brothers in 1880 had been able to play direct from Gesto's written canntaireachd without difficulty, sight-reading without preparation. Center described Bannatyne as a 'crank', and Kilberry rated him a 'vandal'.

The Frasers, both Simon and Hugh, had a high regard for James Mauchline, who composed in 1874 a piobaireachd *Keppach na Faisach* 'The Glen has become Desolate', and also a work [piobaireachd?] *My Heart is Yearning for Thee, O Skye.*

In 1884 Simon himself composed a piobaireachd, *Gilmore's Lament* (for Richard Gilmore, a Melbourne player who had made a pipe for Simon). Although a beginner's work, composed before Simon began tuition with Peter Bruce, it shows that he had already a good understanding of the basic structure of piobaireachd, presumably passed to him by his father.

Easter Leakichan is now Leacachan House, on the south-western side of Loch Duich, on the Ratagan shore road. John MacCrimmon, possibly the composer of *The Glen Is Mine*, lived here.

Leacachan seen from across Loch Duich.

Old houses (restored) at Risgary, Bernera. Mary MacLeod had a house here, said to have been given to her by her chief, Sir Norman MacLeod.

The Gunnery at Risgary, Bernera, where Sir Norman MacLeod kept his weapons. It was described in a Gaelic poem by Mary MacLeod in the late 17th century.

Left. The side-chapel in Rodel Church, Harris. Tradition has it that Mary MacLeod is buried beneath the floor here.

Below. Stone, without inscription, outside Rodel Church, Harris. It is close to the mausoleum where the MacLeods of Bernera were buried, including Sir Norman, the chief to whom Mary MacLeod was devoted. It is perhaps more likely that this stone marks Mary's grave than that she lies within the church, among the MacLeods of Dunvegan.

Right. A likeness supposedly of Patrick Og MacCrimmon, but it was a fanciful print made by R.R. MacIan in the first half of the 19th century, as one of his series of 'MacIan Prints', illustrating Highland dress and weapons.

Below. Hamara House, in Glendale, Skye. Iain Dubh MacCrimmon was the tenant here for a time, in the late 18th or early 19th century.

The old steading at Hamara, in Glendale, Skye. This building may have been part of the former house at Hamara.

All that remains of Gesto House, on the west coast of Skye, home of Niel MacLeod of Gesto in the early 1800s, before he fell out with his laird, the MacLeod chief, and had to move to Waternish.

Mary Anderson in her old age, the mother of Simon Fraser. It has been claimed that her appearance was 'proof' of Italian blood in the family. *By kind permission of the late Dr Barrie J. MacLachlan Orme*

Dugald C. MacLeod (left), with Iain MacFadyen and Bruce McGhie. *By kind permission of Hugh MacDonald, Viewfield House*

'Old Angus' MacLeod, with the Maryhill Pipe Band in 1899. *Photograph kindly lent by Iain MacLeod*

Left. Angus MacLeod in 1899.

Below. Beinn a'Ghriam in Sutherland has two peaks, which give rise to its name. In 1603 it was the scene of a bloodless rout when the men of Caithness fled from the MacKays without a fight.

Above. The old farmhouse at Arnabol, on the western shore of Loch Hope, in north-west Sutherland. The name was later corrupted to Annapool, and two piobaireachd laments were composed by Iain Dall MacKay, commemorating his cousin the Laird of Arnabol, and the Laird's wife.

Right. The gravestone of Charles MacArthur, at Kilmuir, Skye, with its inscription, probably incomplete.

The Peinagown graveyard, with Charles MacArthur's grave, centre, and the memorial to Flora MacDonald in the background.

The small township of Tarskavaig Mor, on the west side of Sleat, Isle of Skye. Here the piper to the MacDonald chief at Armadale had his official home. *By kind permission of Michael Macgregor Photography*

Donald Archie MacDonald, piper to Lord MacDonald, met the Queen in 1956.

Cairn erected by the Skye Piping Society in Glenhinnisdale, in memory of Donald MacDonald.

Looking east up Glenhinnisdale, where Donald MacDonald, the Edinburgh pipe-maker, was born.

Colonel Jock MacDonald (left) with Angus MacPherson and Seton Gordon. *By kind permission of Hugh MacDonald, Viewfield House*

The Fairy Bridge, near Dunvegan, Skye.

The flat green near the Fairy Bridge, where, in the 18th century, a contest was held between a MacCrimmon, probably Patrick Og, and Malcolm MacRobert.

Seumas Archie MacDonald from Hunglader in Skye, in 2004. He had a vast knowledge of piping lore and Skye traditions, as well as being a good piper.

John Bruce, son of Alexander Bruce, Glenelg. John emigrated to Australia, where he became piper to W.P. McGregor on an estate near Benalla. *By kind permission of the late Dr Barrie J. MacLachlan Orme.*

Glendale, in the west of Skye. Here the piping family of MacPhersons lived, with their tradition of a marriage into the MacCrimmons in the 18th century. Danny Campbell also came from Glendale.

Danny Campbell (front row, second from left) at Arras in 1917. *By kind permission of A. A. Fairrie*

Upper Duntulm, the former Manse which was Seton Gordon's home for many years. It is beside the graveyard where Charles MacArthur is buried.

Left. Finlay MacRae beside the cairn in memory of Willie Ross, his former teacher. Finlay raised the money and organised the building of the cairn near the old Ross house in Glen Strathfarrar. *Courtesy of the College of Piping.*

The Isle of Skye Pipe Band. *By kind permission of Skye Media*

Above. Patrick Molard playing at Gesto, the Cuillin Mountains in the background. *By kind permission of Skye Media*

Right. Dan MacPherson, born in Glendale, Skye, emigrated to Australia with his brother Murdoch. He is shown here at a Pipe Band competition in South Australia in 1936.

In 1934, Simon was hit by a motorcycle in Mansfield, and broke his hip. In those days a fractured hip often led to pneumonia, and not long after the accident, in April 1934, he died, aged eighty-nine. He had intended having a book of his canntaireachd tunes published and accepted by the piping world, but this ambition was not fulfilled. A pupil of his son Hugh, Dr Barrie MacLachlan Orme, did the job for him in the 1970s, and the Fraser settings were at last put before the world.

Hugh Fraser, Simon's Son

HUGH ARCHIBALD FRASER, Simon's son, was born at Deuaran Station, Broken River, near Mansfield, in April 1879. At twenty, having been a pupil of both his father and Peter Bruce, he was sent to Hugh MacDonald in Sydney, the Champion Piper of New South Wales who had composed *The Badenoch Highlanders* and *Leaving Glencoe*, two competition marches. Hugh MacDonald, however, refused to teach Hugh Fraser, as he did not himself know the canntaireachd vocables.

Hugh Fraser became an authoritative figure in Australian piping, and Jimmy Jackson's father, who had emigrated to Australia, spoke of memorable drives to the different Games, at which Hugh would be judging. The two of them talked piping (what else?) and had long discussions about piobaireachd. Dr Orme, however, said Hugh was extremely sensitive (presumably about his father's theories) and refused to discuss anything controversial.

Hugh's record as piper in Australia shows that he was regarded as unbeatable for many years (Orme 1985). He was Champion Piper of Australasia from 1900, and Dr Orme lists the many competitions where he was supreme. He tutored many pipe bands, travelling widely throughout Australia. In 1951, when he was seventy-one, Hugh came to Scotland, toured the country with his Australian pipe band and met the Royal family. Back home, he corresponded with Willie Gray for some years, before, in 1970, like his father before him, he was injured in a traffic accident, and died at the age of ninety.

Hugh was always reluctant to have his playing recorded, being over-sensitive about possible criticism. When he was eighty-five, he agreed to play *MacLachlan's March (Mary's Praise)* for his pupil Dr Orme, who was particularly keen to hear it, since his own mother was a MacLachlan. Hugh played it with remarkably agile fingering for one of his age, although his blowing had become a little uneven; he managed to retain his musical interpretation, and we must be grateful that

Dr Orme deceived the old man by secretly recording his performance on tape. Dr Orme did not allow it to be played until after Hugh's death in 1970. Hugh would possibly have been gratified by the appreciation of his playing by those who hear it in modern times.*

Simon Fraser's Theories

One reason why Simon Fraser has not been taken seriously is the miasma of religious and pseudo-historical theory with which he obscured the music. It is likely that these ideas were not his own, but were based on the Gesto manuscript and/or the proof copy of Gesto's book of 1826. Simon Fraser, and later, his correspondent, A.K. Cameron, doubtless developed these theories further, but it seems improbable that Simon himself had the education or the resources to have created them in the first place. The theories have a 'bookish' ring to them, which suggests that they were the work of Niel MacLeod of Gesto, in the years he spent haunting the libraries of Edinburgh (1820s–1830s).

It seems to have been Gesto who linked the MacCrimmon line to that of the Italian family of Giordano Bruno, burned at the stake in Rome in 1600. Some of the material may have come from the writings of the Rev. Dr Norman MacLeod, and some may have been drawn from Angus MacKay's manuscript – but it was probably Gesto who developed the theory from these sources.

Simon Fraser then took it up, and passed it to his correspondents, notably A.K. Cameron in Montana, U.S.A. In 1931, A.K. Cameron wrote to William Gray:

> First of all – *and this is private*, mind that – Piob. Is not Highland music, but Italian music. See? Now. You are mad, – I suppose. Oh ! rest a while till a few things sink in . . . The MacCrimmons were Christians who believed in the Simple teaching of Christ – free from priestcraft – & Theological Dogma. They were always at loggerheads with the clergy of their day. Patrick Mor wrote a Treatise of the failings of religion as then taught, – but was afraid to publish it, as it might bring hardship on

---

* This recording of Hugh Fraser playing *Mary's Praise* is included on a CD, No.3 in a series 'Piobaireachd: Old Settings'. The rest of that CD and the first two in the series have Dr Barrie MacLachlan Orme playing Simon Fraser's piobaireachd settings as he had learned them from Hugh Fraser. Published by Highlander Music, The Beauly Centre, High Street, Beauly, Inverness-shire IV4 7BX, tel. 05603 664899 or 01463 783273.

his family – it was buried with him. – Fraser [Simon] claims. Sheanntair-eachd means: Sing to Christ. See? And every letter in His name is in this word. Canntaireachd is another mutilation ! It is a secret form of singing & playing by which the MacCrimmons were able to worship God in their own manner – & no one was the wiser. Sheann is based in Genesis, Chapter 3 verse 24 as a Key in which are the principal vocables of the System, and also all the letters used in the system. The time marks are taken from verse 24.

He adds 'The system is English'. Elsewhere, A.K. Cameron wrote:

… Now the figure 3 had deep Theological meaning. It was considered the Perfect nonmutable System because the figure 3 could not only be divided.

Now, the Taorluath or '*Tri*'-luadh is a symbol of the Holy Trinity and its three notes – like the three leaves of the Shamrock are symbolic of the Three figures in the Trinity. It is Three A notes on the fundamental note of the Chanter …

It is the Weeping Wall of the Jews till this day. Do you begin now to see what Piob., really is? I daren't use this information in O[ban] T[imes], although I hinted at it. G.F. Ross advised me to keep religion out of the matter entirely, but I cannot see why, because the truth & Secret of it must be imposed before they begin to understand it.

… S. Fraser: – '664 has a deep meaning in MacCrimmon music – meaning 3 or Trinity, as they knew the meaning of this Theological puzzle'. The meaning was given in the book of 1826. – one reason for *Suppression*. – See. Now, I tried to get this meaning from Fraser for years. But he won't come through !! The Pope of Rome has 6 6 6 figures on his cap. – Another Mystery . – See

Is all this based on masonic ritual? While to many people the theories are weird and unacceptable, to others there is no problem – and some who can swallow them appear to be themselves masons. One aspect which is common to the beliefs of Simon Fraser and of the Freemasons is the eclectic mix of world religions: while the combination of Old Norse gods (all with English spellings) and Judaism, and Greek myth mingled with the teachings of Giordano Bruno, strikes the modern reader as ludicrous, the rituals of Freemasonry are even more extreme, yet they are accepted by the members of the society.

Explaining the term Seanntaireachd – which he said was 'so secret it appears in no dictionary' – Simon Fraser wrote that piobaireachd developed in units of three to represent the Trinity. The beats [bars] expressed or conveyed to one another the principles of Christianity. He appears to be attributing the 'principle of three', which is structural in piobaireachd form, to religious theory. Developing this, he claimed that the *Lament for the Only Son* is really the Lament for Christ, because it contains, in its seanntaireachd form, the vocables for *bohim* or *bochim*, which means 'place of weeping'. This is confusing – what language are we in now?

The seanntaireachd system is allegedly based on the Bible, Genesis chapter 3, verse 24 (in the Authorised Version, which reads: ' So he drove out the man; and he placed at the east of the garden of Eden Cherubim, and a flaming sword which turned every way, to keep the way of the tree of life'). It is the culminating verse of the story of the Fall of Man. This was because that verse contains all the sounds of the vocables used in the system. Surely it would be the other way round – that verse was selected because it had the sounds, i.e. the system was not based on the verse, but existed already before being linked to the verse.

Simon Fraser said this verse gave the MacCrimmons the idea of the form of piobaireachd lament. Other vocables, he added, were taken from the Norse gods, *in their English spellings*, Thor and Odin (hence the vocable *thorodin*), as well as from Greek deities and the Druid religion, also with anglicised spellings, which gave us, for example, *dru*, the top G′ note with grip. It is hard to take this seriously, masons or no masons.

Around 1650, said Simon, Patrick Mor went to Italy to study the Italian solfeggio system, and stayed there two years. Does this mean he missed the Battle of Worcester, in 1651? While there he looked up manuscripts of the Bible – what manuscripts? – and discovered they had been altered. This seems an over-simplistic summary of the study of biblical sources, to put it mildly.

On his return home, Patrick 'improved and perfected the canntaireachd'. His tunes 'contained the religious ideas which were sacred to him . . . expressed in stanzas of poetry which explain the reason for composing the music'. The *Lost Pibroch* was 'one of the most sacred tunes, and therefore not often played'. It was made on the Triad System. 'One stanza which Simon Fraser quotes from this tune is most prophetic:

> The missing letter 'l' will be replaced, [what does this mean?]
> The Name of God will be effaced,
> The love of God will die away,
> And love of gold will win the day.

The claim seems to be that this was written by Patrick, to go with his *Lost Pibroch*. Simon Fraser said 'I am the only man living who has this fine tune'. He added 'Note that the word GOD has *three* letters', a somewhat meaningless observation. He went on:

> the true meaning of the 'Lost Pibroch' is really 'The Lost Art' of playing them. There are several lost pibrochs, which will never be discovered now, and we can only make the best of what we have of the originals. The 'Lament for the Great Music' is a Lost Pibroch . . . It was in Neil MacLeod's (unpublished) book. The true 'Lost Pibroch', which I have, is a different tune altogether and I am the only man living who has this fine tune which is very difficult to put into staff notation.

He went on:

> The Lost Pibroch is mentioned in the first verse of 'the Lament for the Children'. The words, he said, were composed by Patrick Mor Mac-Crimmon on the death of seven of his eight children in twelve months. The English version – [do we assume it was translated from Gaelic?] – is as follows:

> > Hear me, dear Saviour, Oh hear me now
> > All my dear children, but one, are laid low.
> > Spare him, dear Saviour, spare him to me,
> > To play the Lost Pibroch in memory of Thee.

> The other name for the Lost Pibroch is The Lament for my Saviour.

The meaning of this is not clear: if it is 'Lost' because it means the art of playing pibroch is lost, was it already lost in Patrick Mor's day? If so, when and how was it lost?

Simon Fraser intended publishing his own book, but never did – he was badly affected by the death of his son Jack in 1914. He had extensive correspondence with A.K. Cameron in Montana, who had emigrated from Scotland in 1902. Cameron had been taught his piobaireachd by J.F. Farquharson of London, said to have been a pupil of Donald Cameron. In 1931, A.K. Cameron wrote to Willie Gray that Simon Fraser's piobaireachd corresponded exactly to what he had learned from Farquharson ('and all other methods are wrong'). He said he had been sent 400 pages of MS of piobaireachd from Simon, but later denied this, saying he had 'a few'.

Dr G.F. Ross in Calcutta published two books, in 1926 and 1929, based on Simon Fraser's material. He published two settings of the *Cave of Gold*, but it is thought he had the tune from Simon Fraser in the first place. It is unknown elsewhere.

Simon Fraser 'replaced' some 'lost' bars in the music, also omitted some bars from existing settings. 'He incorporated the cadence into the bar time-structure, generally making the learning of the tunes much easier'.

Note that many of his settings are widely accepted as being excellent by leading pipers, who generally say they don't care what daft theories he had about the religious significance, the settings justify his being taken seriously. The judgement that he 'knew little or nothing about piobaireachd or piping' cannot possibly be right – he must have had considerable knowledge both to produce these settings and to be able to transcribe from canntaireachd into staff notation, even if he had the originals from Peter Bruce or Gesto via his father. Without the necessary knowledge he could not have made sense of what was passed to him.

The Religious Theories

Patrick Mor's Dream of Love: Simon said Patrick dreamed of the beginning of Creation and his own quest for Love. Then he traced history forward through the ages to the Crucifixion. When he awoke, he composed *The Comely Tune* to represent the different periods of history as in the dream. 'By playing the ground some four to six times, each time with different expressions, the tune represented the different eras.' Simon Fraser's mother knew this work well, and could sing the verses written to it by Patrick Mor. Simon wrote: 'Peter Bruce could play it beautifully, but Bruce said none but a MacCrimmon could do it justice. Neil MacLeod used to say that MacCrimmon must have been inspired when he wrote the lines. He taught them more beautifully than all that had been written by musicians and poets put together.' A wild claim.

Simon then explains the system of triple vocables in the work, and adds 'This tune, or the verses to it, deal with the hidden mysteries of the "Triad" and other secret orders, and it was for mentioning these things and sayings that caused MacLeod's friends to get him not to publish the book that he first intended to. Neither the Scots nor the Irish in the old days cared about admitting their views of Christianity, and while any of the MacCrimmons lived, they had to keep these matters a very close secret.' This seems to imply that his masonic friends prevented him from revealing their beliefs and rituals, the paragraph having a strong whiff of the masons. Or were Gesto's friends merely trying to prevent him from making a fool of himself?

Simon Fraser then quotes several verses in English which he attributes to Patrick Mor, and two more by Gesto which are in exactly the same idiom, leading us to wonder whether Gesto translated all these verses from Gaelic. Or did he in fact compose them himself, in English? Simon continues:

> There is no doubt that mystery seems to be one of the greatest foes of the Human Race. Of course, mystery is a great subject and a dangerous one. Hate and mystery is anti-christ. You will see by the Book [*Gesto 1826*], the fate of those who happen to reveal any hidden mystery, and this spirit is far from being dead yet. I think this largely accounts for the fact that none of the MacCrimmon ideas or writings are to be found now. As they were great scholars, they knew well how to explain the great beauties of Primitive Christianity.

And he adds that it is interesting that Joseph MacDonald never mentioned the MacCrimmons in his Treatise – 'but then, he had strong religious convictions'. Joseph was the son of a most orthodox and strict Presbyterian minister – and he did mention that Skye and Mull were important centres of piping.

It is perhaps ironic that Simon Fraser professed to dislike mystery, when he had surrounded his musical theories with obscure evidence that is not easy to decipher.

This section seems to point straight at Gesto as the origin of all this apparent masonic influence – unless Gesto took it all from Iain Dubh. It should be stressed that there is *no evidence whatsoever* that the later MacCrimmons were scholars, or poets, or that they wrote anything down. Nor do we know which of them could speak English. We must bear in mind, however, Sir Jhone McChrummen, a university graduate, in 1533. Nothing is known for certain of the family's religious convictions, but Sir Jhone may have been a priest.

Simon Fraser said Patrick Mor thought the Old Testament should not be part of the Bible, because it is full of bloodshed and war. His Primitive Chritianity preached Perfect Love, not a mix of Love and Hate. 'Another test of Christianity is the control of selfishness . . . one of the worst passions and difficult to master.' He felt the clergy were selfish and had altered the Bible in order to control people. 'All my sons are Freemasons, but they do not believe in secrets invented by man to delude his fellow creatures . . . Creeds and ceremonies have nothing to do with the simple and sublime teachings of Christ.'

It is interesting that he brings up the subject of the Freemasons in this context. He implies that he himself was not one of them, although his sons were. He said 'the MacCrimmons did not believe in Baptism or any form of ritual, and looked upon it as pagan. They did not believe in the Fall of Man', considering it a silly and ridiculous fable – yet he maintained that the seantaireachd vocables were based on a verse describing the climax of the Fall of Man, in the book of Genesis.

Fraser called the MacCrimmon religion 'Christian Spiritualism', teaching Infinite Love and the after-life in Heaven. 'No man ever trod this earth who knew or understood these teachings better than Patrick Mor MacCrimmon.'

His authority for this must have been Gesto – or Iain Dubh – or possibly Donald Ruadh.

Simon stated that Patrick Og followed Patrick Mor as piper at Dunvegan; then came Donald Bain (sic), Malcolm and John Dubh MacCrimmon. He does not mention Donald Ruadh in this succession. Note that he is wrong about Donald Ban, who was much younger than Malcolm and did not succeed him at Dunvegan, let alone precede him. This at least can be proved, and shows the falliblity of some of Simon's information.

He goes on to say that the MacCrimmon fame spread and pipers got prestige from having been taught by them. 'Finding their number of pupils increasing, they opened a college at Boreraig. Seven years study was prescribed for each scholar.' This is probably not so; nor is the implication that their teaching began at Dunvegan. Elsewhere Simon says that Alasdair Crotach opened the Boreraig college when he brought the Bruno son and grandson from Ireland, long before the MacCrimmons became so famous. Alasdair died in 1547, and no evidence has been found of MacCrimmons, let alone Brunos, at Boreraig earlier than 1710.

The idea of Primitive Christianity is in itself not unpalatable, and indeed might be expected to develop in areas where clergy were sparse or corrupt. What is not acceptable without evidence is that it was Patrick Mor's religion (or that of the Laird of Anapool), nor is it credible that piobaireachd was *composed* (Simon Fraser even says *written*) as a form of religious symbolism. It is more likely that it was made (and not written at all) as *music,* and then, after it was written down centuries later, was studied by fanatics (masons?) who read symbolism into every note.

It was probably Gesto who did this, and it seems unlikely that he had these extreme ideas direct from the MacCrimmons – unless Iain Dubh was the culprit. Did Donald Ruadh perhaps disapprove of the publishing of masonic secrets? Donald was probably a mason – Willie Gray seems to have thought so. He himself was prominent in the masonic movement, and, like Simon Fraser, he laid stress on the religious aspect of the MacCrimmon music, regarding it as vital to the full understanding of the music.

Note that:

1. The alleged Patrick Mor MS was buried with him.
2. The Gesto MS of 200 tunes has vanished, but did exist, some form of it being seen in Edinburgh in 1835.
3. The two proof copies of Gesto's 100-page book (1826) were lost in Australia.
4. The 1828 published book had only twenty tunes, and no theories.

Evidence disappears, but one hard fact remains that we keep coming back to: the 125 Fraser settings, as published by Dr Orme, are widely accepted as being mostly excellent. That is what matters at the end of the day.

Simon Fraser's Notes on Individual Tunes

In some of his notes Simon used forms which show that he was drawing on late sources: his spelling *Anapoole*, for example, is based on the late 19th-century form, as is the designation MacLeod of Colbeck (not the earlier Colbecks). On the other hand he has the title *Millbank's Salute*, in its older form, with the old setting, no Taorluath before the Crunluath fosgailte.

Simon had the only known version (Ground only) of *MacLeod of Talisker's Lament*, 'as played by John Dubh MacCrimmon' – i.e. not composed by him? Was it by his brother, Donald Ruadh?

Simon claimed that the *Bells of Perth* was a warning tune, because it has what he calls the B D C B warning code, as in *War or Peace*, but Dr Ian Cassells has shown beyond doubt that its theme was a 17th-century hymn, the 'signature tune' of the city of Perth.

Two settings of the *Prince's Salute* are given by Simon Fraser, and the work is attributed to John MacIntyre; the second setting is 'as played by Ian Dubh, Neil MacLeod and Peter Bruce, copied from the Mac-Crimmon MSS (sic)'. Willie Gray said: 'This lively tune was popular in masonry. The piper, having put on his bonnet and doing his little shuffle, stood throughout the tune.'

The note on the *Lament for the Children* is mystifying: Simon wrote that it was made by Patrick Mor, and that the setting taken from Gesto's 1826 book. In letters to A.K. Cameron, he said he had added some MacArthur beats (bars). He added: 'The missing letter in Gesto's book of 1828 is the letter "s", and it is in this time [in the high A or high G grace notes] it should occur, but does not.' It is not clear what this means.

Lament for King James Departure 1688: called by Simon '*The Duke of Sutherland's Lament*, from the Gesto 1826 MSS'. There are discrepancies here, as Gesto 1826 was not the MS but a proof copy of the book – and there was no Duke of Sutherland at that time, nor even an Earl of Sutherland. There was the Countess of Sutherland in her own right, married to the Earl Gower, who in 1803 became the 2nd Marquis of Stafford, but he was not created Duke of Sutherland until 1833. Before that, he did not have any Sutherland title. He did not hold it for long, as he died later the same year, and presumably any Lament for him would have been made in 1833 – if indeed it was for the same Duke. The 2nd Duke died in 1861. There can have been no possibility of a Lament for any Duke of Sutherland as early as 1826. Gesto would have known this, although Simon Fraser might not.

About the *Lament for the Dead*, Simon said it was 'composed by a pupil of John MacKay (Raasay). This pupil and Angus MacKay were being taught at the same time'. He said it was composed around 1870, which must be mistaken, as the work appears in Peter Reid's MS of 1826, as well as in the MSS of Angus MacKay and Duncan Campbell, long before 1870. Angus MacKay, born in 1813, would have been his father's pupil probably no later than 1830.

Lord Lovat's Lament was 'as played by Charles MacArthur'. The composer, David Fraser, was a distant cousin of Simon's father, Hugh Archibald, whose grandson Hugh said David 'never gave out the same setting twice'.

Of *The Unjust Incarceration,* Simon wrote: 'I have a tune called *The Black Chanter* which was very similar to this tune, composed by Donald Roy MacCrimmon [Donald Ruadh]. This tune has been altered and claimed as their own by the MacKays. It is a fine tune.' It is in the Campbell Canntaireachd MS of 1790, so unlikely to have been claimed by the Raasay MacKays for whom Simon Fraser had a strong dislike, declaring they had corrupted the music. The work is generally believed to have been composed by Iain Dall MacKay; presumably Simon Fraser included him in his disparagement of the MacKays.

Sources

Dr Barrie Orme, correspondence
Inverness Court Records, Edinburgh
Blanche Jebb
Sir John Dalyell`
Roderick Cannon
Ian Cassells
A.K. Cameron

Alan Lawson, *A Country Called Stratherrick*
Harry Fraser
William Gray
Donald MacPherson

The Silver Chanter

On the Wednesday evening of the Skye Gathering, an event is held in Dunvegan Castle which is billed as a Recital, but is in fact a competition for six invited pipers playing before a single judge. This has gained in prestige to the extent that the winner gains a qualification to play at the Glenfiddich Championships at Blair Castle in the autumn.

Its name comes from a legend about the MacCrimmon pipers receiving the gift of piping from a fairy in the form of a silver chanter. It seems that an early chief, Alasdair Crotach (died 1547) invited chiefs from all over the country to bring their pipers to Dunvegan for a Great Competition. When the time came, Alasdair's own piper was not feeling well and could not blow up his pipe. His apprentice, a young lad named MacCrimmon, had to take over, but was overcome at the thought, and ran outside, weeping. A wee lady dressed in green appeared and asked what was wrong. She then offered him a choice of three gifts: riches, invisibility or piping talent. He chose piping (of course), and she gave him the Silver Chanter – and naturally he won the competition and became the MacLeod chiefs' first MacCrimmon piper.

Dame Flora MacLeod devised the present-day competition in consultation with Seumas MacNeill and John MacFadyen in 1967, after only one piper from outwith Skye turned up for the piping events of the Gathering. The first winner was Hector MacFadyen. Soon the Dunvegan Cup piobaireachd event was so well attended that it had to be divided into two sections, the two winners being invited to play in the Silver Chanter the following year.

Light Music Associated with the MacLeods

Dame Flora MacLeod's Welcome to Cape Breton, by Allan
   J. MacKenzie 6/8 M 2
Lord MacLeod S 2
MacLeod's March 6/8 M 2
MacLeod's Oran Mor 6/8 SA 1
D.C. MacLeod of Stormy Hill, by J.A.C. Fisher 2/4 M 4

and the compositions of D.C. MacLeod (see below)

Other MacLeod Pipers

DONALD MACLEOD, known as The Centenarian of Skye, was said to have been born at Ullinish, near Bracadale, in the west of Skye, in 1688. He was a soldier for more than fifty years. He joined the Royal Scots in 1700, served in Spain in 1740–41, fought at Fontenoy in 1745, and then for the Hanoverians at Falkirk and Culloden, before serving in America. He moved from the Royal Scots to the Black Watch, then to the Fraser Independent Company in 1725, remaining with them until 1736. He was reckoned to be a good piper and a champion swordsman.

After retiring from the Army he became a Chelsea Pensioner, and died in Chelsea Hospital in 1793, aged 105. His Memoirs were published in 1791, and re-issued in 1933.

Minginish Piper

The Contullich Papers, with the MacLeod estate accounts in the early 18th century, record the payment of £10 as 'MacLeod's allowance' for the salary of 'the Minginish Pyper', who is not otherwise named. This began in 1706, and in 1707, the joint salaries of the Ground Officer and Pyper in Minginish came to £72, of which £10 was the piper's. In 1711, a piper named Normand MacLean was given a wage of £20; he was bracketed together with the Harris piper, Hugh MacLeod, who was paid twice as much. Normand (Tormod in Gaelic) may have been the Minginish piper in 1711, possibly based at Carbost, possibly at Talisker. If he was indeed the Minginish piper he would have known Iain Dall MacKay, the Blind Piper of Gairloch, who was a frequent visitor at Talisker in the early 18th century.

Minginish is the part of south-west Skye which contains the Cuillin mountains and the village of Carbost, as well as the estate of Talisker.

JOHN MACLEOD was a Skye piper who is documented in the records of the Celtic Society. He was a pupil of Angus MacKay in the 1840s, and became a good player, but he never competed.

Alexander MacLeod (1829–1903)

ALEXANDER MACLEOD was born in Perth, but was of Skye parentage. He became a piper in the 26th Cameronians, and eventually was Pipe Major, just for one day (to give him an increased pension). He is said in the Notices of Pipers to have composed one piobaireachd work, *MacLeod of Roag's Lament*, which seems to have been distinct from *MacSwan of Roaig's Lament*, and has been lost. He also made many pieces of light music, most of which remained unpublished, but his best tune, *The Drunken Piper* (or *Highland Rory*) is well known.

He died in Edinburgh in 1903, and was given a military funeral at Dalry Cemetery.

Dugald C. MacLeod

The Skye piper and composer DUGALD C. MACLEOD, often wrote as D.C. Macleod, and was known locally as Dougie. He was a joiner by trade, living in Portree, and many, but not all, of his compositions have Skye names; they include both piobaireachd and light music. He published a book of Skye tunes, calling it *The Skye Collection*.

He was not himself a Skyeman, as he hailed from Islay. When a young man he went to London, to work as a joiner/handyman to a wealthy family, and there he met his wife, a Skye girl, and soon after their marriage, they made their home in Skye. For many years he was a staunch supporter of the Skye Games and all the Skye piping competitions.

In 1998, he wrote an interesting letter to the *Piper Press*, about MacRae tuning slides. He said he played MacRae pipes himself, bequeathed to him by his father, ALEX JOHN MACLEOD, who had been the Gaelic teacher at the school in Tarbert, Harris. Dugald's mother, Dolina MacPhail from Bragar in Lewis, told him the history of those pipes. A Harris man, JOHN MACKINNON, had emigrated to North America before the First World War, but returned with the Canadian army in 1914. He remained over here and married a cousin of Dugald's mother, a girl called Effie MacPhail. John used to play the pipes at ceilidhs and dances in Glasgow, along with his friend DONALD RUADH MACLEOD from Arnol. Donald, however, developed miliary tuberculosis, which killed him. Unfortunately the two friends had shared the same set of pipes. On Donald's death, John's wife decreed that he must never share pipes again, so she commissioned MacRae to make him a pipe of his own. It was a silver and ivory set, but the silver was found to be flawed and had to be done again. Dugald attributed the weightiness of them to this mistake. John's wife paid £26 for them – and that included a silver mounted practice chanter.

Not long after he had started playing the Glasgow circuit, John MacKinnon said he had had a vision of himself walking into Hell with his pipes on his shoulder, and he underwent a religious conversion, with the result that he gave up piping, and offered his pipes for sale (could have saved his wife £26). When Dugald's father came back from service in the Second War, he bought the pipes for £50, which, as Dugald said, was quite a price for someone connected with the family.

Dugald played these MacRae pipes, and in the late 1950s had them re-conditioned by Wee Donald (presumably MacLeod, rather than MacLean of Oban). He played them with a Naill chanter and a modern blowpipe with integral valve, and suggested that tuning slides 'do not adjust easily to modern-day central heating and this may be the reason for their present rarity'.

His compositions include:

Colonel Jock, Viewfield 2/4 M 4 (for Colonel Jock MacDonald, Portree)
Doinger 6/8 J 4
D.R. MacDonald's Reel R 4
Duncan MacAskill, MBE, MM 6/8 M 4
Evaporation 2/4 M 4
Faghail Viewfield 6/9 SM 1
A Farewell to the Tilley Lamp (made when Viewfield went electric)
The Fiscal's Reel R 4
Gail MacMillan 6/8 SM 2
Georgina MacLeod, Skebost (sic) 6/8 M4
Iain Andra's March 2/4 M 4
Iain C. Henderson 2/4 M 4
Iain Iasgeir 6/8 J 4
Isla C. MacLeod 6/8 J 4
Lament for Charlie MacEachern of Islay P 7
Lament for Dr Allan MacDonald of Skye P 8
Lament for J. Jersey MacLeod of Skeabost P
Lament for Major J.H.L. MacDonald, QOH P 8 (this was the son of Colonel Jock, Viewfield)
Laphroaig 6/8 M 4
The MacKenzie Girls of Shiader S 4
Peter Fulton, Breakish S 4
Portree Highland Games 2/4 M 4
Smithton Park 6/8 SM 2
Su-Kar-Sal S 4

Note also *D.C. MacLeod of Stormy Hill*, by Dr J.A.C. Fisher 2/4 M 4

Sources

Oral tradition in Skye
The Skye Collection
The Piper Press

The MacLeods of Dundee, Skye and Jersey

ANGUS MACLEOD, DUNDEE was a descendant of John MacLeod (1807–1875) who with his wife and three sons Angus (I), Donald and Norman, left Holm Bay, on the shore below the Storr Lochs, to the north of Portree. They went to Tayside, where they settled. That son Angus (I) himself had a son ANGUS MACLEOD (II), born in 1874, who in turn called his eldest son ANGUS MACLEOD (III), who then called his own son ANGUS (IV), and it is not always easy to distiguish the generations. The second one (II) was known as 'Old Angus', or 'Angus senior', to tell him from his Dundee son; 'Old Angus' was well-known as a piper and composer of pipe music. Angus (IV) lives in Skye, and his piping brother IAIN MACLEOD is in St Mary, Jersey, in the Channel Islands, where he is an active member of the Jersey Pipe Band and has several piping pupils; he also has followed his grandfather in composing lively and unusual tunes.

In the 1880s, Old Angus was taught by Pipe Major John Stewart, uncle of G.S. MacLennan, and later, in 1895, on John Stewart's advice. he went to live in Glasgow so that he could have lessons with John MacDougall Gillies. When living in Glasgow he was Pipe Major of the Maryhill Pipe Band, going on from there to take on the Pipe Majorship of the Grange Thistle Pipe Band in Grangemouth. He died in 1958.

Old Angus' son, Angus (III), was also a good player, but his nervous temperament kept him from competing. He founded the well-known MacLeod Pipe Band in Dundee. After a spell in Cumberland, Angus (III) went to live in Skye where he worked a croft with 200 sheep. 'Eighteen tough years there but I wouldn't have missed it for anything. From my croft I looked straight over two miles of water to the Cairn' (at Boreraig). Pressed into service by Colonel Jock, Angus played for the dancing at the Provincial Mod ('every dancer in Skye from Staffin to Sleat').

On one occasion, French TV was making a programme about the Auld Alliance, and Angus as piper was given the task of marching up a corridor in Dunvegan Castle, then round the dining room where Dame Flora was presiding. 'It took two rehearsals to get the tempo right for the TV cameras. Everything was going fine. I stopped beside

Dame Flora where she (then aged over ninety) poured me a bumper dram. Thought I, this is something that hasn't been rehearsed. Have I got to take that in one? Being a MacLeod I gave the toast and downed it, and was on the point of blowing up my pipe when "CUT!" Charlie the butler appeared from behind a curtain with another dram, so start over again. Success the second time, round the table and out, with two bumpers in me. A good job I didn't have to do it a third time.'

Angus (III) continues: 'On the day of Dame Flora's funeral the four local pipers were asked to take part – Dr Tony Fisher, Nicol Campbell, Donald MacPhee and myself [all lived in or near Dunvegan]. I was asked to lead off from the castle door, playing *MacLeod's Oran Mor* and a few blending variations of piobaireachd. Reaching the main road, Nicol continued with *Flowers o' the Forest,* Tony played *When the Battle Is O'er,* and Donald MacPhee followed. It was a nice morning, but as time went on quite a breeze came up, and some rain. Undoubtedly I had the best of it. Pipes in nice tune, and sheltered all the way up the drive from any breeze by the rhododendron bushes on each side. By the time it came to Donald's turn he was exposed to the elements. It was unfortunate. He chose to play *Loch Duich,* and everything slowed down considerably when he also chose to march in time to the music. He was further handicapped by playing his son Angus's pipes, who, if I remember rightly, plays with the drones on the right shoulder. Tony gave the drones an occasional hoist for him on to his shoulder, and when a gust of wind blew Donald's bonnet off, Tony retrieved it. Unfortunate, but under the circumstances it could have happened to any of us.

'I imagine old Donald will be gone by now (1995), and I know for sure that Nicol died on 10 May 1991, exactly a week after my wife. When she died, I was taken up (from Dundee) to see my son Angus (IV) in Skye, and we went to see Nicol. He was in really good form. About midnight on 10 May, his wife phoned and told me Nicol had died. My son Norman took me to the funeral'.

Another memory of Skye was an occasion when a film was made of Dr Johnson's tour of the Highlands with Boswell. Much of the filmimg was done around Dunvegan. Angus (III) said the introductory scene was Samuel Johnson sitting stroking a black cat, and the background music was Angus himself playing the Urlar of *The Desperate Battle of the Birds.*

Angus (III) retired to live in Ardler, near Blairgowrie, and his son Angus (IV) succeeded to the family croft.

A descendant of this MacLeod family is a brother of Angus (IV), IAIN

MACLEOD, a piper now living in Jersey, in the Channel Islands. He is a vet by profession, who practised in Jersey for over thirty years. A very musical player, he is a staunch advocate of the 'old style' of piping, with open C's and the so-called 'redundant A'. This appears to be a family tradition among these MacLeod pipers, based on the teaching of John MacDougall Gillies.

In January 2000, Iain published two CDs of his own playing of piobaireachd in the MacLeod family style inherited from his grand-father. Played on a 100-year-old set of Henderson pipes, these works are most enjoyable. With the title *Some Piobaireachd As Taught By John MacDougall Gillies*, the first CD has nine piobaireachd works, some incomplete:

MacCrimmon's Sweetheart
Scarce of Fishing
The Children
Bells of Perth
Battle of the Birds
MacIntosh's Lament
MacLeod's Salute (in an unusual setting)
Battle of Waternish
Corrienessan's Salute (an exceptionally good performance)

This CD1 finishes with *Broghan's Song*, composed by Iain for his grand-daughter Broghan, and described by him as a Lullaby.

The second CD also has nine piobaireachd works, mainly incomplete:

Earl of Antrim
MacLeod of Raasay
Struan Robertson
Earl of Seaforth
Wee Spree
Massacre of Glencoe
Unjust Incarceration
Mary MacLeod

All the above played by Iain MacLeod, and the final work on CD2, *Iain MacLeod's Welcome to Brittany*, composed by Jacques Pincet, is played by the composer.

The 'classical' piobaireachd works on these two CDs are most interesting as well as enjoyable, as they represent the teaching of John MacDougall Gillies in the 1890s. The playing might be regarded as a step between the 'old' style of the early 19th century as exemplified by the Frasers in Australia, and the 'new' approach of the Piobaireachd Society in the 20th century.

The sleeve notes to the CDs are of interest, too, and Iain included a Discussion Tape in which he gives an airing to several topics of interest to piobaireachd enthusiasts.

Iain then followed this in 2008 with a first-class book of lighter pipe music, with a CD of himself playing the Ceol Beag compositions of his grandfather, with some of his own works – which stand up remarkably well to those of Old Angus. Entitled *Dundee, Skye and Jersey, Family Compositions and CD,* it contains some forty-four tunes, with interesting notes on their background, and very good illustrations. The music is well-played and most enjoyable, whether from the early 20th century or two generations later.

Sources

Piping Times
Iain MacLeod, Jersey
Iain MacLeod's CDs and Collection of family compositions

A Piper Visiting Skye

A piper was in Skye for the Skye Week competitions, and the town of Portree being busy, he found accommodation in a B&B establishment on a croft outside the town. Over breakfast with his fellow guests, there were comments about the modern way of serving of tiny portions of butter, jam and marmalade in wee plastic containers with peel-off lids. The piper lamented the passing of the old days, when every crofter had his own cow which supplied him with milk, butter and cheese, produced on the premises, with plentiful servings.

The piper then turned to his hostess and asked if she had any honey. She returned with some honey – in a tiny plastic container. He looked at it, and said 'Ah. I see you keep a bee.'

The MacArthurs

The MacGregor–MacArthur Manuscript

In 1820, two men met with the ailing Angus MacArthur, to hear him sing or play tunes on the chanter ('whistle') and to write them down, creating the MacGregor–MacArthur manuscript, also known as the Highland Society of London manuscript. This was published in 2001, by the Universities of Aberdeen and Glasgow in association with the John MacFadyen Memorial Trust and the Piobaireachd Society, as Volume 1 of the series *The Music of Scotland*. It contains the music of thirty piobaireachd works, printed both as they appear in the manuscript and in transposed settings for modern-day pipers to use as a working text.

The manuscript was made at the request of the Highland Society of London, who ran the national competitions in Edinburgh. Angus Mac-Arthur seems to have sung the tunes to John MacGregor, who wrote them down in staff notation, and the third man, Andrew Robertson, checked them. His exact role is not entirely clear, and little is known of him, but John MacGregor was one of the foremost pipers in the country, one of the MacGregor pipers from Glenlyon who had dominated the competitions when they were started in the late 18th century. After winning the Prize Pipe in 1805, John had become the official Piper to the Highland Society, and was acting for them on this occasion.

The manuscript now belongs to the Piobaireachd Society, but is on permanent loan to the National Library of Scotland (MS 1679). It is available on the Internet. There is some doubt about the writing of eighteen of the works, as a note on a sheet of paper inside the cover of the manuscript says '12 Piobaireachds written by John MacGregor, dictated by Angus MacArthur and examined by Andrew Robertson'. Does this mean that the rest of the thirty were not dictated by Angus, or perhaps not written out by John?

Angus MacKay had a loan of the manuscript, and indicated which works were played differently by his father, John MacKay. He did not return it to the Highland Society, and on his death it passed to his pupil Michael MacCarfae, piper to the Duke of Hamilton. That is why on the cover of the manuscript is written 'MacArfrae's Piobaireachd Manuscript Vol III'. After MacCarfrae's death, his daughter sold it to Dr Charles Bannatyne, and in 1926, after Dr Bannatyne had died, it was bought by the Piobaireachd Society, who later lodged it with the National Library.

The thirty works are:

The Big Spree
King James VI's Lament
King James VI's Salute
Beinn a'Ghrian
The Bells of Perth
Hector MacLean's Warning
The Pride of Barra
The Battle of Maol Ruadh (Mulroy, or Red Hill)
The MacDonalds' Salute
The Highland Society of Scotland's Salute
Catherine's Lament (or Salute)
Abercairney's Salute
Beloved Scotland
The MacLeans' March
The Brothers' Lament
Lord MacDonald's Lament (1796)
The Daughter's Lament
Nameless
MacKay's Lament (= Lament for Donald Duaghal MacKay)
Nameless – a Lament
The Bard's Lament
Suarachan (The MacRaes' March)
Sir James MacDonald of the Isles' Lament
Lady MacDonald's Lament
MacKenzie of Gairloch's Lament
The Young Laird of Dungallon's Lament
Lady Margaret MacDonald's Salute
The Laird of Arnaboll's Lament
Nameless (The MacDougall's Gathering)
You're Welcome, Ewen

Background Notes on the Works in the Manuscript

These notes are given with the same reservations as applied to the notes on the MacCrimmon tunes (above): they are personal opinions rather than definitive evidence, and are intended as possible guides to the mood of a piece. No guarantee of accuracy.

The Big Spree

The Big Spree is one of three Spree tunes which seem to be composed in the same style, the other two being *The Little Spree* (commonly called *The Wee Spree*), and *The Middling Spree*. All are attributed to an unnamed piper of the MacGregors of Glenlyon, the famous Clann na Sgeulaiche. The traditions about the tunes are confused and unclear, but seem to involve a drunken blacksmith. Angus MacKay gave the *Big Spree* the Gaelic title '*Tha'n daorach ort 's fearr'd tha cadal*', meaning 'You are drunk, you'd better have a sleep'.

Neil Angus MacDonald from Barra, a leading piper who was prominent in the Roman Catholic community in the north, said that the Spree compositions, and especially the *Big Spree*, had echoes of musical phrases found in the sung Litany of the Catholic church. There is a tradition that during the persecution of the Catholic faith in the mid 17th century, when the holding of Mass was forbidden, sometimes a piper was sent out if a priest was in the area, illegally. The piper would play one of the Spree tunes as a sign to the faithful to come to Mass at some secret location, and they say that playing the *Big Spree* indicated the presence of an important prelate, a Bishop or Archbishop, the *Middling Spree* a fairly prominent cleric, and the *Wee Spree* a mere parish priest or curate.

If there is any truth in this tradition, it might indicate that the three works date back to a time before the middle of the 17th century.

The *Wee Spree* seems to be a favourite work of young players with the urge to experiment, probably because it is so melodic, comparatively short and comparatively easy to play. It lends itself well to playing by a quartet, with one piper improvising seconds. It has also been used by two playing together, each with a hand on the other's chanter. If the audience has drink taken, like the aforesaid blacksmith, their appreciation will be much enhanced.

Sources

Alec Haddow, *The History and Structure of Ceol Mor*
Fionn (Henry Whyte)
Angus MacKay, Manuscript
Neil Angus MacDonald
George Stewart
James Mather
Piobaireachd Society Conference, Bridge of Allan

King James VI's Lament and King James VI's Salute

Both of these appear in the MacArthur manuscript as Nameless works; the name of the Lament comes from Angus MacKay's Index, that of the Salute being a name written in above the score by Dr Charles Bannatyne, on what authority we do not know.

The *Lament for King James VI* appears in the Campbell Canntair-eachd manuscript (No. 12 in volume 1) with the title of *Porst na Lurkin* 'Tune of the Shank', which links it to Sir James MacDonald of Sleat, accidentally shot in the leg while out hunting in North Uist (see below, *Sir James MacDonald's Lament*).

Whether either piece was composed in honour of King James VI of Scotland, known to Englishmen as James I, must be doubtful. James was the son of Mary Queen of Scots and Lord Darnley, and was born in 1566. Almost immediately he was separated from his mother, and was brought up as the heir to the joint thrones of Scotland and England. Mary was beheaded in 1587, but she had been forced by the Scottish nobles to abdicate the Scottish throne to her infant son some eighteen years earlier. James became monarch of the two countries when Elizabeth of England died in 1603. He was said to be 'a learned, stupid ruler', and was known as 'the wisest fool in Christendom'. He died in 1625, and was succeeded by his son, Charles I.

These two works whose titles appear to honour the first Stuart king of Britain may have been given the names in a later age, when Jacobite or monarchist supporters were to the fore as subjects of piobaireachd compositions. Several such works appear in this manuscript: *Abercairney's Salute*, *Lady Margaret MacDonald's Salute*, *The Daughter's Lament*, *The Brothers' Lament*, *The Lament for Donald Duaghal MacKay*, *The Young Laird of Dungallon's Lament*, and probably the *Big Spree*, all have Stuart monarchist associations. Whether Angus MacArthur regarded these two works as pro-Stuart, known to us as works for King James VI but Nameless in the manuscript, we do not know.

Donald MacDonald said in his notes on the tunes that *Lament for the Union* was 'composed by Macriumen', but Colin Cameron wrote that it was the work of Donald Boyd, piper to King James VI. Because James became King of both Scotland and England in 1603, it is assumed that 'the Union' refers to that – but more often 'the Union' is used of the Act of Union in 1707. When James acceded in 1603, the two countries remained separate, with their own governments and institutions. In 1707 they became one kingdom, forming Great Britain, and it was generally this amalgamation that was lamented in Scotland, the

Scots regretting the loss of their identity. For the background to the title of the *Lament for the Union*, however, Colin Cameron's note is usually followed. If Donald MacDonald was correct, it may have been Patrick Og MacCrimmon who made the tune, in 1707.

Presumably because of the name Boyd, Donald is generally said to have been a Lowlander. Some consider that the unusual construction of the *Lament for the Union* is the result of Donald's non-Highland background, but it is not clear whether it was thought to be through ignorance of conventional piobaireachd form, or an accepted Lowland traditional form. And because he was the king's piper, it has been suggested that he might also have composed the two works, *King James VI's Lament* and *Salute*. They seem to have little in common with the *Lament for the Union*.

Donald Boyd's name may suggest he came from the island of Bute. It is not even certain that he was of Lowland origin. There was a family called Boyd in North Uist, who were MacDonalds; their Gaelic by-name was Bodach (long *o*), anglicised to Boyd, because one of them, in the early 17th century, had sent his son to be fostered in Bute. He might later have become the King's piper, but there is no known tradition of his being a piper.

Donald MacDonald was the name of the man who sent his son south, and Donald Boyd was a name which recurred in this line. Some of his descendants were in South Uist and Barra – and William Matheson said that some of them later adopted the alternative name of Johnson.

In North Uist, according to Professor Matheson, another source of the name Boyd as used by English speakers, was the Gaelic name Mac Iain Buidhe, ('son of yellow-haired John'), and branches of this family are found in Benbecula. Many of them were also called Donald. It seems clear that there were Boyd families throughout the islands, and it is possible that Donald Boyd the King's piper was from one of these.

Sources

Angus MacKay, Manuscript
Colin Cameron
William Matheson, *TGSI* LII

Beinn a'Ghriain

Professor Alec Haddow was of the opinion that this title is a corruption of the original name *Beinn a'Ghriam*, and that it was called after the mountain of that name in central Sutherland. A frequent copying error in old maps and documents was the confusion of letters made up of the wee strokes known as minims. The letter i was a single minim (with no dot), n was two minims and m was three – and often they tended to run together as if attached. Small wonder if m was mistaken for in – and it often was. An example is in the list of Strathnaver men pardoned in 1614, where Donald McCrummen's name has been misread as McCruinnien.

Beinn a'Ghriam is a double peak, Beinn a'Griam Mor and Beinn a'Griam Beag (Big and Little Beinn a'Griam). They may be seen from the road near Forsinard and Kinbrace, where the Straths of Kildonan and Halladale meet, on the boundary of Sutherland and Caithness. The name *griam* is obscure: it is probably from an Old Norse word *grima* (with a long vowel, as in Griam), meaning 'double' or 'pair'. There are many Norse names in that part of Sutherland. It probably became readily corrupted, both because *grima* is an obscure word even in Norse and because it was misinterpreted by Gaelic speakers identifying it with *grian* 'sun'.

There seems to be little doubt that the name of the piobaireachd work should be *Beinn a'Ghriaim*, and that its background is in the Sutherland hills.

The mountain Beinn a'Griam Mor has a place in MacKay history. In 1601, in the time of Donald Duaghal MacKay's father, his easterly neighbour, the Earl of Caithness, of the Sinclair family, deliberately provoked trouble with the MacKays by asking permission to hunt near Durness, deep in MacKay country. He knew the permission would be refused, as the Sinclairs had long been a threat to the MacKays, and, as expected, it was.

At once Caithness started to mass his supporters, seeking to avenge this 'insult'. The Caithness men, under their Earl's leadership, advanced to a position just inside the MacKay territory, but only just; the boundaries were so fluid that it was hardly an invasion. They gathered at the foot of Beinn a'Griam Mor. The men were not keen to fight, as the Earl of Caithness was not liked and had no flair for leadership. At daybreak, the Caithness army fled, and there was no battle. This explains why the piobaireachd work is not called the *Battle of Beinn a'Ghriam*.

This bloodless victory was commemorated by the building of a huge cairn, at the foot of Beinn a'Griam Mor. It was called Carn Teichidh, 'the cairn of flight'. It stood for a long time, and was a mockery to the people of Caithness for some two hundred years. There is now no trace of it, although its presence is still remembered; close to the site, on the slope to the north of the Kinbrace–Syre road, between Beinn a'Griam Mor and the Badanlochs, there is an exceptionally large circular fank (sheep-pen), with substantial high stone walls. Local tradition says that this was built 'when the sheep came', in the early 1800s, using all the stones of Carn Teichidh, and that is why the fank is so big, and the walls so high.

If the dating of this bloodless battle to 1601 is accurate, it would seem that the work might have been composed a year or two before the arrival of Donald Mor MacCrimmon in Strathnaver. Perhaps we may take this as evidence that fine piobaireachd music was being composed in the north before he came. Or did Donald Mor make it a few years later, as a tribute to his host and protector, the chief of MacKay, having been told of the MacKay triumph that day? There is no surviving tradition of the authorship of the work.

It is noticeable that the opening bars resemble those of the start of *I Got a Kiss of the King's Hand*, composed some fifty years later, by the elderly John MacCrimmon. He was piper to the Earl of Sutherland at Dunrobin, in East Sutherland, and we might wonder if he was using an older motif, peculiar to Sutherland – or perhaps an older song.

The MacArthur manuscript gives a much fuller setting than is found in Angus MacKay. It is notable for the effective repeat of the Urlar, before the Taorluath variations.

Sources

Register of the Great Seal
Alec Haddow, *The History and Structure of Ceol Mor*
Piobaireachd Society Book 4
Proceedings of the Piobaireachd Society Conference
R.M. MacNicol, gamekeeper, Strath Halladale

The Bells of Perth

At the Conference of the Piobaireachd Society in March 2004, an illuminating talk on the origins of this tune was given by Dr Ian Cassells. He is the carilloneur of the bells of the old St John's Kirk in Perth, and has played the theme tune of the piobaireachd on his bells. He gave an interesting account of his bells and their history in the context of Scottish bell-ringing, and identified the tune which lies behind the piobaireachd.

It should be noted that in Scotland, as on the continent, church bells play tunes, not peals and changes sounded by pulling on ropes, as is done in England. In Scotland, only the clapper moves when the bell is played; in England, the whole bell is in motion. The Scottish system is based on the Flemish carillon tradition.

In St John's Kirk, Perth, the bells high in the tower are linked to a massive keyboard down below, and there the carilloneur sits to play his tunes. This is not like playing the piano or organ: as is a piper, he is restricted in the number of notes available to him, although the bells of Perth cover a range of three octaves. The physical effort of sounding them is considerable; he has to hit the keys forcefully, and timing the lengths of the notes is tricky. There is no opportunity for practice, as every note sounded is heard throughout the town. A surprisingly musical effect is achieved by a skilled carilloneur such as Dr Cassels, and he can play grace-notes, but only in a simplified form.

Some of the bells of St John's Kirk in Perth go back to mediaeval times. St John's now has a total of sixty-three bells, but many of these are at present disconnected. The oldest, called 'Ave Maria', dates from about 1340; the largest, a Flemish bell, is 'John the Baptist', brought from Flanders in 1506. There are other 16th-century Flemish bells, mainly dated 1526, and later bells in the carillon were cast in 1934.

Dr Cassels has discovered that in 1653, the Town Council of Perth held an official inspection of the bells, which included the Ave Maria and six Flemish bells, at that time used for sounding the hour and half-hour throughout the day.

The Council's Report said: 'The notes of the half hour musick being thirty-two notes: The Son of Adam answered them – All Glorie to the Sone of Man, (with) the Father and the Spirit . . . perpetualy.' This refers to the melody played, and Dr Cassels adds 'Presumably the bells had been playing this tune from 1526 on'.

He then made the discovery of a vocal piece called 'All Sons of Adam', whose tenor part is a plainsong Christmas hymn 'Conditor Alme Siderum' (Creator of the Starry Height). This is of mediaeval date.

The words, says Dr Cassels, are almost identical with those given in the Council Report. The melody is thirty-two notes in length, requiring only six bells, and as an Advent (pre-Christmas) hymn would be appropriate for a church dedicated to John the Baptist.

Dr Cassels suggests that the seven-note 'motto-theme' of Perth, the tune or musical phrase associated with the town or the church – just as the tune *Oranges and Lemons* identifies the church of St Clement Dane, in London – was the first seven notes of that hymn-melody, which are also the first seven notes of the Urlar of the piobaireachd. This means that anyone hearing it would immediately think of Perth.

There is no doubt that this tune was played on the bells at the time of the composition of the piobaireachd. The tradition is that one of the MacIntyre pipers to Menzies of Menzies heard the bells playing it as he made his way home to Rannoch, passing the town of Perth (or St Johnston, St John's Town, named for the Kirk); it is said that he was travelling through the neighbouring hills so as not to enter the town, possibly to avoid the payment of a toll, or to escape the closing of the town gates at sunset.

The date is not certain, but the composer of the piobaireachd may have been John MacIntyre, who was a pupil of Patrick Og MacCrimmon, and it is thought that he made it towards the end of the 17th century. He was piper at Menzies Castle, which is about thirty miles from Perth. John's father and son were also pipers there, and some attribute the piobaireachd to John's son Donald. Other works by these MacIntyre pipers include *The Prince's Salute*, *The Battle of Sheriffmuir* and *Menzies' Salute*.

[The above account is based on the talk given by Dr Cassels and reported in the *Proceedings of the Piobaireachd Society Conference* for 2004. I am grateful to Ian and the Society for permission to use this material. As the Chairman remarked at the time, 'We will never think of the *Bells of Perth* in quite the same way again.']

Hector MacLean's Warning

Donald MacDonald junior called this *Brather a'n amhildaich*, which seems to be calling Hector the Brother of the Devil.

Hector MacLean was the illegitimate son of Allan nan Sop, a notorious pirate who ravaged the west coast in the 16th century. Allan had Hector and his brother legitimised, and Hector inherited his father's wealth. He married a daughter of the Earl of Argyll, and began a campaign to discredit his cousin, Lachlan Mor of Duart. Having ambitions to replace Lachlan as clan chief, Hector spread rumours doubting Lachlan's manhood, hoping to convince his relations that Lachlan was unfit to be their leader, but succeeded only in riling him to the point where he seized both Hector and his son, and imprisoned them in Duart Castle. After a year, Lachlan had Hector removed to Breacacha Castle in the south of the island of Coll, where he was beheaded, an execution without trial. This was in 1578, when Lachlan was building up his power as the leader of the MacLeans.

There was a story of a witch making a prophecy of the fate awaiting Hector, and the title *Hector MacLean's Warning* may refer to that.

Sources
Alec Haddow, *The History and Structure of Ceol Mor*

Dr Barrie Orme, correspondence
J.P. MacLean, *History of the Clan MacLean*

The Pride of Barra

There is confusion about the titles of the several piobaireachd works associated with Barra and the MacNeills, which are known as the *Pride of Barra, MacNeill of Barra's March* and *MacNeill is Lord There*. The title in the MacArthur manuscript is *Spaidearachd Bharrach, or the Pride of Barra,* but Angus MacKay's title *Mac Neil of Barra's March* is generally used for this tune, as *The Pride of Barra* was already the name of another work.

In the Campbell Canntaireachd manuscript, volume 1, the tune numbered 6 is called *Spaddarich Bharach,* but it is not the same work as this one in the MacArthur manuscript. This tune appears in the Campbell MS as *Dougald MacRaneil's Lament.*

The spelling *Spaidearachd* is a Gaelic word meaning 'boasting', and there is confusion with another word *spaidsearachd* 'walking, marching'. Iain MacInnes says this is a back formation, i.e. a Gaelic term translating back the English word 'March', and that it 'became popular' around 1820. Joseph MacDonald in his *Compleat Theory* of 1762 used the term 'March' but not in the sense of walking or marching. He did not use *spaidsearachd,* but *slighe,* literally meaning a 'passage, track' or 'craft', and to him a 'March' was what we now call a 'Piobaireachd' (unless we speak Gaelic, in which case it is *Ceol Mor* – but that term did not come in until quite late in the 19th century).

The published edition (2001) of the MacArthur manuscript quotes two Gaelic flyting songs, one called *Spaidearachd Bharrach,* dating from around 1650, in which a South Uist woman is disputing with a woman from Barra. The title of this piobaireachd as given in the Campbell Canntaireachd manuscript (1790) is *Dougald MacRaneil's Lament,* which the editors suggest refers to the discomfiture of the South Uist contestant at losing the dispute. The tunes of the two songs are known, but neither is related to the two piobaireachd works associated with this title.

Sources

Angus MacKay, Manuscript
MacArthur–MacGregor Manuscript
Campbell Canntaireachd Manuscript

The Battle of Red Hill

See also above, *MacCrimmon's Sweetheart*.

The work we know now as *Isabel MacKay*, following Angus Mac-Kay, was given the title *The Battle of Maolroy* by Donald MacDonald, but it bears no resemblance to this tune *The Battle of Red Hill*, which is a translation of *Blar Maol Ruadh*.

The Battle of Maol Ruadh (Mulroy) was fought on 4 August 1688. The battlefield is close to the confluence of the rivers Spean and Roy, across the Roy from the village of Roybridge, upstream from Spean Bridge. It is near Keppoch, where the two MacDonald brothers were murdered in 1663 (see *The Brothers' Lament*, below). Considered by some to have been the last clan battle, it was part of the struggle between pro- and anti-Stuart parties, which culminated in the battle of Killiecrankie in 1689.

At Maol Ruadh, the great leader of the MacDonalds of Keppoch, Coll of the Cows, with 800 men, fought against a force of 1200 Mac-Intosh clansmen and allies, in a fight later described as 'a bloody affray'.

The MacIntoshes and their friends the MacGillivrays had called upon Captain Kenneth MacKenzie of Suddie to assist them, and he brought a troop of his own men to the fight. The MacGillivrays had obtained a Commission of Fire and Sword from the Privy Council in Edinburgh, which said that 'whatever slaughter, mutilation, blood, fire-raising or other violence' might be committed against the enemy 'shall be held laudable, good and warrantable service to his Majesty and Government'. Some government forces were sent, too, as it was thought desirable to suppress the power of the MacDonalds of Keppoch.

This did them no good, however. Keppoch had brought his own allies to add to his own MacDonnells, and launched a fierce Highland Charge with swords and axes, in which Suddie was mortally wounded.

One of Suddie's soldiers, Donald McBane, later wrote an account of the battle:

> The MacDonalds came down the hill upon us, without either shoe, stocking or bonnet on their heads: they gave a shout and then the fire began on both sides and continued a hot dispute for an hour. Then they broke in upon us with sword and target and Lochaber axes which obliged us to give way.

Stuart McHardy has given us a story-teller's account of the battle, adding the detail that as the MacIntosh troops were fleeing, their standard-bearer came to the Roy River, which he had to jump, to make his escape; the place is still called MacIntosh's Leap.

Keppoch was victorious, but subsequently referred to the battle as 'the unhappie accident I had with McKintoshe at Millroy' (quoted by Peter Simpson in *The Independent Highland Companies 1603–1760).*

Sources

Stuart MacDonald, *Back to Lochaber*
Peter Simpson
David Stevenson, *Alisdair MacColla*
John Prebble, *Culloden*
Stuart McHardy, *The Well of Heads*

The MacDonalds' Salute

See also the *MacLeods' Salute*, above.

This work is associated with the MacDonalds of Sleat only on the evidence of Angus MacKay, who attributed its composition to Donald Mor MacCrimmon in 1603. The editors of the MacArthur manuscript think it might be later, basing their judgement on the phrase structure of the variations. These variations might have been added later, of course. The title *Fannet* given to this work in the Campbell Canntaireachd manuscript probably means 'Mockery', which might tie in with the story of Donald Mor and the end of the MacLeod/MacDonald feud in Skye. Possibly the basis was a song-air dating from 1603.

Sources

Angus MacKay, Manuscript
MacArthur–MacGregor Manuscript
Campbell Canntaireachd Manuscript

The Highland Society of London's Salute

This appears in the manuscript under the title *The Highland Club*, and is attributed to 'J: MacArthur'. It was Angus MacKay who told us it was a salute to the Highland Society of London, and that its composer was John MacArthur, known as 'The Professor', living in Edinburgh in 1790. The Highland Society of London ran the Edinburgh competitions at that time, and dominated the piping scene, encouraging the transcription of pipe music into staff notation and publishing several collections of written piobaireachd music.

John 'the Professor' MacArthur was the nephew of Charles (I) MacArthur from Skye, being a son of Charles' brother Niel; he made his home in Edinburgh, where he was a grocer by trade. He was a first cousin of Angus MacArthur of the MacArthur manuscript.

John had a fine reputation as a piping teacher and was recognised as an authority on piping matters. He was acknowledged by his fellow-pipers to be the best of them, and after he had proved his superiority in 1783, he did not compete again but gave demonstrations of his skill, to general acclaim, at the start and finish of the Edinburgh competitions, every year until his death in 1790. That year he played two of his own works, the *Highland Society of London's Salute* and *Salute to the Prince of Wales*. He died a few months later.

Sources

Notices of Pipers
Introduction to 2001 edition of the MacArthur–MacGregor Manuscript

Catherine's Lament/Salute

This is not named in the MacArthur manuscript, but Angus MacKay gave us the name *Catherine's Lament* or *Salute*, causing confusion by calling it *Cumha Chaitrine* but translating that as *Katherine's Salute* (*Cumha* means a lament). Dr Charles Bannatyne wrote on the Angus MacKay manuscript a title *Frasers' Gathering;* his authority for this, if any, is not known.

Willie MacLean told a story about this composition: see below, Malcolm MacRobert.

Murray of Abercairnie's Salute

The manuscript attributes this work to Charles MacArthur, and it is one of several tunes he made in honour of prominent Jacobites who had figured in the Rising of 1745 or its aftermath.

James Murray of Abercairney had been a Jacobite supporter all his life, and contributed money to the cause in both of the Risings, in 1715 and 1745. At the start of the '45, his name appeared in a list of the wealthier lairds of his district, between Perth and Crieff, who could be counted upon to back the Jacobites. He seems never to have appeared in person, and did not join the Jacobite army or take part in any battle, although his brother was captured in a skirmish the night before the battle of Sheriffmuir, in 1715. It may be that Abercairney was too old, or had some physical handicap which prevented his taking up arms, but it did not curb his zeal in supporting those who did. Maybe he was just too canny to risk losing all he had by taking an active part.

His most remarkable act of loyalty was in 1745. On an estate neighbouring Abercairney lived the Duke of Perth, a leading Jacobite. One night a Campbell officer called on the Duke, and was cordially invited to stay for dinner. In the middle of the meal, the officer's men closed in and announced that the Duke was under arrest. The Duke said he must change his shoes and fetch his coat, and went into a closet which, unknown to his captors, concealed a private staircase. He used it to escape from the house, and, still wearing his cloth slippers, ran across country in the dark, to his neighbour, Abercairney, who took him in and hid him from the Campbell troops. The officer, Captain Duncan Campbell of Inverawe, vented his feelings by punishing his men severely.

This seems to have been the closest that Abercairney came to actual conflict, but he reacted with courage to a difficult situation. Later correspondence shows how closely he kept in touch with the Jacobite leaders throughout the campaign, and he sent them money on many occasions.

After the Rising had failed, he retained his estates, presumably because nothing could be proved against him; only a few years later he was petitioning the government for a grant of trees to be planted in Crieff, to beautify the town.

One of his descendants built a Piper's House in the grounds, incorporating a thirty-yard corridor, so that the piper had room to walk up and down in comfort. Unfortunately it is no longer in existence.

Sources
D. Murray Rose, *Prince Charlie's Friends or Jacobite Indictments*
Dr Alasdair MacLean

Beloved Scotland
The full title seems to be *Beloved Scotland I Leave Thee Gloomy*, according to Angus MacKay – but elsewhere he also wrote that *Beloved Scotland* was the wrong title anyway. It is one of a number of possible farewell works, often associated with the departure of emigrants to a new life overseas.

There are a number of references to pipe music being played for emigrant ships leaving Scotland, although seldom is the name of the music mentioned. Possibly the title of *Beloved Scotland I Leave Thee Gloomy* is based on the translated words of a Gaelic song. *Weighing From Land* has been described as a rowing tune or iorram, but it may have been a rope-pulling shanty, if the vessel was ocean-going.

Smaller vessels would work the west coast bringing emigrants to central ports, such as Tobermory, where larger ships awaited their passengers. The *Dubh Gleannach* was a coastal vessel with this function; a fine Gaelic song was made about her.

Seton Gordon, in his book *Hebridean Memories*, wrote of an emigrant ship leaving South Uist in the spring of 1923, the *Marloch*, taking fifty families from the Outer Isles to St John, New Brunswick, heading for Alberta. Seton Gordon tells how 'fully 1500 people' were there at Lochboisdale to see them off, 500 leaving from Uist, another 100 from Barra.

> The sun shone and a piper provided cheerful music upon the pier . . . A piper who was making the long overseas journey played such animated marches as *MacDonald of Glencoe* and *The Highland Wedding*, pacing up and down the after part of the vessel. On shore a second piper was playing in time with the first. . . The tender cast off her moorings. There was a sudden fluttering of handkerchiefs. . . As the boat slipped across the waters of Lochboisdale, one of the oldest of the men who were sailing from his home, snatched his pipes from where they lay on deck at the ship's bow and played with deep feeling the mournful strains of an old Gaelic air. It seemed to voice the sorrow of that company of wanderers. The pipes were not in tune and the execution did not compare with that of the previous players, yet that sad melody will always remain in my mind, *Cha till mi tuilleadh* (*I will return no more*). It was played with a heart that was heavy with sorrow.

As Seton Gordon made clear, the ships themselves often had a piper or pipers on board, encouraged by the masters of the vessels as a means of keeping the passengers entertained and content during the long voyages to America or Australia. There is a strong tradtion about the piper on the *Hector*, in 1783; named as John MacKay, he was possibly one of the sons of Iain Dall, the Blind Piper of Gairloch, though he has also been claimed by Rogart, in Sutherland, and by Lochaber. The story goes that he arrived on the quayside in Ullapool as the ship was about to weigh anchor and leave for Nova Scotia. He had no money for the fare, but the other passengers were so keen to have a piper with them that they clubbed together to pay his passage. Possibly he had come merely to earn a little by playing farewell music on the jetty, but he seized his chance, and found himself in Canada a few weeks later.

Another story is that he stowed away on the *Hector*, and was discovered when the ship was out in the Atlantic. He was spared the usual fate of stowaways – being thrown overboard and left to drown – because his piping skills were valued by the other passengers, who undertook to feed him in exchange for his music.

The famous painting of the arrival of the *Hector* shows John MacKay piping the newcomers ashore after their long voyage. He settled near Scotsburn, Nova Scotia.

Some years later, in 1805, his nephew, another John MacKay from the Gairloch family, left for Nova Scotia, too. As he was rowed out to the waiting ship, the *Sydney Smith*, anchored in deep water off Longa Island, at the entrance to Gairloch, he played a tune which no-one had heard before, saying it was called *The Departure of Piping from Scotland*. Presumably it was his own composition.

In the 1840s, we have a description of two ships lying in Tobermory Bay, one for Protestant migrants, who were quiet, sober and miserable, and had no pipers, the other for the Roman Catholics, loudly bewailing their lot and drinking heavily, with three pipers on board. They were from Moidart, and had been put out of their homes by their landlord.

Another forced emigration was that of the inhabitants of Kildonan in Sutherland, in 1841. The newspaper account stresses the heartfelt grief of the evicted, and says that the piper on the quay was playing *We Will Return No More (Cha Till Mi Tuilleadh)* as the ship pulled away.

Presumably *Leaving Kintyre* was another such emigrant work, though its origin and composer are not known, nor are those of *Beloved Scotland*. Similarly, we have a tune which seems to be the fare-well of a soldier, leaving his wife or sweetheart as he goes to the wars: *My Dearest On Earth, Give Me Your Kiss* starts with an Urlar of ten-der and romantic tone, which soon changes to the grimmer atmosphere of battle, in the variations. This too is a farewell composition, though different from the emigration works.

Beloved Scotland was the tune with which John MacFadyen won his first Clasp, and he asked to have part of the first line engraved on his headstone, in the graveyard at Portree. Unfortunately, it seems, the engraver was given the wrong setting, and, much worse, they say he made a note error, which would have been most uncharacteristic of John – and would not have won him the Clasp.

Sources

Angus MacKay, Manuscript
Donald Archie MacDonald, *Tocher* 15
Seton Gordon, *Hebridean Memories*
Lucille H. Campey, *After the Hector*
J.H. Dixon: *Gairloch and Guide to Loch Maree*
James Robertson, *Mull Diaries*
Inverness Courier

The MacLeans' March

As with other works in the manuscript, this is not named, and we take its title from Angus MacKay. It has been said that its composer was Allan nan Sop, also known as Allan of Gigha, who was a leading MacLean of the 16th century. Allan, however, was a notorious predator who ravaged the west coast, preying on his own clansmen, among many others, and it seems unlikely that he would have composed the clan piobaireachd work. On the other hand, he must have commanded a degree of respect among his clansmen as he was given the honour of burial in Iona, with an ornately carved stone which would rank him among the foremost of the Highland chieftains.

He was not the clan chief, being of illegitimate birth (he was born and brought up in the Treshnish Isles), but by right of force and strength of character he seems to have been accepted as a leader (this is known as tanist succession). He strengthened his position by accumulating considerable wealth, largely ill-gotten, which he bequeathed to his son, Hector, named in the title *Hector MacLean's Warning*. If Allan did compose the *MacLeans' March*, it would be earlier than 1551, when Allan died, in Tarbert Castle, Loch Fyne.

It might have been composed in the early years of the 1600s, when the MacLeans and the MacNeills joined forces in a raid on Islay. The MacLean chief, Lachlan Mor, had been killed in the battle of Traigh Gruinard, in 1598, and in reprisal his clansmen ravaged the MacDonald lands in Islay. This weakened the MacDonalds' hold on the island, and eventually led to its being taken over by the Campbells, during the 17th century. This suggestion, however, implies that the term 'March' means an invasive march by the MacLeans, but we would expect it to mean a piobaireachd work.

Sources

Alec Haddow, *The History and Structure of Ceol Mor*
J.P. MacLean, *History of the Clan MacLean*

The Brothers' Lament

As the story associated with this title involves the murder of two MacDonald brothers in Keppoch, perhaps it should be *The Brothers' Lament*. It seems to be tied up with the *Sister's Lament*, and, at least stylistically, with the *Park Piobaireachd*. Note that the *Brothers'* is here a lament *for* the brothers, while the *Sister's* is a lament *by* the sister: a neat illustration of the two uses of the genitive form in titles of piobaireachd works.

Both the *Brothers'* and the *Sister's Laments* are expressions of grief over the killing of the young MacDonalds of Keppoch in 1663, a deed which resounded through highland story and song.

Alasdair and his younger brother Ranald were the sons of Donald Glas MacDonald of Keppoch who had fought at Inverlochy on the side of Montrose. Donald sent his two boys to be fostered by MacDonald of Sleat, at Duntulm in Skye, and later they went over to the continent, to Rome and probably also to Paris, for additional education. When their father died in 1661, his brother, Alasdair Buidhe, acted as tutor (guardian) and was the interim chief for his nephew, who was still a minor.

Two years later, young Alasdair took over, and at once began to initiate reforms unpopular within the clan, especially affecting their system of obtaining wadsetts, a type of loan based on land-tenure, particularly open to corruption and fraud. He also expressed disapproval of the time-honoured custom of cattle-rustling. This had been part of the old clan system, which by the late 17th century was regarded by progressive clan leaders as hopelessly outdated. Some of the clan, who had benefited from the old ways, broke away, and at the house of the chief's uncle they plotted against young Alasdair.

In September 1663, both of the brothers were murdered at their home in Keppoch. Both were boys in their late teens, and they were set upon in their bedroom. All the attackers thrust their dirks into each corpse, so that they shared the guilt equally. The report of the Royal Commission, established by the Privy Council in 1665, said that the body of Alasdair had 'thirty-three great wounds', and Ranald twenty-eight.

Stuart McHardy has a different story: the young chief and his brother came home from their studies in Rome, and Alasdair took up his position as chief. A feast was held in the great hall of the house at Keppoch, and among the many clansmen attending was a father with his six sons, from Inverlair in Glen Douglas. Known as the Siol Dughaill, they were friends of the young chief's uncle, and they sat with the uncle's two sons at the feast, intent on mischief. The plan was to start a fight when everyone had taken plenty of drink, and to make sure that in the fracas, both Alasdair and Ranald were killed. It all worked out as planned, and when the two young men were found dead on the floor, the Siol Dughaill were foremost in expressing their grief and horror at this tragic accident, saying loudly that that was what happened when swords and drink were involved.

The sister was away at the time. On her return next morning she found her brothers' bodies, but no sign of the killers. One story says she drank their blood and died instantly, but another says she lived long enough to compose the *Brothers' Lament* before she died of grief. Yet another version is that she made not a piobaireachd but a poem, with some seventy-two lines giving a full description of what she had seen. This became a song, and possibly the *Brothers' Lament* is based on the tune to which it was sung.

The family bard, Iain Lom, vowed vengeance for this killing and courageously composed several powerful Gaelic poems which made public the facts. He waged what Alec Haddow called a 'one-man campaign, which finally led to the destruction of the assassins', who included the two sons of Alasdair Buidhe, uncle of the victims.

Iain Lom was the only one of the clansmen who sought revenge, which probably shows both how unpopular the young laird had been and how frightened they were of his uncle, the new chief. Iain's own house was pillaged and what was left of his belongings was scattered on the hill. Iain, however, was not deterred; he went round the powerful clan leaders of his time, asking for help – Glengarry, Seaforth, Macdonald of Sleat. This last, the boys' former foster-father, was eventually roused by Iain's eloquence to raise a force and obtained permission from the Privy Council to attack the murderers and their followers.

The main killer and seven of his men lost their lives, and Iain had their bodies buried, headless. He then took their heads to Invergarry; somewhere in the story the eight heads became seven. At a well beside Loch Oich, he washed them, and seems to have treated them in some way to prevent decay. The well is now called the Well of the Heads, a popular tourist attraction. Since the king had authorised the vengeance, the seven heads were then sent to Edinburgh to be exhibited on the gallows.

If the sister made the *Brothers' Lament*, who composed the *Sister's Lament*? The whole gruesome tale has been corrupted by so much story-telling and poetic embroidery that it is difficult to work out the historic truth in it. The *Daughter's Lament* is a further complication; it is the name given by the Campbell Canntaireachd to the work otherwise called the *Sister's Lament*. A completely different tune known now as the *Daughter's Lament* was always previously given the title *Lament for Clavers* (Bonnie Dundee) – see below.

Sources

Alec Haddow, *The History and Structure of Ceol Mor*
Rev. A. and Rev. A. MacDonald, *The Clan Donald*
Stuart MacDonald, *Back to Lochaber*
Stuart McHardy, *The Well of Heads*

Lord MacDonald's Lament

This is called *The late Lord McDonald's Lament* in the manuscript, and is attributed to Angus MacArthur, one of the compilers of the manuscript, with the date 1796.

Lord MacDonald was Alexander, 17th chief of the MacDonalds of Sleat, 9th baronet, who was created a peer in 1776; he became the 1st Lord MacDonald 'of Slate, Co. Antrim'. He died in 1795, a comparatively young man.

He was the younger brother of the brilliant Sir James, who died aged twenty-five in 1766, while in Rome. Alexander was educated at Eton and St Andrews, and was described in the *History of Skye* as 'a cultured man, widely read, and a genuine patron of learning'. He composed an ode of welcome, in Latin, for Dr Johnson, and was also an accomplished violinist. He composed two tunes still played by fiddlers and pipers, *Lord MacDonald's Reel* (four parts) and *Mrs MacKinnon of Corry* (Mrs MacKinnon was related to him, as she was a MacDonald of Sleat).

Dr Johnson mentioned in his Journal that Sir Alexander's piper played while they were dining, in his house at Armadale, Skye – and Boswell wrote: 'Sir Alexander's piper plays below stairs both at breakfast and dinner, which is the only circumstance of a chief to be found about him.' The piper would have been Charles MacArthur II, probably a nephew of the great Charles.

Dr Johnson was at his most outspoken in his dealings with Lord MacDonald. He told him squarely that his education had made him unfitted for his position as chief of the clan, and both Johnson and Boswell seem to have given their host a roasting on this subject. Boswell commented: 'He bore with so polite a good-nature our warm, and what some might call Gothick, expostulations on this subject that I should not forgive myself, were I to record all that Dr Johnson's ardour led him to say.'

He had, however, recorded a great deal more than was printed in the later editions of the Journal; he had to cut it down, after threats of both violence and legal action.

Boswell reported that Dr Johnson had said that if Sir Alexander had visited Skye in the autumn (instead of his customary early summer), it would have been too much for the people to tolerate – not only the bad weather but himself as well. Stories were also printed of Sir Alexander's meanness. He had been entertained by the Irish harper, O'Kane, but 'could not find it in his heart to give him any money', so instead gave him an ornate harp-key. Later finding out that this was a valuable object, he asked for it back, but O'Kane refused to return it. On being told that the gentleman's relations were angered by his giving away a family heirloom, Dr Johnson said 'He values a new guinea more than an old friend.'

When somebody observed that Sir Alexander was always frightened at sea, Dr Johnson said 'He is frightened at sea; and his tenants are frightened when he comes to land'. And when Sir Alexander told Boswell that he left Skye with the blessing of his people, Dr Johnson said acidly 'It is only the back of him that they bless.'

Once Sir Alexander came on a serjeant and twenty men working to repair the high road, and stopped to speak to them. On leaving he gave the serjeant sixpence for the men to buy a drink. When the serjeant asked who that was and was told it was Sir Alexander, he said 'If I had known who he was, I should have thrown it in his face.'

Boswell published these stories in the original edition of the Journal with Sir Alexander's name included, but had to omit it in later editions, simply calling him 'a Highland chief'. When he quoted the doctor as having called Sir Alexander 'a rapacious Highland chief who 'has no more the soul of a Chief than an attorney who has twenty houses in a street, and considers how much he can make by them', he named him, but was obliged to omit the name later.

Alexander Nicolson, in his *History of Skye*, explained the reasons for this antipathy. He wrote that:

[Lord MacDonald] was wholly devoid of sympathy either with the culture or the manner of life of his own people. In his dealings with them he stood purely in the role of landlord and he had no scruples about increasing their burdens when occasion presented itself. The demand for wool and the boom in kelp had furnished him with ample pretexts for raising rents and he took the fullest advantage of the situation. Great resentment, therefore, prevailed against him and several of his tacksmen actually united, pledging themselves to resist the payment of what they looked upon as unwarrantable impositions. Many were constrained to emigrate.

Even the clan historians were less than enthusiastic about Lord Mac-Donald, writing that 'his sympathies and tastes were, if not wholly English, at least entirely anti-Celtic'.

It is hardly surprising that Lord MacDonald was greatly angered by Dr Johnson's comments on his character and conduct, as reported and published by Boswell; he threatened Boswell with physical violence, giving rise to unkind caricatures and cartoons of them both, in the

London papers. His Lordship smarted under this humiliation, but had to live with it. The very fact that the disagreement caught the attention of the London press tells us that Dr Johnson was right – Lord MacDonald belonged to that world in the south, rather than to his island estate – but we might think the visitors were unmannerly to make their comments to their host, let alone to put their opinions before the public. It was a poor reward for a Latin ode, specially composed.

The newly created Lord MacDonald raised a regiment, the MacDonald Highlanders, which was sent to America in 1778; it was disbanded on its return in 1784. Alexander Nicolson implies that the regiment was raised as 'payment' for the MacDonald peerage, which seems likely enough. Ten years later, when French invasion threatened, he created a defence corps in Skye.

He helped to enrich his family by marrying a beautiful English heiress, Miss Elizabeth Diana Bosville of Gunthwaite in Yorkshire, who is commemorated in the piobaireachd work *Lady MacDonald's Lament* (see below). They had ten children.

Sources
Alexander Nicolson, *History of Skye*
James Boswell, *Journal of a Tour to the Hebrides*

The Daughter's Lament
Even though the Campbell Canntaireachd manuscript uses this title for the work elsewhere called the *Sister's Lament*, it is generally accepted that it is the name used nowadays for a different composition formerly known as *Clavers' Lament*, or *Lament for John Graham of Claverhouse*. This is not the work we call the *Lament for the Viscount of Dundee*, who was the same gentleman, but a different tune.

The Daughter's Lament is not given a name at all by MacArthur, and we take the title from Angus MacKay. His predecessors, Donald MacDonald and Peter Reid, both knew it as a lament for Graham of Claverhouse.

John Graham of Claverhouse (1648–1689), also known as 'Bonnie Dundee', was a relative of Montrose and one of the most hated and the most loved of Scottish leaders. He was a fanatical royalist who detested the Covenanters, and when sent to oppose them in south-west Scotland, treated them so brutally that he earned the by-name 'Bluidy Clavers' and the description 'the ever accursed damnable Bluidy Clavers, the devil incarnate'. On the other hand, as commander of his Highland army, he showed such understanding of the Highland character and such fine qualities of leadership that his men were devoted to him, and followers of the Stuart cause regarded him as a hero.

He attended St Andrews University before crossing to the continent to study military matters. In 1677 he was commissioned into the Duke of York's regiment of Horse Guards, newly raised in Scotland. He served in the struggle against the Covenanters, using the campaign as savage vengeance for the death of Montrose.

In 1679 he had mixed fortunes against the Covenanters. Later that year he went to London, where he enjoyed the patronage of the Duke of York. In 1683 Charles II made him a Privy Councillor, giving him £4,000.

Claverhouse became a Major General in 1686, and was Provost of Dundee two years later, the year that William of Orange came to England. James VII (II) gave him sole command of the army's cavalry, and summoning him to Salisbury, created him Viscount of Dundee.

Late in 1688, when James had been restored to the throne but William was a constant threat, the Privy Council wanted to negotiate a compromise, but Dundee led the opposition to this, hoping to fight on. The king refused, and Dundee's regiment was disbanded; he returned to Scotland with only fifty troopers. He tried unsuccessfully to rally support in Edinburgh. When in 1689 the Special Convention declared in favour of William and Mary, Dundee fled north, and was proclaimed a traitor; Major General Hugh MacKay of Scourie was sent to contain him.

Dundee moved rapidly through Inverness, Perth, Angus and Lochaber, where Cameron of Lochiel promised his support. He was amassing an army, and managed to cut MacKay off, isolating him in Inverness when government reinforcements arrived in Perth.

MacKay then seized Blair Castle, and Dundee waited at Killiecrankie, close by, in terrain which Lochiel had selected as being ideal for the Highland Charge. MacKay's army greatly outnumbered that of Dundee, and were much better fed and rested, but Dundee had the territorial advantage.

The government forces broke under the charge in the narrow confines of the pass, and all but two regiments fled. At this point Dundee on horseback led his men into the fray, raising his sword to wave his men on to victory; a musket ball caught him in the armpit, entering his body behind the armour. He fell at the moment of his triumph, and died soon after. He is buried in the church at Blair Atholl.

Dundee's armour was later taken to Blair Castle, and put on display. To make it appear more dramatic, the Duke of Atholl had a hole drilled in the breast-plate, which was supposed to be a bullet-hole – but the bullet had never penetrated the armour.

Dundee, like Donald Duaghal MacKay before him, was a soldier with remarkable powers of leadership. He was a Gaelic speaker, and it is said that when his Highland troops on the march were half-starved and exhausted he would not ride his horse, but put a fainting soldier on its back, and himself walked with the men, carrying the weapons of a weary supporter, singing Gaelic songs and telling stories in Gaelic to put heart into his troops – and of him, as of Donald Duaghal, it was said that he never sat down to eat until he was satisfied that all his men had food. These stories are probably told of all good leaders, but of Dundee (as he was later known) they are persistent. Drummond of Balhaldie, for example, said that Claverhouse was 'generous to every person but himself, and freely bestowed his own money in buying provisions to his army'. The Duke of York (later James VII) said 'Claverhouse is not the man to say things that are not'. There are stories all over the central Highlands of his kindness and generosity, and of his fondness for his horses; it is only in the south-west and among the more extreme Protestant factions that he is still hated.

Claverhouse swore he would ask nothing of his men that he would not do himself. He once said that no general should fight with an irregular army unless acquainted with every man he commanded, and he made a point of knowing their genealogies, the deeds of their ancestors and the verses of their bards. This is probably reflected in the construction of the *Lament for the Viscount of Dundee*, which is said to be made up of the tunes of Highland songs from two or more different areas.

He had a horror of drunkenness and of womanising: unusually for his time, he drank no wine and kept no mistresses. His household had family worship, in the episcopalian style, morning and evening, and he gave much time to private prayer.

Some time ago the *Antiques Roadshow* on television had a programme in Canada, and one of the objects brought for inspection by the experts was a painting on a wooden board, showing a man with long flowing black locks. It was quite crudely painted, and on the back it said: 'Graham of Claverhouse'. The English expert dismissed it as a poorly painted local portrait of some unknown local man, probably done by an itinerant pedlar in exchange for a meal at a farm. He was wrong, and the programme received letters from indignant Scots – enough to show that Clavers is still a hero, and that he is still recognisable.

John Graham was a good-looking man of great personal charm. He wore his hair long, in the Cavalier style, with his black curls brushing his shoulders. Most who favoured this style wore wigs, but contemporary sources tell us that Clavers wore his own hair. It certainly suited him.

In spite of his reputation as a hater of Covenanters, he fell in love with the daughter of one of their more fanatical leaders, and she married him in the face of her parents' objections. Lady Jean Cochrane loved her husband dearly, and when he was asked if she had been forced to marry him against her will, he laughed and said 'Ask the lady'. They had several children. Was one of them the Daughter named in the title, lamenting the death of her father?

Sources
M.E.M. Donaldson, *Scotland's Suppressed History*
Dictionary of National Biography
William (Benbecula) MacDonald

Next in the MS comes a *Nameless* composition not found elsewhere.

Cumha Mhicaoidh or The Chief Of MacKay's Lament
This is a different version from that of Angus MacKay, and is considered to be better – but Angus is the only one who names Donald Duaghal as the subject. Colin Campbell and Donald MacDonald both, like Angus MacArthur, named only 'the Chief of MacKay', while Donald MacDonald junior said it was for *Eon mhic Aoidh*, taken to be John (Iain), the son of Donald Duaghal who became 2nd Lord Reay.

The MacArthur version has Urlar, 1st Variation and Doubling of the Urlar. There are no other variations.

For the history of Donald Duaghal, see above.

Nameless – A Lament

The Bard's Lament
It is not known who this bard might have been, nor even if this was a lament for him or by him. The name is an apparent translation of *Cumha a' Chleirich*, which might mean *Lament for the Church Officer*. It seems that the positions of bard and church officer were sometimes combined, and there is doubt as to the meaning of the term *Cleireach*. Originally denoting a clerk, it came to mean a cleric or clergyman

(Catholic priest or Presbyterian minister), then a church officer, and by extension, anyone who could read and write. Most bards did not write down their work, but composed and stored it in their heads; anyone who did record it in writing would be worthy of comment, earning the by-name *Cleireach*.

The editors of the MacArthur manuscript point out that the brother of Donald Gorm Mor (who died in 1617) and father of Donald Gorm Og, 8th and 9th chiefs of Clan Donald in Skye, was Gilleasbuig Cleireach, Archibald the Clerk, and the lament might have been for him.

Cleireach, however, became quite a common designation as literacy spread among the upper classes. Another MacDonald called Gilleasbuig, son of Donald Gruamach, had that by-name, and Hector MacLean, laird of Coll (c.1490–c.1560) was known as *an Cleireach Beag*, the Little Clerk. He was noted for having composed a poem on Allan nan Sop (see *MacLeans' March,* above): he had been captured by Allan, and this poem was called the *Caismeachd Ailein nan Sop*. *Caismeachd* usually means 'warning, alarm', but here is simply a 'war-song'. Written around 1537, the poem has survived, preserved in a manuscript compiled by Dr Hector MacLean in 1738. It is of a type known as 'semi-bardic', and was (perforce) an extravagant praise of Allan. It turned out to be flattering enough to do the trick: Allan was pleased, and released his captive. The Little Clerk was also a composer of Latin verse. Clearly *cleireach* could mean a bard or an educated man, or both, and could be anybody.

Sources

Derick Thomson, *An Introduction to Gaelic Poetry*

Suarachan

The work known as the *Suarachan* is also called the *MacRaes' March,* and the title refers to a character who took part in the Battle of the Park, around 1490. The Park is a field on a hillside near Strathpeffer, in Easter Ross, overlooking the wide strath of the River Conon. The village of Contin, on the main road from Dingwall to the west, lies below the battlefield.

Some say the battlefield was lower down, to the immediate east of the village, but local tradition places it higher up the hill. The site is still known as 'The Park'; today it is planted with trees. 'Park' is an English spelling of the Gaelic *pairc,* which means an enclosed field, a piece of fenced land.

The battle was not a big affair but is considered important because it shifted the balance of power in the north from the MacDonalds of the Isles to the MacKenzies of Kintail.

Feelings between the two factions had been running high throughout the 1480s. Kenneth MacKenzie of Kintail had married a daughter of the Lord of the Isles, but after several insulting exchanges between the families, Kenneth repudiated his wife and returned her to the Mac-Donalds. Both sides then gathered their forces, and marched to Contin (where, according to MacKenzie tradition, the MacDonalds burned down Contin church, which was full of MacKenzies taking refuge – see the comments on the *Battle of Waternish*, above).

Among the MacKenzie supporters that day was a man called Duncan MacRae, an orphan brought up by the old MacKenzie chief, Alasdair Ionraic. Duncan was a very large, brave man, known always as the Suarachan 'Worthless One', a term used for someone who is beneath contempt. The name possibly referred to his past as a penniless orphan. The MacRaes were by tradition the bowmen of the MacKenzies, and it was natural for Alasdair Ionraic to take the boy into his household, as a dependant. Normally when a fostering was arranged, there was an exchange of goods or money, but Duncan had no family to supply these.

When the battle began, Duncan killed a man and sat on the corpse, as if he had done his share. When urged to fight on, he said 'Pay me like a man, and I will fight like a man'. The MacKenzie chief (Alasdair's son) said 'Kill your two, and you shall have the wages of two', so Duncan killed another and sat on him. MacKenzie cried 'Fight on, and you will not need to haggle with me over your day's pay', and Duncan stood up and killed sixteen more of the enemy. According to the story tellers, one of the sixteen was MacLean of Lochbuie, an experienced warrior who had come to support his MacDonald allies.

The MacKenzies won the day, and pursued the MacDonalds helter-skelter down the hill and into the Conon river, where many of them drowned. The folk downstream in Dingwall saw the water running red, and wondered whose blood it was, MacKenzie or MacDonald.

Embellishing Duncan's exploits, as was customary, the storytellers said that in the final moments of the battle, Kenneth MacKenzie was resting in a nearby house, and asked what had become of Duncan Suarachan. He was told that he had been last seen chasing four or five MacDonalds near Tor Achilty, to which one of the MacKenzies commented 'If there were only four or five of them, he should be all right.' Presently there was a noise at the door, and there stood Duncan, with one hand holding his axe over his shoulder, the other carrying a large bundle. As he came in, they saw what it was: the heads of five MacDonalds, strung together on a withy.

After this Duncan was no longer the Suarachan, at least not in his hearing. His new name was Big Duncan of the Axe, and he became well-off, the best-known of his generation of the MacRaes. Stuart McHardy tells other stories of him in later life, when he proved his bodily strength, and matched it with native cunning, although he was generally regarded as being a bit simple.

It is not known who made the March, nor who gave it the title the *MacRaes' March*.

Sources

Alec Haddow, *The History and Structure of Ceol Mor*
Alexander MacKenzie, *History of the MacKenzies*
Stuart McHardy, *The Well of Heads*

Sir James MacDonald's Lament

Composed by Charles MacArthur, this is one of several 18th-century piobaireachd compositions which have a Crunluath fosgailte but no Taorluath variations. This seems to have been an accepted form, and was the model for some of the 18th-century piobaireachd poems, based on the structure of contemporary musical works. It was only those with the fosgailte form of Crunluath that had no Taorluath variation. Joseph MacDonald called them 'Gatherings', and differentiated them from other piobaireachd works which he designated 'Marches'.

This was a lament for the young Sir James MacDonald of Sleat, who died in 1766, at the age of only twenty-five. He was the elder brother of Sir Alexander, who succeeded him, to become the first Lord MacDonald (see above). Sir James was only five when his father died. His mother, Lady Margaret, daughter of the Earl of Eglinton, ran his estates for him during his minority. He was brought up as a Gaelic speaker in Skye before being sent to Oxford, where he shone at all subjects, science, languages and philosophy – he was what was known as a polymath. He was also said to be good-looking, of high character, modest, generous and kind, and loved by all who knew him.

The only dissenting voice seems to have been that of Iain Dall Mac-Kay, the Blind Piper of Gairloch, who in his extreme old age visited the young Sir James, then no more than thirteen years old. It was probably in 1753 or 1754, when Iain was in his late nineties.

Iain had been accustomed for many years to visit Sir James' father and grandfather as an honoured guest, bard and piper, and he had always joined the family at dinner. On this occasion, however, Sir James, entertaining guests, made him eat downstairs with the servants. He then sent down a message asking Iain to play his pipes as he had formerly done, but to stay downstairs and play from there (was he perhaps trying to spare the old man the stairs, or did he dislike pipe music? Perhaps he was ashamed to admit to liking it, in front of English friends).

Iain sent back a stinging rebuke in poetic form. We do not have the original verse, but the gist has been preserved in Gaelic prose, and from it we may reconstruct the form as he probably made it. Alexander Nicolson gave us the prose: '*Abair ris mata, gur h-ann a b'abhaist dhomsa bhi toirt aoibhneis lem' cheol do chluais athar anns an talla so; agus nach 'eil mi nise nam' sheann aois a dol a chur a leithid de dhimeas air a' phiobmhoir 's gu'n teid mi 'ga seideadh suas 'na dheireadh-san*'.

Dr Alasdair MacLean translated this: 'Say to him then that I was in the habit of giving joy with my music to his father's ears in this hall, and that I, in my old age, am not now going so to demean my great pipe as to go and blow it up his rear.'

If we omit the introductory *abair ris mata (gur h-ann a)* 'then say to him that', the rest falls neatly into a bardic verse, with a nice internal rhyme scheme and binding by alliteration:

B'abhaist dhomsa toirt
aoibhneis le m'cheol
do chluais athar anns an talla;
chan 'eil mi nise nam' sheann aois
dol a chur a leithid de dhimeas
air a phiobmhoir 's teid 'ga seideadh
suas 'na dheireadh-sa.

This may be loosely translated as:

I played my music for his father
For the pleasure of his ears;
For the son I will not ask my pipe
To blow it up his airse.

This is not a full rendering, but the gist is there, and with a few simple rhymes and alliteration, too.

Sir James at thirteen would have been already an Oxford student, and was probably showing off to his southern friends. He was young, and we may forgive his (apparently) single lapse into arrogance.

A story was told of him in Rome, where he had gone later for the sake of his health. The Pope sent a cardinal to find out if this young man really was as brilliant as he was reputed to be. On his return the cardinal said he had questioned the young man on many different subjects, in seven different languages, and he had answered with fluency and easy familiarity in all of them; and when he left, Sir James gave an order to his servant in yet another language 'which I am sure nobody in the world understood but themselves'.

As an adolescent suffering indifferent health, he was involved in a hunting accident in which he was shot in the leg. In North Uist, local tradition remembers the name of a woman, Marion Cameron (ni' Dhomhnaill mhic Iain mhic Iomhair) who lived near the scene of the shooting, at Airigh na Gaoithe; she brought out blankets to wrap the injured youth before he was carried to the island of Vallay. The anger of his clansmen at this incident shows the affection in which he was held; they said that if Sir James died of his injury, they would kill Roderick MacLeod of Talisker, who had accidentally fired the shot – the trigger of his gun had caught in a sprig of heather. Sir James recovered in the house of his host, Ewen MacDonald of Vallay, who made a jokey poem, *Lament for the Leg*, which must also be a tribute to Sir James' sense of humour. The Campbell Canntaireachd manuscript has (volume 1, tune number 12) *Porst na Lurkin* 'Tune of the Shank', which is the same as *King James VI's Salute* (or *Lament*) – see above.

Sir James toured the continent with the great economist Adam Smith and a scholar called Topham Beauclerk, leaving a good impression on all who met him. On his return he took over the estate management from his mother, and appears to have been genuinely concerned for the welfare of his tenants. It was he who planned the building of Portree as a large village, in an attempt to improve the economy of Skye, and he founded the large school there, as a convenient centre for as many children as possible. He took a keen interest in Gaelic poetry and song, and spent hours with the clan bard, John MacCodrum.

But his health was failing, presumably from tuberculosis, and he returned to the Mediterranean in 1766, trying to prolong his life. He wrote some touchingly courageous letters to his mother when he knew he was dying, and the end came when he was in Rome, in the middle of July. His funeral was the largest Protestant ceremony ever held in Rome. Tributes poured in, from Adam Smith and David Hume, from poets and tenants, all regretting the passing of this remarkable young man. He was succeeded by his brother Alexander, a different person altogether and as much hated as James was loved.

Lady Margaret had an elegant marble monument made in Rome

and in 1768 it was placed in the Kilmore church, in Sleat. A long and magnificent epitaph was composed (in English) by Sir James' friend, Lord Lyttelton. It refers to his erudition, great talent for business, his propriety of behaviour, and his politeness of manner. Part of it goes:

> His eloquence was sweet, correct, flowing,
> His memory vast and exact,
> His judgement strong and acute,
> All which endowments, united
> With the most amiable temper,
> And every private virtue,
> Procure him, not only in his own country,
> But also from foreign nations,
> The highest marks of esteem.

A hard act to follow, and Sir Alexander made little effort to emulate his brother.

Sources

Alexander Nicolson, *History of Skye*
William Matheson, 'Notes on North Uist Families' *TGSI* LII

Lady MacDonald's Lament

This was composed in 1790 by Angus MacArthur, the compiler of the MacArthur–MacGregor manuscript, in memory of Lady MacDonald, wife of Lord MacDonald (who six years later was the subject of *Lord MacDonald's Lament* – see above).

Lady MacDonald was English, and, apart from Queen Anne, seems to be the only Englishwoman commemorated in a piobaireachd work, until the death of Princess Diana in more recent times. There are several women named in the titles – Isabel MacKay, Mary MacLeod, the Sister, the Daughter, Mrs MacLeod of Talisker, the Old Woman (of the Lullaby), Lady Margaret MacDonald, Lady D'Oyley, Lady Anapool, Mrs Smith, Mary and Morag (In Praise of), possibly Catherine (but she was probably a cow), Mabel Thomason and presumably My Dearest on Earth who was to give the kiss – and these were all Highland ladies, or of Highland descent, certainly Scottish.

Lady MacDonald was a Yorkshire heiress, Elizabeth Diana Bosville, daughter of Godfrey Bosville of Gunthwaite, said to be as beautiful as she was wealthy, the perfect match for the chief of the MacDonalds, who had been educated at Eton before going to St Andrews University. He met her in London, where they were both in high society, and although they had a home at Armadale in Skye, they seem to have lived elsewhere as much as possible, visiting Skye only in early summer. Certainly she did not rival her mother-in-law in the affections of the people of Skye, although she left her mark in Portree: Bosville Terrace and the Bosville Hotel are named after her, and through her the Christian name of Godfrey entered the family.

Beautiful she may have been – possession of vast wealth does do wonders for a lady's looks – but Boswell was less than gallant in describing her to her husband as 'neither having a maid nor being dressed better than one'. She was his hostess at the time, and we cannot be surprised that her husband 'was thrown into a passion' by Boswell's ill-mannered criticism.

They had a family of ten children, of whom the youngest, Archibald, is described as a 'posthumous child', but the lament for his mother is dated 1790, and his father died in 1795. Presumably 'posthumous' here means his mother died during the birth.

Another member of the Bosville family later married Henry, the 8th Baron Middleton, who is described in *Debrett's Peerage and Baronetage* as having his seat at Armadale, Skye. He bought the estate of Applecross in 1862, and his family held it for about fifty years. His piper was John MacBean, an Applecross man, taught by Alexander MacLennan in Inverness, of the renowned MacLennan piping family.

Sources

Alexander Nicolson, *History of Skye*
Debrett's Peerage and Baronetage
Notices of Pipers

MacKenzie of Gairloch's Lament

Angus MacKay wrote: 'The lamentations of the clan were perpetuated, by the family Piper, blind John MacKay, when death removed Sir Hector to a better world'. Angus was clearly confused, as Iain Dall MacKay, the Blind Piper of Gairloch who was piper to the MacKenzie lairds of Gairloch, died in 1754, and Sir Hector, the 11th Laird, died in 1826.

Peter Reid called it *Cumha Fhir Eachainn Ghearloch, Sir Hector Mackenzie of Gairloch's Lament,* in his collection dated in the year of Sir Hector's death; and when the work was played in the Edinburgh competitions in 1835, it was specifically said to be a lament for Sir Hector MacKenzie. So Angus MacKay must have been mistaken – but was it composed by another John MacKay? Two possibilities spring to mind: the Blind Piper's grandson, known as John Roy (Iain Ruadh) MacKay, and Angus' own father, John MacKay, Raasay.

John Roy had emigrated from Gairloch to Nova Scotia in 1805, and although it is said that Sir Hector valued his playing highly, he had put the family out of their holding of land in the Flowerdale glen, and had removed them to Slattadale, on Loch Maree. John Roy can only have taken this as a slight, since he was then further from the Laird's house if his services were required, which must have meant they were required less often. When he left for Canada on board the *Sidney Smith* in 1805, he was playing a work which he said was called a *Lament for the Death of Piping in Scotland,* which does not suggest strong support from his laird. He appears to have had little reason to remember Sir Hector with affection.

Another reason to doubt that John Roy made the lament is his son's *Reminiscences.* Known in Nova Scotia as Squire John, this younger John MacKay wrote a detailed account of his childhood and family life beside Loch Maree, and the life they had led since arriving in the New World. If John Roy had made the lament, which would have been the first piobaireachd work composed in America (as far as we know), surely the Squire would have made much of it. John Roy was not known as the composer of any works other than his lament for the death of piping in Scotland.

Yet another consideration is that the work already bore Sir Hector's name when it was written out in Peter Reid's collection of 1826.* Sir Hector died that year late in April (his son said on the 23rd, the clan history says the 27th). The news would then have had to reach Nova Scotia, John Roy would have had to take time to compose the lament, and it would have had to be brought over to Scotland. It must then have been made public in time for Peter Reid to include it before the end of the year. This would have meant it was written down, either by Peter Reid from someone else's playing (but whose?), or by someone who then gave it to Reid. This seems to be pushing things a little, in an age when transport across the Atlantic was still under sail and the voyage could take weeks – but it is possible. There is, however, no evidence that John Roy was a composer of piobaireachd.

---

* A complication here is that recent research claims to have shown that Peter Reid's manuscript is to be dated 1825, rather than 1826. As it names Sir Hector as the subject of the Lament, and Sir Hector died in April 1826, it is hard to accept this judgement.

The evidence seems weighted against John Roy: could the composer of the lament have been John MacKay, Raasay? He and his son Angus were living at Drummond Castle in 1826, and it seems unlikely that Angus, even in his later years of madness, would have confused his father with 'blind John MacKay' (Iain Dall), the family piper to the Gairloch MacKenzie clan. Angus was thirteen years old, and would have remembered if his father had made the lament – and there was no reason for John MacKay to have commemorated Sir Hector. Probably we may discount him as the composer.

So who might have made it? Sir Hector was suceeded by his son, Sir Francis, whose piper, we know, was John MacLauchlan, brother-in-law of Donald MacPhedran. In 1843, John competed at Edinburgh, described as 'piper to the late Sir Francis MacKenzie of Gairloch', who had died earlier that year. We do not know, however, how long John had been with Sir Francis. If he had been the Gairloch piper when Sir Francis succeeded his father in 1826, he might well have been asked by his laird to commemorate Sir Hector with a piobaireachd lament. John MacLauchlan was a composer of pipe music, but is not known to have made any piobaireachd. His collection of pipe music, published in 1854, contains only light music, and there is no reference to any piobaireachd work. He was, however, an excellent player of piobaireachd.

The lament is in a style of the 19th century, and has been described as 'plush and confident', perhaps not the first attempt of a composer of piobaireachd, though it is hard to be sure.

Sources

Angus MacKay, Manuscript
Peter Reid
J.H. Dixon, *Gairloch*
John MacKenzie, *Pigeonholes of Memory*
Alexander MacKenzie, *History of the MacKenzies*

Dungallon's Salute or Lament

MacArthur gives this no name, and the title *The Young Laird of Dungallon's Salute* is taken from Angus MacKay. Colin Campbell called it *Dungalan's Lament*, and in Gesto's Canntaireachd it is *Mac' Vic horomoid, alias McLeod Gesto's Lamentation*. We do not know why Gesto claimed it for his family.

Dungalan is the name of an estate in Sunart which took the designation of an ancient ruined fort, formerly the family stronghold, on a tiny island in Loch Sunart, off the south coast of Ardnamurchan. (There is another Dungalan in Colonsay, but it is not likely to be the one named in this title).

The estate belonged to a cadet branch of the Camerons of Lochiel. Allan Cameron, who had been an elderly supporter of Montrose in the mid-17th century, was the 16th of Lochiel. He had two sons and a daughter called Jean (who married Alasdair Dearg MacDonnell of Glengarry). Allan Cameron's second son, Donald, was given the lands of Glendessary, and Donald's son, John of Glendessary, was an uncle of Allan Cameron of Erracht, who raised the Cameron Highlanders.

John of Glendessary married twice, and his son Archibald, by his second wife, was given the tack (long lease) of the lands of Dungallon. He was the first of a short line of lairds of Dungallon. He married a distant cousin, the daughter of Sir Ewen Cameron of Lochiel. Archibald died in 1719, leaving two sons. The elder was his heir, John, a sickly youth who never enjoyed robust health. He was a young child when he inherited, and was in his twenties when he died in 1739, unmarried. His younger brother, Alexander Cameron, then became the third and last Laird of Dungallon.

Alexander's lands and possessions were attaindered by the Crown when he was captured some months after Culloden. He had been the Prince's standard-bearer, and was lucky to escape execution. In 1757 he was a Captain in the 1st Fraser Highlanders, and died two years later, leaving no children. What was left of his inheritance went to a cousin, Captain Allan Cameron of Glendessary – who was married to a sister of the first Mrs MacLeod of Talisker.

There were only the three Lairds of Dungallon, and the clue to which of the three is commemorated in the piobaireachd work is found in Angus MacKay's manuscript. He quoted the words of a Gaelic song, said to be sung to the Urlar of the salute:

Tha oighre og air fear Dhungalain,
Is fhaicainn fallain togail mail;
Tha oighre og air fear Dhungalain,
'S fhaicinn fallain 's fhaicinn slan.

The laird of Dungallon has a young heir,
May we see him in health round collecting the rent;
The laird of Dungallon has a young heir,
May we see him sound, may we see him in health.

Presumably this song was made before the death of the first laird, when John was very young. Its preoccupation with the boy's health suggests that he was delicate from infancy. It should be noted that neither

Archibald I of Dungallon nor Allan III was born as the expected laird, both inheriting or being granted the lands and title as an afterthought; only John was born to it, and he must have been the heir to whom the song refers.

Although Angus MacKay calls this a Salute, which would mean it was made during the laird's lifetime, that is, in the twenty or so years before 1739, Colin Campbell's title *Dungalan's Lament* might suggest it was made to commemorate the young laird's untimely death. Both of the piobaireachd works we have for subjects described as Young, this one and *Young George's Salute*, are for young men who failed to grow old. Both died in their twenties.

Sources

Alexander MacKenzie, *History of the Camerons*
John Stewart of Ardvorlich
Memoirs of Sir Ewen Cameron of Lochiel
Fionn (Henry Whyte)

Lady Margaret MacDonald's Salute

Lady Margaret Montgomery was the beautiful daughter of the Earl of Eglinton whose mother was a MacDonald of Sleat. She married, as his second wife, Sir Alexander MacDonald, 15th chief. He had previously been married to Ann Erskine, by whom he had a son, but mother and child both died of fever in Edinburgh when the marriage had lasted only a year.

Lady Margaret, with her double links to the MacDonalds in Skye, immersed herself in the life of the island and was dearly loved by the tenants. One of them told Dr Johnson that when she was out riding in the island the people ran to clear stones from her path, for fear of her horse stumbling. She was a staunch Jacobite, who must have been grieved by her husband's conduct during the '45. First of all he hung back, unwilling to commit his clan to the Prince's cause, and then he joined the Jacobites, before suddenly changing sides, bringing shame to his clansmen. Although he seems to have been a reasonably good and benevolent chief until then, he was remembered as a turncoat and a villain. When he died in 1746, a damning ditty made the rounds of Jacobite society:

> If Heaven be pleased when sinners cease to sin;
> If Hell be pleased when sinners enter in;
> If Earth be pleased to lose a truckling knave –
> Then all be pleased: MacDonald's in his grave.

He had the biggest funeral ever seen in Skye, at which the procession was two miles long; three men were killed in the fighting in the graveyard, and fifty were seriously wounded. This seems to have been regarded as the mark of a successful funeral.

Lady Margaret defended his reputation staunchly, and she herself did not swerve from her Jacobite beliefs. She is known for the part she played in helping Flora MacDonald with the escape of the Prince.

Lady Margaret had had Flora in her household, as one of a group of girls she was bringing up along with her own daughters. It was a form of fosterage in areas where well-born girls had difficulty finding an education, and it gave Lady Margaret's own children companionship. Flora knew her ladyship well.

When Flora was in South Uist and was asked to help the Prince escape to Skye (even though she belonged to a family who supported the Hanoverians), she accompanied him in the boat which landed them on the shore to the west of Monkstat in Trotternish, where the MacDonalds were living. [This gave rise in later times to the song known as 'Over the Sea to Skye', or 'Speed Bonny Boat'. Many think it refers to a short voyage from the mainland to Skye, but in fact the sail from South Uist to North Skye crosses the Minch and can be both long and hazardous.]

Flora left the Prince among the rocks on the shore, and made her way up to the house to find Lady Margaret, according to plan. To her consternation, she found a number of soldiers there, and Lady Margaret was dining with the officers. Leaving the table, she came out to speak to Flora and learned what was happening. She took Flora in to join the company, and the two of them kept up a calm front until the meal was over.

Then Lady Margaret found women's clothes for the Prince, and he was brought up from the shore. Flora had a pass to allow her and her servant to travel, and the story was that she was bringing an Irishwoman, a 'grand spinster', that is, a woman excellent at spinning, to the MacDonald household at Kingsburgh, a few miles down the coast.

Flora and the Prince, in his disguise as a servant woman, set off to walk to Kingsburgh, and she had difficulty persuading him not to stride along in manly fashion. Near Glenhinnisdale, they met John MacDonald, the father of Donald the Edinburgh pipe-maker, and he showed them a well where they could have a drink of water. Lady Margaret went back to her guests.

Later she helped more than one Jacobite fugitive, and both she and Flora became well-known as Jacobite heroines, their reputations off-setting the bad taste left by Sir Alexander.

Charles MacArthur composed Salutes to several noted Jacobites, especially those who had not fought in the campaign but had helped in the background.

After she was widowed and left with a family of young children to bring up, Lady Margaret acted as Tutor or Regent to her own son, Sir James, who had inherited at the age of five (see above, *Lament for Sir James MacDonald*). Alistair Campsie, with his innate dislike of the aristocracy, described her as 'both stupid and mendacious', but the evidence suggests she was intelligent, efficient and courageous.

Sources

Alexander Nicolson, *History of Skye*
Robert Forbes, *The Lyon in Mourning*
Alistair Campsie, *The MacCrimmon Legend*

The Laird of Arnaboll's Lament

This work has no name in the MacArthur manuscript. Angus MacKay called it *The Laird of Anapoole's Lament*, but elsewhere gave a note 'qy Arnbol', which shows he had preserved a memory of the original name of Arnabol. Gesto used the title *Lament for the Laird of Ainapole*, which suggests he knew it from a written source, this spelling being a copying error (the usual misreading of undotted minims). Arnabol is a farm on the west bank of Loch Hope, in north-west Sutherland.

Simon Fraser called this the *Lament for Giordano Bruno*, or *for Uncle Giordano*. Was this name a family tradition given to him by his mother, or did he get it from the Bruces? Or from Gesto? An alternative name was *In Praise of the Rainbow* – see above, the MacCrimmons and Simon Fraser. Fraser uses the name Anapoole in his notes, probably following Angus MacKay

This is one of two laments, one for the laird, the other for his lady. Although tradition had always maintained that Iain Dall MacKay, the Blind Piper of Gairloch, was the composer of both, this was doubted – until it was shown that the laird of Arnaboll, on the western shore of Loch Hope, was a second-cousin of Iain Dall, and the laird's wife, Marion, was a relative of Iain's patron, Robert Munro of Foulis.

The Laird was Donald MacKay of Skerray, a great-nephew of Donald Duaghal, 14th chief of MacKay. He was a lawyer who graduated from Edinburgh University in 1678, described in one source as 'a notary public in Skerray and then in Ribigill'. *The History of the Clan MacKay*, published in 1829, says that he 'studied the law and was a writer [lawyer] in 1686', but does not say where he practised, if anywhere. The *Book of MacKay*, in 1896, appears to have confused him with his father in some details, and describes him as the wadsetter of Kinnisid, still living in 1702, with no mention of Arnaboll. Kinnisid, now spelled Cunside, was a stretch of grazing land with a shieling, to the south of Ribigill, a large estate south of Tongue, on the far side of Loch Hope from Arnaboll.

Donald married the girl who had inherited the tack (long lease) of the farm of Arnaboll from her father. Her name was Marion, only surviving child of Donald Munro of Arnaboll. She was Donald MacKay's cousin, his mother being Margaret Munro of Eriboll. This family of Munros had bought Eriboll, part of the lands of Strathnaver, from the MacKay chief when he was in need of cash, in 1632. The Munros and MacKays had a long alliance lasting some three hundred years, and knew they could trust each other.

Donald and Marion had two sons, Hugh and John, neither of whom lived at Arnabol. The *Book of MacKay* says that Hugh inherited the wadsett of Kinnisid, and later was living in Caithness, but this section is a little confused, and may not be reliable. Hugh's younger brother, John MacKay, became a merchant in Inverness, and in 1717 he married Jean Barbour, daughter of John Barbour of Aldowry, and they had nine children, one of whom, Donald, born in 1730, went to live near Halkirk, in Caithness. Many descendants of the family emigrated to New Zealand.

In a corner of the old graveyard above the house at Arnaboll, there is a pair of horizontal gravestones lying side by side which may be those of Donald and Marion, but there is no inscription. The Laments seem to date from the first twenty years of the 1700s, although even this is not certain. When, in 1697, Iain Dall composed his Gaelic piobaireachd poem *Corrienessan's Lament*, the details of the description of his route through the Sutherland mountains make it clear that he was travelling from Arnaboll, and we assume that the laird his cousin, and/or the lady, were living there then, in early summer. Mention in the poem of details of scenery and natural features indicate that Iain Dall made the journey in summer, probably in June, and it is possible that the MacKays visited Arnaboll only in the summer-time, and did not live there all the year round.

This lament for Donald MacKay of Arnaboll has a quality of agonised grief in it which suggests that he and Iain were close friends as well as cousins. That for the lady is more conventional, but is unmistakably the work of Iain Dall, with phrases which remind us of Iain's later works, the *Unjust Incarceration* and the *Lament for Patrick Og*.

Sources

Angus A. MacKay, *The Book of MacKay*
Alexander MacKenzie, *The History of the Munros*

The MacDougalls' Gathering

Both Angus MacArthur and Angus MacKay give no name to this tune, but the title *MacDougalls' Gathering*, pencilled in on the MacKay manuscript by Dr Bannatyne, has been accepted, mainly because any name is better than none. It is not known if the work has any links with the MacDougall clan.

A work called *Latha Dhunabharti* (The Day, or Battle, of Dunaverty) is mentioned in the papers of the MacDougalls of Dunollie, and it was said to have been composed by Alasdair Mor MacDougall of Moleigh. The castle of Dunaverty, at the southern tip of Kintyre, was captured by General Leslie in 1647; MacDougall clansmen who had joined the Royalist forces were in the stronghold, besieged by government troops. When it was taken, the Royalist supporters were savagely massacred, many MacDougalls losing their lives. The *Lament for MacDonald of Sanda* commemorates the leader of the defeated force in the castle, also killed in the massacre, and some say this was the work known as *Latha Dunabharti*.

Alasdair Mor MacDougall is said to have been born around 1635, so it may be doubtful if he was the composer of *Latha Dunabharti*. The work is no longer known under that name, and it is possible that the piece we now call the *MacDougalls' Gathering* is a version of it. Alasdair's son Ranald Ban is said to have composed a work called *MacDougall's Salute*, and this too is no longer known. Were there three works, or one work with three names?

Sources

MacDougall papers
Jean MacDougall, *Highland Postbag*

You're Welcome, Ewen

The Piobaireachd Society Book 2 gives the Gaelic title as *'S e do Bhea-tha Eoghainn*, with no mention of the Camerons, but the English form *You're Welcome, Ewen Lochiel* identifies the work with the Camerons of Lochiel. The Piobaireachd Society editors also mention that they took the Crunluath variation from the Duncan Campbell manuscript, 'and [it] is as played by the Camerons'. They note that the tune appears in the MacArthur, Angus MacKay and Duncan Campbell manuscripts, and 'all three settings are practically identical'.

Other piobaireachd works associated with the Camerons include:

The Camerons' Gathering (CC II 78. It is nameless in John MacKay's MS. The alternative title *Come and I'll Give You Flesh* is the clan motto of the Camerons. Thomason gives the name *The Camerons Gathering* to the work called *Blar Vuster* in the CC MS);

Camerons' March (CC II 83 – which Angus MacKay called *The MacLeans March*);

Ewen of the Battles (Eoghan nan Cath) found in Angus MacKay, John MacKay and Duncan Campbell;

Sir Ewen Cameron of Lochiel's Salute: this is Angus MacKay's title, but Donald MacDonald, followed by Thomason, gave this the name *Away To Your Tribe, Ewen*;

Croan air Euan (CC II 60), apparently a form of Cronan air Euan 'Lullaby for Ewan', may also be a Cameron work, though this is doubtful.

It is not clear who was the Ewen in *You're Welcome, Ewen* nor whether we are justified in calling him Ewen Lochiel. Is he to be identified with the Ewen Lochiel named in the title *Sir Ewen Cameron of Lochiel's Salute*? Donald MacDonald's alternative, *Away To Your Tribe, Ewen* perhaps suggests that he is, but there were many chiefs of the Cameron clan who were called Ewen. The fame of Sir Ewen in the early 18th century probably led to many stories being transferred to him from lesser chiefs of that name.

The Piobaireachd Society Book 10 gives us a story about Sir Ewen Cameron of Lochiel (1629–1718). He was an ardent Royalist, and on one occasion the governor of Inverlochy sent a force of soldiers to ravage Lochiel's estate, killing and plundering, opposed by the Cameron clansmen. In the fierce battle Lochiel was fighting hand to hand with an English officer, and managed to kill him by sinking his teeth into the officer's throat, 'the sweetest bite I ever tasted'.

Years later Lochiel went into a barber's shop in London, to have his beard trimmed. As the razor passed over his throat, the barber asked if he was from the north. 'I am', said Lochiel, 'Do you know anyone from the north?' 'No, sir, nor do I wish to, they are savages there. One of them tore the throat out of my father with his teeth, and I only wish I had the fellow's throat as near me as I have yours just now'. Lochiel said nothing, but he never entered a barber's shop again.

Donald MacDonald wrote that Lochiel was frequently away from

Lochaber on lengthy foreign travels, and one of his clansmen sent him a letter begging him to come home, using a Gaelic phrase translated as 'Away to your tribe, Ewen'. A corresponding phrase on his return might have been 'You're Welcome, Ewen Lochiel'.

Sources

Piobaireachd Society Books 10, 12
Campbell Canntaireachd Manuscript
Donald MacDonald, Manuscript
Alexander MacKenzie, *History of the Camerons*

An Eavesdropping

Overheard in the Ladies' Cloakroom at Bruar restaurant, near Blair Atholl, the day after the Glenfiddich Championship:

> 1st Lady: 'Did you hear those people at the next table, talking about the Viscount? One of them said he was much too slow and shouldn't have won – what could they be talking about?'
>
> 2nd Lady: 'I don't know – must be a race-horse, I suppose. Or a greyhound'.

Other Piobaireachd Works with Skye MacDonald Associations

The Desperate Battle (Cuillin)
The Earl of Ross's March (see above)
The MacDonalds' Salute (see above)
The Red Hand in the MacDonalds' Arms

Notes on the above tunes

The Desperate Battle (Cuillin): Donald MacDonald associated this title with the Keppoch MacDonalds, and told a tale which is clearly related to the story behind the *Brothers' Lament* – the tale of the Seven Heads. Donald gave the work the title 'Angus MacDonald's Attack on the MacDugalls', and it concerns the MacDonalds of Clanranald, rather than those of Skye.

There seems to be no connection here with the *Desperate Battle (Cuillin)*. This title is taken from Angus MacKay, and associates the tune with a battle fought in 1601 between the Skye MacDonalds and the MacLeods. Alec Haddow tells the story:

> Donald Gorm Mor had married a daughter of MacLeod of Dunvegan,

but rejected her after a year. This led to a renewal of hostilities between the two clans, culminating in a battle near Glen Brittle, in which the MacDonalds routed the MacLeods. The next two years saw such bitter hostility that finally the King intervened and the other Highland chiefs brokered a truce [see *MacLeods' Salute*, above].

Fionn (Henry Whyte) in his notes to the tunes published by David Glen, had these comments on Tune 7, *The Desperate Battle*:

> It seems that, in the absence of Rory Mor Macleod in Argyll, seeking the aid and advice of the Earl of Argyll against the MacDonalds, Donald Gorm Mor assembled his men and made an invasion into Macleod's lands, determined to force on a battle. Alexander Macleod of Minginish, the brother of Rory Mor, collected all the fighting men of the Siol Tormoid [MacLeods of Skye and Harris] and some of the Siol Torquil from the Lews, and encamped by Beinn a'Chiulinn [sic]. Next day they and the MacDonald engaged in battle, which continued all day, both contending for the victory with incredible obstinacy. The leader of the Macleods, together with Neil MacAlister Roy and thirty of the leading men of Macleod of Dunvegan, were wounded and taken prisoners, and the MacDonalds gained the day.
>
> Shortly threreafter the Privy Council requested the Chiefs to disband their forces and quit Skye. We find an entry, dated Stirling, 22 August 1601, in which both parties are ordered to dissolve their forces and to observe the King's peace.

The Red Hand in the MacDonalds' Arms: the legend behind this title is told in Book 10 of the Piobaireachd Society's edition. It is taken from a Gaelic poem or song, about the origins of the MacDonalds' claim to land in Skye: *Cumha Lamh Dhearg Chlann Domhnuill*, 'Lament for the Red Hand of Clan Donald'. This poem tells that the great MacDonald leader, Somerled (died 1164), had three ambitious sons, Dugald, Ranald and Duncan, all of whom wanted the lands of Sleat, in southern Skye. It was agreed that they would race in three boats across the Sound of Sleat, and the first to put his hand on the shores of Sleat should have it.

Dugald was soon left far behind, and Duncan was in trouble when the plug came out of his boat, which began to sink. He stopped the hole with his thumb, and began to draw ahead. Ranald, seeing he was about to be beaten as they neared land, put his hand on the gunwhale of his boat and lopped it off with a single blow of his sword. He then threw the severed hand ashore, ahead of his brother's landing. So Ranald won Sleat for himself.

Recent work on the DNA of the major clans has confirmed that the Skye MacDonalds were indeed descended from Somerled.

The composer's name is not known, nor the date of the composition of the music. The Gaelic poem dates from the 17th century, looking back to the 12th. This may suggest that the piobaireachd could be from the same time as the poem, or a little later.

The English form of the title, *The Red Hand in the MacDonalds' Arms,* does not reflect the Gaelic *Lamh Dhearg Chlann Domhnuill,* but is reminiscent of lines in a poem by Iain Dall MacKay, his *Dan Comhfhurtachd, Ode of Consolation* (1734), addressed to Sir Alexander MacDonald on receiving news of the death of the chief's young wife. Referring to the grandeur of Sir Alexander's position as chief, Iain mentions the magnificent coat of arms on the clan's silken flags:

> *Croinn-iubhair le brataichean sroil,*
> *Loingeas air chorsa's ro-siuil*

> *Long a's leoghan a's lamh-dearg*
> *Ga'n cuit suas an ainm an Righ.*

> Your masts with their silken banners,
> Your ships along the coast with full sails,

> War-ship and lion and red hand (the clan symbols)
> Being raised up in the King's name.

The armorial bearings of the different septs of the MacDonalds do not all show the Red Hand. In the 15th century, it appeared on the crest of the MacDonalds of the Isles – the clan chiefs – and that of the MacDonalds of Keppoch, of Antrim and of Tynekill, in Ireland; it was not on the arms of the MacDonalds of Glengarry, Stirling or Ulster, nor of the MacAlisters.

The Red Hand has been associated with the MacDonalds of Sleat through the centuries, up to the present day, together with the war-ship and the lion, as Iain Dall remarked.

Non-piobaireachd Works with MacDonald Associations

The Ardvasar Blacksmith R 4
Armadale Castle, by E.J. MacPherson S 2

Sources

Piping Times
Simon Fraser, *Piobaireachd*
Thomas Pearston
Willie M. MacDonald

Donald MacDonald, Manuscript
Angus A. MacKay, *The Book of MacKay*
Alec Haddow, *The History and Structure of Ceol Mor*
Fionn (Henry Whyte)
Piobaireachd Society Book 10
Iain Dall MacKay

The MacArthurs at Hunglader

The history of the MacArthur pipers in Skye is given in the edition of the MacArthur–MacGregor Manuscript published in 2001. The outlines are well known: in Skye the first known MacArthur piper to the MacDonald chief was Angus, who may have come from Proaig, in Islay. His three known sons were Charles, known as Charles I, living in the 18th century, Niel (died 1762) and John Ban (died 1779 or before). In the next generation we have the sons of Charles I, Donald (died around 1780) and Alexander (went to America c.1801); the son of Niel was a second John (known as 'the Professor', died Edinburgh 1790) and the son of John Ban was a second Angus (died 1820 after dictating the manuscript).

A MacArthur piper to Lady MacDonald in Skye later went to Lord Eglinton in Ayrshire: he was known as Charles II, and is generally thought to belong to the family at Hunglader, though the connection is not clear. Some say he was the son of the second Angus, who with John MacGregor compiled the manuscript of 1820.

Another MacArthur piper was Archibald, on the island of Ulva; he was piper to MacDonald of Staffa. He may have been descended from a brother of the first Angus in Skye, both thought to have left Proaig in the 1690s. Archibald is said to have died in 1834, but the 1841 Census shows him living in Ulva with his wife Janet. He probably died in the mid-1840s.

Charles I MacArthur travelled with his MacDonald chief, to St Andrews and Edinburgh, leaving his sons to carry on the family's teaching tradition in Skye. They had been given land at Hunglader, in Kilmuir, Trotternish, in North Skye, holding it at half-rent by virtue of being the chief's pipers. Donald remained at home, and it is said that the MacCrimmons sent pupils to him, to learn the MacArthurs' 'particular graces'. In the Seafield Papers there is an interesting record of one of his pupils, John Cumming, sent to Skye by the Grant chief in Strathspey in the 1770s.

In or soon after 1780, it is thought, Donald drowned while ferrying cattle from Uist to Skye, and work which he had commissioned, to carve a gravestone for his father Charles, came to a halt.

There are several possible explanations for the apparent breaking off in the middle of the inscription on Charles MacArthur's gravestone at Kilmuir. The inscription, in capital letters, says:

HERE LIE
THE REMAINS OF
CHARLES MAC
KARTER WHOSE
FAME AS AN HON
EST MAN AND
REMARKABLE PIP
ER WILL SURVIVE
THIS GENERATION
FOR HIS MANNERS
WERE EASY & RE
GULAR AS HIS
MUSIC AND THE
THE MELODY OF
HIS FINGERS WILL

There is plenty of space beneath this inscription, which appears to be incomplete. There are at least four possible explanations:

(a) The stone was commissioned by Charles' son Donald MacArthur, in 1780, when his father died. Before the work was completed, however, Donald was drowned, and the mason, fearing he would not now be paid, stopped working on the inscription.

(b) Work ceased when the mason realised he had made a bad error – he repeated the word THE inadvertently, putting it once at the end of a line and then again at the start of the next; did he stop, thinking he would not be paid, or did he intend starting afresh?

(c) The inscription, though flawed, is in fact complete, in the idiom of 18th-century English: Frans Buisman suggested that the final sentence ending with 'his fingers will' is using 'will' as a noun, so that the meaning is: 'His manners were as easy and as regular as his music and [as easy and regular as] the will of his fingers', i.e. he had command of his fingers. This might be regarded as a little strained.

(d) In Trotternish there is a story, reputed to have been an account given by the mason's grandson. According to this, the mason's

name was JAMES MUNRO, and he was a stone mason brought in
by the MacDonald chief to build bridges which are still in use
in Skye. James Munro, known as the Fochad Bard (it seems to
mean a satirist, someone who made satiric verse) was a piper
as well as a mason and a bard; he had a croft by the shore at
Camus Mor, near Bornaskitaig, not far from the Bruce croft
where Calum Piobaire is said by local tradition to have been born.
When Lord MacDonald's piper Charles MacArthur died, it was
His Lordship who commisioned the carving of the gravestone.
He made an agreement with James, and supplied him with the
required wording of the inscription. A price was agreed. And the
arrangement was one often used at that time: after half the work
was done, half the price would be paid, the rest to follow on
completion. James carved half of the wording, but no money was
forthcoming. After a long wait, he went up to Duntulm to see the
factor, who was at the castle, attending a ball held there by Lord
MacDonald for a 'crowd of bigwigs'. James went to the door, and
spoke to one of the servants, saying he had come for the money he
had been promised. Next thing he knew, he had been sent away
with a flea in his ear, and told he could whistle for his money, so
incensed was His Lordship at having his festivities interrupted. So
James refused to complete the work, and it remained half done. It
has to be said that the MacDonalds had left Duntulm some fifty
years before Charles MacArthur died, and in the 1770s Thomas
Penant had said Duntulm was already a ruin, but James may have
gone to their new residence at Monkstat. This story, of course,
ignores the error made in carving the inscription.

[I am indebted to Seumas Archie MacDonald of Hunglader, for this
story.]

In 1972 the Skye Piping Society had a commemorative cairn built
beside the ruins of Duntulm Castle, in Trotternish. The occasion was
the MacDonald Clan Gathering during Skye Week in 1972, and the
piper at the unveiling was P/M Donald MacArthur. It was a day of
beautiful warm sunshine, and Jonathan MacDonald had laid on a great
open-air spread of traditional food – oatcakes, scones, pancakes and
local cheeses and preserves – and after the ceremony, Colonel Jock and
some of his friends retired to the Duntulm Hotel for a long informal
ceilidh which Jock remembered with great pleasure in later years. The
inscription on the cairn reads:

This Cairn
is to commemorate the MACARTHURS
Hereditary Pipers to
The MACDONALDS of the Isles
During the 18th century
Their School of Piping stood at nearby Peingown
'Thig Crioch air an t-saoghal
Ach Mairidh Gaol is Ceol'
(The World will end
But Love and Music endureth)

Purists point out that the MacArthurs were pipers to the MacDonalds of Sleat, who were not the MacDonalds of the Isles, strictly speaking, but presumably the term is used loosely to mean the MacDonalds who were an island clan.

For further detail of the MacArthurs, see the 2001 edition of the MacArthur–MacGregor manuscript.

Sources

Edition of MacArthur Manuscript
Seumas Archie MacDonald
Jonathan MacDonald

Pipers to the Skye MacDonald Chiefs

Lord Archibald Campbell, in his *Records of Argyll*, told a story of how piping came into Skye from Islay. The MacDonald chief of the Isles lived in the palace on Finlaggan Isle, in Islay, and he had a big ploughman. One day this ploughman was feeling hungry when along came an old grey-haired man who offered him food. When he had eaten it, he was given a chanter to play, and at once stood up and began to play it. This was the Black Chanter, and when the Chief heard him playing he gave him a three-drone pipe, and he became the MacDonald chief's piper as long as he lived. The Black Chanter remained with the family in Islay. One of the MacDonalds then went to Skye, and from Skye he took a man called MacCrimmon, and sent him over to Islay, to learn from the Big Ploughman. MacCrimmon began courting the Big Ploughman's daughter, who gave him the Black Chanter on loan – but MacCrimmon took it and left her, and returned with it to Skye.

We might wonder why Lord Archibald weakened his story by specifying a three-drone pipe in pre-MacCrimmon times. It also conflicts with the story of the Silver Chanter (see above).

The *History of Skye* tells us that the MacDonalds 'maintained a piper in each of their three baronies, namely, Sleat, Trotternish and North Uist' – the first two in Skye, the last in the Outer Isles.

In their book *The Clan Donald* (vol III, 124), the two Revs A. Mac-Donald said that in the middle of the 17th century, the MacDonald chiefs had a bard and piper whose name was MAC BHEATRAIS or Mac Beathaig. He was mentioned in John MacCodrum's poem, *Di-moladh Piob Dhomhnuill Bhain (Dispraise of the Pipe of Donald Ban)*, which included a verse:

Bha i treis aig Mac Bheatrais
A sheinneadh na dan,
Nuair theirig a chlarsach
'S a dh'fhailing a pris.

('Mac Bheatrais had a spell of reciting poetry, when his harp would not work and its price failed.')

This, however, refers to his profession as a bard. He was, like Iain Dall MacKay, a piper as well as a poet.

After Mac Bheatrais came a family of bards called MacRuari, but they were not pipers. Alexander Nicolson, in his *History of Skye*, named MALCOLM MACINTYRE as the MacDonald piper in 1723, maintained by the clan chief in his barony of Sleat, in the south of Skye. He 'like all his colleagues, was given a portion of land free in virtue of his office'. We assume that this Malcolm MacIntyre was the one listed in a Rent Roll in 1733, then holding land at Tarskavaig Mor, a small settlement a few miles to the west of Armadale. The Roll describes him as 'Piper to the Laird'. Was he perhaps one of the MacIntyre pipers from South Uist?

When the MacArthurs, as pipers to the MacDonald chief, were given the tenancy of Hunglader, around 1700, they claimed that they had previously been pipers to the Lords of the Isles, in Islay. This would tie in with the traditional association of MacArthur pipers with Proaig, on the east coast of Islay. The authors of *The Clan Donald* were in no doubt that the Proaig MacArthurs were connected to the MacDonalds and not brought to Islay by the Campbells, as has been claimed.

The Rent Roll of 1733 has the MacArthur piping family at Hunglader in Trotternish, a holding valued at 84 merks Silver Duty, 'in virtue of their office'. In 1745. the MacDonald piper in North Uist was IAIN BAN MACARTHUR, brother of the great Charles, and his salary was £33 6s 8d, which was probably equal to his rent. It was Iain's son ANGUS who became the last of the hereditary MacArthur pipers to the

MacDonald chief; he died in London in 1800, and after that there were no MacArthurs at Hunglader.

Jeannie Campbell has drawn attention to a receipt among the Clan Donald papers, dated 1748. On one side of the paper are the words 'Acco' Sir James McDonald to Adam Barclay £3–3 1748', and on the other '19 September 1748. Acco'. The Hon Sir James McDonald to Adam Barclay. To a sett of Hyland pipes of Cocawood mounted with ivory £3=3 Attests Marg MacDonald.'

This is followed by 'Edin 3 Nov 1748 then received full payment of the above acco' from Mr John McKenzie and discharges the same and all preceeding this date by Adam Barclay'. John MacKenzie was the agent for the MacDonald estates in Skye.

Jeannie points out that in 1748 Sir James was only seven years old, and his mother, Margaret MacDonald (named in the title *Lady Margaret MacDonald's Salute*) was acting for him. The pipe made by Adam Barclay was presumably for the family piper, Charles MacArthur. Adam Barclay had his business as a wood-turner and pipe-maker in Edinburgh (see Jeannie Campbell 2011). Later in that century, both the MacDonald and the Grant chiefs were ordering pipes from Hugh Robertson in Edinburgh, who in 1767 charged £3 for a set of pipes mounted with ivory, sold to Sir Alexander MacDonald, Bart.

Norman Anderson was said to be the name of the father of Mary, Simon Fraser's mother. She was born in 1827. The only Norman Anderson recorded in Scotland at that time lived in the tiny settlement of Tarskavaig, on the west side of Sleat, close to the house at Tarskavaig Mor, the home of the MacDonald chiefs' pipers. Mary claimed that her father had a deep knowledge of piobaireachd and its history, and it is thought that he might have learned this from contact with Charles MacArthur, nephew of the great Charles, before he (Charles II) left Skye to become piper first to Murray of Abercairney, and then to Lord Eglinton.

The pipers to the MacDonald chiefs based at Armadale, in Sleat, in the south of Skye later included ALEXANDER ROSS, born at Altnabreac, Achilty, Easter Ross, in 1845, brother of DUNCAN ROSS who was piper to the Duke of Argyll. In 1881, Alexander was at Kilberry Castle in Argyll as butler and piper to Campbell of Kilberry, but moved to Skye and the service of Lord MacDonald in the 1880s. He lived to be an old man, and for many years was a judge of the piping at the Skye Games, well into his eighties. It was his proud boast that he never wore trousers in his whole life, preferring the kilt.

When he was living in Argyll in 1880, he and his brother were asked by John F. Campbell, the eminent folk-lorist, to assist him in deciphering the canntaireachd published by Gesto (1828), which at that time was regarded as being virtually unintelligible. The book had piobaireachd works written not in staff notation but in canntaireachd vocables, and to Campbell's surprise, both of the Ross brothers were able to read them and play the tunes off the page. A pianist had been brought in to play the tunes on the piano and then write them down in staff notation. Campbell later wrote a booklet called *Canntaireachd*, which proved unsatisfactory, adding nothing to our knowledge of the system, but giving us valuable information about the Ross brothers and about John MacKay, Raasay.

Alexander died in 1930 at Allangrange, in the Black Isle, attended by his great-nephew RODERICK ROSS, to whom he bequeathed his pipes. Roderick lived in Brora, Sutherland, for many years.

Another piper to Lord MacDonald was a remarkable man, DONALD ARCHIE MACDONALD, who belonged to Sleat in Skye although he spent many years as a Customs Officer in Kyle of Lochalsh. He was piper to Lord MacDonald, and to the Kyle branch of An Comunn Gaidhealach. Described in the *Oban Times* as 'a handsome, genial Highlander whom everybody wished to meet', he had spent his life since early youth in uniform – in the Royal Navy, the Glasgow Police and, finally, the Customs and Excise.

He was born in the family croft at Saasaig, between the road and the shore, to the south of Teangue, a township on the east side of Sleat. He was the son of Donald and Margaret MacDonald. His father was a joiner, and Donald Archie worked on the croft before, in 1913, he followed his brother Allan into the Glasgow Police. He was not long in Glasgow before war broke out and he went into the Navy, where he began to develop his wrestling skills.

After the war he returned to the police, and as one of those 'huge Highland polis' who were vital to the Glasgow force, he helped to smash the power of the criminal street gangs, and told many stories of those exciting days. And when in the police, he continued to work on his skills as an athlete. He became the Scottish and British champion at catch-as-catch-can (free-style) wrestling, and represented Britain in the Olympic Games at Antwerp in 1920, and again in Paris in 1924, when he won the Bronze Medal at heavyweight level. He was the only British wrestler to win a medal. He was also the Scottish Police heavyweight boxing champion in 1928.

After twenty-six years service as a policeman, he retired to the Customs and Excise in Kyle, where he was much in demand as a popular entertainer at ceilidh evenings, as a singer, story-teller and piper. He composed several tunes, including *The Kyle Ceilidh* and in 1956, a march to commemorate the Queen's visit to Kyleakin.

After competing in heavy events at various Games, where he was the anchorman in Sleat's tug-of-war team, he became a judge of the athletic events at the Games, and even in old age, his great size and strength were a by-word. His neighbour recalled him, after his retirement to Sleat, carrying his clinker-built boat on his back, up the steep hill from the shore to his croft – a heavy, wooden vessel.

He retired from the Customs in 1960, to his croft at Saasaig, near Teangue, in Sleat, after a rousing ceilidh in his honour, run by the Kyle members of An Comunn.

After his death, the next occupant of the house found his two Olympic certificates, and presented them to the Clan Donald Museum in Armadale.

Sources

Alexander Nicolson, *History of Skye*
Rev. A. and Rev. A. MacDonald, *The Clan Donald*
Jeannie Campbell, *Highland Bagpipe Makers*
Seumas Archie MacDonald
Lord Archibald Campbell, *Records of Argyll*
Notices of Pipers
Emily MacDonald
Oban Times
Roger Hutchinson, article in *West Highland Free Press*
Duncan MacPherson

Other MacDonald Pipers

Donald MacDonald, Glenhinnisdale (c.1767–1840)

(Glen)Hinnisdale used to be pronounced 'Heeng-is-dal' and may possibly be derived from Norse *Things-dal,* 'Glen of the Assembly'. Pipers know it as the birthplace of DONALD MACDONALD, who later became a pipemaker in Edinburgh and published a collection of piobaireachd in 1820, one of the earliest collections of printed pipe music known, and fore-runner to the collections of Angus MacArthur and Peter Reid, later in the 1820s, and of Angus MacKay in 1838.

At the head of Glen Hinnisdale, or at least at the end of the present-day road up the glen, the Isle of Skye Piping Society has erected a cairn with the inscription:

> To the memory of
> DONALD MACDONALD
> Born on this croft about 1750.
> He was a pupil of the MacArthurs
> hereditary pipers to Clan Donald.
> In 1822 he published a book of 23
> piobaireachds – the first to commit
> Scotland's classical bagpipe music to
> print and preserve for posterity a
> heritage of music which conveys
> the history of the Highlands.

Every year, the day after the Donald MacDonald Quaich competition at Armadale, a piper comes to play at the cairn one of the works preserved by Donald.

Donald was not the first to commit piobaireachd music to print, as the work of both Joseph MacDonald and his elder brother Patrick, who came from Durness, Sutherland, appeared in print before that of Donald. His, however, was probably the earliest printed full collection in staff notation.

In an article in the *Celtic Magazine* in 1887, the Rev. Alexander MacGregor described a meeting he had had fifty years earlier with Donald MacDonald and his father, John. He met them at their house in the Lawnmarket, Edinburgh, where Donald had his workshop.

Sir John Sinclair, from Caithness, married to a daughter of Lord MacDonald, had long been a patron of Donald, since the days when

Donald served in his regiment, the Argyll and Caithness Fencibles, in the early 1800s. It was Sir John who established him in Edinburgh as piper and pipemaker to the Highland Society of London. Donald was taught by Angus MacArthur, in Edinburgh.

On the occasion of MacGregor's visit, Donald played him 'a fine piobaireachd, *The Gathering of the Clans*'. Donald elsewhere gave this the alternative title of *The End of the Little Bridge,* but some say it was another name for the *Lament for the Children.* The Gaelic word *cloinne* means both 'children' and 'clans'.

Donald was described as 'a small man, extremely corpulent' at eighty-two years of age. Surprisingly, in 1837 he was playing in the critical presence of his father, John, then over 100 years old. Jeannie Campbell, however, has pointed out that Donald's death crtificate gave his age as seventy-three in 1840, so he must have been a mere seventy when he met MacGregor.

John had known many historical characters in Skye, including, as a boy, the Prince, Flora MacDonald and MacDonald of Kingsburgh. When the Prince, disguised as a servant-woman, was being taken to Kingsburgh, on his way from Uist to Raasay, John had shown the party a well near the Hinnisdale River where they could stop for a drink.

Some thirty years later, in Skye, John had seen a stranger wearing an unusual broad-brimmed hat, and asked the minister, Dr Donald MacQueen, who it was. He was told (in Gaelic) that it was the great Englishman, Dr Johnson, who had made the English language, a reference to the famous dictionary – to which John replied *'ma ta, a'Mhinisteir, bha gle bheag aige ri dheanamh'* ('Well, indeed, minister, he had precious little to do'). John described Dr Johnson as 'a lusty, stout man, somewhat like my son, Donald there, but probably stouter'.

In 1801, Donald won 3rd prize at Edinburgh, as 'piper to the Caithness Fencibles'. In 1807 he entered as 'P/M Argyllshire Militia', but did not improve his position. In 1811, he came second, and finally in 1817, as 'late P/M, Argyll Militia' he won 1st prize at Edinburgh. He had competed also in 1806, '08 and '09, simply styled 'Pipemaker'.

He published his collection of twenty-three piobaireachd works in 1822 – it is said that he had completed it as early as 1806, but publication had been delayed. The manuscript is now in the National Library of Scotland, catalogued as NLS MS 1680.

Donald was living in Campbeltown at some point after leaving the army and before he went to Edinburgh. His daughter Margaret seems to have remained there; in 1816 she married James MacCallum, a collateral ancestor of the piping MacCallums of Campbeltown. Their daughter Mary was born there the following year. It is not certain what happened to this family, but the widowed Margaret was probably in Edinburgh ten years later, living with her sister in impoverished circumstances.

Today, in his memory, the annual piobaireachd competition for the Donald MacDonald Quaich is held at Armadale Castle. Four pipers are invited to compete in front of a single judge and a small audience, largely composed, it has to be said, of bemused American tourists who thought they were going to hear jigs and hornpipes. The piobaireachd settings are those of Donald MacDonald's manuscript, but the style of playing is mainly modern.

Sources

Celtic Magazine V
Rev. Alexander MacGregor
Keith Sanger, *Piping Times* 49/6
Jeannie Campbell, *Highland Bagpipe Makers*
Old Parish Register for Campbeltown

William MacDonald

WILLIAM MACDONALD was the piper who played for Thomas Pennant when he visited Kingsburgh in 1769. William was said to be a proficient performer who had studied under the MacCrimmons.

Alexander MacDonald

ALEXANDER MACDONALD, from Skye, was a competitor at the Edinburgh competitions in the early 1800s. 'A melodious player' (NoP), he competed in 1807–09, being placed 3rd in 1808. In 1807 he was described as 'piper to the Skye Volunteers'.

Somerled MacDonald

SOMERLED MACDONALD, of Inverness, was a son of Lachlan MacDonald, Skeabost, Skye, and uncle of Major Kenneth Cameron. Born in 1868, he was a great-grandson of Niel MacLeod of Gesto (see above). Dr Keith N. MacDonald was his uncle. A prominent amateur piper, Somerled won several prizes at the competitions of the Scottish Pipers' Society, between 1888 and 1923. He was a judge at the Northern Meeting, Oban and elsewhere, for many years.

In 1910, he wrote to the *Oban Times:*

> At Fort William one of the judges could neither play the pipes nor had
> he any knowledge of competitions or pipe music whatsoever. To my
> amazement this judge asked me, while the piper was still tuning up
> his pipes if he had begun to play his tune! It used to be a rule in com-
> petitions that the piper should not be allowed to tune his pipes on the
> platform. It has since struck me that perhaps this rule was made in
> order to enable judges to guess with tolerable accuracy when the piper
> actually did commence.

Somerled allied himself with Seton Gordon in dissociating himself
from the early publications of piobaireachd in staff notation as put out
by the Piobaireachd Society; he supported the suggestion that the society should scrap them, and that John MacDonald, Inverness, should
be appointed editor of the replacement settings. This scheme came
to nothing, however, when John MacDonald made it clear he would
decline the honour if it were offered to him. All his life, Somerled
adhered to the 'old' style of playing, and did his best to stem the tide of
standardised modernisation.

In a letter to the *Oban Times*, in April 1910, he said that he was
serving on the Music Committee of the Piobaireachd Society, but 'my
word was not taken on any single point, nor was any advice taken from
any professional player'. Somerled then had the proposed settings of
the Society checked by three leading professionals, and sent the results
to Archibald Campbell of Kilberry – who threw them in the bin, as
'absolute rubbish'.

In his capacity of judge Somerled was embroiled in the infamous
decision at Oban in 1928 when two eminent players, G.S. MacLennan
and John MacDonald of the Glasgow Police (Seonaidh Roidean), were
penalised for so-called 'false fingering' when they played a G gracenote birl in their marches. Somerled was quick to disassociate himself
from the decision, saying he had been over-ruled by his two fellow
judges, one of whom was Sheriff Grant of Rothiemurchus.

D.R. MacLennan told the story:

> Seonaidh Roidean and G.S. played, one after the other, the same set, it
> was *Abercairney Highlanders, Athol Cummers* and *Pretty Marion,* and
> I was standing listening with Willie Taylor and a few others in the lovely
> sunshine, and it was a toss-up to us whether Seonaidh Roidean would
> beat G.S. or not. They were easily first and second.
>
>   When the competition was over, the judges conferred for quite a
> while, and then Somerled MacDonald came over to where we were

standing, and he said 'I'm having nothing to do with the decision here. It's scandalous. They say that George MacLennan is making false notes, and if George MacLennan is making false notes, then God help the rest of us'.

The prize went to Corporal Thomson of the Cameron Highlanders, 'and no one who played the G gracenote birl got into the prize list whatsoever. Willie Ross was playing, Bob Reid and a few more – I don't think old John MacDonald played that day.' The competition was the Former Winners March, Strathspey and Reel.

D.R. pointed out that there was nothing new about the G gracenote birl, it had been played since at least 1880, but 'judges at Oban and Inverness were going round telling pipers that they would never get a prize so long as they played it in their marches'.

> The next thing that happened was pipers running around saying 'My God, don't play a G gracenote birl anywhere'. It got around, I can assure you, like wildfire, with the consequence that it spoiled piping for years and years, up to the present time. Not only did pipers drop the G gracenote on the birl in the march, they cut it out in strathspey and reel playing, where it is absolutely vital, to my mind, anyway. I heard a very prominent piper playing *Blair Drummond* once, no G gracenote in it anywhere, and it was simply lamentable.

To this controversy, Tommy Pearston added his own comment:

> There once was a piper called Cyril
> Who always grace-noted the birl,
> He said 'I'll take some beating
> At the Northern Meeting',
> But he tied for twelfth place with a girl.

Somerled MacDonald, who clearly agreed with D.R., took part in the heated correspondence in the *Oban Times*, basing his argument on the words of Joseph MacDonald's *Treatise*.

Frank Richardson wrote that Somerled, when judging at a Games, was

> fascinated by the cyclists who hurtled round the track whilst we were trying to concentrate on the piping. He always hoped to see a good crash, and if he saw a possible one building up he would leave his seat at the judges' table and peep round the side of the hut. Admittedly he only did this when some very poor player (and we heard many in those days) was grinding his way through a tune which we had easily damned as 'Below Standard'. Any remonstrances were met by some such remarks as 'I know this fellow – he's hopeless' . . .

But Somerled overstepped the unforgiveable limit one day when a 'hardy annual' competitor was laboriously pursuing his annual pilgrimage in search of the Holy Grail – the Gold Medal. Somerled related in a loud voice how at Nairn Games a famous film star had seized him and another Highland veteran by their arms and swung them round to face a press photographer. In case we missed the point he left the shelter and demonstrated what had happened, turning his back on the luckless competitor.

Frank Richardson recalled how, while they were judging at Crieff Games in 1933, 'a troop of the Royal Scots Greys in full-dress uniform solemnly trotted up and stationed themselves between the platform and the judges. With a roar like an enraged Highland bull, old Somerled charged and routed them, his fine white hair and whiskers streaming behind him with the speed of his advance, his *cromag* waving wildly'.

Somerled was a well known artist of his time, specializing in portraits. He lived for many years in Inverness, and died there in 1948.

Sources

Piping Times
D.R. MacLennan
Frank Richardson, *Piobaireachd*

The MacDonalds of Viewfield

The MacDonald family who lived at Viewfield House on the outskirts of Portree took an active part in the piping life of Skye, and Colonel JOCK MACDONALD, himself a good amateur player, became a respected judge at some of the Games in the west.

Harry MacDonald

Colonel Jock's father, Harry MacDonald, and his uncle, Alexander MacDonald, were founder members of the Skye Gathering, inaugurated in 1877, and they were both on the original Committee of ten 'elevated persons' drawn from the Skye gentry. Harry was the proprietor of the Treaslan estate, to the west of Bernisdale, in Skye.

Harry was the second son of Harry MacDonald of Treaslan, and inherited the Treaslan estate from his elder brother, Colonel Alexander MacDonald, who was childless. Harry junior had been a planter in India, and on his return to Skye he made his home at Viewfield, on the outskirts of Portree, rather than in the ancestral home at Treaslan. He set about enlarging Viewfield, and let Treaslan fall into ruin; local people were surprised, as Treaslan and its lands of several thousand acres belonged to the family, but they held Viewfield on a long tack from Lord MacDonald.

Colonel Jock's mother was Flora MacKinnon, sixth child of John MacKinnon, born 1811, 4th of Kyle (near Kyleakin) and his wife Isabella MacLeod of Orbost. Isabella's father William was 2nd of Orbost, son of Captain Norman MacLeod of Bernisdale, and he married his first cousin. Jointly they inherited the estate of Orbost from their aunt, Isabella MacLeod, and she was the grand-daughter of the Old Trojan of Bernera, so that there was a family connection to the MacLeods of Bernera, descended from Sir Rory Mor MacLeod, the MacLeod chief at Dunvegan.

John and Isabella MacKinnon lived at Kyle House and ran the Kyle farm of about 1,000 acres. John, like his grandson Harry after him, was a vast man, weighing some twenty stone, but an excellent dancer, and very musical. He loved sailing, and kept his own brig anchored in the Kyle below his house. He was over-fond of whisky, and his face was so ruddy that he was known as 'The Kyle Lighthouse' as people living on the mainland opposite Kyle swore they could see his face glowing when he sat in his garden.

He and his wife had six children, and also brought up the two sons of his brother who had died in India.

A large glossy booklet was produced in 1998, giving the history of the Games, and from it Harry MacDonald junior emerges as a great local character. It is evident that, like his son Jock, he was above all an enthusiast, a man who flung himself wholeheartedly into any enterprise which interested him, and a man who got things done.

It is largely due to his hard work and inspiration that the Skye Games have become an institution, and through his persistence the Skye Gathering Hall was built in 1879. It was intended to accommodate the social side of the Games and of the community, but is now used every year for the piobaireachd competition, when the pipers compete for the Dunvegan Medal and the Clasp.

Harry MacDonald had spent his working life in the tea plantations of India, 'but he had always retained the exile's love of the song, dance and language of his homeland. A huge man who had a bath especially made to accommodate his great bulk, Harry MacDonald and the Skye Games became synonymous' (Roger Hutchison, in the Skye Games booklet).

When the Centenary Games were held, Harry's son, Colonel Jock, said how happy his father would have been to think that his innovation, the Games, had lasted for 100 years.

Colonel Jock MacDonald

Colonel Jock had joined the Games Committee in 1920, and was to become as closely linked with them – 'and as greatly loved a local figure' – as his father had been. His comments on the Centenary gave his views on the piping of the 1970s. 'The pipers are very good now, especially the younger ones. There are probably more good pipers around than there were in 1877, and I have only one complaint. There is less individual style around now; no longer can you tell who is playing as soon as you hear them. Something of the Highland lilt has been lost, and I think the reason is that almost none of the pipers today can dance. Then they could all dance, and they all had the rhythm.'

John MacKinnon MacDonald, later known to all as 'Colonel Jock', was born in 1890, at Viewfield, the son of Harry MacDonald. Jock had his early education at the school in Portree, and it would be interesting to know who taught him to play. He was a Gaelic speaker from boyhood.

His sisters, Meg, Joanna and Flora, took a great interest in piping, and when their brother was away living in Assam in the 1930s, they remained at Viewfield. They formed a group of musicians known as the Viewfield Players, who played at dances and balls in Skye. They excelled themselves at a ball at Dunvegan Castle in 1933, when the Duke and Duchess of York (soon to become the King and Queen) were visiting the island, and Seton Gordon waltzed with the Duchess.

One of the sisters was behind an excellent scheme to bring top pipers to Portree each year, to teach local youngsters. Each boy paid half-a-crown (2/6d old money), but if the family could not find the money, the lessons were free. Under this scheme, players such as Willie Ross, 'Wee Donald' MacLean and Willie 'Gruids' MacDonald spent time in Portree, and among their distinguished pupils were Peter MacFarquhar, Finlay MacRae and Peter Bain. Finlay said that Willie Ross began with a class of fourteen, but eliminated half as no-hopers after the first lesson. Willie Gruids made a strathspey, *Miss MacDonald of Viewfield*, as a tribute to the lady who had organized the scheme. The finances received assistance from the Piobaireachd Society (see also below).

For his secondary schooling, the young Jock MacDonald was sent to Fettes College, near Edinburgh, Scotland's leading Public School. There he became an excellent rugby player, and in 1911 he played for Scotland against Wales. In this match, however, he suffered a severe knee injury which ended his rugby career. He was unable to play for his university. He continued his piping at Fettes, a school with a good piping tradition.

He went on to Brasenose College, Oxford, and then embarked on a career as a tea planter in Assam, India, but on the outbreak of war in 1914, he joined up, entering the Inns of Court Regiment, which was sent to France. He was wounded that same year, but on his recovery was commissioned into the Queen's Own Cameron Highlanders, and then seconded to the Persian Rifles, as a Captain. He recalled a mission on which he was sent to capture the Shah, with his family and retinue, as they were German sympathizers. They were all duly taken, but Jock had to intervene personally to prevent his Persian troops from murdering the lot of them, there and then.

He used to tell another tale of his adventures in the Middle East. He had to have a serious abdominal operation, and was in hospital, still on the danger list, when he decided to discharge himself, saying he was more likely to survive somewhere else than if he remained where he was. As he was leaving, feeling grim, an orderly presented him with his death certificate, already completed, and insisted on marking it 'Cancelled'.

Jock seems to have had a war quite different from anyone else's, and in 1917 he was sent on a training mission to St Petersburg, in good time to witness the start of the Russian revolution. During his stay he was awarded the Order of St Stanislav, but forty years later could not recall what it was given for; he thought it might have been for a record consumption of vodka.

After the war he served on the North-West Frontier of India, and was awarded a medal.

Between the wars, he was, as his father had been, a tea-planter in India, living in Assam. In 1935 he met and married his wife, Evelyn Logan, who was an auxiliary nurse. She was a daughter of Judge Logan of Restalrig, and in 1978 she was awarded the MBE for services to the Red Cross and in the community. She has often, but needlessly, been called 'long-suffering', but was a character in her own right and well able to take her husband's eccentricities in her stride, in her forthright, kindly way. His sisters kept Viewfield going while he was away.

In 1941, Jock re-joined the army as a 2nd Lieutenant in the Royal Engineers, and served in India, Iraq, and Iran, eventually becoming a Lt-Col in command of a Pioneer Group in Burma. He was awarded the OBE for this work.

On his return to Skye in 1946, he and his cousin Maj. Gen. Harry MacDonald of Redcliffe, late of Probyn's Horse, 'played a considerable part in local affairs in Skye'. Unusually for one of his background, Jock was a fluent Gaelic speaker, an enthusiastic attender at the Mods, local and national, and a keen piper. He regularly attended the Piobaireachd

Society Conferences, which he enlivened with his wit, anecdotes and friendliness.

There was no 'side' to Colonel Jock, and he was friendly with everyone, regardless of status. I recall an occasion when my husband and I were in Portree for the Games, a few months after attending the Piobaireachd Society Conference, at which we had briefly met Colonel Jock, but only as two very minor figures in a crowd. As we were walking across the Square in Portree, we were passed by an ancient tractor and trailer. It stopped abruptly, and the driver, in a ragged old kilt, jumped down and hurried back to greet us, shook our hands, said how pleased he was to see us again, and hoped we would enjoy the piping. After a little friendly chat, he hopped back onto his tractor and roared away through the town, leaving us feeling surprised and gratified by his unaffected kindness. His attitude was all the more pleasing for being in contrast to the stand-offishness of many Piobaireachd Society members at that time.

The *Piping Times* described him as 'a witty and entertaining companion, a lover of good piping and fine whiskies and all that is best in Highland life'. His lack of pomposity and his insouciant attitude to protocol was often a surprise to more particular colleagues, especially the military purists. One of his foremost characteristics was his enthusiasm for any ploy in which he was engaged.

David Murray gave us an affectionate portrait of him in Oban: Colonel Jock had persuaded him to join in the march of the pipers and stewards from the centre of Oban out to the Games Field for the Argyllshire Gathering. Lt. Col. Murray 'duly reported outside the Royal Bank next morning, to be greeted by Jock Viewfield wearing his everyday kilt (in which he used to gut salmon), three pullovers, his old jacket and his home-knitted bonnet and hose. The state of his shoes is best left undescribed. He had clearly recently visited a byre. In one hand he held a gnarled ash plant, and in the other a young collie on a rope. He explained that he was getting the collie used to the pipes'. He must have been a sore trial to the Admiral (Roddy MacDonald), who was a stickler for correct form, but to Jock mere appearance mattered not a jot. He cared nothing for what others would think, and sensible practicality was his criterion.

In 1947, Jock and Evelyn returned to Viewfield, and it was necessary to find some form of income. They turned their large house into an hotel, doing most of the work of running it themselves. Raymond Eagle said 'The hotel gave early American visitors a true Highland experience . . . Jock had a great sense of fun, and the guests were sometimes greeted by the Colonel himself, along with his tame owl, who sat so still that many thought the bird was stuffed, until it winked. Jock would play his pipes and entertain them with his anecdotes'.

Jock once had an American couple staying at the hotel, and offered them a dram of his best single malt whisky. They declined, but when pressed, the husband said he would have a taste of it. His wife insisted it be just a splash on the bottom of the glass, then to be filled up with water. Jock asked 'Would you perhaps like a piece of soap and a clean towel with it?' This sounds more ill-mannered than was Jock's normal habit: he must have been sorely tried.

Food was still rationed, and the MacDonalds became more and more self-sufficient, growing their own vegetables and raising livestock, including pigs. 'Jock made a very sensible arrangement with other Portree hotels to collect their left-over food to use as swill. For this purpose he bought the tractor and trailer. News filtered back from one hotel that an American guest had complained that the only man she saw in Skye wearing a kilt was driving a 'garbage truck' – it was Colonel Jock collecting his pig swill.

In Portree it was known that if Colonel Jock signalled he was turning left, he was just as likely to turn right, and people allowed for that. Once, when down in Perth and driving along the main street, he went through a series of traffic lights at red. The police caught up with him, and asked if he was aware of what he had done. 'Red lights?' said Jock, all innocence. 'We don't have any of those in Skye.'

Colonel Jock often used to share a piping session at Viewfield with Seton Gordon. Jock did not share Seton's interest in nature or walking the hills; he was, however, equally enthusiastic about Skye and its history, and supported Jonathan MacDonald's creation of the Duntulm Croft Museum. He even converted a room at Viewfield into a bothy interior, to show his guests what life was like in the old days.

He had brought back from Burma a large ivory carving of an elephant's foot, and one day it disappeared. Colonel Jock heard later that the culprit was William Stewart of Ensay, and that he had had it made into an ivory chanter. This he eventually presented to Colonel Jock – rather to Jock's regret, as he said he had no use for an ivory chanter, and had been rather fond of the elephant's foot. Any Colonel other than Jock would have been apoplectic with rage at the fellow's cheek, but that was not Jock's way; he accepted the chanter with a smile, and said nothing.

He became legendary, both as Convener of the Skye Games and for his many eccentricities, but he never fell into the trap of showing them off, as if to say 'I'm unusual, look at me being a character'. His was genuine eccentricity, and he was oblivious to the effect his oddities had on others. His enthusiasms remained undiminished, and when the Admiral succeeded him as Convener, he commented that Jock's was a hard act to follow, as not everyone has the stamina, or the inclination, for listening to Jigs and Hornpipes until two o'clock in the morning.

Jock and Evelyn had one son, John Harry Logan MacDonald, who after Wellington College and Sandhurst became a career officer in the Queen's Own Cameron Highlanders, later the Queen's Own Highlanders. He developed cancer and died, leaving three children. One son, Allan, was a Captain in the Queen's Own Highlanders, the other, Hugh, returned to Skye to run the hotel at Viewfield.

Jock used to judge the piping at Glenfinnan, often on the bench with Angus MacPherson and Seton Gordon. On one occasion it was calculated that their combined ages added up to 271 years. They sat all day out in the open without shelter, and after a soaking in the morning would sit in wet clothes all afternoon, a tribute to the properties of Harris tweed. A competitor (probably not on the prize list) made the comment that all three were too old, two were too deaf and one of those was biassed as well. Jock, the youngest at a mere eighty-four, was the exception, regarded as a fair and honest judge whose criticisms were helpful and constructive. He could be outspoken, however: he once said that Lord Dunmore, who often judged at the Northern Meeting and at Oban, between 1883 and 1906, had not been a good piper, indeed, he didn't know one end of a chanter from the other, and sometimes used to blow into the wrong end.

The MacDonalds started a piping competition for local youngsters, held in the hospitality of their hotel at the end of the tourist season, usually in early November. The young MacFadyen boys, especially John and Iain, benefited from these. After Jock's death, a trust was formed so that it continued as the Colonel Jock MacDonald Memorial Piping Festival.

Colonel Jock died at Viewfield in 1980, aged ninety years, and piping lost one of its nicest characters. Always full of humour, he had none of the childishness shown by many Public School boys who have never really grown up. Jock's was the wit of a mature adult, full of knowledge, wisdom and anecdote, kindliness and, above all, enthusiasm.

In 1976 he had attended the funeral of Dame Flora MacLeod, and was helped down the slope from the graveyard by a young fellow, to whom he said 'I suppose it's not really worth my while going home at all, I might as well stay here' – but he still had another four years to go.

In his memory, as well as by the re-naming of the piping festival at Viewfield, he was honoured when the Clasp competition, held on the Tuesday evening of Skye Week and open to any holders of the Dunvegan Medal, was named the Colonel Jock MacDonald Memorial Clasp. A worthy memorial. In 1984, Brian Donaldson of the Scots Guards won the Dunvegan Medal during the day, and went on to win the Clasp in the evening.

Works made for Colonel Jock and his family include:

Colonel Jock, Viewfield, by Dugald C. MacLeod 2/4 M 4
Faghail Viewfield, by Dugald C. MacLeod 6/8 SM 1
A Farewell to the Tilley Lamp, by Dugald C. MacLeod
Lament for Captain J.H.L. MacDonald, QOH, by Dugald
    C. MacLeod P 8
Miss MacDonald of Viewfield, by William MacDonald S 2
Mrs Evelyn MacDonald, Viewfield, by Dr J.A.C. Fisher 2/4 M 4

Sources
Piping Times
Donnie MacKinnon
Colonel Jock MacDonald

The Admiral

Vice Admiral SIR RODERICK MACDONALD, KBE (1921–2001), known as 'The Admiral', came of a Skye family, and made his home there after he retired, to settle at Ollach, near Portree. Although he reached high rank in the Royal Navy, he had served at sea in destroyers in the Atlantic during the Second World War, and was far from being a desk-bound sailor.

Like Colonel Jock, he had been a pupil at Fettes College, where he was taught his piping by Pipe Major James Sutherland. In 1936, James composed a 6/8 March, *Roddy MacDonald, Fettes College*, which was published in John M. MacKenzie's collection.

The Admiral's obituary in the *Piping Times* (March 2001), written by David Murray, says Roddy 'had no illusions about his own ability as a piper', but he continued playing throughout his service in the navy, and this must have given him some understanding of pipers' problems, unusual in a high-ranking officer. He was, however, both a stickler for correct form and a good organizer, and in November 2000 wrote to the *Piping Times* complaining that two competitors at Skye had 'rolled up to collect their awards wearing jeans'. He added 'Had I not been unavoidably detained elsewhere I would have loosed off a broadside on the spot. Only once before, when the same clanger was dropped by one well-known piper on the circuit, I generously attributed his disreputable appearance to an excess of modesty (ho, ho!) about his performance on the day'.

Clearly he could be pompous, but in person the Admiral was surprisingly unstuffy, and was always approachable and friendly. He was a large man, full of humour and enjoyment of life.

He became a member of the Clan Donald Trust, and set himself to promote Donald MacDonald's reputation, being a leading light in the establishment of the Donald MacDonald Quaich competition, held every June in Armadale, South Skye.

The Admiral became President of the Isle of Skye Piping Society, at the time when they had a cairn erected at the head of Glen Hinnisdale, to commemorate Donald MacDonald. An annual ceremony is held there, the day after the Quaich competition, with a piper playing one of the piobaireachd works preserved in staff notation by Donald.

Roddy MacDonald was a painter whose work was exhibited in Edinburgh and Naples. Pipers will remember his portraits of Colonel Jock, and of Duncan MacGillivray, both of which cleverly capture the essence of his subject.

Succeeding Colonel Jock as Convener of the Skye Games, he managed to transform enjoyable chaos into something closer to naval organization, to the great benefit of the pipers, especially those who had come great distances – as David Murray put it, 'he brought in several overdue innovations which made the games somewhat less of a marathon endurance test for pipers and judges alike'. It was said that one reason why he was elected Chieftain of the Skye Gathering was that he was the only member of the Committee who could be trusted to hand over the sponsor's product to winners without a wee taste to determine quality. His large and genial presence at the Skye competitions is missed.

Sources
Piping Times
Skye Games Booklet

John MacDonald

JOHN MACDONALD, the Ardvasar Blacksmith (Seonaidh a' Ghobha, or a'Ghabhar) lived not far from Sabhal Mor Ostaig, which is now the Gaelic college in the south of Skye. John ran 'an embryo piping school' at Ardvasar, and among his pupils was Evan MacRae, who became the first instructor at the Sabhal Mor piping courses (see the *Piping Times,* August 1996).

John was taught by Alexander Ross, who for many years in the late 19th century was piper to Lord MacDonald and lived at Armadale (see above).

There is confusion about a piobaireachd composition, the *Cave of Gold,* which appears the collection published by Dr G.F. Ross. Some attribute this work to the Ardvasar blacksmith, others say it was made by another Skye blacksmith, Archibald MacDonald, while Simon Fraser gave Donald Mor MacCrimmon as the composer. But are these the same tune?

George D. MacDonald

The Pipe Major of the Millhall Pipe Band, Stirling, in the 1920s, was GEORGE D. MACDONALD. Although born in Dunoon, he was of a Skye family, and was a pupil of John MacDougall Gillies. George took the band to many honours, making it one of the leading pipe bands of his generation.

Dr Allan MacDonald

Dr ALLAN MACDONALD, the GP in Uig for many years, taught SEADAN (JOHN) MACKENZIE, who as a youth began to show more enthusiasm for girls than for music. For a spell he did not turn up for lessons, and when the latest affair fell through and he returned to the fold, Dr Allan greeted him with two tunes, *The Rejected Suitor* and *The Stool of Repentance.*

Dr Allan, known as An Dotair Mor, or The Allan, was a large man in every sense. He always wore a kilt and stout brogues, and was prepared to wade through bog and heather to reach his patients. On one occasion, recalled by Seumas MacNeill, he had invited Seumas and several of the Skye summer school pupils to dinner, and had just asked Seumas to play a piobaireachd before the meal when the telephone rang. The son of the manager of the Skeabost Hotel had got a fish hook embedded in his hand, and the doctor was needed. Dr Allan said he would come, but then turned to Seumas and said 'We'll go as soon as you have finished your piobaireachd'. Seumas said that he would wait until they came back, but Dr Allan insisted ('he was the senior man and more determined'), so Seumas rattled through *The Company's Lament* in record time, that being the shortest piobaireachd he knew. And then they set out.

The doctor was inclined to drink too much, and his wife tried to restrict his alcohol intake. One day Seumas was at his house when Allan came in, complaining that his feet were wet, so he poured himself and Seumas a generous dram. In came his wife from the kitchen, saw the drams and asked what the occasion was. 'Oh, I got my feet wet, I needed a dram.' She returned to the kitchen, and when she came back, they were into the second dram. Dr Allan explained that he had got both feet wet. When she found them with yet another, she said 'Grown a third foot, have you?'

Before he went to Uig, Dr Allan was the GP at Carbost, near the Talisker distillery. The manager of the distillery was a friend of his, a man who did not drink whisky but was fond of a sup of beer. The doctor and he had an arrangement: Dr Allan would buy a crate of twelve screw-top bottles of beer and deliver it to the manager's office; when he had drunk the beer, the manager would have the bottles filled up with whisky, the tops screwed on, before returning the crate to the doctor. Eventually, the empties went back to source and the process began again.

Jonathan MacDonald

JONATHAN MACDONALD runs the Croft Museum at Kilmuir, indeed he created it, and wrote all the admirable and interesting explanatory notices displayed among the exhibits. As a boy he was drawn into the Kilmuir tradition of playing the chanter around the fire, and he confirms what Seumas Archie MacDonald said, that, until around 1950, all the families in Kilmuir played. He himself learned ('I had no choice, everybody in Kilmuir played'), taught first by his father, who was hugely enthusiastic about piping, and then by Seton Gordon.

Jonathan says that the Kilmuir piping families used to pass tunes among the townships, and each would play a tune in a slightly different way, adding little embellishments of their own, so that if you heard a tune played, you could tell which township that setting came from. He agreed with Seumas Archie MacDonald that very few played the full pipe, and almost nobody played piobaireachd, except Seton Gordon.

Jonathan's nephew is HECTOR MACKENZIE, a good piper and a composer. He is considered one of the best players of his own generation of Skye players.

Seumas Archie MacDonald

SEUMAS ARCHIE MACDONALD, who lived in Hunglader, Trotternish, had a wide knowledge of Skye piping and its traditions, but said his distant ancestors came to Skye from Uist. He judged at local competitions and was known for his outspoken criticisms of poor playing ('he shoots from the shoulder', said his friends). When asked if he played as a boy, he said all the families in Kilmuir played, not necessarily the full pipe, but everyone played the practice chanter, and a few played pipe music on the whistle. Asked how many of his own family were pipers, Seumas Archie was able to name at least twelve in his immediate kin, father, uncles, brothers, nephews and first cousins.

Seumas' mother used to sing pipe music, both Ceol Beag and Ceol Mor, in canntaireachd, and Seumas said his father and his uncle Walter (who for thirty years was conductor of the Glasgow Gaelic Choir) used to sing canntaireachd 'for two days every New Year's'. This is a variation on those who, having no Gaelic, burst into Gaelic song at a certain stage of the New Year celebrations.

This proliferation of players in Kilmuir lasted until as recently as 1950. Very few attempted piobaireachd, however: there was no teacher of piobaireachd until Willie Ross and other tutors came to Skye in the 1930s, but they concentrated mainly on improving the standard of small music playing.

Seumas Archie had a set of pipes which he bought for £25 from a man at Uigshader. He thought they were MacDougalls, and were really easy to set up. When he gave up playing a full pipe, he sold them to America, for £2,000.

Seumas Archie died in 2004, and is much missed.

Dr Angus and Emily MacDonald

Today the best piper in Skye is Dr ANGUS MACDONALD. He is one of the three piping MacDonald brothers from Glenuig, Moidart, and he and his brother ALLAN MACDONALD have each won both of the Gold Medals as well as Clasps and Senior Competitions at Inverness and Oban. Allan has moved more into experimental and reconstructed music, aiming to reproduce piobaireachd as it was played in the old days. IAIN MACDONALD, the third brother, does not compete but is well known in the folk group circuit, and is an excellent piper. Dr Angus says that Iain has the best musical ear of all three brothers.

Angus' career as a competing piper is still at its height, and therefore no further details will be given.

Angus' wife EMILY was born in Nova Scotia to a family of MacLeods who came originally from Seilebost, in the west of Harris, north of Scarista, home of the piping MacCrimmons. They emigrated to Nova Scotia, where Emily was born. After their marriage she and Angus lived for a time in Nova Scotia, before moving to Skye, in order to bring up their children in a Gaelic environment. They live outside Portree, where Angus is a partner in the GP practice. Emily is active in the piping life of the district, teaching some beginners, and was for some years Secretary of the John MacFadyen Trust. She is now the Steward of the Skye Gathering competitions, a thankless task which she carries out with calm and pleasant efficiency.

Bruce/MacPherson Pipers

Angus Cam MacPherson

The Bruce family from Skye and Glenelg enjoys a considerable reputation for fine playing and teaching. There is unquestionable documentary evidence that some of them used the names Bruce and MacPherson interchangeably, mainly in the 18th century but also well into the 19th. The explanation that Angus Cam Bruce changed his name to MacPherson at his chief's request when he went as piper to Cluny MacPherson at Cluny Castle, near Newtonmore, in the 1840s, is probably mistaken, though it is possible that Cluny asked him not to use Bruce as well.

According to MacPherson family tradition, Calum Piobaire's father was ANGUS CAM MACPHERSON (his by-name is used to distinguish him from his grandson Angus MacPherson of Inveran – Cam means 'with a droopy eye', or sometimes 'with a cast in the eye', and implies a certain lop-sidedness of the face). He was himself a good player. Angus' father was PETER BRUCE or MACPHERSON, who had several Bruce brothers, all good pipers, who taught Angus. As far as we can tell, they all lived in the Trotternish area of Skye, though they seem never to have been numerous.

The 1841 Census lists a few Bruces around Uig, and there were Bruces in Glendale, who had come from Uig, but by that time the piping family of Bruces had gone, first to Glenelg in the early 1800s – ALEXANDER BRUCE (1771–1840) was a pupil of Donald Ruadh in Glenelg in 1814, and had won second place in Edinburgh in 1807; he was described by Angus MacKay as 'Piper to MacLeod of Gesto' – and then to Australia, where PETER BRUCE is said to have taught Simon Fraser and Simon's son Hugh their piobaireachd. Peter and his uncle, JOHN BRUCE, were taught in Glenelg by Donald Ruadh MacCrimmon, between 1811 and 1822.

Calum Piobaire said his father was taught by his Bruce uncles in Skye. We cannot trace the family further back, as the Skye Registers begin very late – 1823 in the case of Kilmuir Parish.

The name Bruce is of Norman origin, and the powerful Bruce family had huge lands in Nithsdale and Annan, in the western regions of the Scottish borders. A branch must have come to Skye, where the name would have been alien in the Gaelic world. Probably they had used MacPherson first as a patronymic, then as a Gaelic alternative to Bruce. In a similar way, the Rankins in Mull had Condullie as a secondary, alternative name, and in the Skye Registers there are instances of Mac-Queen and MacDonald being alternates. Sometimes by-names took on full surname status, as with the name Vass among the MacKays, in Sutherland and Easter Ross. Around Beauly, there were instances of tenants changing their name to Fraser, under pressure from their Fraser chief. The use of alternative family names was by no means uncommon, especially in the period when patronymics were giving way to surnames, during the 18th century.

Calum Piobaire MacPherson

See also *Piping Traditions of the Inner Isles*
In Skye the 1841 Census shows MacPherson families living alongside those who called themselves Bruce, often in the next house, and both are remarkable for the prevalence of the two names Peter and Angus. At Barn of Monkstot, in Kilmuir, the household of Norman MacPherson, thirty-one, Cottar, had two women called Catherine, aged thirty-five and forty, one presumably his wife and one possibly his sister, as well as a child Marion MacPherson, nine, and a boy Malcolm Bruce, five. It is possible that this last was Calum Piobaire, living with an uncle after the death of his mother (the ages in the 1841 Census are often inaccurate).

In 1851, a piper called MALCOLM MACPHERSON, aged forty-six, was visiting the family of a farmer called John MacLeod, living in the big house at Ollach, near Portree. He was listed as having been born in the parish of Snizort. Born in 1805, he cannot have been Calum Piobaire himself, but may have been his uncle, brother to Angus Cam.

The Bruces in Braes and Glenelg

Dr Barrie J. MacLachlan Orme deposited in the National Library of Scotland (Accession 11613) a pamphlet about the Bruce family, compiled in March 1999 for the centenary of the purchase of the first land for settlement at Savernake, in Australia (10 February 1898).

This pamphlet gives the descent: Murdo Bruce married Flora Matheson, and his children were Alexander, born c.1781, John c.1812 and Flora (in 1841 Census) c. 1801 or a little earlier.

Alexander, aged twenty-three, married Christian MacKenzie, nineteen, on 12 July 1803. His home was at Camustianavaig, almost adjacent to Achnahanaid, Braes, where subsequent generations of the Bruce family lived on their croft (some of them still there in 1999).

Christian MacKenzie was from Ollach, Braes, the daughter of Kenneth MacKenzie and Mary MacQueen; she died 8 May 1869 at Kirkton, Glenelg.

Known members of the family of Alexander and Christian were

Malcolm, c.1806
Peter, c.1818
Murdoch, c.1823 – or earlier?
Mary, c. 1829
Patrick, born 1815 at Glenelg (= Peter Bruce, went to Australia)
Ann, born 1819 at Glenelg
John, c.1825

Peter Bruce in Australia said he did not really know his age.

Alexander and Christian were living at Kirkton, Glenelg, when the Census was taken in June 1841, and were clearly there by 1815 when Peter was born. The pamphlet says that apart from writings in the *Oban Times* by Dr Keith MacDonald, no other information on their life has been found, but Alexander Campbell wrote of meeting Alexander Bruce in Glenelg in 1815.

Of their family, Malcolm 1806 married Jane Stewart 24 May 1836 in Daviot and Dunlichty Parish. He was at Moy Inn as proprietor in the 1841 Census, and died of cholera in October 1849 – he is buried in Daviot churchyard.

Writings held by the Australian Port MacQuarie Historical Society suggest that Peter went to Australia with Colin MacLeod as his piper – time and ship still unknown – and he was employed by Major Innes in 1843 as overseer of property and personal piper.

Peter married Hellen Sandison 4 July 1844.

Flora Bruce was in 1841 living with her brother at Achnahanaid, Braes, Skye.

John Bruce, a crofter/fisherman, married Catherine MacIntosh and they lived at Achnahanaid, Braes. Their family, born between 1845 and 1855, were Murdoch, Christy, Murdo, Norman, Alexander, Lachlan and John.

This Lachlan, born 1853, married Janet Nicolson, and they had Christina 1895, died 1897, and Christina, born 1898.

Christina (John's daughter, or Lachlan's?) married Donald MacIntosh, and as a young person corresponded with Janet and Bobby at Savernake, while her father wrote to George.

Christina and Donald had Norman, born 1927, and he married Murdina Nicolson – they lived on the Bruce croft at Achnahanaid. In 1999 their family, Lachlan, Janice, Donald and Norman were all living with their families in Portree.

Christina died in 1969, Donald in 1986, and both are buried in Portree cemetery.

Alexander Bruce and his Family

The Notices of Pipers describe ALEXANDER BRUCE (1771–1840) as 'a native of Skye, a very good performer', piper to Capt. MacLeod of Gesto. He came second in Edinburgh in 1807, first at St Fillan in 1823 when piper to Bruce of Glenelg.

On 12 October 1815 Alexander Campbell paid a visit to Donald Ruadh MacCrimmon, who was then living at Kirktown, Glenelg, near Bernera Barracks. The manuscript account of this visit is held by the library of Edinburgh University. It tells how, after leaving Donald Ruadh's house, where Bruce played *The Prince's Salute*, Campbell and Bruce adjourned to the inn in which Campbell was staying, and there Bruce 'over a glass, communicated to me many interesting particulars regarding the mode of training pipers by his celebrated Preceptor, which I have taken notes of and may hereafter prove useful'.

The youngest son of Alexander Bruce, JOHN BRUCE, born in 1825, is named in the 1851 census when he was living in Glenelg with his widowed mother, Christian, and his sister Mary. John was already describing himself as 'Piper'. He went to Australia, and died there in the 1890s (K.N. MacDonald). He was presumably named after his father's brother, JOHN BRUCE (1775–1847), said (by some) to be a good piper, 'often employed by Sir W. Scott who took a kindly interest in him'. He 'competed at gatherings with success', according to the Notices of

Pipers. Walter Scott referred to him in his diaries as 'John O'Skye', and he seems to have become part of the pseudo-Highland household created by Scott at Abbotsford. Somebody said his position at Abbotsford was 'more picturesque than musical'. There seems to have been agreement that John played light music better than piobaireachd.

In 1832 John senior entered the Edinburgh competitions, describing himself as a piper employed upon the *United Kingdom* steamship. All entrants had to produce a certificate that they were good enough, and John had one from MacDonald of Staffa. He had competed some years earlier, in 1818, recommended by Scott as 'my wood Forester and occasionally my piper,' and 'a pupil of MacRimmon'.

In 1832 John produced another certificate from John Nicolson, late tacksman of Clachanish, Isle of Skye, saying John Bruce had been employed by him as a cowherd in 1807 and 1808, which seems a curious recommendation for a piping qualification.

MALCOLM BRUCE, born around 1806, the eldest son of Alexander, was a capable player, piper at Moy Hall to two successive MacIntosh chiefs. A silhouette of him was included in the sale of Moy Hall in 1944. The 1841 census lists under Moy Hall a piper named MURDOCH BRUCE, then aged thirty. He was the first in the list of servants at Moy Hall, which is unusual – the piper is usually last to be named of the employees at big houses. Was Murdoch a son of Alexander and Christian in Braes, said to have been born around 1823? Or is his name at Moy a mistake for Malcolm?

PETER BRUCE son of Alexander, was born in Glenelg, probably in 1815. He taught a number of pipers, including Simon Fraser in Australia (some sources say that Simon was his only pupil, but it is thought that Simon may have been his only pupil at the time that Bruce took him on). Peter Bruce came fourth in Edinburgh in 1838. He emigrated to Australia, where he won many prizes. He is said to have had a wide knowledge of MacCrimmon canntaireachd, learned from his father Alexander.

The Bruce Family in Australia

[The following account is based on that of Dr Barrie MacLachlan Orme in his edition of the piobaireachd settings of Simon Fraser, and is used here by kind permission of Dr Orme.]

Dr Orme quotes from an article in the *Oban Times*, published on 11 and 18 January 1913, written by Dr Keith N. MacDonald, a grandson of Niel MacLeod of Gesto ('Some Famous Pipers, the Bruces of Glenelg, Contemporaries of John Dubh MacCrimmon'). Dr MacDonald lived at Ord, in Skye, where Alexander Bruce and his son John often visited. All of them later went to Australia.

Around 1811–14, Donald Ruadh MacCrimmon was living in Glenelg – he had moved there in 1811 – and in those years he taught piobaireachd to Alexander Bruce, who was piper to the Gesto estate. Sandy, as Alexander was known, seems to have been taught by both of the MacCrimmon brothers as well as by Gesto himself. In 1807, he competed at Edinburgh, playing as 'Piper to Captain MacLeod of Gesto', and came second to Donald MacNab; clearly he was at that time already not only Gesto's piper but a very fine piobaireachd player who could hold his own with the top players. Alexander Campbell, who called on Donald Ruadh in 1815, heard his pupil Alexander Bruce play: it seems that he was not then currently a pupil but had been taught by Donald – and lived handily close by.

Dr MacDonald gave us a description of Alexander (Sandy) Bruce: he was a sturdy man, five feet seven inches tall, clean-shaven, with a ruddy face. He usually wore a tartan coat, with flaps decorated with silver-gilt bullet-shaped buttons, and trews (tartan?). He would start his day at 8 a.m. by playing his pipes, and again during dinner, and afterwards for dancing – but for dancing he used a bellows pipe. When playing piobaireachd on the Great Highland pipe, he walked up and down in a stately manner until he reached the quick movements, for which he stood perfectly still.

In 1823 he is known to have competed at St Fillans, where he took first prize, a new pipe. His employer at that time was Mr Bruce of Glenelg, who owned the Glenelg estate. In 1913, Dr Keith MacDonald said he had heard John Bruce say that Sandy had competed against Angus MacKay, and Angus had 'admitted that Bruce was the better player of piobaireachd'.

Alexander Bruce became a pupil of Captain Niel MacLeod of Gesto, who taught him piobaireachd from canntaireachd. Another pupil, John MacAskill of Rhuandunain, said Gesto used the words of instruction '*gribad is bogaill is togall*' ('grip and dip and lift').

Alexander taught his own three sons, Peter, John and Malcolm, and then sent them to Gesto for polishing. John liked the light music, his favourite tune being *The Lass of Glenshee*. Dr MacDonald recalled in particular the night of his sister's wedding, when John Bruce played superbly all evening. John became piper to Keith MacAllister on Loch Awe, then to MacAllister's son-in-law, Dr Crichton of Fort William, before emigrating to Australia.

There John was the manager of the Highland Chief Hotel in

Melbourne, until his wife died. He moved to Glen Lyon Station near Wilcanna, NSW, where he was piper for six years, and then had a long association with the piping MacGegor family in Victoria. John taught some piobaireachd, but did not have many pupils. He had a son and three daughters. He competed at Melbourne, usually being beaten by his brother Peter.

Lachlan Bruce, a nephew of Sandy, said in 1915 that Gesto, John Dubh MacCrimmon and Sandy Bruce had competed at Kyleakin (when?), and Sandy was the winner.

Peter Bruce was taught by his father and by Gesto, and was 'the greatest piobaireachd player to go to Australia'. He was held in great respect in his own time, especially by his pupil, Simon Fraser, who said he had learned the MacCrimmon canntaireachd from Peter for some twenty years. When Peter died, he left one of his pipes to Simon, usually an indication of a favourite pupil.

Before he emigrated, Peter had competed in Edinburgh in 1838, at the age of sixteen, and came fourth, winning himself a silver-mounted pistol [imagine the outcry today if a sixteen-year-old was awarded a pistol]. He had been one of a short leet of fifteen players who had won through from the preliminary heats, along with his brother John, and Kenneth Stewart. In Peter Bruce's opinion, Kenneth played the best, but the winner was John MacBeth, second was Donald Cameron, and third Duncan Campbell. Kenneth later went to Australia, too.

After he emigrated, Peter Bruce, when in full Highland dress, used to wear two eagle feathers in his bonnet, either because he was the champion piper of Australia or because he claimed to be a direct descendant of King Robert the Bruce, or possibly both, one feather for each. His father wore only one feather. It is not certain when Peter Bruce left, but some say it was in 1837, although he competed in Edinburgh in 1838; others believe it was after 1846, when thousands in the Highlands were starving after the failure of the potato crop – but Peter is known to have been in Australia by 1843, employed by Major Innes.

Dr MacDonald said Peter Bruce spent most of his time on his 300-acre farm near Benalla, Victoria. He won innumerable prizes and medals for his piping in Australia, most of which remained in the family. He excelled in both piobaireachd and light music – and won a dirk for Best Dressed piper at one of the competitions.

He had two sons, Robert (who had four sons, two of them pipers) and George (who lived in Perth). Peter's silver-mounted pipe was passed down the family.

Dr Orme gave us a list of the tunes submitted by Peter Bruce at the

Highland Society of London's competition in Edinburgh in 1835. As he says it was for the occasion when Peter came fourth, the date was probably 1838. The spelling appears to be his own. The tunes he entered were:

1.	Cluaig Phairt	(*The Bells of Perth*)
2.	Failte a'Phraonsa	(*The Prince's Salute*)
3.	Chelli Chriosda	(*Glengarry's March*)
	or	
4.	Cumha Dhonnaell Bhain cc Cremmon	(*Lament for Donald Ban*)
5.	Cumha Blar Bhatarnish	(*Battle of Waternish* – note that he calls it a lament)
6.	Piobrachd Bennaomheg	(*Old Men of the Shells*)
	or	
7.	Tulloch Ard	(*MacKenzie's Gathering*)
8.	Faelte na Donnalach	(*MacDonald's Salute*)
9.	Ghlasmheur	(*Finger Lock*)
10.	Faelte Ullean dhuegh cc Cunnech	(*Black William MacKenzie's Salute* or *The Earl of Seaforth's*)
11.	Cumha an Unen	(*The Union of Scotland's Lament*)
12.	Cumha cc an Tosich	(*MacIntosh's Lament*)

How many of these did he have to play, to reach the Final?

The Macphersons in Badenoch and Glendale

In the district of Badenoch, especially around Newtonmore, where the piping MacPhersons lived, there was a strong oral tradition that the MacPhersons were cursed by the MacCrimmons; it was believed that any MacPherson who played the pipes would suffer some misfortune, probably a physical disability. It is not clear when or why this curse was thought to have been laid, but some descendants of Calum Piobaire felt so strongly about it that they would not allow their children to be taught to play. One let his daughter learn, and she suffered a partial collapse of her face, which was attributed to the MacCrimmon curse. It seems more likely there was a genetic weakness, as Calum Piobaire's father was called Angus Cam, his face being lop-sided. None of Calum's children seems to have been affected by the curse. The tradition has preserved no motive for the curse, and in most stories concerning the MacCrimmons and the MacPhersons, they appear to have been friendly enough – apart from the tale of poor Annag MacCrimmon having her fingers chopped off because she gave away family piping secrets to the Glendale MacPhersons, in the 18th century. In that story there is undoubtedly a certain tension between the families (see below).

Sources
Dr Barrie MacLachlan Orme, correspondence
Angus MacKay (James Logan)
Angus MacPherson

Dan MacPherson, Australia – see below, Glendale

Donald Ewen MacPherson – see below, Glendale

Donald MacPherson

The well-known 20th-century piper DONALD MACPHERSON, who holds nine Gold Clasps and is renowned and revered in the piping world, is probably of Skye origin, but says the link is far back, and not through his father. His mother was a Bruce connection, but Donald does not think there was piping in her family, either. He learned his piping from his father, Iain MacPherson.

In Skye, three good pipers also called Donald MacPherson are still remembered: DONALD (DAN) MACPHERSON, from Fasach, Glendale, emigrated to Australia, served in the First World War and later taught piping at the Scotch College in Victoria; his cousin, another DONALD MACPHERSON from Glendale, also went to Australia, probably around 1910, and nothing more was heard of him; and DONALD MACPHERSON from Broadford, a piper in the 5th Camerons, in the Second World War. Col. David Murray tells how his regiment took part in the advance at El Alamein, to secure the objective known as 'Inverness', and Donald was ordered to play *The Inverness Gathering*; he found it insufficently inspiring, so he 'soon broke into *The Cameron Men,* which saw the company on to their goal. The 7th Black Watch then appeared through the dusty moonlight. It was clear that the Black Watch blood was up, from their battle cries and shouts. To ensure that the Camerons were not mistaken for Germans, Donald was ordered to play *Pibroch o' Donald Dubh* which luckily the Black Watch recognised'.

During this attack, Duncan MacIntyre was killed while playing the regimental march, *Highland Laddie,* and next morning, of the last day of the battle, Donald MacPherson of the 5th Camerons was also killed.

Skye Tunes not Associated with the MacLeods/MacCrimmons or the MacDonalds/MacArthurs

(possibly) *Catherine's Lament*, by Malcolm MacRobert P 7 or 8
(possibly) *Catherine's Salute*, by Malcolm MacRobert P 11 or 12

– see Malcolm MacRobert, below.

The Cave of Gold P 7. There are three caves called the Cave of Gold in Skye, an island with a wealth of caves. One is at Harlosh, south of Dunvegan, another at Bornaskitaig, in Trotternish, and a third at Greshornish, on the coast between Waternish and Bernisdale. It is not clear why they are called 'of Gold'. All three have stories of a piper who entered and was never seen again. The accompanying dog seems to be optional.

Tony Oldham describes the Greshornish cave as being thirty feet high and five to ten feet wide, the first seventy-five feet of it being awash at high tide. The rest is a dry passage, five feet high and five feet wide at the floor, 'ending in a narrow tube occupied by a rabbit'.

Ethel Bassin's book on Frances Tolmie quotes a song which she had learned as a child, called *Uamh'n Oir – The Cave of Gold*. In English it goes:

Ere I return,
Ere I attain,
Ere I return from the Cave of Gold,

the young of the goats
will be goats of the crags,
and the little calves great kine.

Creel-bearing horses
will be riding-steeds,
and babes on the bosom men bearing arms –

But never more shall I return.

(Note the *Cha Till Mi Tuilleadh* ending: some of the tales have the piper playing the tune of that name as he enters the cave.)

The source for this piobaireachd work is Simon Fraser, in Australia. It was published by Dr G.F. Ross, but he seems to have got it from Simon Fraser, who said it was made by Donald Mor MacCrimmon. Others claim it for much more recent times. It has been attributed to John MacDonald, the Ardvasar Blacksmith.

The Coolin Hills 2/4 M 2
Donald MacKinnon of Uig, by Murdo MacKenzie
James MacDonald, Totescore, by Murdo MacKenzie 2/4 M 4
John MacKenzie's Farewell to Brea Uige, by Murdo MacKenzie 2/4 M 4
Journey to Skye, by Donald Thomson P (?) 9
Farquhar MacRae, by William Ferguson 2/4 M 4
John MacLeod of MacLeod, by Iain MacCrimmon 6/8 M 4
Kenneth MacKenzie of Culnacnoc, by James MacKenzie 6/8 M 4
Kenny Gillies of Portnalong, Skye, by Peter MacFarquhar J 4
Keppoch na Faisach, or *The Glen has Become Desolate*, by James
    Mauchline P
Loch Langabhat, by William (Gruids?) MacDonald 2/4 M 4
MacKay from Skye, by Roderick Campbell R 4
MacKinnon of MacKinnon's Lament Setting I P 1, Setting II P 9
MacKinnon's Salute Setting I P 8, Setting II P 2
Miss MacDonald of Viewfield, by William 'Gruids' MacDonald S 2
Mrs Sutherland's Welcome to Portree, by William (Gruids?)
    MacDonald S 2
My Heart is Yearning for Thee, Oh Skye, by James Mauchline P

Portree Bay, by J. MacKenzie 6/8 M 4. There is a rumour that this
    was in fact composed by one of the MacRaes, known as the 'Com'
    brothers because they had fought at the Battle of Commassie. The
    composer had set his heart on an outboard engine for his boat, and
    to raise the money sold the tune to John MacKenzie who published
    it as his own, but the fact that he never made another tune was
    regarded with suspicion. The details are not clear.

Passing Portnalong, by Allan J. MacKenzie, 1996 2/2 M 2
The Portree Men, by R. MacKenzie/J. Mauchline 2/4 M 3 (also known
    as *The Skye Crofters*)
Prince Charlie's Farewell to Skye 6/8 M 2
Prince Charlie's Welcome to Skye 2/4 M 2
Scorriebreck Falls, by Peter Bain R 4
Skye Boat Song 6/8 SM 2
The Skyeman's Jig (sett.) by Duncan Johnstone 6/8 J 4
Strathspey Dance Party in Skye, by J. Pincet S 6
Will You Go To The Isle Of Skye? R 2

See also lists of compositions by Danny A. Campbell, Dr J.A.C. Fisher,
Dugald C. MacLeod, Evan MacRae and Finlay MacRae; also lists of
MacLeod-associated works and MacDonald-associated works, above.

Pipers in Skye other than MacLeods/MacCrimmons or MacDonalds/MacArthurs

Malcolm MacRobert

In his tapes recorded for the School of Scottish Studies in the 1950s, Willie MacLean refers to a man called MALCOLM MACROBERT who, he says, was living in Skye, probably in the 17th century. Malcolm was not, however, a Skye man himself, but had come in from elsewhere. He was a craftsman by trade, making articles in metal and wood by hand, mainly household utensils, but it is not clear whereabouts in Skye he lived. MacRobert was probably a patronymic, that is, not his surname but an indication that his father's name was Robert (see below). This patronymic 'son of Robert' may have given us the modern surname Robertson, which is found quite frequently in Skye. The name is spread pretty evenly over the island, with two main concentrations, in the Broadford area, especially Harrapool, in the parish of Strath, and around Teangue, in Sleat. Does this suggest that Malcolm MacRobert lived in either of these places? We cannot tell.

Malcolm was a fine piper, and a good composer of pipe music, which in those days was what we now call piobaireachd or Ceol Mor. He prospered, breeding and selling cattle, but one of his cows, which he had raised from a calf and named Catriona, was his favourite, and he did not want to sell her. Times grew harder, and in the end he was obliged to sell his beloved Catriona, and was so affected by the parting that he composed *Catherine's Lament* to express his grief.

A few weeks later, the story goes, he heard a lowing at his door, and told his wife to go out and see what it was. She came back to tell him that Catriona had come home – whereupon he composed *Catherine's Salute* in her honour. The fact that Angus MacKay gave the title *Cumha Chaitrine* but translated it as *Katherine's Salute* might suggest that there was just the one composition, and it was played as either a lament or a salute.

An 'old Highlander', with whom Willie shared a journey by mail-coach which took them over the Fairy Bridge, near Dunvegan, told him a story about MacRobert. It seems that MacRobert, though a fine piper, was not taught by the MacCrimmons, something which was worthy of comment in Skye and was mentioned whenever MacRobert's name came up in stories: how could he be so skilled yet not Mac-Crimmon-taught? His friends believed he was just as good a player as MacCrimmon (which MacCrimmon? Patrick Mor? Patrick Og?). So a contest was arranged, to take place on a little 'green' beside the burn, just downstream from the Fairy Bridge. This small flat green 'platform' is still to be seen, and it has steep banks on both sides of the burn, forming a natural small amphitheatre.

The acoustics here are exceptionally good. In the 19th century, before the Disruption of the Churches in 1843, a preacher, known as Maighstir Ruairidh, used this green when the landlords forbade him to preach on their land, regarding him as a dangerous subversive. The triangle of land at the Fairy Bridge is not in any of three estates which meet there, Dunvegan, Waternish and Greshornish, and he preached on horseback, from that green below the bridge, addressing a crowd estimated at nine thousand. (The amphitheatre does not hold nearly as many as that.)

Back in the early 18th century, on the day of the piping contest, the followers of the players, armed with claymores, just in case, ranked themselves on opposite sides of the burn, and MacRobert and Mac-Crimmon each played in turn. It is not clear how the contest was judged, nor what tunes were played, but after the first round, honours were even, and both were held to be equally good. So another round was played, and this time MacCrimmon had the edge, being judged to be marginally the better of the two. MacRobert agreed he had met his match, the thing was settled amicably, and the claymores were not needed.

Willie MacLean was notorious for exaggeration, but in speaking of Malcolm MacRobert and his presence in Skye, he was probably right, for there is corroboration in the traditions of Mull: Neil Rankin Morrison gave us a story of the Rankin piping school at Kilbrennan, Mull, to which was sent a boy, Calum, son of Robert (= Calum Robertson = Malcolm MacRobert). The Mull tradition was that the Campbell Laird of Muckairn, in Argyll, had brought over from Ireland two men, David and Robert: David was an Irish harper, and Robert was an armourer ('*na ghobhainn-arm*). Robert brought his son Calum with him, and sent him to Mull, to learn piping from the Clan Duiligh (the Rankins at Kilbrennan). Neil Rankin Morrison tells the tale of the young Calum having his fingers 'unlocked' by an encounter with a supernatural being, making it clear that Calum then became an excellent player, but giving no hint as to his eventual career.

Neil quotes an old song (*seann oran*) associated with Torloisg, a place close to Kilbrennan. It goes:

Thug mi cion gu de 'm fath	I gave love for whatever reason
Ho ro hug o	(ho ro hug o)
Tomhais thusa co dha	You guess to whom
Ho hao riri hoireann	(ho hao riri hoireann
Ho ro ho hug o	ho ro ho hug o)
Do mhac Raibeirt an ceard	To the son of Robert the metal-worker
Chan e 'n ceard a ni spain	Not a tinker who'll make a spoon
No dh'fhiaclaicheas card	Or cut the teeth of a carding comb
Ach an ghobhainn ni 'n t-arm	But the smith who makes weapons
Claidheamh geur is sgiath dhearg	A sharp claymore and red shield
Leis an cinneadh an t-sealg	With which the hunt is prepared,
Coileach dubh is boc earb.	For blackcock and roebuck.
Thug mi gaol, cuim' an ceileam,	I gave love, why should I conceal it,
Do namhaid na h-eilid	To the enemy of the hinds
'S roin mhaoil a thaobh sgeire	And of the smooth seals beside the skerry
'Nuair a dhireadh tu 'n stuc	When you would climb the crag
Le d'ghille le d'chu	With your gillie and your dog
Le d'chuilbheir caol ur	With your new narrow-bore gun
'N uair a lubadh tu ghlun	When you would bend your knee
'S a chaogadh tu 'n t-suil	And close one eye
Bhiodh an eilid gun luth	The hind would be without strength
Call fal' air an driuchd.	Losing blood on the dew.
Thug mi cion cuim' an ceileam	I gave love, why should I hide it,
Do mhac mnath a tir eile.	To a woman's son from another land.
C'ait am bheil e 's a'chruinne	Where is he in the world,
Aon mhac mnatha thug ort urram	A single mother's son, to surpass you
ann am boidhchead 's an gilead	For the beauty and clarity (of your music)
Ann an uaisle 's an grinnead	For its dignity and neatness?
Mach o phearsa Chloinn Duiligh	Apart from the persons of Clan Duiligh
'S Phara MacCruimein	And Patrick (Paddy) MacCrimmon.

The Gaelic used in this poem is old and difficult, with many Irish characteristics, and probably dates from the 17th century.

The persons of Clan Duiligh were the Rankins in Mull, master-pipers and critical teachers of Calum. The mention of them and of Paddy MacCrimmon indicates that the preceding lines refer to pipe music, Calum's ability as a piper rather than his looks and character.

Calum appears to have followed his father's trade as a metal-smith, which accords with the Skye tradition related by Willie MacLean. Some of Willie's tales were taken, he said on the tape, from Gesto's manuscript, but this one he had from the old man on the mail-coach in Skye.

The story of Calum was told by Neil Rankin Morrison to illustrate the origins of the title *The Finger Lock,* and there is no indication of the date. The second part of the tale about young Calum tells how he was taken by his teacher Rankin (which Rankin?) to cut kelp on the shore. This might suggest a date late in the 18th century, if it was during the years when kelp was a lucrative crop, but we cannot put too much reliance on this, as kelp was used as a fertiliser in the fields long before the potash trade needed it. In any case, the version involving the cutting of kelp could be a later re-casting of the story.

We know that the Rankins gave up their school around 1756, and that it had been struggling since 1692, when the Campbells took over Duart Castle. It seems likely that the boy Calum was in Mull in the late 17th century. When he grew up to become Malcolm MacRobert in Skye, the contest at the Fairy Bridge would have been in the early 18th century, and so the MacCrimmon would have been Patrick Og.

Sources

Angus MacKay, Manuscript
Willie MacLean tape
Neil Rankin Morrison, *TGSI* XXXVII

Donald MacKay

DONALD MACKAY was piper in 1745 to Hugh MacDonald of Armadale, stepfather of Flora MacDonald. It was said that Donald was a good player of reels and jigs, but was also a piobaireachd player. We do not know where he originated.

Angus Mor MacKay

ANGUS MOR MACKAY was said to have been the piper who took over as piper to the (absent) MacLeods of Dunvegan, after the MacCrimmons had left their employ. He was considered to be inferior to his predecessors. Was he related to Donald MacKay, 1745?

The Rev. Alexander MacGregor

The Rev. ALEXANDER MACGREGOR (1806–1881) was the son of a Perthshire minister, and became the minister at Kilmuir, in Skye, for some years before he went to the Gaelic Church in Edinburgh, and then to Inverness. He was 'an excellent amateur piper and violinist' (Notices of Pipers), and for years was a piping judge at the Northern Meeting. A Gaelic scholar and writer, and an excellent preacher, he was a well known figure in Highland life.

In 1837 he paid a visit to the home of Donald MacDonald, the pipe-maker, where he met both Donald and his father, John. An account of this visit was published in the *Celtic Magazine* in 1887.

In 1880 he was asked by the folk-lorist, J.F. Campbell, to write an account of his memories of Niel MacLeod of Gesto, whom he had known in Edinburgh in 1835, shortly before Gesto died. This letter is valuable testimony to the existence of Gesto's manuscripts of some 200 piobaireachd works, written out in canntaireachd vocables. The manuscripts were later lost, and some had doubted their existence, but the Rev. Alexander MacGregor had seen them (see above, Gesto).

Angus MacSwayd

ANGUS MACSWAYD (1804–1881) was a Skye man who joined the Ross-shire Buffs (78th Regiment) in 1823, and became piper to the Grenadier Company, later Pipe Major of the 78th in Ceylon, from 1833 to 1837. Around 1856, he was made Pipe Major of the Ross-shire or Highland Rifle Militia (later to become the 3rd Seaforth Highlanders), based at Dingwall. He was a good player who competed at the Northern Meeting in 1860–62. He was also said to be a good teacher.

From 1825 on, he was compiling a manuscript of both piobaireachd and Ceol Beag, presumably for his own use, but he never completed it. At one time it belonged to Lt John MacLennan, and then to William Gray of the Glasgow Police.

Angus MacSwayd died at Dingwall around 1851.

Norman MacSwayd

NORMAN MACSWAYD was the son of Angus, also a piper in the 78th, and later Pipe Major of the Stirlingshire and Highland Borderers Militia (which after 1851 was the 3rd Argyll and Sutherland Highlanders). Norman competed at the Northern Meeting in 1874, 1877–79 and

1890, also at Oban in 1890. He is perhaps best remembered as the composer of the march *Cuidich an Righ*, which was published in the Seaforth Collection. Presumably he made it when he was in the 78th regiment, as it became the regimental march – 'Cuidich an Righ' (Help the King) is the motto of the Seaforths, referring to an incident in the regiment's past.

Donald Muir

DONALD MUIR, born in Skye, was an army piper who enlisted in the 42nd Highlanders (the Black Watch) around 1840. He served in the Crimean War, and afterwards, being a fine looking man as well as a good piper, he was one of those chosen in 1858 to be photographed, at the Queen's request, by the London photographers, Cundall and Co. Queen Victoria wanted a photographic record of her brave Highland soldiers who had fought in the war – the handsome ones, anyway.

Thomas Hardie

THOMAS HARDIE is said by some to have been a native of Skye, but, although of a Skye family, he was born in Greyfriars, Edinburgh, in 1828. He became Pipe Major of the 79th Regiment (Cameron Highlanders) from 1860–68. Before this, he had been chosen to replace Angus MacKay as the Queen's Piper, after Angus went mad in 1854 and had to be confined.

Thomas was transferred from his regiment to Windsor Castle, but soon became the prey of the other royal servants, who mocked his Gaelic accent. According to Robert Meldrum's *Reminiscences*, 'after vainly warning them, he at last threw off his coat and gave two of them a hammering'. The Queen was not pleased, and Thomas was returned to the 79th, no doubt to his relief. He is described as a fine-looking man with a black beard. He was succeeded at Windsor by William Ross, from the Black Isle.

Angus Ross

ANGUS ROSS, the father of Alice Ross, was born in 'Kilmuir by Uig', in Skye, on 22 February 1845, to Donald Ross, a Skyeman, and Diana MacKenzie, from Easter Ross. Angus went to London where he joined the Scots Guards. He married an English woman, before he went as piper to Cluny MacPherson at Cluny Castle, near Newtonmore. Angus

MacPherson's father and brothers were also pipers at Cluny, and Angus married Alice Ross: she was Mrs MacPherson of Inveran.

This Ross family seems to have links with the Rosses to whom William Ross the Queen's piper belonged, and with Duncan and Alexander Ross, pipers respectively to the Duke of Argyll and Lord MacDonald. The family links are not clear, however, and seem to have been deliberately obscured to conceal one or more illegitimacy.

Donald and Roderick Nicholson

DONALD NICHOLSON was the grandfather of RODERICK DANIEL NICHOLSON, a piper at Gillanders Mountain, Middle River, Victoria County, Nova Scotia. Roderick was born in 1891, second of the six children of Neil Nicholson and Catherine MacLeod. Neil's father Donald was born in Kilmuir, Skye, before he emigrated to Cape Breton – he died at Middle River in 1898.

Donald was married to Christine Matheson, born in 1813 in the Glen of Uig, Skye. They had two children in Skye before they emigrated in 1843, and five more after they settled in Middle River.

Roderick Nicholson, who served in the trenches in World War I, had a big influence on piping in Nova Scotia.

Ronald Mackenzie, Ord

RONALD MACKENZIE (1841–1911) from Ord in Skye is often confused with his contemporary, Ronald MacKenzie, known as Ronald Seaforth, nephew of John Ban MacKenzie. This confusion is increased by the fact that Ronald Ord was taught by Pipe Major Alexander MacLennan, son of Donald Mor of Moy, a close friend of John Ban's family. He had first been taught in Ord by 'Lachie the Grieve', starting at ten years of age.

Ronald Ord became piper to Neil W. MacDonald (a grandson of Neil MacLeod of Gesto) at Dunach, near Oban, shortly before John MacColl was there, and then Ronald moved on to be piper to Duncan Darroch of Torridon. He was known as 'The Piper of Ord'.

Going into the Black Watch as a piper, he served in the Egyptian Campaign.

A story was told about him in those army days. While playing for a company of recruits he had given them an Irish tune, *The Boyne Water*, and was hauled up before his commanding officer for playing a prohibited tune (certain Irish tunes were regarded as subversive). He got off by denying the charge, saying no, no, it was a very old air, *The Girl I Left Behind Me*. They are the same tune.

Later, he was Pipe Major in the Black Watch – but in 1952, Archibald Campbell of Kilberry was told by Mr MacInnes, a retired London policeman and native of Drumfearn in Skye, that Ronald lasted only a week as a Black Watch Pipe Major, and ended up playing on the streets in Glasgow. He retired from the army in 1891. His home was at 130 Taylor Street in Glasgow.

His heyday seems to have been in the 1870s when he won the Prize Pipe at Inverness (1875) as 'piper to Neil MacDonald of Dunach'. He was a good player of both piobaireachd and light music, and won many prizes at the Games and bigger competitions.

Ronald Ord died in 1911, and was given a military funeral at Sighthill Cemetery, Glasgow. The *Oban Times* for 18 March 1911 published a photograph and obituary, saying the funeral was accompanied by two pipers from Maryhill Barracks, 'who played *The Flowers of the Forest, Lochaber No More*, etc'.

Glendale

Glendale, a beautiful glen in the north-west of Skye, is to some extent cut off by the hills from the rest of the island, although Boreraig is not far away. Its comparative isolation seems to have encouraged the people to become self-sufficient, and Glendale has produced many fine pipers and other musicians, as well as poets, writers, singers, teachers, ministers, scholars and craftsmen. It was also well-known for the 'Glendale Martyrs', land-reformers whose leaders served prison sentences in the late 19th century.

Danny A. Campbell

DANNY A. CAMPBELL, as he was known, was christened plain Donald, and it is thought that the initial A. stood for his father's name, Alexander, that is, the letter was a means of identifying to which of the many Campbell families in his township he belonged. His brother and sisters would have had the same distinguishing letter; it was a form of patronymic which existed alongside the surname. (It is not the same as the B. of Donny B. Macleod's name: this popular broadcaster explained that when he was at school in Lewis, there were eight Donny MacLeods in his class, and the teacher designated them A, B, C, etc. When he grew up Donny B. was already labelled, so retained the distinguishing letter. It did not stand for anything.)

Donald Campbell was called Danny, as were many of that name in Skye – it is based on the pronunciation of Donald in Gaelic. Danny was the third of five children born to Alexander Campbell and his wife Ann MacDonald, in Lower Milovaig, Glendale, in the west of Skye. He had two elder sisters, Ann and Jessie, a younger sister Annabella and a brother John, six years his junior.

Their home was not far from the pier at Loch Pooltiel, used by local fishermen. Alexander was described in the Census as a crofter/fisherman, who spoke no English, only Gaelic. There was little necessity to learn English at that time, in Glendale, since his wife, Ann MacDonald, had both Gaelic and English. She came from the parish of Strath, in the east of Skye, an area which includes Broadford. Alexander may have met her when landing his catch there, or possibly through the church – weddings and funerals were social occasions when young folk met those from other communities. Alexander's children spoke both Gaelic and English, as did all the Glendale youngsters (not permitted to speak Gaelic in school).

Danny was born on 14 July 1867, and named after his father's father, who had died a few years earlier. Donald senior had been born in 1801 at Waterstein, about a mile and a half to the south-west. The great-grandfather, Kenneth, was born in Milovaig in 1771, so the family had roots in Glendale.

Pockets of Campbells are found along the west coast of Skye, mainly in fishing communities, and nobody seems to know where they came from. They were settled in MacLeod country, by the end of the 18th century. Alexander Nicolson said that in the 17th century, fishing of both herring and salmon was profitable to the clan chiefs, but the local people were 'not inclined to engage in it'. The result was that Lowland crews were brought in, and these may have included Campbells, from Argyll or elsewhere.

Marriages in the family are not recorded in the Old Parish Register, which starts in 1817 and goes on into the 1870s but is sporadic. As did many Highland families, the Campbells in Glendale tended to have the eldest child of each generation baptised and therefore registered, but since a fee was charged, the younger siblings are found only in the Census returns. The recorded baptism of the first child was enough to establish the legitimacy of the family. The fact that the marriages are not there probably means that they were not married in church by the minister, but relied on the Scottish form by declaration in front of witnesses, marriage completely lawful until 1855, but not usually one that was recorded officially on paper.

Donald senior married Catherine Campbell, who belonged to Milovaig – she was born there around 1806. She and Donald had a croft of four acres at Milovaig in 1851. They had eleven children, of whom Alexander (1837) was the sixth. The first eight were all born at Milovaig, while the youngest three, were born at Holmisdale, in Glendale proper, beside the Hamara river. So we conclude that the family moved to Holmisdale from Milovaig in 1841 or thereabouts, but they went back to Milovaig around 1850, possibly when Donald's father died.

Alexander and Ann lived at Lower Milovaig until some time between 1873 and 1881, when they moved about half a mile east along the coast, to Polasgan (pronounced Pol-OSH-kan), a house which remained in the family until recent times. When Danny Campbell left home in 1882, at the age of fifteen, it was from Polasgan that he went. He was living there in 1881. Archie Campbell, a descendant of the family, presumably from Danny's brother John, was living in Milovaig in 2004, and remembered visiting his three elderly maiden aunts at Polasgan, as a boy.

The date 1882 is significant in the history of Glendale. This was the year that the Glendale crofters made their stand against the tyranny of their landlord. Three of their leaders, regarded as trouble-makers, were arrested, tried and given two-month prison sentences. There is a memorial stone to them, beside the hill-road to Glendale from Colbost.

Danny A. left home in 1882, at the height of the trouble, when he was only fifteen. Possibly he was a hot-headed adolescent, and his parents shipped him out of harm's way before he could land himself in prison. In later life he was always eager to take part in active service with the army, and seems to have relished the thought of battle.

He was already a piper when he went south to join the army. He was taught by one of the piping MacPhersons of Glendale, probably Finlay, at Fasach, or possibly by Finlay's cousin (brother?) Murdo MacPherson, at Holmisdale. The MacPhersons had MacCrimmon blood from a marriage in the 18th century, and were skilled in the MacCrimmon style of teaching.

We know from Angus MacPherson that his father, Calum Piobaire MacPherson, also taught Danny, but we do not know when. Could it have been when Danny was a boy in Skye and Calum was visiting his people in Skye and Raasay every summer? Or was it later that Danny went to Calum, as Willie MacLean did, at his home at Catlodge, near

Newtonmore? Calum died in 1898, so if Danny went to him at Cat-lodge, it must have been when on leave from the army.

This may be supported by another tradition, that Calum Piobaire did not teach beginners. When John MacDonald, later of Inverness, went to Catlodge, he was taught by Calum's son Jockan until he had won the Gold Medal at the Northern Meeting; not until then did Calum agree to take him, saying to Jockan (so the story goes) 'You have made him good, now I will make him great'. This was quite late in Calum's career, however, and he may have been more ready to start beginners when he was younger. There were family links through both MacPhersons and MacLeods, so perhaps Calum made an exception for family reasons.

In 1888, however, John MacDonald wrote to Archibald Campbell of Kilberry: 'The last time I heard D. Campbell, Glendale, play at Por-tree, he finished *The Kiss of the King's Hand* the same as Malcolm [= Calum Piobaire] MacPherson. I asked him where he got it, and he said from Keith Cameron who was in Hamilton Barracks when Campbell was there with the Scottish Rifles, and from whom he learned several tunes'. That comment certainly suggests that Danny Campbell had not yet been to Calum Piobaire for tuition.

Danny was something of a legend in army piping, because when he joined up at fifteen years old, his piping was so good that regimental pipe majors began to vie for his services. He had some tuition while at the Hamilton Barracks in Falkirk, but was still only fifteen when he went as a Boy Piper to the Cameronians (Scottish Rifles), and was immediately put into their Pipes and Drums – and their standard was exceptionally high. This suggests he had been well grounded as a boy in Skye.

Col. Angus Fairrie, in his notes on Danny Campbell in the 1994 programme for the Northern Meeting, mentions that the Hamilton Depot at Falkirk was 'a focal point of piping in central Scotland' at that time. Col. Fairrie continues: 'A strong fraternity of Militia Pipe Majors offered tuition to young pipers and vied to enlist the best of them in their own battalions. And so Dannie Campbell duly joined the Cameronians . . . and in 1889, at the age of only twenty-two, he was accepted for the post of Pipe Major with the Permanent Staff of the 3rd Militia Battalion The Cameronians'. (The spellings Dannie and Danny are found interchangeably throughout his career; Willie Gray used both.) He was at that time the youngest Pipe Major in the army.

He had begun competing as a solo player, and in 1888 he played at the big three-day event, the Great Exhibition in Glasgow, competing against, among a host of other piping stars, Calum Piobaire, who was the eventual winner. Was this perhaps where Danny met Calum? Did this lead to his going to Calum for tuition?

In 1892 Danny came second in the Gold Medal competition at the Northern Meeting. Throughout the 1890s he was regarded as a leading player of both piobaireachd and light music, and in 1894 he won the Gold at Inverness, against formidable opposition.

Col. Fairrie writes: 'As a military piper he had always been keen to see active service, and he achieved this in the Boer War when he went to South Africa as a reinforcement with the 3rd Militia Battalion Highland Light Infantry.' The Queen's Own Highlanders book, *Cabar Feidh*, says that he changed regiments in 1899 in order to get to the war, because he had not been chosen to form part of the Boer War contingent.

It is with Danny Campbell's career in the First World War that the accounts appear to differ. Correspondence with Col. Fairrie sheds light on this, and the notes in the Notices of Pipers, apparently written by Major Ian MacKay-Scobie, add to the picture.

Col. Fairrie writes:

> The service record of Pipe Major Donald Campbell is almost impossible to verify. The book 'Pipes of War' lists him in the 5th Camerons, but with no dates. Historical Records of the Cameron Highlanders list him as Pipe Major of the 6th Camerons in 1914, which could be wrong. The entry in 'Notices of Pipers', in Major MacKay-Scobie's handwriting, says that in 1914 he became Pipe Major of the 5th Camerons, then served with the 6th, and was invalided out in 1916. Richard Crawford in his 'Pipers of the Highland Regiments 1854–1902' states that he was invalided out of the service with rheumatism, and on recovery he joined the Royal Navy and served aboard minesweepers. The Notices of Pipers say he served as a piper on various ships and shore bases when in the Navy.

Col. Fairrie goes on to say that he found two 'pretty reliable' sources in the Library of the QOH Regimental Museum. The Enlistment Books of the Cameron Highlanders show Pipe Sergeant No. 27434 Donald Campbell transferring to the Cameron Highlanders from the 2nd/2nd Lovat Scouts in 1916 (tradition says he left the Lovat Scouts in disgust on finding himself the only piper in the battalion). Col. Fairrie also has the photograph album belonging to Captain Malcolm Moffat, Adjutant of the 6th Camerons in 1917–18. The Captain was a 'meticulously accurate diarist', and his album includes a number of photographs inscribed as having been taken at Arras in November 1917. One of them, printed by Col. Fairrie in his Northern Meeting programme-note, names Pipe Major Campbell on the front row. 'The only point in doubt was the absence on his tunic of the ribbon of the Queen's South Africa Medal, earned with the 3rd (Militia) Battalion HLI, but this could be explained by the unavailability of the necessary medal ribbon in France in 1917.'

If Danny Campbell was in Arras with his regiment in November 1917, however, he cannot have been invalided out in 1916. Col. Fairrie says his guess is that Danny started the war with the 5th Camerons, but being aged about forty-seven, and possibly not fit enough for active service in the trenches, he was moved to the 2nd /2nd Reserve Battalion Lovat Scouts. However, after the losses suffered by the Service battalions at Loos and the Somme, he returned to the Camerons, and was appointed Pipe Major of the 6th Camerons in 1917–18. By then aged about fifty, and suffering from the hardship of the trenches, he was invalided out of the army. 'He may possibly have served in the Royal Navy at a shore establishment, such as Invergordon or Kyle of Lochalsh, and gone to sea with his pipes from time to time.'

In 1939 Willie Gray wrote in *Piping and Dancing* (vol. 5, no. 4) that

> Danny was in his hey-day over forty years ago and was one of the leading performers. He was popularly known to older pipers as 'Danny' or sometimes 'The Cocky Boy'. . . he particularly excelled in Strathspeys, Reels and Jigs and had many excellent sets of Highland airs all of his own arranging. He was exceedingly nimble in fingering, and he could use the thumb grace note with great dexterity.

Willie Gray went on:

> I remember years ago at the old Waterloo Rooms, Glasgow, where piping and dancing competitions were then held, being run for two successive evenings on such occasions. Here on one particular occasion Danny played Cameronian Rant Strathspey and Reel. It was a great performance. Right from the start he took the audience with him and before the finish of his reel Danny's playing was lost in the uproar and din of applause. 'He took the house down'.
>
> Danny had a habit of jerking and also of changing his foot frequently to beat time while playing to dancing as if stressing emphasis in an effort to assist the dancers. On one occasion while playing to the 'Swords' in the same Waterloo Rooms, Danny while going through these evolutions with his back partly to the audience and near to the edge of the platform side-stepped and toppled over (a five foot drop), pipes and all, amongst the audience. However, none the worse of his sudden disappearance, Danny was soon up at his allotted place, piping as if nothing had happened.

Danny insisted on open and round playing, particularly in the common shakes or doublings which had to be distinctly heard. This is quite in contrast to the common fault of performing doublings too closely . . . In rendering 'Gillie Calum', he stressed all the E's, thus giving effect to the pointing of the melody. The G and D shake in A followed by melody note E were made big and open so that the doubling could be heard to effect. He was particularly crafty in the application of the little finger burl and grip.

Writing in *Piping and Dancing*, vol.6, No.1, September 1940, Willie Gray was discussing a 'bind' of three notes – C E A with D grace note upon C, no grace note on E and G grace note on A – in the third part of *Lady Loudon's Strathspey*:

> While I have no fault to find with the gracing of this bind, I remember very well how that crafty little player, the late D.A. Campbell (Danny) substituted a G grace note instead of D grace note on the C of this bind. The result was most effective and produced a distinctive technique on the large chanter. . . . Another movement which Campbell often used was a double thumb (or high A) shake on high G instead of the ordinary throw or doubling of high G. He often followed this shake with the doubling of top A and if the student cares to attempt this piece of gracing, he will probably appreciate the absolutely marvellous dexterity and control of finger possessed by this piper. It is doubtful if any piper could excel Campbell in his use of the top A grace note.

Nobody seems to know what became of Danny Campbell after the war, nor where and when he died, nor where his burial place might be. Any information would be welcomed.

As for his playing, he was highly regarded by army pipers and his fellow competitors. Angus MacPherson said he was an excellent player, and was considered to be a worthy pupil of Calum Piobaire. With tuition from both MacPherson and Cameron teachers, he had a background similar to that of John MacDonald, Inverness.

Danny Campbell was not a prolific composer, but he made some good tunes. They include:

Braeriach 6/8 J 4
The Cockie Lad J (William M. MacDonald found this in the MS of Willie Sutherland, Airdrie, dated 1901. Willie Sutherland used to sign himself 'The Earl of Skye'.)
Danny Campbell's Walk Round 2/4 M 2
Dunvegan Castle 2/4 M 4
Glendale 6/8 M 2 (There are two 6/8 marches by Danny Campbell

called *Glendale*; they appear in Books 3 and 4 of Donald
MacLeod's Collection.)
Jig 6/8 J 2
Louisa Campbell S 2

Also note:

Donald Campbell's Welcome to Glendale 6/8 M 2
and *Danny Campbell of Glendale*, a Reel in 2 parts, appears
anonymously in Neil Angus MacDonald's Collection.

It is not easy to distinguish between different Donald Campbells, and
other tunes may be connected with Danny A. Campbell. It is a puzzle
that he seems to have composed two 6/8 marches and called both of
them *Glendale*. Perhaps one of them was not intended for publication.

Sources

Census and Old Parish Register Records for Glendale (Duirinish parish,
  Skye)
Jeannie Campbell, *Highland Bagpipe Makers*
Lt Col. A.A. Fairrie
Alistair MacLeod, Inverness Library
Notices of Pipers
Cabar Feidh, Regimental Music of the QOH
James Jackson, Alness
William M. MacDonald
George MacPherson

Dan Macpherson, Portree (1879–1959)

Thanks to Dr Barry Maclachlan Orme of Southbank, Victoria, Australia, we know of this excellent piper who left Scotland around 1898.
Not only has Dr Orme supplied biographical notes and photographs,
but has sent a tape of the playing of this Skye piper, proving to be true
the assertion that he was a fine player of both light music and piobaireachd. His playing was recorded first on wire, then later re-recorded on
reel-to-reel tape, and then recorded again on audio tape cassette, the
latest transfer being to CD, so that the quality of the recording is poor,
but its faults cannot conceal the fineness of the music and the excellent finger technique of the player. It is an interesting example of the
'old' style of playing, unaffected by access to the Piobaireachd Society
settings. Dan recorded it in 1952, when he was seventy-three.

This account is based partly on Dr Orme's notes, for which we are grateful.

Dr Orme was taught his piping by Pipe Major DONALD (DAN) MACPHERSON. He wrote a note on the life of his teacher, now in the memorabilia of the Pipe Bands of Victoria, vol. 19, no. 5, dated June 1989. It is held by the Scotch College, Victoria, Dr Orme's old school.

His account is quoted here with his kind permission. He wrote:

Donald MacPherson, always nicknamed 'Danny', was born and brought up at Portree, Skye, where he spoke Gaelic only, until he attended the local school. He was a very strongly built man, with dark, olive-coloured skin, black hair and eyes, and a round face with high cheekbones. His eyes portrayed a sharp character with a very quick wit. To compete at the various Games, he used to practise the pipes for three hours each day in an upper room, facing Portree's main street, so that people used to stop to listen and admire his playing. He became a champion at all three fields of endeavour: piping, dancing and wrestling.

He joined the Seaforth Highlanders as a drummer boy aged 14. All his life he loved the Seaforths and was always delighted to meet up with any member from the regiment. [He must have later become a piper in the regiment].

For a short while he worked at Henderson's Music Shop in the Golden Mile in Edinburgh, where he repaired bagpipes and tuned them. It was here that he met the great Colin Cameron who eventually gave him pibroch lessons.

Just before the turn of the century, he left Scotland to become a piper to a Malayan Sultan, and to my knowledge, he never returned to Scotland. This position did not last, and he went to South Africa to participate in the Boer War campaign. It was here that he once played for a forced march of a company of troops until all the men had collapsed . . . Danny was still fresh and still playing!

It may have been the friendship with Jack Senter in Africa which encouraged Danny to come to Australia at the conclusion of the Boer War. Jack Senter was cousin to the famous Jimmy Center, who also made pipes and who himself came to Australia in 1907. (Jack's family chose to alter the spelling of their surname to show their individuality from their well-known Center relatives.) In Australia, Danny joined the Royal Caledonian Pipe Band under Pipe Major Hugh Fraser (he was the son of Simon Fraser).

When the 1914–18 War began, Danny re-enlisted. When he was not doing Band work, his duty was to carry the wounded as a stretcher-bearer on the field of battle. It was during the war that Danny had the opportunity to practise and develop his unique piping style which has never been duplicated. This style was extremely good, with lots of lift and very accurate fingering.

In Australia, after 1918, Danny couldn't settle down. He travelled extensively from pipe band to pipe band, from one Highland Gathering to the next. He would stay several days at each competition, and the nights were spent at the local hotel, where he had a great time piping and chatting. On one occasion at Portland, he was challenged by six Irishmen to a fight. A drinking friend held his pipes, while Dan deliberately dropped each of his challengers, one by one.

It was in Millicent, South Australia, while playing with that pipe band, that Dan met Clarice, who became his wife. She was the daughter of a local farmer, and she played the drums. She could also play classical music on the piano very well, and she eventually played for the Country Dancing for the Melbourne Scots Dancing Circle. Clarice helped to steady Dan's life, and they had one daughter, Angela.

Dr Orme adds that Dan's brother MURDO(CH) MACPHERSON lived with him and his family in Melbourne. Murdo was also a piper, but a very shy man who avoided the limelight. Another brother – or possibly a cousin – was Donald Ewen MacPherson (see below).

In the tape of Dan MacPherson's playing, it will be heard that he played the 'old style', with what Dr Orme calls 'the middle A in the Crunluath', now known to the establishment (and despised) as the 'redundant A'. Dan had left home long before this became controversial, and as Dr Orme put it, 'had not been involved with the changes in this music after that time'. He also played the 'he iririn' movement.

Apart from Dr Orme, Dan taught a man called Jock Duguid, who had been a Lt. Col. in the Seaforths. Jock was learning piobaireachd from Dan, but was such a strong personality that he soon began to teach Dan what he had of piobaireachd himself. Dan was not amused.

As an old man, Dan MacPherson was a judge, and a tutor of piping at the Scotch College. 'No-one knew his age, but he would have been in his eighties when he died, in 1959.' He loved piping, also he loved Camel cigarettes and Scotch whisky. A lesson with him usually consisted of five minutes chanter, followed by a long period of stories and finishing a packet of cigarettes.

Dan died of stomach cancer in 1959, when he must have been eighty.

This Australian account of Dan MacPherson's career is not fully borne out by local written records (Census and Parish Register) or by family tradition among relatives still living. Discrepancies after the passage of time often appear in oral tradition, especially after a period overseas. This slight distortion of tradition is normal.

The Census records of Portree for 1881 and 1891 show no MacPherson families with children of the right age.

George MacPherson, of Fasach, Glendale, and Alasdair MacPherson of Glen Feochan, near Oban, are grand-nephews of Dan MacPherson, and they confirm that Dan came from Glendale, in the west of Skye. As Portree is the nearest town of any size, it could be said loosely that Portree was his birthplace, as his birth would have been registered there. The son of FINLAY MACPHERSON and his wife Ann Campbell, he was born in their house, at 20 Fasach, in 1879. He is listed as Donald, a boy of twelve, in the Census for Duirinish in 1891, with his father Finlay (born 1843), and mother Ann (nee Campbell, born 1847 – she was a daughter of Peter Campbell in Fasach, and his wife Catherine, and was related to Danny A. Campbell). Finlay and Ann were married in 1874.

Finlay was the son of Donald MacPherson, who in 1851 was aged forty, farming two acres, married in 1839 to Flora MacSwein, the daughter of a neighbouring family. Finlay was their second child, born in 1843, after a daughter Rachel in 1841. After Finlay came Mary (1845), Murdoch (1847) and John (1852).

In 1861 Finlay, aged seventeen, was living with his uncle Neil MacPherson, then thirty-eight, a 'merchant grocer' who was consistently described as being unmarried but had daughters Mary (1851), Flora (1855), Peggy (1859) and Ann (1863), as well as a son Neil (1861), with no indication of who the mother might be – but she was a woman living nearby, with her own house, and it seems that although she and Neil had several children, they were not married and did not live together. Neil's nephew, Finlay, described as his 'servant', was assisting him. They lived beside Finlay's parents in Holmisdale.

Finlay had seven children, of whom Donald (Dan) was the third, born in 1879. All were born at Fasach, Glendale. Were his brothers Murdo and Donald Ewen older or younger? Finlay's brother Murdo(ch) (1847) was the father of Donald (1889), who was probably Donald Ewen who went to Canada: that would make him a first cousin of Donald MacPherson in Australia, but this is not certain.

As Dan was living at Fasach in 1891, it is unlikely that he went to live in Portree before 1892, and he was probably there for only a couple of years, at the most. He may have stayed with a widow from Glendale, Jain MacPherson, and her children, in a house in Bosville Terrace, which is central enough in Portree to merit the description given by Dan later in life. But he was not born or brought up in Portree itself. He would certainly have been brought up as a Gaelic speaker who spoke no English until he went to school.

His great-nephew, George MacPherson, says that the MacPhersons in Glendale, living in Fasach and Holmisdale, had good pipers in every generation from way back, and they were the piping teachers for all the youngsters in Glendale.

The Fasach MacPherson piping tradition was MacCrimmon-based, and George (who is a professional story-teller and is steeped in the traditions of the district) tells how one of the ancestors in the mid-18th century, Hugh MacPherson, married a MacCrimmon girl called Annag (Annie). Her family was not pleased by the match, but she defied them, and settled with Hugh at Holmisdale. She had taught her piping husband the secrets of the special MacCrimmon fingering, to the fury of the rest of the piping MacCrimmons, who lived just over the hill, at Boreraig. They held a family meeting and decided that she must be punished by having all the fingers cut off her right hand, and this sentence was carried out. She soon developed skills with her left hand, and remained in Glendale.

It would seem that her family maimed her before she was finally married, perhaps during a 'handfast' union, because the story says that Hugh 'stood by her' and they were married anyway. The MacPherson family tradition is that, since then, every generation of each family descended from Hugh and Annag has had one person who is left-handed, and one who is a piper. This is certainly true of the modern generations, among George's siblings as well as his own children, but the left-handedness would be genetic. The story of the maiming was possibly symbolic, to explain the persistent left-handedness in the family.

The marriage of Hugh and Annag has been dated, from other detail in the tradition, to some time between 1731 and 1749, so it is likely that Annag was a grandchild of Patrick Og, possibly a daughter of Farquhar MacCrimmon, and sister of Donald Donn MacCrimmon of Lourgill.

The MacPhersons in Glendale were intermarried with the Campbells and other local families, so that both their piping genes and their piping tuition helped to create an enclave of piping ability similar to that of Kilmuir – but with a stronger tradition of piobaireachd (Ceol Mor).

In the case of Dan MacPherson we are fortunate in having the tape of his playing – showing that his style was not as 'old-fashioned' as that of the Frasers in Australia, which was based on the early 19th-century teaching of Gesto and Peter Bruce, and passed on to Dr Barrie MacLachlan Orme; Dan's was probably influenced by the style of the Seaforths in the 1890s, but is still of great interest to pipers today.

Donald Ewen MacPherson

Donald Ewen MacPherson is described in the Notices of Pipers as being 'of Skye and Uist'. It is not known what the connection with Uist may have been. He was related to Donald (Dan) MacPherson in Australia (see above), possibly a first cousin, but some say he was a younger brother.

A pupil of Calum Piobaire MacPherson and of Robert Meldrum, he was a good piobaireachd player who could have made a name for himself as a piper, but preferred to concentrate on the athletics and wrestling at the Games. He was a Pipe Major in the Royal Scots, and won the wrestling championship of the services. When he went to Canada, he became Pipe Major of a band in Toronto. In his honour, Dan (Donald) MacPherson made a 2/4 march *Pipe Major D.E. MacPherson's Welcome to Canada*. This later became a fiddle or accordion tune, now known as *Donald MacPherson, New York*.

In 1920, he was a foreman on a construction crew in the Toronto area. A Canadian contemporary of his said 'Most people thought Donald Ewen quite unapproachable, but I wish I had known him better'.

He composed a 'solo march' in 1947, called *Alex MacMillan*.

Sources

Dr Barry Orme, correspondence
Census Records
George MacPherson
Dr Roderick Ross
Bill Cromarty, South Orange, New Jersey
David Murray

More Skye Pipers

Farquhar Beaton

The Notices of Pipers record FARQUHAR BEATON, of a Skye family, a first-rate piper who went to Canada in the late 19th century. 'When at his best he excelled as a player of piobaireachd and marches.'

William Sutherland (1844–1903)

Although WILLIAM SUTHERLAND came from a line of seven generations of pipers in Caithness, and he was born and reared in the Lowlands, he was known as 'the Earl of Skye', for reasons unknown. It has been suggested that his remote ancestor might have been a by-blow of Donald Mor MacCrimmon, in the early 17th century, during Donald's exile in northern Sutherland, but this seems somewhat far-fetched. William once sent John MacDonald, Inverness, a manuscript copy of the jig *Rattlin' Roarin' Willie*, which he said he had found in an old manuscript of pipe music. He signed his letter to John 'the Earl of Skye', so it may have been a self-awarded title – but why?

He worked as an engineman in a coalmine at Airdrie, where he was regarded as an eminent piper and composer; he often competed at the Games and won many prizes.

His father had been born at Clarkston, in Airdrie, and became a professional piper at the age of twenty. William went to Canada, and won more prizes in the USA and Canada, becoming Pipe Major of the 48th Highlanders of Toronto. In 1897 he enlisted in the Royal Scots (in Britain) and served in Burma with the 2nd Battalion in 1898. He won the Piping Championship of India in 1901 and 1902, and was Pipe Major of the 2nd Battalion from 1902 to 1904. He retired to live in the mining town of Plean, near Stirling, and died there in 1941.

Among those killed in the First World War were several pipers from Skye. These included ARCHIE MACKENZIE, a private in the 2nd Cameron Highlanders, who was born in Portree and lived at Sligachan. He was killed at Ypres in 1915.

Another piper lost was WILLIAM MACDONALD, of the 5th Cameron Highlanders. He was born at Harrapool, Broadford, and died of his wounds, aged twenty-one, in 1917.

The Rev. Neil Ross and Dr Roderick Ross

The Rev. NEIL ROSS was from Fasach, in Glendale, a keen amateur piper with a special enthusiasm for piobaireachd. He did much to encourage piping, when he was the minister at Laggan, near Newtonmore, in Inverness-shire. He clarified and corrected many of the Gaelic titles of piobaireachd works, and emended the faulty Gaelic of many piping publications. In 1933 he was awarded the CBE for his services to Gaelic literature and language. He died in 1943.

His son RODERICK ROSS is a medical doctor who was a friend of Malcolm MacPherson, grandson of Calum Piobaire. Together they devised and published the well known series, *Binneas is Boreraig (Music from Boreraig)*, which pipers like for three reasons: the settings are musically pleasing, the lay-out of the music in a three-line stave is clear and easy to read, and the music is divided into phrases, not bars, with imaginative use of colour to make the patterns clearer. This scheme seems to have been the work of Dr Ross, based on the playing of Malcolm MacPherson. A tape of Malcolm's playing accompanied each of the six volumes issued in the 1930s.

In recent years, the College of Piping in Glasgow has issued a one-volume edition, edited by Dugald MacNeill, with Malcolm's playing transferred to CD.

Roderick Ross said his father retained the family cottage at Fasach after he had left Glendale, and 'his spirits would droop unless he returned there each year'. Neil was the son of a stone-mason who had built many houses in Glendale, probably in the 1840s, and grandson of the mason who had 'constructed, almost single-handedly, the famous drystone Drynoch Bridge, which tour-buses still stop to admire'.

The Cairn at Boreraig

In 1933, a big cairn was built at Boreraig, to commemorate the Mac-Crimmon family of pipers. The two pipers who played *MacCrimmon's Sweetheart* for this occasion were John MacDonald and Robert Reid. In his account for the *Times* newspaper, Seton Gordon said: 'It is probably safe to say that never before has this classical piece, full of melody and difficult to express except by the highest exponents of piping, been played in unison by two pipers, but so perfectly did MacDonald and Reid play that it seemed as though only one pipe was heard sounding over the hills and over the sea'. *MacCrimmon's Sweetheart* is an odd choice for this occasion: its claim to be a MacCrimmon composition is dubious at best, and it has had that title only in comparatively recent times – long after the MacCrimmons had left Boreraig.

Every year a piper plays a MacCrimmon piobaireachd at the cairn as a mark of respect for the family. In recognition of the landlord of the site, a token rent of one penny is paid annually to the Skeabost estate. One year it was ALEXANDER MACDONALD, of South Uist origin, playing at the Cairn.

The *Piping Times* tribute to him said: 'His performances were always of the highest musical quality . . . a well remembered example of his fine playing was at the Cairn at Boreraig when in a driving wind of rain and sleet he gave a splendid interpretation of the *Lament for Donald Ban MacCrimmon*. On that day he seemed impervious to the weather, though the MacLeods had serious worries about the effect on his health. A quick rush to the car and a liberal intake of well deserved whisky and coffee staved off any serious effects. This was one of the most outstanding performances of piobaireachd ever heard at the Cairn.'

Angus MacPherson at Inveran, in Sutherland, composed a piobaireachd work which he called *Salute to the Cairn at Boreraig*. He later (after keeping it 'behind the clock' for a year or two) entered it for the composing competition organised by the BBC in 1965, and it won first prize, out of sixty-six entries in the piobaireachd section. One of the other sixty-five entrants made the sour comment that it had won only because it was on a 'sacred subject' – the MacCrimmons.

Source
Piping Times

Seton Gordon

[The following account of Seton Gordon's life is based to some extent on the biography by Raymond Eagle (*Seton Gordon, The Life and Times of a Highland Gentleman*, published by Lochar, Moffat, 1991). I have been unable to contact Mr Eagle for permission to use his book as a source, as my letters, c/o the publishers, have been returned unopened. I would like to acknowledge my debt to him, and to assure him that I did try. Any opinions which appear to be critical of Seton Gordon are, however, not drawn from Mr Eagle's book.]

SETON GORDON (1886–1977), although born in Aberdeen and educated at home in Aboyne and at Oxford, lived in Skye for so long that he came to be regarded as one of the Skye piping fraternity, almost as a Skyeman. He and his wife Audrey lived from 1930 to 1959 at Upper Duntulm, formerly the Kilmuir Manse in Trotternish, beside the Kilmuir graveyard where Flora MacDonald and the MacArthur pipers are buried.

His father, William Gordon, was Town Clerk of Aberdeen, an Aberdeenshire man, and his mother, daughter of a gardener from England, was well-known locally as a poetess and a singer. They made their home in Aboyne in Deeside, to the west of Aberdeen, and Seton did not go to school but was educated at home. He was brought up with a keen interest in natural history, photography, fishing and golf; his parents' gardener at Aboyne was a piper, who talked to him about pipes and piping. His outdoor interests took him to the Balmoral and Invercauld estates, where he met ghillies and stalkers, and from them, too, he developed his interest in piping.

There is a persistent rumour, possibly fostered by Seton Gordon himself, that he had royal blood, being a by-blow of the Prince of Wales (later King Edward VII), whose first public scandal was when he was still in his teens. This possible paternity was not acknowledged openly (Mr Eagle does not refer to it at all), but it is widely believed. Seton Gordon does seem to have claimed acquaintance with members of the Royal Family as if by right, with a confidence which seems otherwise unwarranted.

Mr Eagle explains the royal connection as friendships made by Seton at Oxford, but there, of all places, the entree into royal or noble circles was a carefully guarded privilege, and there must have been some reason why a Scottish town clerk's son was accepted by princes – if indeed he was. He was, however, equally assiduous in maintaining correspondence with the Prime Minister and in seeking the friendship of influential Highland gentry, so it could be that his social climbing was merely an instinctive career move.

It is undeniable that the Prince of Wales left many offspring in the Highlands, some of whose mothers were married off respectably to other men. The royal child would then be accepted as if the husband were the father, even though everyone knew he was not. There was little of the usual stigma of the time attached to these illegitimate children or their families, as it was recognised that the mothers were reluctant victims rather than loose women, many of them being servants who had no choice but to submit to the Prince's advances. One of these sons was a piper, JOHN PETER MACLEOD in Tain, who won the Gold Medal at Inverness in 1907; his mother had been a maid in a local 'Big Hoose' where the Prince had stayed, and as such she was not permitted to refuse him. She lost her job, of course, when her pregnancy became obvious, but she would have been given financial compensation privately, whether or not she was married off.

It was not necessarily the Prince of Wales who may have been responsible. Any member of the Royal Family, however minor, might have given Seton Gordon the feeling that he had the right to claim acquaintance. We have no way to prove or disprove the rumour of Seton Gordon's royal blood, unless local tradition knew of it at the time. In the vicinity of Balmoral, loyalty to the Royal Family might have kept mouths closed. Further away, in the north, local people had no such inhibitions, and royal connections in certain families are well attested, and still remembered. The Chief Constable of Edinburgh, in the 1920s, for example, a Ross who came from Kildonan, in Sutherland, was not allowed to travel through the city in procession in the same carriage as King George V, because the resemblance was so marked. They were half-brothers.

In 1908, Seton Gordon went up to Oxford, where he was in digs in the same house as Prince Felix Youssoupoff, a cousin of the Tsar of Russia and related to the English Royal Family. This proximity would probably not have been tolerated unless there was some kind of family link. Through this prince, Seton met another Prince of Wales (later Edward VIII, grandson of Edward VII) who was also an undergraduate at the time. Their common interest in piping led Seton and the Prince to share piping tuition from Willie Ross, then Pipe Major in the Scots Guards; he travelled up by train from London to give them their weekly lesson. The Prince was 'a competent and enthusiastic piper and a very apt pupil' (who struggled to play *Invercauld's March)*. He later became Hon. President of the Scottish Pipers' Association. 'On one occasion,' wrote Raymond Eagle, 'Pipe Major Ross and Seton Gordon piped the Prince down the High [Street] to his college [Magdalen] at midnight, and the proctors [university police] went, too, across the street, but did not interfere because the Prince was there. Curfew for the colleges was 11 p.m.'

Raymond Eagle goes on: 'The Prince continued his enthusiasm for the pipes, and in 1935 he composed a slow march, which he called *Mallorca*. His original handwritten manuscript was presented to the Scots Guards. It was so enthusiastically received that it was put into the regular music programme, and included in the Changing of the Guard ceremonies at Buckingham Palace.' The Prince later gave up playing.

His own account of his playing is more modest: he wrote that he 'never became very proficient', although he took his chanter wherever he travelled. His description of the composing of *Mallorca* makes it clear that all he did was find himself 'breaking into an air of my own invention' when playing his pipes in a lonely spot on the coast of Mallorca. He then 'had it set to music by my father's old Pipe Major, Henry Forsyth'.

That was the year 1935, when the Prince joined a practice meeting of the Royal Scottish Pipers' Association in Edinburgh, and played with their band. The *Piping Times* account (January 2005) says:

'Afterwards he played a solo slow march' – and someone else played *Mallorca*.

It may have been the influence of Willie Ross which later led Seton Gordon to join the ranks of the 'old-fashioned' players who disliked the 'modern' style of piobaireachd published by the Piobaireachd Society. Although friendly with Archibald Campbell of Kilberry, and a faithful correspondent exchanging frequent letters with him, Seton Gordon, to his great credit, aligned himself with the professional pipers on this subject. His objections led to his being ousted from the Society's music committee, and his place given to one of Kilberry's sons (see William Donaldson, 2005). He wrote sympathetically to John MacDonald, both of them strongly disliking the Kilberry Book. And he joined forces with Somerled MacDonald to try to have the Piobaireachd Society books scrapped and re-issued under a new editor, preferably John Mac-Donald, Inverness. This came to nothing, but Seton Gordon had done his best. His efforts were little known until Dr Donaldson brought them to light.

Around 1912, when Seton was still a student, he met Colin Cameron at the funeral of the Duke of Fife (whose piper Colin had been). They had a long talk about piobaireachd. It is not clear why Seton Gordon should have been attending the Duke of Fife's funeral, but links with Mar Lodge may have been the reason, allied with his possible blood connection to the family.

It appears from Seton Gordon's career that the shared weekly classes with Willie Ross, in the three short Oxford terms of eight weeks maximum, were virtually his only piping tuition, apart from a few lessons from Willie Ross in Edinburgh when Seton was living in Northumberland. Much of his Oxford tuition was for light music. He seems to have built up his knowledge of piobaireachd mainly from chance conversations with people such as Colin Cameron, the 'Two Bobs', Colonel Jock MacDonald and others. He was noticeably defensive if questioned about his knowledge.

He judged at Games and Gatherings for many years, in spite of his increasingly profound deafness, and the dreadful tuning of his own pipe became a by-word. Many of the excellent pipers who played in front of him were not satisfied, questioning his experience, his knowledge and the accuracy of his hearing, especially in his old age. There is little doubt that he continued to judge long after he should have retired, but how could the pipers challenge the presence of members of the gentry, considered to be their superiors?

Seton Gordon was one of what present-day players call 'the Jolly

Boys', appointed as judges on account of social position and education rather than professional expertise. This appointing of judges for social reasons has bedevilled the judging of competitions ever since they began in 1782, and to some extent still does. In the old days an ignorant Lord would often be flanked by two other judges with the necessary experience and knowledge, but some, including Seton Gordon, regarded themselves as authorities who needed no guidance. Even today, a degree in medicine is considered to be part of a qualification for judging a piobaireachd competition.

At the outbreak of war in 1914, Seton was not conscripted into the army, nor did he volunteer, presumably exempted by his deafness. Many expected him to volunteer for the Lovat Scouts, for which his wide knowledge of field craft and his fitness on the hill would have made him ideal. Instead, he seems to have gone into the Royal Navy, in a non-active capacity. He became a 'coast-watcher', not exacting work. It entailed living in Mull with his wife, Audrey, and organising a net-work of observers of the movements of shipping up and down the west coast and among the islands. One of his watchers was John Johnston of Coll, who gave him valuable information about piping in the old days.

In 1916 the Gordons moved from Mull to Aultbea in Wester Ross, when Seton was appointed Base Intelligence Officer to the naval establishment there. He was commissioned as a Lieutenant in the RNVR, but he did not go to sea.

After the war, the Gordons moved around as Seton, failing to obtain forestry work, had to support his family with his writing. He and Audrey had twenty-one different homes in ten years. In the year 1920–21, he had a few more lessons with Pipe Major Willie Ross, travelling from Northumberland to Edinburgh for the purpose.

All through the 1920s, Seton was assiduously cultivating friendships with the Highland gentry, who seem to have accepted him on his own evaluation. This was probably for professional purposes, to enhance his writing career and help him to build himself a name; it also enabled him to gain access to remote estates otherwise not open to the public. Some of the gentry undoubtedly found him tiresome, and Robert Wolrige Gordon, a grandson of Dame Flora MacLeod, remarked that he always felt that Seton Gordon sought publicity for himself too much. The birth of the Gordons' second daughter in 1925 may have lent a certain desperation to his social climbing, when his career was still uncertain. Both he and his wife Audrey took many lecturing engagements to help make ends meet.

An exchange reported with glee by General Frank Richardson is revealing: the General remarked to Seton that if he went for a walk in the country he never saw any of the exciting wildlife that Seton described in his books; he never saw so much as a sparrow, while Seton was marvelling at golden eagles. Seton replied that he had to see them, it was no good his writing that he'd been out and seen nothing, his public wanted something more colourful. While this says little for his integrity, it does probably reflect the anxiety of a freelance writer struggling to make a living. As someone remarked, at least he was honest about his dishonesty.

In 1926 the death of his father eased Seton's financial problems. He inherited two houses, so he let one and sold the other, buying a substantial family house with land, at Aviemore. At once he began to be accepted as a Highland gentleman, and he was invited to judge at some minor piping competitions. Judging later at Braemar and in Skye led to friendships with Skye families, including the MacLeods of Dunvegan and the MacDonalds of Viewfield, Portree.

Summers in the late 1920s were spent in Skye and the islands, and Seton met the Prime Minister, Ramsay MacDonald, at one of the Games in the north, probably Dornoch, which MacDonald attended every year. They began a correspondence, enthusiastic on Seton's part, which lasted until MacDonald died in 1937.

When Norman MacLeod of MacLeod died in 1929, Seton played a big part in the running of the funeral, and he arranged the piping by Angus MacPherson and his son Malcolm. In the same year, Angus composed a piobaireachd work, *Salute to Seton Gordon*.

In 1930, the Gordons moved to Skye, to make their home at Upper Duntulm, in Trotternish. During the next ten years Seton formed friendships with Viscount David Fincastle, son of Lord Dunmore, and with Francis Cameron-Head of Lochailort, with whom he shared a love of piping and Highland history.

The Duke and Duchess of York (later King George VI and Queen Elizabeth), touring Skye in 1933, called in at Upper Duntulm. By now Seton was making a respectable living from writing books and articles about wildlife in the Highlands, and had a regular income from the renting of his house in Aboyne. At the Ball held for the Yorks in Dunvegan Castle, Seton waltzed with the Duchess.

Arguably 1932–39 were the golden years of Seton's life. When the MacLeod chief, Sir Reginald MacLeod, died in 1934, the piper, Robert Reid, was held up on his journey north, and arrived too late to play as the cortege left the Castle. Seton stood in for him, and Reid arrived in time to play at the graveside. We have to assume that Seton had brought his pipes and had them ready, more or less in tune.

He was now judging all over the country, including the Highland Society's competitions in London. 'Special trains', he wrote to Ramsay MacDonald, 'are bringing pipers from Glasgow, Edinburgh, Aberdeen and Dundee'. His three children were all in boarding school, at their grandparents' expense, and he was free to travel.

In 1938, the 'Two Bobs', Robert U. Brown and Robert Nicol, started their tuition with John MacDonald, Inverness. Seton Gordon took the credit for having persuaded the King, George VI, to send them. He said that the King was not sure he could spare Brown, his gamekeeper, who had trapped 3,000 rabbits the previous winter. 'Greatly daring, I replied "Well, sir, I would rather have a piper who had been under John MacDonald than a man who had trapped 3,000 rabbits". The King said "I will see they go to John MacDonald".'

In June 1939, Seton was awarded the CBE for services to natural history and literature. He had made his name with his books on the Highlands and the Hebrides, which were becoming hugely popular.

At the outbreak of World War II, Seton once more became a coast-watcher, and later a weather-observer for the RAF. His two daughters were called up, one to the Land Army, working on farms, the other as a driver for army officers in the Highlands. Seton visited Edinburgh to give lectures to the troops, and called on Willie Ross at the Castle.

In 1945, his son Alistair Gordon became an officer in the Scots Guards, and saw action in Europe in the last months of the war. He survived the fighting with only a minor wound.

In 1943, Seton's wife Audrey, an Oxford graduate in biology, had been called up and sent to work on scientific research for the government, in England. She was away for nearly three years, to her husband's great dismay. For company he turned to his friends the Cameron-Heads, and when the Games resumed after the war, he took up his judging career again. He was appointed Chieftain of the Glenfinnan Games.

Audrey returned to Skye, and both were aghast when in 1949 the Inveran Hotel in Sutherland burned down, leaving their friend Angus MacPherson without a home or a business. Seton organized a presentation, at which he made the principal speech.

The 1950s brought sorrow: in 1957 his friend Francis Cameron-Head died suddenly, and two years later, when Seton and his wife were both acting as lecturers on a National Trust cruise ship, Audrey was found dead in her bed. Her memorial service was at Kilmuir, and her ashes were scattered on the top of Cairngorm.

A few months later, Seton met his second wife Betty, and they were married in 1960. She was well off, and had a manor house in England and a house in Glenshiel; she and Seton divided their time between these and Upper Duntulm.

Seton in his old age had some disagreements with naturalists attached to the RSPB (Royal Society for the Protection of Birds). They regarded his methods as hopelessly outdated and unscientific, but he could not resist expressing his (unwanted) opinions. One of the scientists used to refer to him as 'Old Satan'.

He was still very active on the hill in his latter years, and one July day in 1966, when he was past his eightieth birthday, he made a memorable walk in the Cairngorms with his friend Alwyne Farquharson of Invercauld: they left home at 5.30 a.m., and walked until midnight, covering a distance of some twenty-five miles.

At his English home he enjoyed visits from James Campbell of Kilberry, when both played their pipes and had endless discussions about piobaireachd. He also made pleasant visits to Skye, where he called on his friend Colonel Jock MacDonald.

In 1972, the piping world was shocked to hear of the sudden death of Robert U. Brown at Balmoral. Seton wrote to Prince Charles about it, receiving a moving reply:

Dear Mr Gordon,
You were very kind to write about Brown. I was absolutely shattered by his death, and burst into floods of helpless tears. I had no idea how much he meant to me and how much of a Highland friend he had been. He taught me so much – he was the first person I used to go fishing with when I was small, and he taught me all I know about stalking.
     He was what I call a 'nature's gentleman', a man of the forest and mountains, and thus one of the greatest pipers Scotland has known . . .

About this time Seton experienced his first hearing-aid, and to his joy began to hear birdsong again, for the first time since he was in his twenties. Presumably the quality of his judging at the Games was also improved. His eyesight remained as keen as ever. In 1975, he judged at Glenfinnan, Invergordon and Skye, but he was beginning to fail.

When Angus MacPherson died in 1976, at the age of nearly ninety-nine, Seton wrote an appreciation in 'The Field', referring to his friend as 'a piping aristocrat, for he was descended from generations of celebrated pipers.' The same year saw the death of Dame Flora MacLeod; John MacFadyen and Seumas MacNeill were asked to play at Dunvegan Castle, and four pipers from Dunvegan district played the cortege from the castle to the church. Seton wrote a tribute for a memorial book.

He was still writing, and still active, but said he looked forward to death and meeting old friends again. He died at his home in England on the night of 18–19 March 1977, being found lying at the bottom of the staircase.

Among tributes to him, a friend wrote: 'I don't think there ever was a more lovable character. Always so gentle and kind and so entertaining and full of fun!' Reference was made by others to his 'wisdom and kindly advice, and also his courtesy'. His protégé, Jonathan MacDonald, speaks of him with devotion and gratitude, saying how strong was his influence for the good of the district.

He was not always so well appreciated by the pipers competing before him. They found his deafness trying, and did not trust his judgements – and they were scornful when he habitually judged without a score. They also disliked his social attitudes. He was gentle and kind to those of social rank he considered his equal, but he could be brusque to the point of rudeness when approached by a stranger or a youngster.

Once, in Skye, he was due to judge a junior competition, and a row of young boys was sitting on a bench, waiting for the start. One of them inadvertently made a loud fart, and, as little boys will, the lads all burst out laughing. Seton Gordon had not heard the cause of their mirth and assumed they were laughing at him. He at once cancelled the competition, and sent the boys home, a high-handed action which some of them remember ruefully to this day. The decision was, of course, the result of his deafness, so might merit our compassion – but it was resented.

In the post-war years he was judging regularly in Skye. On one occasion he had been at the Dunvegan Medal, where one of the pipers was Donald MacGillivray, from Calrossie, near Tain, in Easter Ross, a pupil of John MacDonald (Donald won the Gold Medal at Inverness in 1948). After the competition, Donald was keen to leave Portree for home as soon as possible, having a farm to run, but Seton Gordon approached him, saying 'You're going east, aren't you? You can give me a lift to Inverness'. Donald was planning to go by Achnasheen and Dingwall, and a diversion via the Great Glen and Inverness would add considerably to his journey, but Seton Gordon had already climbed into the car – and after all, he was a judge and Donald did not want to offend him. So off they went.

They had to go up Glen Shiel to reach Invermoriston and the Great Glen road, and as they reached the summit, Seton suddenly cried 'Stop!

Stop!' with such urgency that Donald slammed on the brakes in an emergency stop. Out hopped Seton, saying he simply MUST play a piobaireachd, which he duly did, giving his rendering of *The Glen Is Mine* while Donald quietly fumed. On they went, and half an hour later, the urge came on him again, another work had to be played (by Seton), and half an hour later, yet another, while Donald waited, trying to contain his impatience. After all, he was a far better piobaireachd player himself.

On reaching Inverness, Seton said he was staying at an hotel in the Queensgate, and 'if we hurry, I'll be just in time for dinner'. At the hotel, he dived out of the car, seized his suitcase, and disappeared through the door without a word of thanks, leaving Donald to drive home to Easter Ross. 'Not even the offer of a cup of tea,' said Donald, recalling his annoyance, years later.

Another aspect of Seton Gordon which Raymond Eagle does not explore is his correspondence with Archibald Campbell of Kilberry. Campbell asked Seton to report to him (in England) any opinions on piobaireachd expressed by John MacDonald, Inverness, and Seton seem to have embraced the role of Kilberry's spy with some relish. This, had it been known at the time, would not have endeared him to the players. He was secretly reporting back to Kilberry and passing on information and letters which he could use as ammunition in disagreements with John MacDonald – who had a vastly superior knowledge of the music. Both Kilberry and Seton Gordon were mere amateurs, in both playing-skill and understanding of the music, but being more highly educated were not keen to admit that John MacDonald, steeped in the traditions and the music itself, could tell them anything. They were 'Gentlemen' and John was a 'Player', a distinction only too meaningful in those days.

We must give Seton credit, however, for his brave and principled stand against Kilberry's settings and style in editing piobaireachd. It cannot have been easy for such a conventional member of the gentry to set his face against the Piobaireachd Society, and all credit to Seton Gordon that he attempted this. He showed that his great love of piobaireachd was even more important to him than consolidating his social position. He expressed himself so forcefully that he was removed from the Music Committee of the Piobaireachd Society.

Another of Seton Gordon's achievements was as piping correspondent to *The Times* newspaper in London, the only daily paper which has a piping correspondent (the *Oban Times* is weekly). It is also the only British daily which takes piping seriously, and Seton Gordon must take credit for establishing that tradition. After his death, his place was taken by Fred Morrison, and later by Angus Nicol.

It was Seton Gordon who urged the Prime Minister to give John MacDonald an award in the Honours List of 1932. Ramsay MacDonald said 'If he would promise to walk up and down the House of Lords every afternoon playing some martial air, I might make him a Peer' (if John MacDonald would have accepted). In the end it was the MBE, and Seton Gordon continued to exchange letters with John – who, of course, was unaware that his views were being passed on.

At John MacDonald's funeral in 1953, Seton Gordon gave one of the many funeral eulogies, praising the great player in suitably extravagant terms. Raymond Eagle quotes a passage from this: '. . . having heard him play for two or three hours one went back and played probably 100 per cent better than before hearing him, because the ear had taken in the beauty and the skill and the brilliance of his playing', but in fact Seton was here quoting the words of Somerled MacDonald. He added his own praise, of course.

Seton Gordon taught the last of the MacArthur piping family in Skye, Donald MacArthur, from Kilmuir, as well as giving Jonathan MacDonald a grounding in piobaireachd. Seton was the only piobaireachd player in the district at that time. He was also active socially. Raymond Eagle tells how Seton was once at a ceilidh, at which the Fear an Tigh announced that the programme would start with a tune from a local piper, who seems not to have been rated highly. He had scarcely taken the pipes from their box when someone in the audience shouted 'Sit doon, ye boogger!' The outraged Chairman was on his feet, calling disapprovingly 'Who called the piper a bugger?' which brought the reply 'Who caa'd the boogger a piper?'

[This seems to be based on a humorous poem in the Doric, written in 1932 by W.D. Cocker.]

Sources

Raymond Eagle, *Seton Gordon*
Muriel Spark
Donald MacGillivray
Seton Gordon, *Hebridean Memories*
Finlay MacRae
Proceedings of the Piobaireachd Society Conferences

Farquhar McIntosh/Sue MacIntyre

[This account is included in the Skye volume because it was there that Farquhar McIntosh made his name as the first official schools piping instructor in Scotland, a significant step forward for piping.]

Born in Inverness in 1930, FARQUHAR MCINTOSH began his musical career as a lad there, playing the drums with the cadet corps of the Camerons; having no aptitude for drumming he was soon thrown out, but was asked if he would like to try the pipes. He took to them at once, and within three months was playing the full pipe. He was encouraged in this by being allowed to play along with John Allan, who lived nearby.

The young Farquhar used to attend the meetings of Inverness Piping Society, where he met Sheriff Grant of Rothiemurchus, Donald MacLeod, Mickey MacKay, Willie M. MacDonald, Neil Angus MacDonald and other well-known pipers.

Farquhar joined the Scots Guards, and the Pipe Majors, Kenneth and John Roe, took his piping in hand; after two years he was competing in the light music at the Northern Meeting. He also had lessons from J.B. Robertson, which he shared with John Riach. He had a six-month course with Willie Ross at the Castle, emerging with his Pipe Major's certificate. Willie Ross attended Farquhar's wedding in 1954, but Farquhar admitted 'He used to scare the living daylights out of me, though there was always a twinkle in his eye.' Farquhar and Elizabeth had two daughters, Fiona and Elizabeth.

After a spell in the Parachute Regiment, he was then transferred to a Guards detachment in Oman, where he was Pipe Major to the Trucial Oman Scouts for a time, before returning to the U.K., to become a piping instructor at Pirbright. There he taught, among others, 'Big Angus' MacDonald and Tony Wilson. Farquhar left the army in 1961, on medical grounds.

His civilian life began inauspiciously, as he found work in various shops, in the shoe trade in England and then back in Inverness as a trainee manager in Woolworth's. He did not take to this, but resumed his piping, and again competed in the MSR at the Northern Meeting. Meantime, rumours were circulating about the possibility of appointing a schools piping instructor, so Farquhar asked for an interview with the Education Committee of Inverness-shire County Council. After it he heard no more, so assumed the plan had fallen through.

In 1969, however, pressure on the County Council from Neil Angus

MacDonald and Finlay MacNeill led to the setting-up of a pilot scheme, and they recommended Farquhar McIntosh for the post of instructor, in Skye. Although it was only part-time at first, over 200 children put their names forward, and this had to be reduced to 140. Until then, the only instructor in Skye seems to have been Andrew Stoddart, who, although he had no training as a teacher, had managed to keep Skye piping alive, with a struggle.

The pupils were in nineteen different schools all over Skye, and Farquhar had to travel long distances, often on very narrow and twisting roads, averaging about 100 miles a day. He was a good teacher, and soon settled into the piping life of Skye, and with a group of enthusiasts – who included Colonel Jock, Dougie MacLeod, Peter MacFarquhar, Peter Fulton and Calum Robertson – formed the Skye Piping Society.

He supplemented his teaching, especially of piobaireachd, by bringing in 'Wee Donald' MacLean, Dougie MacLeod and Peter MacFarquhar, both to teach and to play for the youngsters. He often consulted other Skye pipers such as Dr Tony Fisher and John MacKenzie, Uig, and he started local piping competitions. Although frequently working from 9 a.m. to 9 p.m., he himself took piobaireachd from Wee Donald, and later, in Ayrshire, learned twenty works from Willie M. MacDonald. Willie was always willing to help with piobaireachd tuition, as was Andrew Wright. Pupils used to send tapes of their playing, which were returned with helpful comments.

When Farquhar had left the army in 1961, he had been suffering from a duodenal ulcer, as well as increasing strain and unhappiness about his gender. He had been unfortunate enough to have received too many of his mother's female hormones when in the womb, and although born with a male body, he knew something was wrong, as all his life he felt he was really a woman. This condition of transexuality is better understood now than it was then, and those who have it, through no fault of their own, are able to discuss it and if desired change their gender. In Farquhar's day it was not unknown, but was less well understood, and it attracted more attention and prurient comment, especially in the press.

He went to see a consultant, who did tests on his hormone levels and explained his condition to him. After treatment lasting some years, he had the final operation, and changed himself from Farquhar McIntosh into Susan MacIntyre. His wife Elizabeth stayed with him, and became his lifelong friend and companion. Although for legal reasons they had to be divorced in 1980, Elizabeth kept faithfully to her marriage vows, retained her married name and supported her partner loyally. Sue was most fortunate in having that unfailing support for all those years. The sex change gave Sue peace of mind at last, and she said she never regretted it.

It is a remarkable story, and we can only guess at the suffering and heart-searching which lies behind it. That the two of them were still together and came through it is a tribute to their good sense and mutual loyalty. The change lost them a few of their friends who could not accept the transformation, but most took it well. Sue paid tribute to John D. Burgess in particular: he was the first to greet her when she went back among the pipers, and proved himself to be 'a thorough gentleman'. When she was struggling to establish herself as a piping instructor in Ayrshire, he twice went down there to give a recital, drumming up support for her as the new instructor, and by his very presence endorsing her status. 'I can't speak highly enough of him', she said.

She came to Ayrshire as she had to Skye, to find local piping in the doldrums, and she was determined to revive it by encouraging youngsters to play, to compete and to join pipe bands. There too she started a society, the Dailly and District Piping Society, and running classes and competitions, she breathed life back into Ayrshire piping. Gordon Walker, Kenneth MacLean and Ross McCrindle are the best known of Ayrshire's pipers.

Sue retired in 1998, returning to Inverness, where she and Elizabeth lived in Abban Street, in a house they called Tigh a'Phiobair (the Piper's House), not far from Perceval Street where John MacDonald, Inverness, had his home. Sue started classes for adult learners, which proved popular. In 2002 she was awarded the MBE for services to piping, an award which was presented to her by the Lord Lieutenant of Inverness-shire, at a ceremony in Inverness. The piper on that occasion was one of her pupils, Gordon MacLean, and many other of her pupils were present. Possibly her most distinguished pupil is Ross McCrindle, now a piper in the Scots Guards. Another was Malcolm Jones, who went on to join the group Runrig.

Sue composed a slow air in two parts, *Denis Reid's Farewell to Skye*: Denis was one of her friends in Ayrshire, and Vice President of the Dailly and District Piping Society.

In 2003, Sue suffered a heart attack, from which she recovered, but she was forced to slow down and give up some of her piping activities. It is typical of her enthusiasm that when illness prevented her from attending the memorial recital of piobaireachd to mark the fiftieth anniversary of the death of John MacDonald, Inverness, she sent a generous donation to the organizers, 'to help with the expenses'.

Sue MacIntyre died in June 2010. Four of her pupils, playing together, led the funeral cortege, before Ross McCrindle piped the coffin into the crematorium, later playing the *Lament for the Children*.

In recent times the Skye schools piping instructor was RON MONK, who has now returned to his native New Zealand. He was replaced by LEWIS BARCLAY, formerly a piper in the Queen's Own Highlanders, and when Lewis moved to Badenoch, NIALL STEWART took his place. EMILY MACDONALD also teaches piping in Portree.

Sources

Sue MacIntyre
Elizabeth McIntosh
Piper Press 1998 (May–July)
Piping Times Nov 1990, Sept 1992, Jan 1997, July 1998, Feb and July
   2002

Some 20th-century Skye Pipers

Lewis Fraser Beaton (1890–1944)

LEWIS BEATON was born in Glasgow, but came of a Skye family, his grandfather having been a noted Skye fiddler. In Glasgow, Lewis started his piping at the age of eight, in the Boys Brigade, taught by Pipe Major Edwin MacPherson, and later he had lessons from John MacDougall Gillies and William Ferguson, composer of *Australian Ladies*. He became an accomplished player, and a leading competitor at the Games. During World War I he fought at Gallipoli with the 52nd Division.

He was a dentist by profession, practising in Twickenham, London, where his house was a centre for pipers. Soon after 1919, he was a prime mover in the founding of the Piping Society of London, and became its first President. The Notices of Pipers say 'He stood up inflexibly for the dignity of piping. When playing at a London concert, if he saw people talking he would stop and decline to go on, stating the reason plainly, no matter how many hundreds there were in the audience'.

Lewis Beaton's name will always be associated with the London competitions, and he was a stalwart of London piping for many years. When he died in 1944, his favourite tune *Dutheich nan Craobh (Loch Duich)* was played at the funeral.

Major Kenneth Mackenzie Cameron, RAMC

Major KENNETH CAMERON, an army doctor, was a capable amateur player, according to the Notices of Pipers. He was a nephew of Mrs Lachlan MacDonald of Skeabost, where he spent most of his boyhood. He was an uncle of Somerled MacDonald, related to Dr K.N. MacDonald – they were all descended from Niel MacLeod of Gesto.

He was a pupil of John Cameron, of the Cameron Highlanders, and served as an army doctor, mainly overseas. To mark the Siege of Ladysmith, he composed a 2/4 March in four parts, *The Relief of Ladysmith.*

He went on to become doctor to Lord Kitchener when he was Commander-in-Chief in India. In 1907, during his stay in India, Major Cameron became one of the 'Seven Pipers of Simla', all army officers except one, Archibald Campbell of Kilberry, who was a lawyer in the Indian Civil Service. Kilberry's elder brother John was also in the group, along with two MacKinnon brothers-in-law of Major Cameron.

The Major died in 1910, in Aldershot, from tetanus he contracted after being thrown off his bicycle by a dog.

IAIN NICOLSON from Portree was a piper in the Scots Guards. He died in 1938.

Roderick Campbell

Born in Skye, RODERICK CAMPBELL was a first-class player who served in the Lovat Scouts in World War I. The Notices of Pipers describe him as the winner of many prizes, who was a good teacher and composer of many tunes. D.R. MacLennan described him as 'a very nice, sweet player'. He won the Gold Medal at Oban in 1908, and was for a time instructor to the Scottish Pipers' Society. He taught John Wilson before he (John) went to Canada, and among his other pupils were Alan Calder, Hans Gates and Ian C. Cameron He died in Edinburgh in 1941, after a long spell in Liberton Hospital. His ivory-mounted pipes went to Dr Angus MacDonald.

Roddy Campbell was a great friend of another Skye piper, GEORGE MACKAY, known as 'MacKay from Skye' and described by D.R. MacLennan as 'a great worthy'. Roddy composed a reel called *MacKay from Skye*, in his honour. D.R. said George lived in Edinburgh with his sister and elder brother 'and I think they kept their thumb on him very well'. George is credited with being the origin of a hoary piping quip: one day Roddy Campbell said to him 'Hello, George, I hear you're getting married.' 'Oh no,' replied George, 'not me – I have enough trouble with my reeds'.

George played in the Gold Medal competition in Inverness in 1902. As he was leaving, someone shouted to him 'Who won the medal today?' 'I did', said George, 'but who did they give it to but Jimmy Center?'

Although George was known as 'MacKay from Skye', he seems to have been the same George who was one of three brothers born in Tongue, Sutherland. It is not known why he had the Skye by-name. Was he in fact a Skye piper? (See the Earl of Skye, above.)

Malcolm MacInnes

In 1940 MALCOLM MACINNES published a book of 120 'bagpipe tunes, gleanings & styles'. He had previously written several books of Hebridean music, including *Songs of the Isle of Skye* and *Lilts from the Western Isles*. In a later volume, *Traditional Airs of Skye and the West*, he wrote that he had collected the tunes from the singing of elderly relatives in Drumfearn, in the Isle of Skye. D.R. MacLennan told Roderick Cannon that he undertook the final preparation of the manuscript of pipe music for the press, and had some difficulty, as 'in some places MacInnes insisted on his own particular renderings, even though these appeared unorthodox'. He died in 1951, and was remembered as 'a thrawn man, very firm in his opinions'.

Dr J.A.C. Fisher

Following on after Dr Murdo MacLean, brother of Wee Donald MacLean, Dr J.A.C. (TONY) FISHER was a G.P. in Skye, based in Dunvegan, and seems to have been a live wire in the post-war piping life of Skye. He was a leading light in the formation of the Duirinish Piping Society, and helped Farquhar McIntosh to found the Skye Piping Society, and to hold piping competitions in the 1960s. He ran the Silver Chanter evening in its early days, and occasionally competed on Boreraig Day. By 1980 he was living at Dalchuirn, Lochcarron, Wester Ross. Although it is said locally 'he talked a good tune, but playing a good tune was another thing altogether', and his compositions are not rated too highly ('more enthusiasm than talent'), his appetite for piping made him a valued member of the community. He and Dougie MacLeod used to get together for joint playing and composing sessions.

In September 1970, the *Piping Times* published the words of Dr Fisher:

> To me, it is as futile to ask why drone reeds double-tone as it is to ask why a baby cries. Both are demanding attention, possibly because they are having wind troubles or their bridles are too tight, or they need to be wetted or are too wet, but usually they both do it out of sheer malice, to test their owner's moral fibre.

Dr Tony's pipe tunes included:

Angus Munro's Jig J 4
Bruce MacPhie 2/4 M 4
David C. Henderson 6/8 M 4
David Meek's Welcome to Skye 2/4 HP 4
D.C. MacLeod of Stormy Hill 2/4 M 4
Donald MacMillan's Can 2/4 HP 4
Ed Garton's Cat 6/8 J 4
Mrs Evelyn MacDonald, Viewfield 2/4 M 4
Murdo Lamont's Spree R 4
The Padlock 2/4 HP 4
Tullochard 4/4 M 4

Evan Macrae

EVAN MACRAE was born in the Black Isle, but was brought up in Sleat, in the south of Skye. He is, however, generally associated with Lochaber, from his long stay as Schools Piping Instructor in Fort William, after leaving the army; he is not considered a Skye piper, although his teacher was John MacDonald, the Ardvasar blacksmith.

Some of his compositions have Skye associations, including:

The Ardvasar Blacksmith R 4
The Duirinish Piping Society S 4

The Stoddart Family

GEORGE STODDART, Edinburgh, told Norman Johnston that his family came from Skye, and that there are still piping Stoddarts there. In the 1841 Census for Kilmuir, there is listed a George Stoddart, living at Erisco (just north of Duntulm). He and his wife Jean were then both forty, and their children were Isabella twenty, Ann fifteen, Walter fourteen, George twelve, James nine, Andrew eight and Margaret five. The parents are listed as not having been born locally, but all the children were. The implication is that this was probably the first generation of Stoddarts to live in Skye, and they came around 1820, probably brought in as shepherds from the Borders.

A Pipe Major JOHN STODDART was killed in action in July 1917; it is not known if he was related.

Today there are Stoddarts still in the Portree and Broadford districts. In the 1920s, the Portree Pipe Band included piper ANDY STODDART and drummer George Stoddart. When Farquhar McIntosh came as piping instructor to the Skye schools in 1969, he took over from Andrew Stoddart, who with no training had valiantly been teaching the youngsters, to keep piping going. In the 1990s the Games Committee included Andrew's nephew, Pipe Major NORMAN STODDART, who now lives at Torrin.

Andy Stoddart was a piper in the 4th/5th Camerons, and told a story against himself when serving with the band in France. They were marching along a road in Northern France, playing at full pitch, when they passed a field in which there were two pigs of a type which Andy had not seen before. Being interested in pigs, he was studying them closely as they marched by, without pausing in his playing. When he eventually brought his attention back to the music, he found he was the only man still playing.

Andy Stoddart was the uncle of Norman, and one of three brothers who were all pipers. Andy developed a special sheep-dip, which he sold to a big agricultural concern for the price of a drink; it was marketed as Stoddart's Special Dip and sold widely, earning a fortune – but not for Andy. Charles Stoddart was an excellent drummer.

The related piping Stoddarts, George and his son Gavin, who became Major GAVIN STODDART, formerly Director of the Army School of Piping, later made their home in the Edinburgh district. GEORGE STODDART was married to Margaret Sutherland, daughter of Pipe Major JAMES SUTHERLAND. She was for many years a staunch supporter of the Piobaireachd Society Conferences, which she livened up considerably with her witty poems and lovely singing.

Nicol Campbell

NICOL CAMPBELL, whose parents came from Glendale, was the piping teacher of the son of the Morrisons, who ran the Dunvegan Hotel. Nicol taught both light music and piobaireachd. He was based in Dunvegan, and was a founder-member of the Duirinish Piping Society. He was probably related to Danny A. Campbell (see above).

He was one of four Dunvegan players chosen to play at Dame Flora MacLeod's funeral. Nicol died in 1991.

Peter Bain

PETER BAIN was a native of Portree and lived across the bay, at Penfiler in Braes. He was not only an exceptionally good piper but also a Gaelic singer – many of his family were talented in both forms of music. He left Portree to live in Glasgow, where he workd for the Post Office. He joined the Scots Guards as a piper, and told D.R. MacLennan he had done so because he had heard D.R. playing at the Skye Games. He won the Gold Medal at Inverness in 1934 and at Oban in 1946. Today there is just one descendant of that family left at Braes. (See also p. 281)

Farquhar MacRae

FARQUHAR MACRAE was born in Portree, Skye, in 1854, but went to Glasgow where he spent most of his life. He lived at 52 Napiershall Street, between Kelvinbridge and St George's Cross, on the west side of Glasgow. A pupil of Sandy Cameron, son of Donald, and probably of Keith Cameron, too, he became a good player who won the Gold Medal at Oban in 1898.

For twenty-five years Farquhar was Pipe Major of the 3rd Volunteer Battalion of the HLI, based in Glasgow, and his band won the World Championships at Cowal in 1913. He formed the City of Glasgow Pipe Band in 1910, and was influential in raising the standard of playing in Glasgow pipe bands in that era. He became Pipe Major of the Clan MacRae band, and was a good teacher who taught Donald MacLeod from Eigg, introducing him to piobaireachd. Donald emigrated to Canada in 1911.

Farquhar was a great fan of Donald MacPhee, then living in Glasgow, and once described MacPhee as 'the finest piper I ever heard'.

Willie Gray, writing in *Piping and Dancing* in October 1940, was discussing the reel *The Sheepwife*. He said: 'This reel reminds me of the late William MacLennan, Edinburgh, who on one occasion, when competing at certain games, was rehearsing it before his turn to compete. Pipe Major Farquhar MacRae (Farrachar, as he was generally called by his many admirers), who had been listening, drew Willie's attention to the manner in which he was snapping the reel and pointed out that the phrase 'Ho do ro chin' should be played round and not cut as MacLennan had been playing it. MacLennan at once acknowledged the point, and when his turn came attempted to benefit by Farquhar's advice. Alas, Willie got confused and did not make a good job of his performance, and on coming down from the platform made straight for Farquhar. 'What's the matter?' enquired Farquhar, and was met with the exclamation 'Damn you and your ho do ro chin'. Gray added that he had no doubt that Farquhar was right, and Willie went on later to make a splendid job of this reel, which won him many prizes.

Craigie Calder, in a tape recording for the College of Piping, said that Farquhar used to play every Saturday night for dancing at the Waterloo Rooms in Waterloo Street, in the centre of Glasgow, a useful source of regular income for him. After playing, he would walk home through the city, but one night of dense fog in 1916, he missed his way and fell into the Forth and Clyde Canal, near Port Dundas, and was drowned. After that tragic event, he was always referred to as 'poor Farquhar' by pipers in Glasgow.

The SPA named a trophy for him, the Farquhar MacRae Trophy for junior piping in their amateur competitions.

Finlay MacRae

FINLAY MACRAE was born in Skye, at Flodigarry, and his great-uncles and grandfather were a well known family of pipers and composers. His great-grand uncles were born on the island of Ensay, near Harris, and Finlay was named after one of them. Another was Angus MacRae, who became a highly acclaimed piper winning many prizes. Angus' brother was piper/valet to Cameron of Lochiel.

Finlay learned his piping in the classes run in the 1930s by Miss MacDonald of Viewfield, sister of Colonel Jock. She brought in a succession of excellent pipers to teach summer classes in Portree. The Piobaireachd Society assisted financially, and pupils had to pay half-a-crown (two shillings and sixpence, old money), but only if their families could afford it. The poorer boys had their tuition free.

Finlay has happy memories of classes in the Drill Hall with 'Wee Donald' MacLean. He recalls Donald, a fervent supporter of Partick Thistle football team, listening avidly to a wireless commentary during a piping lesson; when Partick won the match, Donald threw his chanter high into the rafters of the hall (not recommended).

Many years later, after Donald had been to Tasmania and then returned to Scotland, Finlay happened to see him on the street in Beauly, and renewed his acquaintance. Finlay went to Donald for many lessons in his home in Inverness. Finlay became a leading teacher of piping, including piobaireachd, at his home in Dingwall. He was also a judge at many of the Games in the north, until he retired in his eighties.

In 2006 Finlay decided that there should be a memorial to his former teacher, Pipe Major William Ross of Edinburgh Castle, near to his birthplace in Glen Strathfarrar. Launching an appeal for funds, Finlay raised the money to pay for the building of a fine cairn in the glen, just behind the Ross family's house (now derelict) at Ardcuilc, in the glen. A crowd of enthusiasts attended the unveiling by Willie Ross's granddaughter, Mrs Lesley Alexander. Rain failed to spoil the occasion, which was later continued at a ceilidh organised by Finlay in a Beauly hotel.

In 2011, Finlay had to have part of his leg amputated, because of circulation problems. With his usual spirit and courage he is tackling the task of learning to walk again, and all pipers will wish him well.

Finlay's compositions include:

Megan's Wedding 2/4 M
John and Sarah Dewar of Johannesburg 6/8 M
Donald Smith of Uig 6/8 M
Joey's Tune SA (Joey is Finlay's wife)
Leaving Glen Affric SA
Fiona's Tune SA
Leisa's Wedding Air SA

A cousin of Finlay is Colonel PATRICK (PATSY) MACPHERSON, who lives in England. He is an expert on the history of the Portree Pipe Band, of which he was a founder member.

George D. MacDonald

GEORGE D. MACDONALD was the Pipe Major of the Millhall Pipe Band, Stirling, a band which won many honours. Although born in Dunoon, his father and forebears were from Skye. He was a pupil of John Mac-Dougall Gillies.

Peter MacFarquhar

PETER MACFARQUHAR was the first Pipe Major of the Isle of Skye Pipe Band, of which he was the energetic and hardworking Secretary. Although living in Skye, he belonged originally to Tiree. He was a leading light in the Duirinish Piping Society. His grave is in Portree.

The MacPhees

ANGUS MACPHEE, who lived at Arpafeelie, North Kessock, near Inverness, came from a Skye piping family in Dunvegan. His grand-uncle, Pipe Major ALEX MACPHEE of the H.L.I., was Champion Piper of Australia in the 1930s, and his father, DONALD MACPHEE, was a solo player and a bandsman in the 1930s, playing in the Glasgow Transport band. His uncle, CALUM MACPHEE, lived in London and Edinburgh after the second World War, and was well-known as a solo competitor and tutor of piping.

Angus himself was taught by Pipe Major Peter Bain of the Scots Guards, who was an enthusiastic piobaireachd player. For some years Angus was President of the Inverness Piping Society, and he also joined the Royal Scottish Pipers' Society, the Drumnadrochit Piping Society and the Piobaireachd Society. An amateur player, he won the R.S.P.S. Ceol Mor competition. He was an art teacher, and until his illness he was a respected judge on the bench at the Northern Meetings as well as presiding at Highland Games, judging both junior and senior piobaireachd. Angus was Hon. Piper to the Gaelic Society of Inverness, and wrote on piping and Gaelic topics, with several poems, in both Gaelic and English, to his credit.

Angus named his house in the Black Isle 'Crunluath', and on one occasion, Iain MacFadyen addressed a letter to him simply with a Crunluath movement written out in staff notation. To the credit of the Inverness Post Office, it reached its destination. There must be pipers in the Royal Mail.

In 2006, he published a book, *The Crunluath Collection*, an attractive volume of Gaelic songs 'based on bagpipe music in both Ceol Beag and Ceol Mor'. It gives the words of the songs in both Gaelic and English: he wrote most of them himself and set them to pipe music, some of it his own composition, as well as illustrating them beautifully with his drawings and photographs. He even included a CD of his own singing of the songs. The over-all effect is of an unusual, very musical and pleasing collection, warmly recommended.

Angus died in 2011.

Donnie MacKinnon

DONNIE MACKINNON, of Braigh Uige, is the son of ANGUS MACKINNON, who was a piper in the 51st Highland Division during the Second World War, after being PM of the Portree Band from 1933–39. He

volunteered for the army at the age of forty-five, and served throughout
the war, but when he returned home, he never so much as mentioned
his army days. Angus had the honour of piping as the first plane to land
in Skye came in. It landed at Glen Brittle, but the occasion was not an
unqualified success as the ground proved both rough and soft, and the
plane had great difficulty in taking off again. It was the only landing
ever attempted there.

Angus married a Ross descended from the family of William Ross,
the Gaelic poet, who was a grandson of the Blind Piper of Gairloch,
Iain Dall MacKay. Iain's daughter married John Ross from Broadford. So Donnie has the genes of William Ross, Iain Dall and Donald
Duaghal MacKay in his blood.

Donnie is not a piper, but is important to the local piping world for
his extensive knowledge of Skye piping. For many years he has run the
summer ceilidhs in Portree which have proved popular with tourists
and locals alike. He presents all the local talent in music, dance, poetry
and story-telling, bringing in both the schoolchildren and their elders.
His considerable effort to sustain a good level of entertainment over a
long period has helped to keep the standard of performance high.

John MacKenzie

There were two good pipers of this name, both associated with Trotternish. One of them, who had a brother in the Scots Guards, went
to Australia. He is the reputed composer of the tune *Portree Bay*, but
some say he bought it from someone else. The other, known as Seadan,
lives at Sheader, near Uig, in Trotternish, and runs a taxi business and
a school bus. He is knowledgeable about the piping life of Skye. He
was previously a postman, and a man of so many interests that he had
no time for competing. His pipe is one of seven made for the Glasgow
Exhibition in 1888. He was a pupil of Dr Allan MacDonald, the Uig
G.P., and held by some to be the best piper in Skye since Peter Bain.
He is a first cousin of Seumas Archie MacDonald, and a close friend of
Murdo MacKenzie, piper and composer.

Flora Macneill

FLORA MACNEILL returned to live in Uig, where she was born in 1918.
She had left at the age of fifteen, to settle in Beckenham, Kent. She was
active in the piping life of London, acting as Secretary to the London
Piping Society for many years. After the Second World War she moved

to Glasgow, where she was Secretary to the Scottish Piping Society. She had always kept up her links with Skye, and eventually retired to Uig, joining her brother and sister. Nobody was surprised when she took on more administration, becoming Secretary of both the Skye Piping Society and the Games Committee. Full of energy and enthusiasm, she was always most efficient, and well-liked by the pipers and the audiences alike, for her informal and helpful friendliness. After some months of illness, Flora died in 2004.

When she eventually stood down as convener of the piping committee, she was replaced by 'Andy' Anderson. The latest convener is Cailean MacLean.

Allan Beaton

ALLAN BEATON was for many years living in London, where he was a stalwart of the London Piping Society. A native of Skye and a Gaelic speaker, he returned to the island on his retirement, and made his home at Stein, in Waternish. For some years after his return he served as a Highland Councillor for Skye, but has now retired from that, feeling he has made his contribution. He is a good amateur piper, and has a wide knowledge of the history of both piping and Skye. A member of the Piobaireachd Society, he takes charge of tape-recording the talks and discussions at the conferences.

Events and Associations

Reeds in Skye

At the Piobaireachd Society Conference in 1992, Seumas MacNeill was speaking about the Summer Schools held by the Glasgow College of Piping. These started under canvas, at Dunvegan, and local boys could attend free of charge. One boy 'came from a place several miles past Dunvegan [was this perhaps Glendale?], and walked to the camp. He had a practice chanter, and his reed was making a nice sweet sound. I said to him "Where did you get that reed?" and he said "I just picked it out of the field in my way down." It was a straw which he had pressed together at the top, with no staple, nothing at all. It was a perfectly good practice chanter reed, but every day he had to go and pick another one.'

Experiment has shown that the straw of bere barley gives the best results, being tougher than the barley grown today – and of all the straw types available, barley does seem to be the best; but no doubt straw differs in all parts of the world, just as reeds do.

Skye Gathering

(See also above, the MacDonalds of Viewfield.)

In June 1959 (the Games were held earlier in the year then) a competitor in the 16lb Hammer event at the Skye Games made an erratic throw, and a competing piper, Donny MacKenzie, had to step back smartly, in mid-tune, as the missile flew past him. It bounced on the piping platform before passing between the two judges, Seton Gordon and Dr Allan MacDonald. No-one was hurt.

Skye Piping Society

The Isle of Skye Piping Society was founded in 1926 by Miss Joanna MacDonald, known as 'Miss Toonie', a sister of Colonel Jock. She gave it the Gaelic title Comunn Piobaireachd an Eilean Sgiathanaich (the CPES). The aim was to promote piping on the island by bringing in expert pipers from the mainland. Life membership cost 3 guineas, and the annual subscription was 5s. Thirty people at once took up life membership, and some gave donations as well.

William MacDonald, from Sutherland, had previously held some classes in Skye, and there is a report by John MacFadyen that Andrew MacDonald, brother of the great John MacDonald, Inverness, had taught in Skye earlier in the 1920s. General Frank Richardson came to Skye in 1926, to give piping tuition to local youngsters, but this must have been a private arrangement.

In 1926, the new Society appointed Willie MacDonald for a period of six months; his salary was £4 10s a week. The Skye and Lochalsh Archive Service has the Minutes of the Society as part of the Viewfield Papers (ref. SL/D1062/etc), which show that Willie taught for a month in each of several places in Skye: Portree, Dunvegan, Skeabost, Staffin (where the Free Presbyterian Missionary was hostile) and Strath, for five evenings per week. Each of these places was required to start a branch of the Society, and to raise £20 for the expenses of the classes.

The scheme was soon in trouble: in 1928 funds were low and the Committee asked Willie to take a lower salary, but he refused indignantly. After heated correspondence, the Society approached other noted pipers – Willie Ross in Edinburgh, then J.A. Gordon – but both were too busy. William Ferguson was available but wanted £5 10s plus his travel costs. They had to go back to Willie MacDonald, and settlement was reached. They contacted the Highland regiments hoping for donations, since many of the trained pipers from Skye went on to join the army, but only the 1st Battalion of the Scots Guards responded, by sending one guinea (Willie's brother, John D. MacDonald, was their Pipe Major).

In 1932, Willie was unable to complete the six months' tuition for family reasons, so his ex-pupil Peter Bain took over, at a salary of £2 10s. He taught for a season, and was replaced in 1933 by Angus MacKinnon.

An approach to the Piobaireachd Society brought Skye into the scheme whereby they sent instructors to remote venues, paying the salaries but requiring the locals to pay for travel within the island and to arrange board and lodging at their own expense. The first teacher sent up was Willie Ross, for one month in the winter of 1933–4. He had big classes (25 in Kilmuir, 'very keen' he said) – but in Portree he reduced the numbers by half, sending away the 'no-hopers'.

In 1938, Peter Bain was still teaching for £2 a week, but piping tuition was now on its last legs. It folded before the outbreak of war.

In 1950, the dormant CPES was resurrected, with Colonel Jock in the Chair, and a committee which included General Harry MacDonald, Dr Allan MacDonald, Angus MacKinnon, Donald MacKenzie and Pipe Major Donald MacLean. Seton Gordon was invited to become Vice-President.

By December 1950 Donald MacLean, from Oban and Glasgow, was teaching in Skye. The response was gratifying: twenty-eight pupils in Portree, seveteen in Uig, eight in Kilmuir, fourteen in Broadford and eighteen in Dunvegan. Donald received £15 a week, but had to pay for his own lodging and travel. Pupils were charged 2s 6d for adults, 1s for juveniles, but Finlay MacRae, who was one of the Portree class, said that anyone with genuine hardship could have help with the fees. Dancing instruction was given free of charge to those enrolled for piping.

Colonel Jock lent the Society £120, and the Education Authority gave £5 per week all winter, provided that the full programme was maintained, but there was a substantial deficit which had to be reduced by holding concerts, dances and sales. The local MP contributed £5, and was asked to become the Society's Patron. This time the regiments, the Camerons, Seaforth and Black Watch, were more generous, sending sums of between £3 and £5.

It was in vain. By April 1951, Donald MacLean extended his teaching at a reduced rate of £12 a week, but once he had completed the course, the Society folded once more, unable to cope with the increasing costs. In some places the tuition had been free, but pupils had to buy their own chanters and books, an outlay of 12s per pupil. Some of them walked as much as four miles to attend the classes. None had their own pipes, but the Society acquired five sets and lent them to boys as long as they were living in Skye, until they could buy their own by instalments.

Since the Society had begun, six boys had gone to the Scots Guards as pipers, one of whom became Pipe Major. Two more had positions as personal pipers, and four were pipers in the Territorials. And the local Pipe Band had eight excellent players.

In the 1960s, under Dr Fisher and Dougie MacLeod, the Duirinish branch of the Piping Society flourished for a time and had a strong influence on Skye piping, before it too fell into abeyance.

In 1969 Highland Council introduced school tuition in piping, with Farquhar MacIntosh as the first instructor, so that every child in Skye could learn to play. The response was immediate and gratifying. Today the need to cut Council spending has led to the charging of fees for tuition, and numbers have dropped somewhat.

In 2000, a decision was made to re-form the Skye Piping Society, which had been 'in abeyance' for some years. An open meeting was well attended, where, according to the report in the *Piping Times*, 'it became abundantly clear that there was a continuing demand within the community for an organisation to promote interest in piping within the island'. Donald MacLeod from Kinlochfollart, Dunvegan, was elected Chairman, and a committee was set up to plan a series of events.

The first step was to re-establish the annual tribute to Donald MacDonald, at his birthplace in Glenhinnisdale, Trotternish. It was decided that, as had been done previously before the Society lapsed, a piobaireachd would be played there by a leading piper, the day after the Donald MacDonald Quaich competition at Armadale, then run by the Clan Donald Lands Trust. The piper in 2000 was Colin MacLellan, who had to play, in steady rain, the appropriately named *Too Long in This Condition*.

The Duirinish Piping Society was another which fell into abeyance, but was a strong influence on Skye piping in the 1960s.

(See also Col. Jock MacDonald, Farquhar MacIntosh, Dr J.A.C. Fisher, Peter MacFarquhar, Flora MacNeill.)

Sabhal Mòr Ostaig

Sabhal Mòr Ostaig is the Gaelic College at the south end of Skye. It was founded in 1973, and named after former farm buildings on the site. It is unique in Scotland in that it offers higher education through the medium of Gaelic, as well as a variety of summer courses and what are known as 'immersion' courses to teach the Gaelic language by having the pupil live with a Gaelic-speaking family near the college, to speak no English at all.

Initially offering HNC and HND courses, the college is now part of the University of the Highlands and Islands, with degree courses as well as a thriving post-graduate research department. Piping scholars such as DECKER FOREST are resident; he has completed his PhD thesis on 'Changes in the Performance/Practice of Ceol Beag, c.1820–1966', and specialises in teaching his pupils the different styles of playing pipe music through the centuries.

Another distinguished post-graduate scholar was ROY WENTWORTH, who uncovered much new information about the life and homes of Iain Dall MacKay. Roy died in 2002, and his PhD was awarded posthumously.

HUGH CHEAPE is also on the staff. When he was at the National Museum of Antiquities in Edinburgh, he did valuable work in collecting and preserving anything to do with pipes and their maintenance (much of his material is now in the museum of the Piping Centre in Glasgow). Hugh continues to research the background and history of piping.

Isle of Skye Pipe Band

An interesting account by Margaret MacKenzie of the Isle of Skye Pipe Band appeared in the booklet published by the Skye Highland Games Committee to commemorate the 121st Anniversary of the Skye Games.

It began as Portree Pipe Band in the late 1920s, under the Post Master, William Watson. In those days no uniform was worn, and the band played every Saturday night in summer, marching from the Drill Hall, through the village and round the Square. They bought their first uniforms in 1932: Glengarry bonnets with blackcock feathers and Clan MacDonald crests, dark blue tunics with white piping, red tartan hose with buckled shoes, and kilts and plaids of the tartan MacDonald of Sleat. This kit was stored and carefully maintained throughout the war years.

A highlight of the early years was when the band was invited to play at the wedding of General Harry MacDonald of Redcliff to Sheila Ross of Cromarty, in Cromarty (the Black Isle). As payment, each band member received £10 and two bottles of whisky, and as a group they were given the bottom layer of the wedding cake, on its silver base. Their return from Cromarty was delayed, and the coach arrived at Kyle too late for the last ferry – and the only food they had was that cake. Not much of it was left by morning.

There was a post-war lull during which the band was disbanded, but in 1961 it was re-formed by the initiative of a piper, Ewen MacKenzie, a former Cameron Highlander who had newly returned to work in Portree. The first Committee President was Colonel Jock MacDonald of Viewfield. Members came from all over the island, and the new band was given the name of the Isle of Skye Pipe Band.

They had no money, but managed to acquire ex-regimental Cameron of Erracht kilts with red tunics, worn with Cameron hose tops, white spats and garter flashes. Raising £201 over a ten-week period of fund-raising, they bought four side drums, a tenor drum, Drum Major's white buff gauntlets and a scarlet gold braided sash. Later they added ostrich feather bonnets costing £65 each, and ex-regimental Seaforth kilts were added to the drummers' uniforms. George Stoddart was the leading drummer in the band, and after the twelve young drummers had had instruction from the instructor of the Queen's Own Highlanders, George took over the drumming classes.

Chanter and pipe classes were started, aiming to consolidate the position of piping in Skye. Pipe Majors of the past included William Watson, Peter MacFarquhar, Angus McKinnon, Donnie MacKenzie, Norman Stoddart and Ron Monk. The band plays regularly in Skye and other islands, and makes occasional trips abroad. It has been affectionately described as 'amateur in status, professional in playing'.

Source
Article in the Skye Games booklet

Bibliography

[*TGSI* = *Transactions of the Gaelic Society of Inverness*]

BASSIN, Ethel (ed. Derek Bowman) 1977: *The Old Songs of Skye – Frances Tolmie and her Circle.*

BOSWELL, James 1785: *The Journal of a Tour to the Hebrides with Samuel Johnson.*

BUISMAN, Frans and WRIGHT, Andrew (eds) 2001: *The MacArthur-MacGregor Manuscript of Piobaireachd (1820).*

CAMPBELL, Lord Archibald 1885: *Records of Argyll, Legends. Traditions and Recollections of Argyllshire Highlanders.*

CAMPBELL, Jeannie 2001: *Highland Bagpipe Makers* (2nd edition 2011).

CAMPBELL, Robert Bruce 2000: *The MacCrimmon Pipers of Skye: A Tradition Under Siege.*

CAMPEY, Lucille H. 2004: *After the Hector: The Scottish Pioneers of Nova Scotia and Cape Breton 1773–1852.*

CAMPSIE, Alistair 1980: *The MacCrimmon Legend: the Madness of Angus MacKay.*

CHEAPE, Hugh 1999: 'The MacCrimmon Piping Dynasty and its Origins', *TGSI* vol LXII.

CONNOLLY, S.J. (ed.) 1998: *The Oxford Companion to Irish History.*

DICKSON, Joshua (ed.) 2009: *The Highland Bagpipe, Music, History, Tradition.*

DIXON, J.H. 1886: *Gairloch and Guide to Loch Maree*

DONALDSON, M.E.M. 1935: *Scotland's Suppressed History.*

DONALDSON, William 2000: *The Highland Pipe and Scottish Society 1750–1950.*

EAGLE, Raymond 1991: *Seton Gordon, the Life and Times of a Highland Gentleman.*

FIONN (WHYTE, Henry) between 1900 and 1907: *Historic, Biographic and Legendary Notes* to tunes in Glen's Collection, 5th edition.

FLOWER, Robin 1947: *The Irish Tradition.*

FORBES, Robert 2007: *The Lyon in Mourning.*

FOSTER, R.F. (ed.) 1989: *The Oxford Illustrated History of Ireland*

FRASER, the Rev. James 1905: *The Wardlaw Manuscript, Chronicles of the Frasers, 916–1674.* Published by the Scottish Historical Society, ed. William MacKay.

FRASER, Simon, ed. B.J. Orme 1979: *The Piobaireachd of Simon Fraser, with Canntaireachd* (2nd edition 1985).

GIBSON, John 1998: *Traditional Gaelic Bagpiping 1745–1945.*

GORDON, Seton 1925: *Hebridean Memories* (re-issued 1995).

GRANT, I.F. 1959: *The MacLeods, the History of a Clan.*

GRIMBLE, Ian 1965: *Chief of MacKay.*

HADDOW, Alec 1982: *The History and Structure of Ceol Mor.*

HALFORD-MACLEOD, Ruairidh 1986: 'Everyone who has an intrigue hopes it should not be known: Lord Loudon and Anne Mackintosh, an intrigue of the '45', in *TGSI* LV.

HILL, J. Michael 1993: *Fire and Sword, Sorley Boy MacDonnell and the Rise of Clan Ian Mor 1538–90.*

HUTCHINSON, Roger, undated article on Donald Archie MacDonald, in the *West Highland Free Press.*

JOHNSON, Samuel 1775: *A Journey to the Western Isles of Scotland.*

LAWSON, Alan 1987: *A Country Called Stratherrick* (2nd ed. 2001).

LAWSON, Bill 2002: *Harris in History and Legend.*

LETFORD, Stuart, 2004: *The Little Book of Piping Quotations.*

LOVE, Dane 2007: *Jacobite Stories.*

MACCULLOCH, John 1819: *A Description of the Western Isles of Scotland.*

MACCURDY, Edward 1945: 'Norman MacLeod – Caraid nan Gael' in *TGSI* XXXIX–XL

MACDONALD, Rev. A. and Rev. A. 1896: *The Clan Donald* (3 vols).

MACDONALD, D.A. 1974: article 'An Dubh Ghleannach' in *Tocher* 15.

MACDONALD, Joseph 1760: *Compleat Theory of the Scots Highland Bagpipes* (ed. R. Cannon).

MACDONALD, Dr K.N. 1900: *MacDonald Bards from Mediaeval Times.*

MACDONALD, Stuart 1994: *Back to Lochaber.*

MACDOUGALL, Jean 1984: *Highland Postbag, The Correspondence of Four MacDougall Chiefs 1715–1865.*

MCHARDY, Stuart 2005: *The Well of Heads and Other Tales of the Scottish Clans.*

MACINNES, John 1985: 'Gleanings from Raasay Tradition' in *TGSI* LVI.

MACKAY, Angus: Manuscripts, now in the National Library of Scotland, Edinburgh (MSS 3753–4)

MACKAY, Angus A. 1906: *The Book of MacKay.*

MACKENZIE, Alexander 1897: 'Mairi Nighean Alasdair Ruaidh', in *TGSI* XXII.

MACKENZIE, Alexander 1884: *History of the Camerons.*

MACKENZIE, Alexander 1889: *History of the MacLeods.*

MACKENZIE, Alexander 1894: *History of the MacKenzies.*

MACKENZIE, Alexander 1898: *History of the Munros of Fowlis.*

MACKENZIE, Bridget 2001: 'The Life and Works of Iain Dall MacAoidh' (with the texts of Iain's poems in full, with translations), in *TGSI* LXII.

MACKENZIE, John 1877: *Sair Obair nan Bard Gaelach, or the Beauties of Gaelic Poetry.*

MACKINNON, John 1995: *The MacKinnons of Kyle and their Connections.*

MACLEAN, J.P. 1889: *History of the Clan MacLean.*

MACLEAN, Somhairle 1974: 'Some Raasay Traditions', in *TGSI* XLIX.

MACLEOD, Dugald C. around 1960: *Isle of Skye Collection of Bagpipe Music.*

MACLEOD, Fred T. 1933: *The MacCrimmons of Skye, Hereditary Pipers to the MacLeods of Dunvegan.*

MACLEOD, Norma 2002: *Raasay, The Island and its People.*

MACLEOD, the Rev. Dr Norman 1899: *Cuairtear nan Gleann.*

MACLEOD, Canon R.C. 1938–9: *The Book of Dunvegan* (2 volumes).

MACLYSAGHT, Edward 1957: *Irish Families.*

MACLYSAGHT, Edward 1964: *The Surnames of Ireland.*

MARSHALL, Rosalind 1973: *The Days of Duchess Anne.*

MARTIN, Martin 1697: *A Voyage to St Kilda.*

MARTIN, Martin 1703: *A Description of the Western Isles of Scotland.*

MATHESON, William 1938: *The Songs of John MacCodrum.*

MATHESON, William 1951: 'Notes on Mary MacLeod' in *TGSI* XLI.

MATHESON, William 1970: *An Clarsair Dall, The Blind Harper.*

MATHESON, William 1982: 'Notes on North Uist Families', in *TGSI* LII.

MIKET, Roger 1998: *Glenelg, Kintail and Lochalsh, Gateway to the Isle of Skye. An Historical Introduction.*

MORRISON, Alick 1962: 'The Contullich Papers', in *TGSI* XLIII.

MORRISON, Alick 1966: 'The Contullich Papers 1706–20' in *TGSI* XLIV.

MORRISON, Alick 1967: 'Harris Estate Papers' in *TGSI* XLV.

MORRISON, Alick 1974: *The MacLeods, the Genealogy of a Clan.*

MORRISON, Alick 1978: 'Early Harris Estate Papers 1679–1703' in *TGSI* LI.

MUNRO, R.W. 1962: 'Some Hebridean Hosts: The Men Behind the Travellers' Tales', in *TGSI* XLIII.

NICOLSON, Alexander 1930: *A History of Skye*, revised edition edited by Alexander MacLean 1994; third edition edited by Cailean Maclean 2012.

NOTICES OF PIPERS in the *Piping Times* throughout 1968, originally compiled by Captain John MacLennan, with later additions by Archibald Campbell, Ian MacKay-Scobie, D.R. MacLennan and others.

O'BAOILL, Colm 1971: 'Some Irish Harpers in Scotland' in *TGSI* XLVII.

O'DONOVAN, John (ed.) 1856: *Annals of the Kingdom of Ireland by the Four Masters*, volume V.

OLDHAM, Tony 1975: *The Caves of Scotland.*

OSBORNE, Brian H. 2001: *The Last of the Chiefs: Alasdair Ranaldson MacDonnell of Glemgarry 1773–1828.*

PARKER, Derek 2007: *Outback, The Discovery of Australia's Interior.*

PENNANT, Thomas 1774: *A Tour in Scotland and Voyage to the Hebrides.*

POULTER, George C.B. 1936: *The MacCrimmon Family Origin.*

POULTER, G.C.B. & FISHER, C.P. 1936: *The MacCrimmon Family 1500–1936.*

PREBBLE, John 1961: *Culloden.*

REGISTER OF THE GREAT SEAL, ed. J.H. Stevenson 1984.

RICHARDSON, Frank and MACNEILL, Seumas 1987: *Piobaireachd and Its Interpretation.*

ROBERTSON, James 2001: *The Mull Diaries of James Robertson 1842–6*, transcribed by J.B. Loudon.

SANGER, Keith 1992: 'MacCrimmon's Prentise – A Post graduate Student Perhaps' in the *Piping Times* 44/6, March 1992.

SANGER, Keith 2007: 'From the MacArthurs to P/M Willie Gray, Glasgow Police', in the *Piping Times* 49/6 March 2007.

STEVENSON, David 1980: *Alasdair MacColla and the Highland Problem in the 17th Century.*

STEVENSON, David 1988: *The First Freemasons: Scotland's Early Lodges and their Members.*

TEMPERLEY, Alan 1988: *Tales of the North Coast.*

THOMSON, Derick 1974: *An Introduction to Gaelic Poetry.*

THOMSON, Derick (ed.) 1983: *The Companion to Gaelic Scotland.*

WATSON, J.C. 1934: *The Gaelic Songs of Mary MacLeod.*

WATSON, W.J. (ed) 1937: *The Book of the Dean of Lismore* (Scottish Gaelic Texts Society).

Index of People

In this index, Mac, Mak, Mc and M' are all treated as Mac.

Abbreviations: br. = brother, d. = died, dr. = daughter, f.= father, gf. = grandfather, gs. = grandson, jr = junior, m. = mother, mar. = married, NS = Nova Scotia, p. = piper, s. = son, sr = senior, w. = wife, sis. = sister(s), st.f. = step-father

Index of Places

Wappin Station, Victoria,
  Australia 132
Warnambool, Victoria,
  Australia 133
Waternish, Skye 5–6, 75, 77, 82,
  231, 234, 279
Waterstein, Skye 241
Well of the Heads, Great Glen 171
West Africa 86

West Indies 30
Wilcanna, NSW, Australia 228
Windsor, England 238
Worcester, England 11, 21–22,
  30–1, 40–1, 67, 71, 77, 83,
  138

Yorkshire 174
Ypres 253

Index of Tunes

This index does not include the alphabetical lists of works associated with particular composers, as follows: